Fractured Horizons

S.P Mercer

For those who have lost, those who fear loss,
and those still searching for what they've lost
- may you find the strength and the courage
to keep going, no matter how fractured the
path may seem.

FRACTURED HORIZONS

I

Prologue

Elizabeth stands stiffly at the edge of the gathering, a lukewarm beer in one hand, the other buried deep in her pocket. The backyard is crowded, littered with relatives, neighbours, and a large number of people, the majority of whom she doesn't recognise.

To her left stands her father, flipping burgers with the kind of exaggerated focus that comes when deciding whether or not to voice what's on your mind. Eventually, he gives in. "You could've done more, you know," he finally says, avoiding her gaze.

His tone as always, is sharp, not unkind, but not sympathetic either, like a blade that has been dulled by years of sly use.

"Worked a little less, been home a little more. Things might've turned out differently."

Elizabeth takes a slow sip of beer, feeling the bitterness settle on her tongue. She should've expected it. Some sort of comment that would imply failure. Some neat little equation that he'd formed in his head, where time spent at work was directly proportional to everything that goes wrong.

"Right. Because it's that simple."

He shrugs, poking at the grill with unnecessary force, clearly unhappy with her sarcastic response. "Never said it was simple. Just that maybe you could've tried harder."

She exhales through her nose, forcing herself to look out at the yard instead of at him.

Why do I do this to myself?

Children catch her eye, darting between lawn chairs, shrieking with laughter. Nothing repulses her more than out-of-control children, not that they are out of control, just having fun. Still, she finds herself wincing at the sounds they make. Following their path, she glances at a group of women huddled near the patio, wine glasses in hand, whispering conspiratorially between sips as she notices how some throw occasional glances her way.

Yeah, keep chatting about me. I don't care.

The men, husbands and boyfriends, stood further in the distance, are of course, clustered in a tight group, rotating between beers and half-finished stories about work, sports, and whatever else they can muster. Anything to fill the silence and avoid any real conversation.

"You still in that lab?" her father asks, flipping a patty as he watches the flames lick at the meat.

"Yes." *You know I am.*

He makes a noise in the back of his throat, something between acknowledgement and disapproval.

"Figured that now you're the big boss, you'd be delegating all the jobs."

"Science doesn't work like that, Dad."

"Maybe not."

Elizabeth feels her jaw clench. There is no winning with him. Not really. If she worked too much, she was absent. If she didn't work enough, she was wasting potential. The line she was supposed to walk was always just out of reach.

"Lizzie!" Her mother's voice cuts through the tension like a splash of cold water. "Can you help me with the drinks?"

A lifeline. Gratefully, Elizabeth leaves her father behind with his grill, his opinions, and his quiet, persistent disappointment. Entering the house, she is met by the scent of roasted vegetables, fresh bread, and a lingering warmth from the oven that had been turned off hours ago.

Her mother moves gracefully through the kitchen, opening the fridge and pulling out a pitcher of homemade lemonade.

"Don't do that face Lizzie. You know what he's like," she says without looking up, as if continuing a conversation they'd already been having. "You know he means well."

A quiet laugh escapes Elizabeth's lips as she leans against the counter. "Does he? Because it doesn't feel like it, it never has."

Her mother sighs, setting the pitcher down. "You know how he is. He doesn't say things the right way, but he worries. And when he worries, he... pushes."

"That's one way to put it." Elizabeth crosses her arms and stares at a crack in the kitchen tile. "It's like no matter what I do, it's not enough. He always finds a way to make me feel like I should have done more."

"That's not what he means." He just... doesn't know how to say he's proud of you. So, he says it the only way he knows how, by challenging you."

Elizabeth shakes her head. "I doubt he's proud of anything I do, and if he is, that's a terrible way to say it."

Her mother chuckles, pouring two glasses of lemonade and sliding one toward her, before noticing the beer in her daughter's hand. "Maybe. But it's the truth. You know, when he talks about you to other people, he makes it sound like you're the smartest person alive. Says you're changing the world."

Elizabeth arches a brow. "He never says that to me."

"Of course not. That would be too easy."

"And I'm not changing the world, far from it."

For a moment, the pair just stand there, the hum of the refrigerator and the hushed sound of chatter on the radio filling the space between them. Outside, laughter rings out, as her father's deep voice rises over the others and she guesses he is launching into some story from years ago, no doubt one where he makes himself the hero.

Her mother's hand reaches across the counter and gives Elizabeth's palm a brief, reassuring squeeze. "He loves you, Lizzie. He just has a hard time showing it."

Is it hard to show your kids you love them, Elizabeth thinks? She nods but doesn't respond. Not sure what there is left to say.

Her mother lets out a defeated sigh. "He took a long time to come to terms with it, you know. Longer than he let on."

Elizabeth feels her grip tighten on her beer. "It isn't my fault he's unaccepting of my choices"

"He accepted it eventually, you know that." Her mother's response is sharper than intended. "I just think he's sad to see it failed."

Letting out a slow breath, Elizabeth wills herself to un-clench her fingers. "I didn't fail. We failed."

"I know that, but it was hardly amicable, was it? coming here in tears every week." Her mother smiles sadly at her.

"Well, I will make sure my next divorce is easier for him to deal with."

"Lizzie."

"Yes mum."

"Don't."

A scolding look is thrown Elizabeth's way, and the weight of the conversation presses against her chest; that familiar feeling of a child being scolded coming rushing back.

"Come on, let's get these drinks outside before he burns the burgers again."

I'd rather stay in here thanks.

As they step outside together, her father glances up from his grill, and his face instantly softens. "There she is," he says with an exaggerated smile as he wipes his hands on a towel. "The woman who keeps this whole place running. What would I do without you?"

He places an arm around his wife's shoulder and presses a quick kiss to her temple. The warmth in his voice seems effortless, natural. Filled with kind affection that has never seemed to extend to Elizabeth.

He throws a sideways glance at her, but doesn't say anything. No nod or acknowledgement that she had also re-entered the garden. Instead, he turns to the gathering and raises his spatula like a trophy. "Alright, food's ready!"

The kids are the first to rush forward, of course, lining up eagerly at the grill, followed by the adults in a slow trickle, chatting as they reach for plates and compliment the smell of the food.

Elizabeth stands on the edge of it all, finding comfort in the feeling of her beer in the grasp of her hand, watching, watching him smile and joke and be so damn nice to everyone. She quickly ends up lost in her thoughts, staring at nothing, until her father's laughter erupts like a gunshot across the yard.

At the grill stands Tina, the most recent arrival to the cul-de-sac. Elizabeth hated Tina from the moment her father had called to tell her about his amazing new neighbour. Young, attractive, the quintessential stay-at-home wife to her hard-working, always pleasant, annoyingly rugged-jawed husband. The kind of woman her father probably no doubt wished she had become, hence the phone introduction. She's a devout Christian, apparently, not that that mattered.

But it was her father's unique choice of words that made her hate Tina the most. "Happily married with a husband. I bet she obeys her man without question".

Good for her, Elizabeth thought.

No wonder her own career choices, independence, love life, and entire existence seemed to irk him so much.

Gratefully, her phone rings, vibrating silently in her pocket. *Oh, thank god.*

She assesses the caller ID, frowns, and answers, pressing the phone to her ear, as she steps further away from the chatter and laughter of the gathering. "Sarah, how are you?"

Sarah's return is sharp. Unexpected. "I don't have much time. We found something."

"What do you mean?"

"It's not just in the debris anymore. It's been found in people."

The words halt Elizabeth's pacing. The sounds of the BBQ, of her father's laughter, of plates clinking together, all begin to fade into static.

"What? That's not possible. It isn't native to Earth; it shouldn't even be able to survive in our biological system."

"I know," Sarah continues. "But we got hold of the blood samples from two men, both unrelated cases, in different regions. It's there. The same structure."

Swallowing hard, Elizabeth's mind begins to race. "Who are these men? How and why did they get tested?"

"The first one was a patient at a private clinic, mid-thirties, healthy, with no pre-existing conditions. Went in for dizziness, headaches, and mood swings. The doctor ran a routine blood test, noticed something unusual in the cellular structure, and flagged it. The sample got sent to a secondary lab for analysis, and that's when we intercepted it."

"And the second?"

"Military personnel. Collapsed during a training exercise. It was written off as dehydration until they scanned his blood. Again, they flagged it. Sent to the same lab for analysis. The results were identical to the first case, so we intercepted again."

Elizabeth's pulse quickens. "And both of them, there's no connection? No shared environmental exposure? Travel history?"

"Nothing obvious. The civilian hasn't left the country in years and works a desk job. The soldier has only been in controlled environments, barracks, and training facilities. No field missions outside the usual rotations."

Elizabeth presses her fingers to her temple. "Okay, let's step back for a second. How do we know this isn't contamination from the lab? Cross-exposure between samples?"

"We checked that too. They were sent in on different dates and were handled by different teams until comparison. There's no way the samples could have mixed, and if they were mixed. One still contained it regardless."

Elizabeth inhales sharply. "Fuck. That means it's out there already."

"That's the only conclusion we can come to. But here's the worst part:" Sarah hesitates. "It's latent."

"Latent?"

"It's there, but it's not doing anything. It doesn't behave like an infection. It doesn't seem to multiply, and it doesn't trigger any immune response. It's just sitting there, embedded in their cells, completely inert. If those samples hadn't been looked at under high-resolution spectrums, they wouldn't have even seen it. So, there's no way of knowing who has it."

Elizabeth's mind races, a headache instantly surging in her forehead. "And you're sure it matches the meteor sample?"

"Perfectly. The molecular signature is identical."

Elizabeth keeps her voice low as she steps further away from the noise of the gathering, her fingers gripping the phone tighter. "Okay, so, the doctors flagged the samples as anomalies and forwarded them for further testing, standard protocol. The problem we have is government interception. Our intercept. They don't even know what they've found." Elizabeth feels a knot tighten in her stomach. "So, we're keeping them in the dark?"

"Surely we have to, for now, until we know more. You know as well as I do that once the wrong people start asking the right questions, this thing gets buried. Hard."

Elizabeth rubs at her growing headache. "So, what's the plan? What does the clinic get told? The military? They're going to want answers, especially when their patients start asking why their blood work has disappeared into a black hole."

Sarah hesitates. "I don't know. Control the narrative maybe. Standard deflections, misidentified markers, contaminated samples. Just enough to stall them while we figure this out. But Liz, there's another problem."

"Of course there is."

"Other governments intercepted their own debris sites."

Elizabeth feels a sudden shift in the air, "Shit. This isn't just our problem. If we've found it in humans, either they already have, or soon will as well."

"My thoughts exactly. But no one's talking, at least not yet. If there have been other findings, they're being buried just as fast as ours will be".

Elizabeth stares blankly at the darkened tree line beyond the yard, her mind racing. "Okay, Sarah, I need to make another call, then I'm coming straight back."

II

Escape

The darkness is almost entirely Black, save for hints of occasional moonlight. Clint breathes heavily as he nearly drags his young son Ezra by the hand behind him. The sounds of madness continuously haunt his thoughts, fresh in his mind as he desperately seeks refuge in the untamed hills that lie beyond the city's concrete streets. Under a canopy of broken clouds, he struggles to lead the boy through the wilderness. His son continuously fails to keep his footing, pulling hard on his father's arm and shoulder with each misstep.

"Move your feet faster, Ezra," he struggles to say, breathing heavily as he lifts the boy back to his feet with a single, swift movement.

"But I can't see anything," Ezra responds, whimperingly.

Although hurried and purposeful, their footsteps are surprisingly quiet. Masked by fallen leaves and moss-covered soil beneath them as they continue to make further descent into the darkness. The occasional sound of birds fluttering from branch to branch reaches their ears, each rustle in the darkness grabs their attention as they simultaneously try to observe the sources in the darkness. The air in the wilderness is different; the smell of concrete is replaced with earthy scents, where each heavy footstep upon the living floor throws new and unusual aromas into the air. The wilderness in front of them rises, their trek becoming steeper with each step.

Even with his surroundings seeming vaguely familiar, Clint struggles to navigate the occasional crevices that hide beneath the foliage as his eyes water and burn, struggling with the constant strain of adaptation as the clouds above either allow or block small beams of moonlight to break through the canopy above.

Eventually, silence entirely embraces them, the only sounds their heavy breathing and the occasional calm wind that passes through the trees.

"Where are we going?" Ezra suddenly asks.

"Just wait a minute." Clint snaps back at the boy, regret instantly flowing through him. "Sorry, buddy, just. Give me a second, alright." He says softly, as he tries to assess his surroundings. To follow a map etched deep into his memory.

Fuck, I didn't think it would be this difficult. Regret now replaced with doubt. "Come on, this way".

He continues to drive them forward, ignoring the sighs and huffs and puffs from his young son behind him. The darkness surrounding them masks his tall and imposing figure; his once jet-black hair is almost entirely hidden, save for the peppered hints of silvered grey that shimmer in the occasional moonlight. His scruffy and already greyed beard adorns a square jaw. His frame is thin, but his shoulders are broad, built naturally during the physical trials of this new world. Beside him, out of breath and panting heavily, his young son, Ezra, clutches desperately to his father's hand. The darkness is a stark contrast to the city lamps that he has become accustomed to over the last few months, and the unfamiliar sounds of the wilderness are keeping him constantly on edge, his eyes constantly and forever searching his new surroundings.

Eventually, Clint stops their progress. Breathing hard, he untangles himself from the young boy's grasp, places his hands on his hips, and looks at the dark canopy above.

Where are you?

"Are we nearly there?" Ezra asks, "It's really dark, and my hand hurts".

"Your hand?"

"Yeah, you've been squeezing it."

"Sorry buddy, " Clint responds, ruffling the boy's hair, as he suppresses a wave of panic while continuing to study his surroundings for a few more moments.

Come on.

Eventually, there's a break in the clouds, and he spots the telltale sign he has been searching for as moonlight reflects off twisted metal amid the dense foliage.

"Yes. Come on. This way". He grasps the boy's hand once more and begins to drag the child through the wilderness.

Before long, a hulking wreck looms before them, its silhouette taking on an eerie and almost ghostly quality in the darkness.

"Finally," he says as he scans their destination. Gently, he squeezes Ezra's hand. "We made it, buddy."

Ezra, feeling like he is forever attempting to catch his breath, strains to make out the shape of the new discovery. As he squints into the night, his eyes struggle to clearly see the shadowy shape. Then, another influx of moonlight hits the shape, its beam bright, no longer threading through a canopy of trees above. He takes in the sight, his heart beating heavily, not with exhaustion, but now, with anticipation.

Curious, he takes a hesitant step forward. "What is it?"

"It's a plane," *or what's left of one.*

"What's a plane?"

"We used to use them to fly."

"Like superheroes?"

"Not exactly, but sort of."

The boy gazes in awe at the once sleek aircraft before them. Battered and broken, its aluminium skin is ripped and dented from a violent and sudden impact. Its wings, once its proud extensions of flight, are now mere short stubs. Over time, nature has attempted to reach out and claim the metal bird as its own, wrapping it in an array of vines, ivy and wildflowers.

As Clint cautiously proceeds forward, muffled footsteps are suddenly replaced with a crunch of shattered glass breaking beneath his feet.

The sound startles Ezra, causing him to look down in panic, but to his relief, he's met with a mosaic of colour as moonlight reflects from the pieces. As the pair get closer, more of the plane emerges from the darkness.

"What happened?" Ezra asks.

"It crashed. It's safe now though." Clint says, pre-empting Ezra's next question.

"How do you know? "

"Do you remember when they selected me to do a supply run? We found it then. It's not got anything useful in it, but it will make a good shelter for the night."

Though the night air is warm, there's a sense of unease that permeates the atmosphere. The smell of rain, for the first time in a while, hangs in the air.

Clint would welcome its fall, offering relief from the oppressive heat that has loomed over the land recently, but deep down, he knows rain, at this moment, would only worsen their current situation. As he takes a glance back into the darkness, he notices, far into the distance, the faint sight of embers as they begin to rise in the sky, painting an eerie orange glow that has begun to light up the horizon. The sight is an instant reminder of the chaos they have fled. Faint sounds of gunfire and distant screams, laughter and death begin to whisper within his ears, paranoia toying with him, sounding a chilling symphony of terror and madness.

Jesus.

He turns back towards the aircraft and continues his approach with Ezra in hand, pulling the hesitant boy towards the metal carcass. He places a hand on the cold metal exterior and peers into a gaping hole where the cockpit had once been. He takes a single deep breath as he begins to take his first steps inside, but his progress is halted by Ezra's hesitation at the threshold.

He turns to his young son, whose eyes are wide with fear as he stares into the dark abyss of the plane's interior, his body trembling with apprehension. "I will check it out first, okay?"

"What if one's in there?"

"There won't be."

"How do you know?"

"I just know. Okay"

"Okay. " The boy says, breathing deeply.

Taking another deep breath, Clint gently unwinds Ezra's hesitant hand from his own and steps cautiously through the torn opening. *Please be nothing here.*

The darkness envelopes him like a heavy blanket, and for a moment, he is blind, but as his eyes adjust, he begins to make out the faint shapes of seats, luggage, and other debris strewn throughout, just as he remembered. The air within the craft smells stale, with the lingering scent of oil and decay.

"See, nothing to worry about," he says encouragingly, his voice echoing through the wreckage.

"You promise?"

"Yes, Ezra, I promise."

The boy takes a momentary glance back at the wilderness behind him and then, hesitantly, follows his father's example. As he enters, his entire body shivers at the sudden temperature drop and his breathing intensifies as he is momentarily surrounded by complete darkness. Thin, silvery strands of moonlight seep through the wreckage's small windows and cracks in the fuselage frame, creating ghostly patterns on the floor and walls, which frighten him even further.

"I don't like this."

Hearing his son's panicked whispers, Clint reaches into the darkness. "Hold your hand out, feel for my mine."

The boy reaches out into the darkness, searching desperately until he eventually grasps his father's hand tightly.

Carefully, Clint guides him to a row of passenger seats and positions the boy on a seat before seating himself, the worn fabric beneath them offering some much-needed comfort.

As they sit together in silence, Ezra's breathing finally begins to slow, and Clint's mind begins to relax.

Finally, in a reluctant state of composure, Clint's thoughts begin to turn away from immediate survival, back to the days before the emergence of the Pathogen. His mind floods with memories of his lifetime before, the hustle of trying to hold down a job, and all the meaningless complaints he once had. He thinks of Ezra's mother, lost to them just before the Pathogen's emergence, succumbing to a violent strain of influenza, and in that moment, can't help but wonder if her premature departure has been a mercy from the horrors that now plague the world.

Suddenly, his brief thoughts of the past are violently interrupted as echoes of an explosion in the distance startle the pair, jolting him back into the present and the darkness of the plane's interior as Ezra clings nervously to his arm.

"Is it them?" The boy asks, almost in tears.

"Probably, but they are far, far away. You're safe here".

"Was that a Legion?"

"I'm not sure".

Clint had heard that word before, Legion. Heard it whispered in muted conversations, too dangerous or frightening to be mentioned aloud. He thought them a myth, a story told by battle-worn women and naysayers, wanting to claim some sort of survival recognition. That was, until one descended upon the camp like a relentless storm. He remembers their eyes, burning bright with a twisted hunger, and their movements, unpredictable and driven by insatiable madness. He remembers how they had armed themselves with various crude makeshift tools that they swung through the air with ferocity. He remembers the deafening roar of gunfire that reverberated through the camp as survivors opened fire, spraying bullets, hoping that some may have lethal intent. He remembers the violent strength shown by those without any weapon and the way they used their bare hands to inflict as much pain and suffering as possible, and the sounds, as savage strikes lead to bone-crushing blows. What haunted him the most, however, was the nonsensical screams and the manic laughter that erupted from their lips as they revelled in the pain and suffering. In his mind's eye, he relives the carnage, witness to a sickening irony as a group of madmen seemingly turn their violence against one of their comrades. Were they driven by the unpredictable whims of their deranged minds, or perhaps as a pack, ridding themselves of a pretender? He wasn't sure, but they attacked without remorse and with deadly precision. It had been a while since he had heard such noises, and now it would be an even longer journey to forget them again.

He attempts to shake the disturbing memories from his mind, glancing thoughtfully into the darkness as he tries to force his mind to happier thoughts of the past and back to the camp before the attack. It was his haven, a sanctuary not only for himself and Ezra, but for those who dared to fight against the Pathogen and its effects on men.

Still, this sanctuary had come at a cost. To gain the trust of the camp members, predominantly female, he and the four other men granted to stay within its walls were subjected to mental challenges. Their thinking processes were put to the test. Those of them who failed even one test were immediately banished, their families, if they had one, given a simple choice: to remain or depart with them.

He had tested flawlessly, proving himself eligible for the camp, but it was more than just a safe place to him; it was a community filled with people who would help educate and protect his son when the looming darkness of the Pathogen eventually came for him, after all, this Pathogen didn't kill, it twisted minds, and turned men into something far worse than feral animals, so for Ezra, it was home.

"Ezra," he says softly, "In the morning, we will continue to move away from the city, try to plan our next steps, and perhaps find another place for us to stay."

Ezra's eyes reflect in the moonlight, showcasing the boy's innocence and resilience as he nods in understanding. Then, as the clouds above shift again, blackness. Clint hears the young boy fidgeting, and although the darkness conceals it, he knows his young son is holding a tattered and sacred photograph of his mother. His last remaining link to a life and to a woman, he barely remembers, but he seems to find peace within it.

Jeez, what would she do now? Ezra's Protection would be the most important thing. Obviously. Even from me. Yes, especially from me, Fuck.

"Ezra," his voice is severe yet gentle. "I need to talk to you about the camp and the tests I had to face; I want you to understand why I had to go through them."

Ezra remains silent.

"In the camp, they were worried about the Pathogen. So, they created these sorts of tests to ensure the men could make sane decisions."

"I know," Ezra responds bluntly, catching Clint off guard, "and if you failed, you had to leave."

"Erm…. yes, that's right. It was a way to protect everyone."

Ezra contemplates his father's words for a moment. "What were the tests like?"

Clint lets out a profound sigh as he attempts to find the words to describe the mental challenges he had to face. "Well, there were word association games, where they would give me a word, such as field, and I would have to give them a response that was relevant to a field, so the correct answers would be grass or cows."

A small smile forms in the corner of Ezra's mouth, "Well, that doesn't seem hard."

"That's the point; it's a test of the simple things to ensure we can associate them correctly. But there were riddles and other things."

"Oh, I like riddles", Ezra interrupts, excitement in his voice. "Give me one?"

Clint sits back against the soft seat as a swell of love for his son fills his heart. "Not right now, Ezra; I need you to listen, just for a moment."

Ezra's expression drops from excitement to worry.

"I need you to help me stay sharp and make good decisions, just like those tests."

"How can I do that?"

Clint affectionately places his arm over his son's shoulders, "When you can, I want you to give me some tests, like the ones in the camp, any sort you like."

"Okay, sure," says Ezra, seemingly excited about his responsibility.

"But", Clint then begins again, "If you ever think my answer is strange or even worse, completely wrong," he stops mid-sentence, the words catching in his throat.

"What?" asks Ezra impatiently.

"I want you to find a safe place, away from me."

Ezra, startled by his father's words, retreats a few inches into his chair as tears build up in his eyes. "You want me to leave you?"

Ah shit.

The realization of his demand on his young son hits Clint violently and unexpectedly, and he struggles to find any further words. After a few moments of silence, he gently pulls his son towards him again and squeezes him tightly, feeling a wild mix of emotions. Ezra sits leaning into his father's chest, his gentle sobs and sniffles prompting a wave of desperation to enter Clint's mind. His need for a new sanctuary and community for Ezra begins to weigh almost suffocatingly heavy.

How the hell am I going to do this? Where do we go?

After a few moments, Ezra pulls away from his father's embrace and gives him a loving glance, "I will give you the tests, Dad, I promise."

Ezra's words cause Clint's chest to tighten, both with pride and sadness; even when forced to mature far beyond his tender years, his young son's resilience and unwavering spirit still make his heart burst with pride, and they sit together quietly in the tranquillity of the night.

Under his father's arm, the boy withdraws to sleep within a few minutes, exhaustion claiming him quickly, leaving

Clint awake in the darkness, battling his tiredness and a mind that races with thoughts and potential plans for the future. Moving north and away from the raided city camp seems to be his only option.

He knows that the West is barren, with miles and miles of open land, no shelter from the elements, and exposure to any danger. If they could safely get back through the city, the south would still only be full of the remnants of modern civilization, and most likely littered with further individuals consumed by madness. Far too dangerous to attempt without any provisions. The East, he knew, was always the preferred area for supply runs of the city camp, while it offers some small towns and shelter, it will be void of any easily found supplies. As far as he could tell, the north was mainly wilderness, but what lay beyond that was a mystery.

III

Tests

Soft, gentle beams of light begin to pierce through the broken windows and cracks of their resting place. Outside, a gentle breeze begins to sway branches ,and the sound of bird song begins to fill the air.

Clint awakens abruptly, startled, breathing heavily and sweating profusely. He holds his head. The sudden transition from dream to reality makes him feel dizzy and nauseous. His stomach churns as if someone is pulling on his lower intestines. As his surroundings begin to come into focus, the truth of his predicament hits him with a forceful fist to the chest.

What the hell, oh, you idiot.

He scolds himself for failing to fight off the tiredness that had lingered over him until he notices Ezra is no longer beside him. With a panicked look, he quickly discovers that the small boy, whom he hadn't felt move during the night, is repositioned in a passenger seat directly opposite, still surrounded in the shadows.

Oh, thank god.

Clint eases himself up with cautious and measured movements and begins to stealthily move between the rows of seats. As he emerges into the morning light, he allows a moment to adjust his eyes and breaths in deeply, savouring a mixture of long-forgotten scents. He can taste the lingering aroma of smoke on his tongue, no doubt from the remnants of the city's fall, but through that, he can taste fresh grass, old wood and pine. As he turns his gaze back towards the plane, sunlight bathes the wreckage, highlighting a quiet beauty that lies hidden in the darkness. The broken fuselage no longer looks as it did the night before.

Long shadows dance with the breeze, and the darkened tendrils of the vines and wildflowers have now transformed into a vibrant display of colours and shapes. Taking a few steps back to admire its view, he takes a moment for himself and leans against a nearby tree. He notices its top is partially severed, then in the distance, another, and another.

Wouldn't have wanted to be a passenger when that was happening.

He walks a small way from the plane, following the severed trees, until suddenly the city's outline is visible on the horizon, the early light just reaching its outer edges. He knew their survival depended on their quick retreat, but he couldn't shake the unease of the unknown challenges ahead.

The sounds of terror from the night before have dwindled, replaced by an eerily quiet, and in his mind's eye, he pictures himself wandering through his garden, a cup of warm coffee in his hands as he eagerly awaits Ezra's calls for breakfast. As the morning sunlight unveils more on the horizon, more of the city emerges, and he strains his eyes to discern any familiar landmarks, recognizing nothing.

I wonder who else got out? If they got out?

Taking a few deep breaths, he turns away from the haunting view and returns to the plane. As he re-enters, he moves carefully between the seats and debris, slowly approaches the passenger seat where Ezra is resting, and softly sits beside his son. His hand hovers over the boy's shoulder as he prepares to wake him, but he hesitates, absorbing the view of his son at peace for a few seconds before gently placing his hand on Ezra's shoulder.

Let him sleep Clint, at least asleep; he's at peace. God, I envy peaceful sleep. No, we need to go.

"Ezra," his voice is soft. "Time to wake up, buddy."

Ezra stirs wearily, blinking and stretching as he emerges from his sleep-induced haze. He looks up at his father, then at his surroundings, and Clint can tell that confusion has momentarily clouded his mind.

Eventually, he nods at his father and pushes himself up, his body stiff from the makeshift rest, "I'm up".

"Come on outside, I want to show you something when you're ready."

As Clint takes a few steps back into the soft light of morning, he glances backwards toward the plane, expecting Ezra to be close behind. But to his surprise, the young boy has paused at the opening, his posture hesitant, like a nocturnal creature caught in the sudden brightness of day.

"Take as much time as you need; there's no rush."

Ezra nods gratefully, thankful for his father's understanding, and the tension in his posture instantly eases. Eventually, with measured steps, he emerges into the morning light, his eyes blinking rapidly as he looks around at the night's resting place.

His father walks in the distance, just a few feet away, and he rushes to join him.

"What did you want to show me?"

"This," Clint responds, pointing out to the horizon.

The boy's gaze sweeps over the sprawling landscape, his expression a mixture of awe and contemplation. "We came pretty far, didn't we?" he murmurs,

Clint hums in agreement before answering, "Further than I remember it being. You did well buddy, sorry if you were scared".

"It's Okay, it's not your fault".

Obviously, it's not my fault. Clint holds his hand out, awaiting Ezra's comforting grasp.

Ezra's hand, trim and tender, reaches out slowly, hesitating briefly as his fingers hover just below his father's palm. "Where are we going?"

That is the question. Clint kneels to Ezra's eye level. "Somewhere, but no matter where we end up, I'll be right here with you and we'll tackle every challenge together."

Ezra tries to absorb his father's words, his young mind trying to process the concept of an unknown journey. A nod comes slowly, as his eyes meet his father's, filled with trust. "Okay."

The wilderness unfolds as they begin to embark on their new journey, their steps purposeful and full of renewed energy. Conversation flows easily between the pair as Clint shares stories and lessons, attempting to fill the air with wisdom. Clint shares memories of the world as he remembered it before the pathogen, and stories of human achievement. He explains things like the concept of a job, work, money, and television. As they venture further into the wilderness, long grass begins to give way to thick bracken and dense vegetation. As the underbrush grows thicker, each step becomes more challenging, especially for Ezra.

It doesn't take long for Clint to recognize his son's new struggle, playfully lifting the boy and placing him down upon his shoulders.

Ezra's eyes light up with his newfound perspective of wilderness. The treetops seem closer, and the dappled sunlight seems warmer on his soft skin.

Clint's balance and perseverance are tested as the terrain continues to be a formidable challenge, with the uneven ground and dense vegetation almost causing him to fall on several occasions. While navigating the deep wilderness,

Clint's keen eyes eventually discern a narrow trail, snaking its way through the thickets and trees, offering a hidden lifeline for tired feet.

Ezra's surprise is tangible, and his eyes widen as he experiences the unexpected change of his father placing him back on the ground suddenly. "Hey".

"Look," Clint's voice breaks slightly with excitement. "There, do you see it?"

Ezra's eyes follow his father's pointing finger, his gaze struggling to find the elusive trail. Eventually spotting it, "Is that a path?"

"It could be Ezra; it could just be". Clint reaches for Ezra's hand, his broad palm almost entirely consuming the boy's hand and wrist.

With newfound optimism, he quickens their progress, hoping the trail will lead them out of the wilderness. The small, narrow trail proves to be a welcome relief to their weary feet. The ground beneath has already been flattened, making it a more forgiving and welcome respite from the rugged terrain they've endured thus far. Thorny thickets and tangled underbrush no longer seem to impede their progress. Yet, while easing their physical burden, its hidden destination keeps Clint on high alert. As time continues to pass, the pair continue to faithfully follow the trail through the wilderness. Now at its highest in the sky, the sun unleashes a suffocating heat, and while he is desperate for the wilderness to end, Clint is partially grateful for the tree canopies above and the shade they provide.

God, I hope this trail doesn't go in circles. "Not much further," he lies to the boy.

Although Ezra has been unwavering in his steps through the wilderness, Clint's subtle glances backwards have revealed that his son's youthful curiosity has begun to wane.

"How about a nature scavenger hunt?"

"What's that?" Ezra asks curiously.

"We each take turns calling out something to find, and whoever spots it first wins a point".

"Oh, that sounds like fun", Ezra says as he skips in excitement, closing the gap between himself and his father. "You go first."

"Alright, how about...." Clint places his hands on his hips and hums.

"Come on, Dad, pick something," Ezra says impatiently behind him.

Clint giggles and hums a little longer, holding his son's impatience to ransom. "Okay, first one to find a feather."

Letting out an excited squeal, Ezra frantically begins to scan the ground at his feet, lifting twigs and branches, reminiscent of a crazed pirate searching for promised loot.

Less enthusiastic Clint slowly drags his feet amongst the undergrowth, moving small amounts of dirt and moss in a poor attempt at participation in his own game. *That will keep you occupied for a while.*

"Got one, "squeals Ezra as he chases after his father, waving it frantically.

"What?"

Turning and kneeling at Ezra's eye level, Clint admires the boy's found feather.

"Oh wow," he exclaims, *Bloody hell.* "That was quick; you've got a sharp eye."

"One point to me," Ezra says, eagerly bouncing, "what next?" he says, ready for more of the same.

"How about a sup dad. "

"What's a sup dad?"

"Nothing, what's up with you?" *God, I'm hilarious.*

"Eh, what?"

God, I'm old. "Nothing buddy, can you find me a yellow flower?"

"Okay."

With Ezra's renewed enthusiasm, the duo continues their journey. Ezra continues to search for the wonders of the wilderness while Clint keeps a watchful and ever-fearful eye on the wilderness around them. As time continues to pass, the landscape eventually begins to change. The thickets surrounding them begin to wane, replaced with spans of open areas that are filled with wild grass. Eventually, Clint catches sight of something promising in the distance, and his heart lifts with relief. He beckons for Ezra to quicken his pace, much to the young boy's huffs of mild annoyance. After a few moments of brisk pace, the object comes into clearer view.

"Look," Clint says, pointing his finger with a sense of triumph in his voice. "A road." *Thank god.*

The abrupt end to Ezra's scavenger hunt seems momentarily forgotten as a surge of excitement propels him forward.

As the pair approach the road, the trees give way to a sudden and immediate clearing, offering them a clear view up and down the tarmac. Clint stops their progress a few feet short of it, keeping them as hidden as possible while deciding which direction to travel. He examines the surroundings, makes a decisive call on which way to head, and then, much to Ezra's protests, makes a further decision to walk in parallel to the road rather than directly on it, hoping to avoid any contact with other travellers, especially when trust is a rare commodity.

It doesn't take long for Ezra though, to voice his protests, as he begins to make audible and deliberate huffs and sighs, the challenging wilderness taking its toll on his young frame. "Why are we still walking through the stupid woods? The road looks so much easier. I'm tired, and my feet hurt," he says, his patience wearing thin as he casts longing glances at the road.

"I know it's tough," responds Clint with a gentle yet firm tone. "But we need to be cautious. Others could be on the road, and we don't know who to trust. It's safer to follow the road from here for now."

"But the really bad ones could be in the woods, couldn't they, you know, the silent ones"

Ezra's comment shakes Clint to his core.

Shit, of course, what an idiot, why didn't I think of that? "There's none of those near here", he lies, again.

The Pathogen may send them mad, but it is when the madness evolves into silence that the real danger lurks. Reluctantly, Ezra nods, his youthful trust in his father's judgment trumping his aching feet. Together, they continue to follow the road, the relief of the smooth tarmac remaining tantalizingly close.

As the day continues to press on, Clint decides to try and impart some of his knowledge to young Ezra, believing that teaching his son a few survival skills would be valuable not just for their current situation but for life in general, and he motions for Ezra to join him as he gently kneels by a small stream of running water coming from under the surface of the road.

"Come here, Ezra," he commands, "time for a lesson".

"Ahh, do we have to?" responds a weary and tired Ezra.

"Yes, we do; now come and see".

Reluctantly, Ezra approaches his father and bends his knees, lowering himself to the soft floor.

Do you see anything unusual here?" begins Clint,

"Muddy water."

"No, it's all about looking for signs, see, look at this", he says, pointing to the ground near the stream. "That's an animal footprint, which means something has passed through here."

Ezra looks at his father curiously, his eyes widening with interest. "What sort of animal?"

"That's a deer track," *Or a dog, or a cat,* "I think."

"Is it far away?"

"I don't think so, you can tell it's fresh because the edges are still crisp and not yet filled with leaves or debris."

Ezra leans closer, studying the tracks intently as he runs his tiny fingers over the indentations left in the mud. "Oh yeah."

Clint nods as he scoops a small amount of water into cupped hands. "See, I know a few things," he says proudly as he begins taking small slips and motioning for Ezra to do the same.

As they continue, Clint continues to try to impart some knowledge to Ezra, pointing out various plants and berries and showing the boy which ones he knows are safe to eat and which ones to avoid.

He gathers some edible wild berries and gives them a taste, greatly exaggerating their appeal. "Yum, try these; they're sweet," he says, offering a few berries from the palm of his hand.

Ezra, eager to eat, snatches hastily and drops some of the berries to the floor. "Sorry," he says as he quickly attempts to make amends for his mistake.

"Just remember, never eat anything you're not sure about".

Ezra pops a berry into his mouth, his face hesitant about the taste as he chews. After a few bites, he dons a sly smile. "I don't like it; can we find something else?"

Clint sniggers as he watches the boy's expression change from intrigue to disgust. "Hopefully, soon".

He continues with his lessons as the road continuously stretches into the distance. Its appearance is eerie, utterly free from the remnants of the world left behind. The absence of vehicles brings a strange sense of liberation, reminding him of where they spent the night, as if nature is reclaiming anything and everything that was manufactured and not natural.

Suddenly, the mood shifts as Ezra's inquisitive nature surfaces once more. "Dad, can you tell me another story about Mum?"

The question catches Clint off guard, and suddenly, his chest begins to feel heavy as memories flood back. "Erm, sure, buddy," he says with a tinge of sadness. "Did I tell you about when we were shopping and stumbled upon a rack of silly hats? "

"No, what hats?"

Those goddamn hats. "Well, they are things you put on your head, anyway. She found some silly hats in this old clothing store, and without a second thought, Mum plucked this bright pink flamboyant and feathered hat from the shelf, plopped it on her head, and twirled around, pretending to be a glamorous movie star. I couldn't help but burst into laughter, and in the end, the shop owner asked us to leave". Clint chuckles to himself at the memory.

Probably because she knocked over half the shelving.

Ezra doesn't speak; instead, he listens intently to his father's story.

Clint's chuckles begin to wane as he notices a change in his son's demeanour. The boy is now dragging his feet, shuffling the leaves and twigs before him. "She loved you fiercely, Ezra. As do I," he says as he reaches down and pulls the boy tightly into his side. "She's with us all the time, you know, in our hearts and memories."

Ezra listens intently, and a bittersweet smile forms on his lips. "That was a test, Dad. You passed."

Clint stops suddenly, his surprise evident in his expression. *Clever Ezra, very clever.* "Smart Ass, "he says, pulling the young boy's hood over his eyes.

"What's a movie star?"

Soon, dusk is upon them, and the last remnants of sunlight begin to paint rays of golden light on the road, illuminating its patches of vibrant moss and transforming it into a carpet of Emerald Green. Evening birdsong fills the air with melodies as the feathery creatures begin to flitter between the branches, their vibrant colours and erratic movements startling Ezra repeatedly as they dart between the trees.

Clint spots a gathering of deer beyond them, grazing in the last sunlit remnants of a clearing far on the opposite side of the road. As he points out his discovery to Ezra, the graceful creatures lift their heads momentarily, seemingly acknowledging the pair's invisible presence before returning to their gentle feast.

"See, I told you it was a deer track," he whispers, secretly proud of himself.

Turning to his father, his eyes bright with anticipation, Ezra breaks the moment's tranquillity, "Dad, do you think I could try a test?"

"Sure, "How about a riddle?"

"I'm good at riddles", replies Ezra with an excited skip.

"Okay then, you ready?"

"Yep."

"I can be cracked, I can be made, I can be told, and I can be played. What am I?"

"Oo, Eggs, they can be cracked, made, and told." Ezra responds rapidly, "Oh, wait."

Clint chuckles softly as he watches the boy strain his mind, working through the possibilities.

"Oh, I know, I know, it's jokes?"

"Wow, that was quick," Clint says, surprised and annoyed by Ezra's quick solution, "You are good at riddles".

"Give me another one."

"Ok, hang on, I need to think."

As dusk turns into night and darkness begins to cloak the land in black, Clint's weariness suddenly settles upon him like a heavy blanket. Ezra, who had already grown tired, is fast asleep in his father's arms, and although Clint finds solace in the weight of his son's trust, the warmth of their shared body heat has only rushed his own tiredness. As he continues to progress slowly, he becomes lost in his thoughts. The silence of the night and his young sons' trust have only increased the gravity of their situation in his mind. They had fled hastily, Ezra's safety being his priority, but in his haste, he had forgotten to gather any supplies.

Why the hell didn't I think?

Their vulnerability has begun to worry him, and relying solely on their wits, determination, and luck to protect one another wasn't going to cut it. His eyelids grow heavier each minute, and as his body yearns for rest. Yet his mind remains alert, vigilant that even though the day has been event-free, dangers may still be lurking in the shadows. Eventually, he gives in to his body's protests and finds respite beneath the sheltering branches of a towering tree. He leans against its sturdy trunk and lowers himself gently to the ground, carefully placing Ezra on the woodland floor beside him. Soothingly, he brushes a lock of Strawberry blonde hair away from his son's eyes and stares at him, his heart aching with love and concern.

As he closes his eyes, anticipating his exhaustion to wash over him, he sits peacefully in the night's serenity. His mind continues to race, the cogs of survival denying him the instant relief of sleep. Eventually, as it finally begins to calm him, a faint sound reaches his ears, shattering his moment of tranquillity. He opens his eyes, alert again, and instantly he grasps the small hand on his thigh. He can see Ezra's wide eyes in the darkness, filled with caution and fear. Clint remains still, following Ezra's instruction as he notices a hushed finger on his lips. The sound begins to drift through the night, carried on by the wind, and he strains his ears, trying desperately to discern its context. Questions race through his subconscious: are they madmen, consumed by the darkness that has infected so many, or is it a band of weary survivors clinging to their fragments of sanity? The unknown hangs heavy in the air. His gaze meets the boys, and he knows the same questions linger.

He leans in close to Ezra, their breath mingling in the night air. "Don't make a sound," he whispers, his voice barely audible. "Be ready to move if we need to."

Ezra nods silently, his grip on his father's thigh tightening. Straining his ears against the night.

Clint tries to absorb every sound and every tone that drifts from the shadows. As the sounds increase in volume, finally, he can hear words spoken. They speak of weariness and desperation, and he notices an undercurrent of sanity. He can't discern their number, guessing a small group, perhaps four or five men, on the road beside them. As the group approaches, he notices the tiny light of a torch, its strained beam barely noticeable against the darkness.

Come on, be sane, be sane.

A simple conversation takes place among them, and he believes his mind is made up. He glances at Ezra, their eyes meeting briefly once more as he begins to rise to his feet. But the boy's grip tightens further. Clint can feel the fear lurking beneath his son's brave facade. At that moment, the decision in his mind changes; instead, he lowers himself to the floor again, opting to remain hidden, to gather at least some resources before exposing themselves to any potential danger.

Alright, Kiddo, sane men and good men are different things entirely, good choice.

As the voices begin to recede further into the darkness, he releases a breath he didn't realise he had been holding. The pair remain as statues, listening intently for a few moments in the silent blackness, the soft movements of the wilderness's innocent residents and the wind their only companions, until Ezra cautiously relaxes, placing his head in his father's lap, and together, they both embrace the silence of the night once more.

IV

Power

Elizabeth's small laboratory is hidden in a quiet, modest corner of a more extensive research facility. Though compact, her office exudes an aura of scientific curiosity and innovation. It is neatly organised, with each instrument and piece of equipment carefully arranged with precision and organisation. Its stainless-steel countertops gleam under the soft glow of overhead lights, and glass beakers, test tubes, and other apparatus stand in orderly rows. The walls are busy with shelving, each cramped with scientific texts, reference materials, and meticulously hand-labelled containers of fluids, powders and other chemicals. The centrepiece of her lab's scientific apparatus is a giant microscope, which sits prominently and proudly on a central workbench. A small whiteboard adorns one wall, covered in a symphony of equations, diagrams, and hastily scribbled notes that would be impossible to discern for non-likeminded individuals. The rhythmic tapping of Elizabeth's fingers on her keyboard echoes off the walls as she struggles to establish a proper connection. Her face displays concentration and frustration as she tests her problem-solving adaptability.

Perhaps I should have asked one of the tech guys to do this for me, no, come on Liz, for Christ's sake.

Finally, she lets out an exasperated sigh, punctuating her efforts. "Bingo".

As she carefully watches, the laptop's screen begins to fill with small blue boxes, each bearing a daunting message, 'awaiting connection,' she feels a growing apprehension. After navigating through a few technical issues, she had successfully entered the online chat room and now, awaits her audience, her anticipation transforming into anxious restlessness with each passing moment.

Oh god, did I miss it?

As the seconds turn into minutes, she can't bear to stare at the screen any longer and begins to pace the small lab. Despite having spent many hours a day in it for years, at this moment, the room feels suffocating. She scrutinises her watch more frequently than usual, each glance conveying her growing impatience.

"Dr Stevens," sounds a sudden and professional voice.

The intruder's intrusion momentarily stuns Elizabeth. *Really? Can no one read signs anymore?*

She turns angrily towards the office door, expecting a visitor, but no one is present. Then, it suddenly dawns on her, and she rushes to the laptop, eager to engage with the virtual visitor. She inspects the screen of Blue Boxes and notices they have now been joined by a single Black box, proudly stating 'Connected'.

"Hello, I'm Dr Stevens." She greets her newfound virtual colleague.

"Yes, I know. That's why I addressed you as Dr Stevens," the voice replies.

Elizabeth feels a warm flush in her cheeks as a momentary state of embarrassment overcomes her. *Oh God, I'm such an idiot.*

"We are going to transfer you to a secure line. Please wait." The voice announces, clearly unfazed by the blunder. Then, just as quickly as the conversation began, it was over. The visitor's black 'connected' box once again became pale blue, branding the words 'awaiting connection'.

"Great start," she mutters as she attempts to regain her composure.

She knows this is critical, and self-assurance will be vital to making a solid impression and she begins to pace the small laboratory again, taking occasional, impatient glances at the laptop in anticipation. Before long, a tiny tone of noise catches her attention, and she eagerly approaches the laptop once more. She watches in awe as the screen begins to come to life, rapidly filling with a digital presence of personalities. She recognises a few faces, representatives of some of the most influential companies on the planet, alongside a few esteemed scientists, most of whom she has only read about in academic papers, and then more known government officials begin to enter. The gravity of the situation is palpable, and while her nerves begin to tug at her resolve, she refuses to let them get the better of her.

The presence of so many distinguished individuals and the kaleidoscope of backgrounds and nationalities leaves her in a state of wonder and excitement. *Well, this is more than I was expecting.*

The voice Elizabeth recognises as the one with whom she made her earlier blunder resonates again.

"Another minute or so, and we shall get underway."

As Elizabeth eagerly awaits the commencement of the on-line meeting, a blend of anticipation and fascination swells within her. *Okay, speak clearly and intelligently.*

Again, the voice, its origin still unknown, speaks: "Everyone is present, Dr. Stevens. Please present your findings."

Shit, right to it then.

With a deep breath, Elizabeth gathers her thoughts and inhales deeply in a final attempt to compose herself. "Ladies and gentlemen. I come to you today to address a deeply troubling and perplexing issue that is gripping our societies worldwide. As you are all no doubt aware. In recent times, we have all borne witness to a startling and abrupt surge in violent and irrational behaviour, predominantly and almost exclusively exhibited by males. We have made a significant discovery: identifying a foreign agent. This agent is present within a substantial number, almost ninety-nine per cent of the male subjects I have had access to, and I believe this to be a key determining factor behind the rise in this alarming behaviour".

Elizabeth inspects the screen, attempting to gauge her audience. *Are they even listening?*

"The truly alarming part of this is not only its genetic composition, which remains elusive, as does the mechanism by which it's selectively affecting males. But the fact that male children appear to be immune to its effects. We haven't yet significantly tested why this is, but it could add further complexity to this issue. I have, however, managed to test another theory to some quite startling results".

She observes the faces in the crowd once more. *Now we are listening, good.*

"The rise in these behavioural episodes coincides with the recent passing of the Borrux 4 meteor; through extensive tests of the small debris fragments left by its passing, I can conclude that the protein I believe to be the culprit of our dilemma is present amongst debris particles".

She scrutinises the occupants on the screen once again. Each one of them is now eagerly anticipating her following words.

"We're dealing with something we barely understand, and this situation is spiralling fast. I suggest we take immediate action, something drastic, to protect our societies." Elizabeth breathes deeply; her words have been carefully thought over many times. "I suggest that all male-held authoritative positions are temporarily placed under the oversight of women."

Audible gasps come from the screen, but she powers on despite their surprise. "This is not a recommendation I make lightly, but one born out of a profound sense of responsibility."

Some of the figures onscreen lean back, their body language hovering somewhere between disbelief and disdain.

"I believe we should halt all international travel, set up quarantine zones, and safeguard infrastructure. I thank you for your attention and would like to share some of my findings for further understanding".

As she explains her recent research, she can perceive the audience's perplexed expressions and sense their unsatisfied groans. Nonetheless, she presses on, displaying the evidence gathered by herself and her group of diligent researchers. She explains the Pathogen's unknown genetic makeup, its insidious influence on what she assumes to be the prefrontal cortex and frontal lobe of men's brains, and its devastating consequences on society. The extent of her words is not something she took lightly; an entire shift in power dynamic worldwide, although temporary, is bound to cause leading figures, especially men, to become defensive. However, the response she receives is beyond any of her expectations. Instead of receiving the constructive criticism she expected, she faces mockery and dismissive laughter. The screen, predominantly male, is unwilling to entertain the notion of relinquishing their positions of power, especially to women. Masculine pride overshadows any reason, and suddenly, a torrent of negativity begins to stream from her laptop screen with such intensity she finds herself slipping into a trance as the voices become distant and muffled, and she feels an immediate headache begin to take hold.

Of course, what did I expect?

Abruptly, a stern male voice rises above the cacophony, cutting through the disarray and jolting Elizabeth from her trance. "Enough."

Elizabeth swiftly scans the screen, looking frantically for the upspoken participant. He demands respect, whoever he is, after all, his firm command almost immediately silenced the others.

"Dr Stevens, thank you for your research, but with all due respect, are you seriously suggesting that men should simply hand over any position of moderate power or significance without considering their contributions and capabilities? And what about other countries? There are no such reports."

The screen falls silent as the weight of his words hangs in the air. Elizabeth notices that his voice carries a tinge of scepticism, still, her mind is ready to respond, her words measured and thoughtful. "Sir, I appreciate your perspective and fully understand your concerns about fairness and meritocracy, but that is the least of my concerns. You are correct, there's a lack of communication between nations, my question to you sir, is why? We have all seen the news reports about the war in the Middle East. China and Japan are in a technological crisis as workers go missing."

"No one's reporting anything because there's nothing to report," says another voice sarcastically.

Oh, here we go. She ignores the comment, maintaining her professionalism as she continues, "There is a crisis, one that is tearing at the very fabric of our societies, and it's affecting the lives of men and women alike." She continues, her voice steady. "The intention behind my proposal is not to undermine or dismiss the contributions of men. It is about acknowledging the vulnerability and susceptibility that men currently face due to this unknown threat. Temporarily shifting power to women is to mitigate its influence at the highest levels and create a safer environment for all."

The screen falls silent once more, its inhabitants pondering Elizabeth's response.

"I believe we should take Dr Steven's proposal into consideration,"

What. Elizabeth, shocked and thankful, searches the screen, looking for the upspoken participant.

His continued addressing of her concerns allows her to eventually discover the occupant. Much younger than the others, maybe mid-30s. From what little she can see, his attire is seemingly impeccable, underscoring status and professionalism. His crisp white shirt adorns broad shoulders, perfectly tailored.

"The increase in violent behaviour is a pressing issue, and if there is a potential solution that can help mitigate it, we should explore it further."

Who are you? Elizabeth feels a surge of gratification for this unknown man, finding herself studying the upspoken participant a little too intently until her admiration is interrupted.

"Ridiculous! This proposal is just an underhanded way of getting less-qualified women into positions of power! We can't simply hand over positions of authority based on gender!"

"Other countries are reporting no such behaviour, anything we have seen is media exaggeration. I agree, this is a poor attempt at feminism wanting to take control."

"Oh, of course, because men have done such a fantastic job in preventing violence and creating equality thus far!" responds a lone female voice.

"This is absurd! Men and women are equally capable, and we should not entertain the idea of discriminating against one gender for the sake of solving a societal problem! says another.

The onscreen room erupts into chaos as participants begin to shout over one another, exchanging heated words, accusations, and insults. "You're just afraid of losing your privilege! "

"Privilege? Oh, stop it, it's nothing but discrimination! We should focus on addressing the violence, not targeting one gender!"

"The violence is committed by one gender."

This is what I expected. Elizabeth's moment of thanks and hope is over, and she opts to try to restore some form of order. "Please, let us engage in a constructive dialogue."

Still, the online room has spiralled into a vortex of name-calling and chaos, where any potential for productive dialogue has been entirely eclipsed by hatred and division. She begins to feel invisible, her heart aching with disappointment. She leans on the desk, her head held low as she listens to the sound of the deeply ingrained misogyny erupting from the screen. The walls feel as though they start to close around her, and then, frustration begins to boil in her veins. "Thank you for your time," she suddenly roars, slamming shut her laptop.

Elizabeth strides through the bustling corridors of the research centre. Glass walls framed the labs she passed, offering glimpses of scientific pursuits in motion, teams clustered around microscopes, colourful chemical reactions swirling in glass beakers, and lines of code streaming across high-powered monitors. One laboratory, though, holds her attention, and she stops to observe the team within as they carefully tend to plants in an artificial ecosystem. Despite her attempts to distract herself with the admiration of her peers, her mind reels from the disastrous online meeting. It had become abundantly clear that the male-dominated world was not ready to listen, no matter how compelling the argument or the situation's urgency. She sighs heavily and continues through the facility, eventually entering a small corner office and closing the door behind her. She settles haphazardly into the only available chair at a solitary desk in the room's centre, knocking a few pieces of paper from the desk in the process. She allows herself a few moments of respite, hoping to find peace with her failure. Instead, she finds further questions entering her mind.

Even if I had managed to sway a few sympathetic men to join my cause and fight my corner, would it be enough to shift the balance of power? Even if it was, how would she be sure that any advice from a man would have been that of a sound mind?

Feeling overwhelmed, she reaches into her lab coat pocket, retrieves her phone, and dials a familiar number, her heart pounding.

Come on, pick up. After a few rings, the call connects. "Hi, Mum. "

"Lizzie, dear! It's so good to hear from you. How are you?" her mother replies warmly and cheerfully.

"Mum, I don't have much time, so please listen. It's about my research on this pathogen I was telling you about, the one that affects men. The representatives in the meeting think it's nonsense."

"Lizzie, should you be sharing such things on the phone?"

"The time for discretion has passed," Elizabeth insists. "Even when hard evidence has hit them in the face, the old buggers won't listen; hell, half of them were probably mad enough anyway, without something from space making them even more damn delirious". Her voice grows increasingly frustrated. "Just do me a favour, keep an eye on Papa; we women are going to have to protect ourselves,"

Her mother sighs audibly, "Protect ourselves, darling? Your father is perfectly fine. We can't let fear consume us."

Elizabeth's frustration mounts, and her voice begins to rise slightly. "Mum, this isn't just fear. If the Pathogen affects Dad, it's a matter of life and death! It's not if, it's when he becomes a threat."

"Don't you dare suggest that your father is a threat! He would never harm me. I will not abandon him when he needs me the most; you know he's not been well."

God, the world's full of noble idiots today.

Elizabeth's patience finally wears thin. "I'm not suggesting he's a threat, but you must consider the probability. This thing is unpredictable, and we can't afford to take unnecessary risks. Please go and stay with a friend, even if it's for a few days, Mum. It's for your safety."

Her mother's voice trembles with anger. "How dare you make such assumptions and demands! I will not abandon your father, no matter what you say. Family stands together in times of crisis!"

"You're being stubborn and naive! I am trying to protect you; protect us all! If you don't take this seriously, then don't blame me when something terrible happens!"

There's a tense silence on the other end of the line. "I can't believe you would say such things." Her mother's voice is strained with emotion. "You've crossed the line; I won't entertain this discussion any longer."

Elizabeth rubs her forehead gently, regretting losing her temper, then the phone call ends before she can muster a response. Her mother's voice was replaced with the dry hum of a dial tone, leaving her in stunned silence. Tears begin to well up in her eyes as a feeling of hopelessness takes over her. She knew contacting her mother and issuing a warning was the right choice, but the price of her refusal burdened her heart. She never understood her mother's steadfast loyalty to her husband, considering his terrible behaviour, multiple affairs, and poor fathering skills. Abruptly rising from the chair, she pushes it awkwardly away from the desk, causing a poorly balanced stack of paperwork to go airborne.

She watches the papers flutter in disarray, landing in a scattered, chaotic mess around the room, and chuckles at the sight. "You can go to hell, too," she mutters. With a firm sigh, she reaches for her phone again, dialling another number from memory.

"Hello?" a curt voice answers on the other end, their tone expectant.

"It went as you suspected. We cannot afford to wait any longer."

The person on the other end of the line listens intently, their voice offering reassurance and support. As the conversation progresses, Elizabeth's voice remains steady and determined as the pair lays out the logistics, assigning roles and responsibilities to individuals who have either already been briefed or are about to be. "What are other countries doing?"

"Nothing, no one is talking about it, blaming toxic masculinity mainly. This can't go on." Elizabeth retorts.

"This isn't like an illness or a pandemic. The only people being treated in A&E are the victims."

The phone call goes on for nearly an hour as the pair discuss any necessary actions to be taken, and with each passing moment, the pieces begin to fall into place. "See you soon", Elizabeth says, hanging up the phone.

Doubt, fear, and determination merge in her mind, forming a potent cocktail that feels like it is tearing her apart from the inside out, but things are in motion now, and she's determined to execute everything they have meticulously crafted. With renewed purpose, she takes a deep breath, her hand on the small office doorknob, ready to begin. The power shift she envisioned was a distant dream, and she was now focused on a more realistic future, an imminent catastrophe. She opens the door and exits the office, leaving the paperwork and her doubts behind. As she walks purposefully back through the research centre corridor, more focused than ever, she immediately heads for the "Human Research Lab," a specialised facility dedicated to studying the intricacies of human biology and behaviour. Upon entering, she can sense an aura of scientific precision and sophistication. The room is spacious, unlike her lab, and well-equipped, with state-of-the-art technology scattered across its gleaming steel countertops. She admires advanced microscopes and analytical instruments as she approaches a small group of female colleagues huddled together, engrossed in their work. As she nears, her authoritative presence commands the group's attention, their eyes widening and their discussions falling deafly silent as they notice her presence. Urgently and methodically, Elizabeth delivers her briefing, conveying the failure of the online meeting and the need for immediate action, finishing her words with an urge for the scientists to leave the lab without delay and to await her call. The team exchanged glances, concern flickering across their faces. One by one, each nods silently, and then the room begins to bustle with purposeful movement as they begin to swiftly gather research materials. They begin to shut down the lab's delicate experiments while simultaneously taking measures to maintain the integrity of their work. With the lab prepared for their absence, they turn to Elizabeth, ready to follow her next instructions. Their eyes meet, and a silent understanding passes between them. Then, together, Elizabeth and the team depart the lab, their steps determined, their minds focused.

V

Screams

Ezra remains fast asleep, his small form nestled against his father's side. Clint's sleep was again troubled. Night terrors continue to haunt his subconscious, an unwanted and unwelcome reminder of the horrors he has seen since the pathogen's emergence. He gazes peacefully at the canopy of leaves and branches above him, watching as the sun's beams gently break through the foliage barrier. After enjoying a few minutes of peace, he gently untangles himself from Ezra's slumbering form, slowly rises to his feet, and stretches his weary muscles. He takes a brief moment admiring his son and feels a mix of love and protectiveness welling within him.

We must keep moving, and we desperately need supplies.

Still, rather than hastening too much, he allows the boy to continue sleeping.

I wish I could sleep like that.

As he begins to wander just a few steps towards the road, Clint is startled by a quiet rustling sound from the nearby bushes. He feels his senses sharpen, instinct urging caution, and he begins to carefully step backwards, back towards Ezra. His eyes remain fixed on the rustling of the undergrowth as he extends his hand behind him and rouses Ezra from his slumber. As the young boy begins to stir, Clint directs his attention towards the origin of the sound with a hushed finger to his lips. Ezra's eyes widen in fright and surprise, but his father's calm presence and demeanour seem to reassure him. Together, they gaze towards the rustling with stressful anticipation. After a few tense moments, a wave of relief sweeps over the pair, their tense shoulders easing in unison as they witness a small rabbit emerge from the undergrowth, it's delicate movements mirroring their own cautious existence. Clint offers Ezra a reassuring smile, which Ezra returns, and the pair watch the small creature intently.

After a prolonged silence, Clint's voice shatters the tranquillity. "We'll keep following the road today."

Both Ezra and the small rabbit are startled by Clint's sudden words, and Ezra follows the rabbit's movements as it makes a swift retreat back into the foliage. "Ah Dad, you scared it away."

"Sorry buddy, but we couldn't sit here all day watching Mr Rabbit."

"How do you know it was a Mr?"

"Erm, I just do. Anyway, we are going to need some food, and especially water," Clint says, "But if we don't find anything, we may have to return to the city."

I can't think of anything worse than going back, well, I can, but I don't want to.

The mere suggestion of a return paints Ezra's expression with a blend of disgust and apprehension. "I don't want to go back."

Clint extends his hand to Ezra and pulls the boy to his feet with a firm yet gentle tug. "Neither do I buddy," he responds, patting down the boy's clothes. "Everything will work out."

It has to.

The pair resume their journey through the untamed wilderness once more, using the road beside them as a guide. The terrain remains rugged and uneven, bordered by wild vegetation on one side and tall grasses on the other. As the morning continues to come to life, Clint can hear unseen rustles in the undergrowth around them, and his senses are instantly back on high alert. Hours seem to pass, and although Ezra has yet to voice complaints, he has begun to hear the low rumblings that emanate from the boy's hungry stomach.

What do I do? We can't go back, I won't go back.

Suddenly, Ezra's excited voice echoes through the wilderness. "Dad, look!"

Clint follows Ezra's outstretched finger. As the boy bounds towards him.

"There, do you see it?"

"I see it, good boy." Anticipating Ezra's sudden eagerness to approach the road. Clint takes a single large stride with an outstretched arm and stops the young boy from further progress before it begins. "Slowly and behind me."

As the pair emerge into the open space and approaches the car, its details begin to come into sharper focus. The car sits upon the tarmac in stasis. Its tyres are devoid of air and now lean heavily against the tarmac. Its windows are empty of glass, offering a glimpse of its interior, which reveals worn and decomposed seats.

"Don't touch anything", Clint advises as he carefully examines the car's interior, leaning in and peering through an empty window frame. With a heavy sigh, he further examines the car, then the road, both up and down. "There's nothing here, buddy".

Ezra casts his gaze along the road, scrutinising it in both directions, mimicking his father. "This is so cool, where were they going?" he muses aloud, his eyes scanning the expanse of tarmac.

"I'm not sure," Clint concedes. "But it appears we should continue in this direction."

They press on, leaving behind the discovery of the abandoned vehicle and returning to the wilderness. As they traverse the terrain once again, Clint notices an increasing frequency of abandoned cars.

This is hopeful, surely they were headed somewhere?

Ezra playfully frolics amidst the wilderness, just a few steps beside his father, until his youthful exuberance leads him to a misstep. With a sudden tumble, the young boy finds himself sprawled on the floor, his giggles replaced with a surprised yelp.

Witnessing the unexpected fall, Clint can't help but burst into laughter, "Careful there, little adventurer!" he manages to choke out between bursts of laughter.

Both surprised and mildly embarrassed, Ezra huffs in annoyance as he lies in the dirt. He looks over at his father, who is still laughing and begins to feel the tug of a smile on his lips. Ezra's laughter doesn't take long to harmonise with his father's as he sits himself up and brushes the dirt from his face. Clint approaches the boy and offers a helping hand. As he rises to his feet, Ezra's gaze wanders upward, fixing on the towering trees surrounding them, and a spark of curiosity ignites within him.

"Are you ok buddy?"

"Yeah," Ezra responds, looking to the sky.

"What is it?"

"If I climb one of these trees, maybe I can see where the road goes".

Clint, still steadying himself from his laughter, gazes upwards and considers Ezra's proposal; he scans the wilderness and then the canopy above again. *Smart, that would be a great way to gather a broader view.* "Great idea. You stay here, don't move."

"Hey, it was my idea; let me climb."

"Absolutely not, you could fall and break your neck."

"So could you."

"Ezra."

"And you say that children bounce, let me do it. Please."

Of course, you remember me saying that. "Okay. Fine, you can do it."

"Yesss." Ezra punches the air in excitement.

Clint begins to search the area, assessing the trees. Finally, he picks one: "Come on then, this one." Ezra excitedly bounces over to his father, delighted to have his own mission. "Right, calm down," Clint instructs in a stern voice. "Now listen, be careful, stick to the thicker branches, and move slowly. We don't want to attract any unwanted attention, and we certainly don't want any accidents."

"I know how to climb a tree, Dad."

Well, I suppose that told me. "Right ready."

Clint cups his hands and gives the young boy his first step. With a grunt, he hoists Ezra into the air, much to the young boy's excited giggles. With agile movements, Ezra begins to scale the sturdy tree. "Slowly," he says as he watches with pride and trepidation as Ezra's small, slight frame scales the tree and starts disappearing into the canopy above. He knows he must sometimes let Ezra explore to foster his independence and resourcefulness, but it doesn't lessen the anxiety that grips him.

Your mother would have a fit if she could see this.

Minutes seem to stretch into an eternity as he anxiously waits for Ezra's return. Finally, he sees his son's figure begin to descend from the heights. He holds his hands up, offering a helping hand, but Ezra opts to go it alone and leaps from a branch a few feet up, landing heavily on the ground. "Ezra, no. That was a stupid risk to take."

But the boy doesn't listen. Rising to his feet, excitement bubbles over as he relays his discovery. His words spill out in a rush. "I could, I could see roofs and chimneys, and a tower, a big, tall, pointy tower."

A church. "Excellent work, buddy. I'm so proud of you," Clint says to a positively beaming boy. "How far?"

"Far, but not that far."

I'm not sure what that means. How far is not far, but far at the same time. "Okay. Listen to me, we must be careful. We can't go rushing; we must observe from a distance first. Just to make sure it's safe."

With the promise of potential supplies, Clint quickens their pace as they make their way towards the clearing. The road now has a steady stream of cars littered on the tarmac, with at least one always in sight, and Clint's mood seems to have lightened. Their journey remains uneventful, peaceful almost, until a piercing scream shatters any positivity. Clint's instincts kick in, and he bundles Ezra clumsily to the floor. The young boy knows his role in this situation, remaining entirely still, not making a sound. Clint listens intently, his heart pounding as the pair lie as statues. Another scream pierces the air, carried on the wind, and it echoes through the trees.

I hate that sound.

Another scream pierces the wilderness. The scream carries a raw sense of desperation. Then another, filling the air.

Clint knows it's different, less guttural than the anguished cries of an infected madman trapped in the clutches of his torment.

That's not a man.

Uncertainty weighs heavily on him as he tries to balance his instinctive desire to lend a helping hand against his need for self-preservation. "Ezra, I think those are a woman's screams," he whispers.

"Are you sure?"

"Pretty sure?"

"Then, we have to help; we can't just ignore someone in trouble," Ezra pleads.

We can. We shouldn't. But we can. Clint's heart wavers. He understands Ezra's impulse; he feels the same, but he can't afford to be reckless.

"Dad?"

Oh, Fuck it. "Okay, no matter what, my priority is your safety. We'll move closer but remain hidden. I will assess the situation before deciding how and if to intervene, okay?"

Ezra nods reluctantly. Together, they rise to their feet and move swiftly through the underbrush. Another scream pierces their ears, and Clint uses it as a guide; they're getting closer. Then laughter.

Clint signals for them to stop, holding his hand up in a silent command. *Shit. What was I thinking?*

The pair crouches behind a cluster of bushes, and he peers through the leaves, hustling Ezra tight against his side as he peers through the bracken. After a few seconds, he notices a young woman stumble into view in the distance. Then, further behind her, is a prominent and menacing figure. Her screams for mercy seem to have given way to heart-wrenching sobs as she stops and turns to face her pursuer, fatigue taking over. Clint's heart sinks. He turns to Ezra, his expression resolute, but Ezra's eyes convey a mixture of determination and panic.

"We have to help," the boy whispers.

I know kiddo, I know. "Stay here, and stay hidden," Clint whispers in return, his gaze locked with his son's. "Watch where she runs; it's crucial. Remember everything about her movements."

"Are you going to help?"

"I'm going to try, but she's going to run. She's going to think I'm one of them".

Ezra nods proudly, his small hand gripping his father's arm momentarily before releasing it. Clint slips away from their hiding spot and with a final glance and blends into the wilderness. As he stealthily approaches the scene, his heart pounds in his chest. The woman's soft sobs have begun to tear at his core. Her breaths come in ragged gasps as she stumbles forward, her legs threatening to give out. In front of her, the madman releases guttural growls. Tears well in her eyes. Suddenly, a blur tackles her pursuer, and she freezes, unsure if this is salvation or just another nightmare. A fierce struggle ensues, each movement fuelled by desperation and survival instincts. Fists connect with bone, and grunts of pain and exertion fill the air. Her pursuer fights back with everything he has. The taste of blood mingles in his mouth as the pair wrestles for control, a battle of wills taking place. Ezra watches from the safety of his hidden vantage point, his eyes darting between his father's fight and the woman. Fear and admiration mingle within him as he witnesses his father's fierce determination, and his tiny hands clench into fists in an unspoken promise. The woman, sensing an opportunity, just as his father had predicted, seizes the moment, sprinting away as fast as her tired body will allow. Ezra follows her path, committing each turn and twist to his memory. Clint's struggle intensifies, his muscles have begun to protest with each exertion, and his body feels as though it is failing him. His gaze briefly locks on the woman's retreating figure. Victory or defeat hinges on this moment. With a final surge of strength, he manages to create space between himself and the madman, the brief moment allowing him to search his immediate surroundings. He picks up a single rock and waits eagerly for the madman's next attack. When it happens, he delivers a decisive blow, incapacitating his opponent. Gasping for breath, he quickly surveys the area, his eyes searching for any signs of further danger. Satisfied that the madman is alone and there are no further threats, he turns his attention to Ezra's position and makes a swift hand gesture, signalling for him to come to him. The young boy obliges, stepping out cautiously from his vantage point into his father's view.

"Ezra, did you see where she went?"

Ezra nods, his eyes wide.

"Show me," his voice is firm and breathless "She's going to seek safety, and there's a good chance she knows where to find it."

Together, they set off in pursuit of the fleeing woman. Clint follows Ezra through the dense woodland, following the woman's hurried path, until Ezra's excitement overshadows his focus, and he tumbles clumsily to the floor.

"Stay focused," Clint whispers as he approaches the sprawled-out boy.

Ezra's eyes snap back to his father, and an apology crosses his face. He gives his father a silent nod, refocusing on the task at hand as he raises himself back to his feet. As they continue to push forward, A sharp pain flares in Clint's side, and he draws a sharp breath. He brushes it off as post-fight exhaustion, but with each step, the ache seems to grow, gnawing at him like a warning. When the pain strikes again, sudden and overwhelming, his legs falter, and he drops to one knee. The adrenaline that had fuelled his fight has quickly begun to wane, leaving behind a searing aftermath of aches and pains. He pushes through, forcing himself to rise to his feet and ignore his body's cries of protest. Then another sudden and sharp surge shoots through him. This time, he staggers as he fights to maintain his balance; his face is etched with agony.

What the?

Ezra continues to lead the way, unaware of his father's predicament. Another bolt of pain hits, overwhelming Clint and stealing his breath away. His pace slows to a walk, and after a few steps further, he lowers himself to one knee, desperately trying to fight the darkness that encroaches on his vision.

What have I missed?

He can hear Ezra's voice calling to him, but the sound seems distant, echoing from a faraway place. Getting louder and louder, but still echoing.

The boy's heart races as he drops to the floor and cups his father's face. "Dad, dad,". Then he notices a new scarlet-coloured marking on his father's shirt, "What's happened, Dad? "

Clint drops entirely to the floor and rolls onto his back, his breathing frantic. *Oh god, not like this, not now.*

"Dad, what do I do?" Ezra pleads, his voice laced with desperation. He presses his small hands against the shirt, feeling for the wound as fear begins to consume him.

Clint's strength continues to fade; he begins slipping in and out of consciousness. "Ezra, I need you to be brave," he manages to say, "find the woman."

With those final words, Clint's eyes close as he succumbs to the darkness of unconsciousness.

"Daddy, please wake up, " Ezra pleads as he rocks his father's body with all his strength, "Please".

As he sits tearfully beside his father, Ezra tries to take a series of deep breaths and attempts to wipe away the tears on his cheeks. He musters all the courage a young boy can and then suddenly, with his father's ferocity, rises to his feet, casting a determined gaze deep into the woodland. "Please, someone help." He screams at the top of his lungs, but there is no response. He looks around erratically for a few moments, then, with determination, begins to drag small branches from the undergrowth and uses his feet to create piles of dry leaves and moss. He hastily places his collected items on top of his father in an attempt at camouflage. Then, he presses a single large branch into the soil, using his entire body weight, creating a makeshift marker for reference. With a heavy heart and heavier sobs, he sets off in his search for the woman. Navigating through the dense woodland alone proves daunting, every minute feeling like an eternity as he clumsily attempts to make his way through the tangled underbrush. His slight frame moves stealthily, and his body reacts to every slightest sound. It's not long before a faint rustling reaches his ears as he ventures deeper into the woods.

He freezes momentarily before stealthily following the sound. "Hello, is anybody there?" his voice trembles, echoing through the stillness of the woodland, but again, he's met with nothing but silence. His brave facade begins to fail, as more sobs begin to echo through the stillness of the trees. As it fails completely, he drops to his knees, his young shoulders trembling. His hands and fingers are scratched and sore, and suddenly, he feels a deep sense of vulnerability and fear.

He attempts again to compose himself, taking long and deep inhales, until the sound of rustling from the bushes causes his heart to skip a beat. "Who's there?" Silence hangs in the air for a moment; the only sound is the boy's sniffles and gentle sobs.

"I'm not going to hurt you," a soft female voice reassures him.

Ezra's gaze darts toward the voice's origin, and his eyes widen as he sees the figure emerge from the foliage. He watches as it approaches, unable to see clearly through the water in his eyes.

Stopping directly in front of him, the figure kneels and gently lifts the boy's chin, directing his sight. Ezra can see her now, and her kind eyes begin to soothe his troubled soul. "Are you alone?" she asks, gently removing some dirt from his tear-stained face.

Ezra stares at her, his chest heaving with suppressed sobs.

"What's your name, sweetheart?" she whispers, her voice like the first warm breeze of spring.

For a moment, the boy says nothing, his lips trembling as he fights to find his voice. Then, unable to hold back, he collapses into her arms, his tears soaking her shoulder.

VI

Water

As Elizabeth grips the steering wheel with tense fingers, her eyes scan the once-familiar streets. The world hasn't gone, yet, but it is rapidly unravelling before her eyes. Reports were that almost 50% of men had fallen to the infection, their minds slipping into the clutches of madness, yet life seemed to persist in a strange, fractured way. While some people had gone to ground, barricading themselves in their homes, avoiding the streets unless necessary, and retreating from their lives altogether, she continues to see the remnants of a fully functional world. She drives past a man in a suit, sitting on a bench on the sidewalk, staring blankly at a newspaper as if he is either willing for normalcy to return or is just too ignorant to care about all that surrounds him. Further down the road, a woman calmly pushes a stroller, she and her child are either oblivious to the growing danger or unwilling to believe it. Yet, as she continues her drive, there are moments that shatter the illusion of a functioning world.

Violence erupts in plain sight. She can't help but gasp as she witnesses a man tackle a passerby to the pavement with brutal force, unprovoked and rageful, his eyes wild with something feral. Some bystanders hurried away, while others lingered, unsure whether to intervene or accept it as just another one of the world's increasingly random surges of aggression. Elizabeth's mind reels. The first news reports had come weeks ago, confirming all that she had argued before. And now the infection was not only real but public. She was convinced that the only solution had been made clear: power and control needed to be placed in the hands of women if society was to survive. However, public knowledge of the pathogen itself only seemed to accelerate its spread. As more experts spoke up and did interviews, even on the occasional chat show, more and more warnings were issued, but somehow, for some troubling reason, each warning only seemed to make things worse. She presses her foot to the gas and weaves through streets that are neither abandoned nor fully alive, caught in a state of limbo, hovering to a slow collapse. Questions gnaw at her: how had it spread so quickly? Was it airborne? She wasn't convinced that it transmitted through touch. And yet, the infection rate had surged almost in response to understanding it. As she passes another intersection, she sees a woman standing outside a boutique, calmly tending to her hair in the reflection of the display window. Just across the street, a man screamed at nothing, pounding his fists against a lamppost.

The world isn't gone. Not yet!

But deep down, She knows she is watching its last, fragile moments regardless of her denial.

Her phone rings, the sharp sound cutting through the noise of the engine. She answers it with a steady hand and puts it on the loudspeaker.

"Elizabeth." The voice on the other end wastes no time. "It's everywhere. The pathogen has spread worldwide. Even the regions farthest from the meteor's debris are showing signs now. Whatever delay there was, it's over."

She inhales deeply, her mind racing. "What about military intervention? Any progress?"

A pause. Then, a resigned sigh. "Some countries tried. Mobilised forces and attempted some form of containment. But, being male-dominated, it was futile. Their own ranks had collapsed before they could do anything meaningful."

Elizabeth grits her teeth, and adjusts her grip on the steering wheel. "Then we're on our own. I don't mean us personally, I mean Women."

"For now. But Elizabeth, it's only getting worse. If we don't get together soon."

"I know," she cuts in. "How's everything coming together?"

The line goes silent for a moment. Then, the voice speaks again. "Currently poorly, but we still have time."

"Poorly in what way?"

"Just get as many as you can; we will need everybody we can get."

The call ends abruptly, and Elizabeth presses harder on the gas. There isn't a moment left to waste. Before she could set the phone down, it rang again.

The same voice, this time with an edge of certainty. "Society is going to collapse. It's inevitable, you know that, don't you?"

She shakes her head, unwilling to accept it. "No. We can still hold things together. We just need to act fast."

"You're not seeing the bigger picture. This was always going to happen. The imbalance in power, the way society is structured. It was built on a fragile foundation. Men hold too much control, and now that they're falling, everything is crumbling with them."

Elizabeth's grip tightens on the wheel again. She was sure it was going to twist and break. "That's not true. We can adapt. We can rebuild."

Silence on the other end of the line.

She exhales sharply. "If you're right, and everything does fall apart, then we need a place, a date, a time. I want to stay as close as I can. I need to see it unfold."

The voice doesn't hesitate. "Your roof. Midnight of the 5th."

"That's only two weeks away."

"That's the date; if you're not there, there's no coming back."

She clenches her jaw, frustrated but knowing there would be no argument. "Fine." This time, Elizabeth abruptly ends the call, tossing the phone onto the passenger seat as anger simmers.

She hates the certainty in that voice, the authority it carries, but she hates herself more because deep down, she fears it is right. Her mind circles the conversation like a vulture. Total collapse? Was the balance of men and women not only in power, but in society as a whole, the reason every attempt to intervene had failed? The military was vast and organised - surely women were stepping in, leading where the men had fallen. Surely there were pockets of resistance, places where people were coming together. But the voice had been so certain. This wasn't something that affected 50% of the population; this was something that made 50% of the population turn on the other 50%, the adult population. She exhales sharply and picks up her phone once more. She hesitates for a few moments before dialling her mother's number. It rings. And rings. And rings. No answer. She swallowed down the frustration rising in her throat. She'd tried three times already today. Had her mother barricaded herself in? Lost power? Or worse? Elizabeth rubs at her temple.

Supplies. Do I have enough? I need to stop somewhere, to grab what I can before things spiral any further. But where?

Where would still be safe? She drives on, passing streets lined with people who walk in a daze, some clinging to their routines, others staring blankly at the shifting world around them. Her city, much like every other, was unravelling, but so many refused to see it. Before long, a superstore appears on the horizon.

As good a place as any, I suppose.

The parking lot of the superstore stretches before her. Some cars sit idling, with wide-eyed women and men at the wheels. Others are parked neatly in spaces as if nothing is amiss. Some people move in and out of the building as if it's any other day, pushing carts filled with groceries, bottled water, and - she notes with some unease - the occasional pack of ammunition.

Near the entrance, two men have another man backed against a concrete pillar, their voices raised in anger. "What the hell is wrong with you?" one of them shouts.

"You think it's Okay to behave that way? What the fucks the matter with you!"

The man in question just stands there, staring at them with wide, unblinking eyes. He doesn't speak, doesn't move, doesn't flinch.

Elizabeth parks clumsily. Hastily. She hesitates, gripping the door handle. Is this feeling fear or just paranoia? She sits in the car, her hands pressed against the door to the outside. She swallows hard, forcing herself to move before taking a deep breath, pushing the door open and stepping out. She walks briskly across the parking lot, her eyes darting around, every sound that enters her ears scrutinised.

Get in, Get out.

The world had felt unpredictable for a while, but today, at this precise moment, it feels like a cornered animal, ready to snap with one final push. Every sound, every movement, sends a jolt through her nerves. As she steps into the supermarket, she is immediately met with chaos. Cashiers and security guards shout, their voices lost in a mixture of the cries of women and children and the obscenities of Men. She watches some men move manically through the store, overturning shelves, throwing goods, and shouting curses. Possibly infected, possibly looters or teenagers taking advantage of a failing world. Others - sane men, she assumes – make attempts to tackle them, trying desperately to restore some sort of order. She pushes forward, focusing her mind as she navigates through the frenzied aisles, weaving between panicked shoppers, looters and everything in between and heads towards the back of the store. She desperately tries to take in her surroundings, to familiarize herself with the layout.

What are you doing? you've been here a million times before.

Her eyes eventually land on a sign: Soft Drinks, Tea & Coffee, and she hurries to the aisle, searching the shelves, her fingers trailing over scattered cans and boxes.

What am I even looking for?

Her mind races back to the conversation in the car. "Water, that's what I need to secure, just in case." She reaches the bottled water section, only to find the shelves have been stripped bare. "Fuck," she mutters under her breath.

If there is no bottled water, I will have to make do. Fill the kettle, the pans, and every cup in the house once I get home.

It wasn't ideal, but it was something. Then, a gunshot. Screams. Panic. Elizabeth needs no further excuse to leave. Pushing forward, she reaches the end of the aisle - only to find her path blocked.

A man stands in front of her, still, unmoving. She tenses and tries sliding past him nonchalantly, keeping her head low, but as she moves, his arm shoots out, barring her way. Elizabeth freezes. "What's a pretty thing like you doing alone?" His voice is smooth, almost casual, but there is something behind it that makes her skin crawl.

She sterns her face as she takes him in. He isn't like the others, the ones whose minds have begun to rot from the pathogen. He isn't wild-eyed, and he isn't muttering nonsense or screaming obscenities. He can string sentences together. He seems calm. "You're not infected," she says, more observation than question.

He smirks. "No, not yet love. But I've heard we are all doomed anyway, well, men are. I'm just making the most of a shitty situation."

Her stomach twists. Just what she needs. The world is rapidly filling with madmen, and she's managed to stumble across something almost worse. A man who still has his mind, and yet, is choosing to be a threat anyway. She contemplates her next move. Violence wouldn't seem out of place the way things are unravelling, but overpowering him wasn't an option. She needs to be smart. "And what's making the most of a shitty situation?" she asks, forcing a flirtatious lilt into her voice.

He grins, taking a slow step toward her. "I can think of a few things."

"Oh really, you wanna fuck is that it? Go at it while the world ends."

His posture relaxes "Well, we could start with that", he says, says as his weight shifts forward.

She strikes with every ounce of force she can muster. She drives her foot into his groin. The man lets out a strangled groan as his body folds in on itself. She doesn't hesitate, shoving past him as he feebly tries to grab her, his pain too overwhelming to cause her any hindrance. Heart pounding, she bolts from the store, weaving through the chaos and sprinting straight to her car. She climbs in, slams the door shut, and starts the engine with trembling hands. As the tyres screeched against the pavement, she realised she was crying.

Journal Entry
March 17

It took me a while to write this down. Why? because I didn't want to. I still don't want to, but I will. Why? Because this journal never seems to fill with positivity, so why ruin a good thing? Now that things are beyond repair. Do I say I told them so? Do I say, Oh well, I tried? No. I will say, they laughed. Of course they did, well, not all of them, but most. But it was the smirks that pissed me off the most. That, and the deep, familiar feeling of dismissal, not because I was wrong, but because they didn't want to listen.

I feel like I laid everything out for them. The data. The genetic analysis. A clear, undeniable link between the meteor's debris and the neurological changes in men. It was all there. A foreign agent, completely unlike anything in our biological history. Others must have known and informed their counterparts, so why did we fail so catastrophically?

It wasn't theory. It was a fact. But facts obviously don't matter when they threaten your power or your wallet, no matter your nationality. Greed means greed in all languages, I suppose. Governments have always been notoriously slow to act. Climate change. "It's not real." "It's not urgent." Wars, famines, economic collapses. "We never saw this coming." But, they did. They just didn't care until it affected their pockets. It was textbook political cowardice. No one wanted to be the first to say, "We're losing control." So, instead, they did nothing. Stalled. Denied. Blamed. Then, when the streets began to flow red with blood, they pretended they were "caught off guard."

Of course, it was the men who objected the loudest. Who scoffed at the idea that they might be at risk. Because to them, it was impossible. "Men are strong." "Men are rational." "Men don't just lose control."

Except they do, and they have, and there are just not enough women to punch a hole big enough to make a difference. Our fault? No, I don't think so. Our choice? Maybe, but if the pathways to the top were even and fair, maybe more wouldn't have given up. No, not given up, perhaps become uninterested.

I should have known what would happen; she did say it would. But a part of me, a stupid part, thought that maybe, just this once, logic would win over ego. That once they saw the evidence, they'd understand.

They didn't.

So here I am. Sat in my apartment as I have been for days now, witnessing the world race straight past every warning and directly into an explosion. Society is unravelling rapidly, piece by piece, and still, the men in power, the ones still sane, refuse to see it. I don't understand the pacing. Some seem to change overnight, others slowly, but the results are the same. Erratic, Violent, Manic.

I've watched it happen in real time. Reports flooded in for weeks. Women in power, CEOs, scientists, and politicians are being threatened, overpowered, and murdered by the very men who were once their colleagues, their friends. Articles obviously only started to pop up more frequently once the stories became more violent, or the victims were important enough to make headlines, to make sales. A female senator beaten to death by her own security detail. A police officer, murdered, dragged from her bed in the night and ravaged by her own husband. But nothing about little old Joan, beaten to death in the streets.

Eventually, countries did begin trying to form some sort of resistance. None of it worked. International flights were banned, and a state of emergency was declared. The United States imposed curfews and quarantined major cities, but all they did was lock the madness in. China attempted to enforce strict isolation measures, using its surveillance infrastructure to monitor signs of aggression. It didn't matter. When their security forces began turning, chaos erupted. Europe tried diplomacy, but of course they did. They pushed for research, medical solutions, treatments. But the process was too slow. Their leadership was already compromised. The French president vanished. The German chancellor was found murdered in her own office, her own guards responsible. Russia took the most extreme approach. When they realized containment was impossible, they resorted to mass executions. Men showing the slightest signs of instability were eliminated. Entire towns saw their male populations wiped out. It proved effective until it came to executing those who were giving the orders. Africa is faring better, apparently, as are Norway and Sweden. The governments have fallen and so has infrastructure. But at least survivor enclaves have been reported, led by women, trying to rebuild in the ruins, hopefully, others did the same. Israel, that's the place to be.

Do you know what worries me the most? I still don't know how the pathogen spreads. I have theories. And if I'm right, it's already too late. Airborne? Likely. The meteor brought it here, so it must have been dispersed the moment its debris hit the atmosphere. Physical Contact? Again possible. Our first findings were from different regions, maybe it's carried. But not by women, I've already checked that. But the infection seems to intensify in crowded spaces, where people touch, breathe the same air, and share the same surfaces. But who is infected? There are no early symptoms and no warning signs. One moment, a man is fine; the next, he's something else. Some resist longer, trying to hold the last shreds of civilization together, but it won't last. How are they doing that? We're not guessing anymore. This isn't theory. It's observation. And the observation is simple: We're fucked."

The only exception? Boys. Why?

Children are immune. How? I don't know yet. Maybe there's something hormonal at play. More research is needed.

So, what now?

The world is changing, whether we accept it or not. When more history books are written, assuming there's still anyone left to write them, they won't say we didn't try to warn them. They'll say: "They had a choice. And they chose to do nothing." Which brings to my mind procreation. Sex. We can build, we can fight, and we can survive. But we can't create life, not without them. We can replace a cock, but we can't replace childbirth. Is that the next fight? When do we start thinking about it? How do we even begin to think about the future?

VII

Awaiting

Elizabeth's small apartment resembles a chaotic collage of survival and hurriedness. Books and literary works are stuffed un-neatly upon shelves, while sticky paper notes are scattered haphazardly across most of the surfaces in the apartment. Dirty plates and unfinished ready meals are stacked precariously on the corner of her coffee table, any idea of cleanliness already pushed firmly to the back of her to-do list. The rest of the coffee table's surface is covered with a map, highlighter pens, markers and a lone flickering candle that fights solely against the darkness. She sighs heavily as she carelessly stuffs another textbook on the bookshelf. The opposite wall, painted in a pale grey hue, is now almost entirely covered with newspaper clippings and handwritten notes in a handmade mosaic of despair and desperation. Bright-coloured circles and post-it notes highlight articles of importance, especially those that chronicle the unravelling of society and the collapse of infrastructure. Amidst the chaotic mural, a single photograph catches her attention – a trip with friends and a reminder of happier times.

What I would give to be back atop that mountain now, away from the world.

On a small table beside the couch lies her trusted and well-worn journal. Reaching for it, she begins to scour its pages. Filled with her thoughts and observations, it has expanded from a mixture of nonsensical thoughts about daily life to an agonising eyewitness account of everything she had predicted would come to pass. Its pages are now filled with scruffy penmanship, as she struggled to document her thoughts at the speed at which they came. She falls haphazardly onto the couch and considers writing another entry.

Journal Entry
April 5th

How long do they last once it takes hold? Days? Weeks? Will they wither and starve? The ones I've seen - none seem to show signs of hunger beyond the rage itself. No instinct to eat, no instinct to drink. Just madness, pure and consuming. If their bodies no longer call for sustenance, then does each man just starve to death in his own madness? Are we witnessing the slow extinction of the male population?

She closes the journal angrily, rests her head on the couch's armrest and stares at the apartment ceiling, watching the dancing light from the candle. The power grid had collapsed just days before, plunging the once-vibrant city she called home into darkness. Deep down, she knew it was coming; there were reports of failures in smaller districts weeks ago, but these last few days without electricity had made everything feel a little more final. *I don't think this apartment has ever been this silent. Damn that bitch for always being right.* The hum of the fridge and the constant low buzz of neon lights from the off-licence below were all sounds she had grown to hate. Now, they are much-missed memories. She spends a few moments reflecting on her endeavour to influence a shift in power dynamics and her desperate plea with those in authority, and the scepticism and denial she received. *If they had just done something, rather than nothing at all.* Now, the consequences of that collective failure were all too apparent. The collapse of infrastructure has been relentless. Roads and buildings lay in various states of disrepair, the streets were littered with refuse sacks and debris, and communications systems had crumbled quickly. Military operatives and government officials had managed to retain the capability to operate on a satellite telephone network, but she wasn't important enough to have one. Once news of the Pathogen broke worldwide, panic and absence of order quickly followed, and the madness too spread unchecked. Like wildfire, once the first news reports of the Pathogen entered the mainstream news. There seemed to be no immediate impact. But within a week, men had either started refusing to go to work or were unable to. Power stations that relied on human supervision had started to fail. Nuclear plants had automatic shutdown procedures that were activated, and some grids began to experience blackouts due to a lack of oversight. Within 4 weeks, Internet services began to fail in many places due to the power failures and loss of maintenance. Renewable sources like hydro and wind kept running, but power plants began shutting down, leading to widespread blackouts. Within a month, there was a total power & network collapse. Without intervention, most power grids failed, and no electricity meant no internet, no cell phones, and no functioning electronic devices. Even major cloud providers relied on human maintenance. Without it, their servers began to overheat or fail due to a lack of power. Survival had become the priority. Some women fought, but most didn't. Without power, water purification, and supply chains, infrastructure had decayed. As she lay watching the candlelight shadows dance on the ceiling, she found herself falling deeper into her moments of reflection and, oddly, a rare and unusual moment of relaxation. Now that society has unwoven, she can't help but repeatedly question her efforts to sway the power balance at the government level, but with a little less self-blame.

Even if they had heeded my warnings, would it have genuinely prevented the collapse? Oh, I don't know, perhaps I should have had a man present the findings. Don't be ridiculous. There's nothing anybody could have done. Perhaps we women should have challenged the status quo much sooner. No, surely it was so embedded in society as a whole that it would have been almost impossible. "I'm going to send myself mad at this rate," she whispers to herself.

The societal structures that had once seemed unshakable had entirely crumbled, and from the ashes rose not women, not science, but only deep-seated imbalances that had allowed the madness to plunge humanity into a spiral of demise.

Elizabeth awakens abruptly, startled by an alarm. Anxiety and anticipation etched across her face. *Where is it?*

Eventually, she finds it stuffed down one of the couch cushions and examines the time, 11.50 pm. Elizabeth doesn't waste a moment, wrapping the watch around her wrist and hastily rising to her feet.

Ten minutes. Ahh, what was I thinking?

She grabs her drawstring backpack from the floor and begins stuffing essential belongings into the bag in a frantic hurry. Documents, a laptop, and other necessities find their place as she moves frantically through the apartment. Finally satisfied that she has all she needs, she checks the watch as she approaches the apartment door and snatches a flashlight from the kitchen side, along with her dark green waterproof jacket from a hook selection on the way. With the jacket draped over her arm, the backpack secure on her shoulders, and the flashlight in one hand, she is poised to take her next steps. Yet, at the threshold, she pauses, nostalgia gripping her. As she turns back to survey the apartment for the final time, her gaze lingers momentarily as memories begin to flood her mind. She closes her eyes and can see the apartment bustling with people. A birthday party. Whose, she can't remember, but there's laughter and friendship. Savouring the bittersweet taste of goodbye, she reaches into her pocket and finds the familiar coolness of her keys. As she stares at the now insignificant metal objects, she lets out a defeated breath and, with a firm swing of her arm, tosses the keys back into the apartment, their metallic jingle echoing in the silence. She leaves the apartment, not bothering to close the door behind her. She checks her watch again. *Four minutes is loads of time.* She ascends the building's staircase, leapfrogging every other step with long and powerful strides. Each footstep reverberating through the abandoned stairwell. As she approaches the summit, her gut churns.

Will I ever see the inside of this place again?

She shrugs off any doubts, opens the door and steps onto the rooftop. Instantly, a wave of night air surrounds her, filling her nostrils with the distinct scent of the city after dark as she lets the doorway slam shut. Cool, damp concrete with a subtle hint of smoke salivates her taste buds as she walks to the edge of the building, absorbing every scent, as she admires the view of the transformed cityscape beyond. A blackened canvas of shadows, the view only offers muted outlines of distant buildings and the occasional tall tree. She stares at the sky, revelling in the sight of the celestial spectacle above.

What have you bought upon us?

Sliding the backpack from her shoulders, she drops it to the concrete floor and scrutinises her watch once more.

Two minutes to go.

She looks out to the city's blackness again and notices a small, faint glimmer of light amongst the dimness. She strains her eyes, trying to focus on its source. She imagines the light's occupants, likely a woman like herself, struggling to stay hidden from the madness.

God, I hope you're not alone up there.

As she stands silently, the distant hum of a helicopter's rotor begins to pierce the quiet night air as its rhythmic buffeting grows increasingly louder with each second. She casts her eyes skyward, searching for the approaching vehicle, and after a few moments, notices a distant cluster of lights on the horizon. She checks her watch again.

Talk about punctual.

As the cluster of lights emerges from the horizon, she quickly begins to gather her belongings, tightening the drawstring backpack, placing it back on her shoulders, and ensuring her trusty jacket is clutched tightly under her arm once more as she shines a single burst of torchlight into the sky, indicating her position. Now, directly above the rooftop, the helicopter begins a graceful descent. The rotating blades churn the night air, and Elizabeth battles to keep her hair from blowing in her face. As the helicopter touches down on the rooftop, she eagerly approaches it, heading directly for the cockpit, hoping to catch a glimpse of the pilot. To her annoyance, she can only see a shadowy figure behind the cockpit glass as they signal for her to board via the side door. With a final glance at the city in the distance, she makes her way to the door, slides it open and climbs into the waiting aircraft. After finding a seat, she puts on the headset hanging beside her and takes a deep breath and clutches her stomach as the helicopter rapidly ascends.

Christ, I think my stomach is still on that rooftop.

"Dr Stevens, welcome aboard," the female pilot's voice crackles through the headset.

Elizabeth peers into the cockpit, where a selection of bright switches and other apparatus illuminate some of the pilot's features. A seasoned female military professional, with short-cropped hair framing her face, and her eyes, sharp with focus, display a calm confidence. "Thank you. I don't think we've met."

"Warrant Officer Rodriguez, but you can call me Rigs," the pilot introduces.

"Thank you, Warrant Officer Rodriguez, I appreciate your assistance."

"Seriously, just Rigs is fine".

"Thank you, Rigs".

"So, you were the one who tried to warn everyone of this?" Rigs says, attempting to start a conversation amid the hum of the helicopter's engines.

"No, well, sort of, I suppose", responds Elizabeth, her gaze now focused on the view out of the window. "But having had more time to think about everything, I don't think we could have prevented this anyway."

"Is there a way back from this, Doc?"

"Oh God, I hope so," Elizabeth replies, her eyes fixated on the city below. "If the affected still have an understanding of self-preservation, then we have a chance. I'm hoping it's just the rationality that I think is affected."

"So, essentially, it's as if someone tampered with their wiring."

"Well, our understanding of it is still pretty basic," Elizabeth replies, "but yes, but I also believe there are stages."

"Stages?" Rigs repeats.

"The evidence seems to point that way."

"What kind of stages?"

"At first, I thought it made them act irrationally, impulsively, unpredictably, and that was it. But as things have progressed, it looks like there's more to it."

"More to it? How?"

"Early on, some become erratic, saying and doing strange things. Others start mumbling, speaking in a way you can barely make out. Then there are the ones who are completely silent. They seem to be far more dangerous," Elizabeth says, her voice wavering. "From what I've seen and heard, they're the ones to fear, the ones who have completely fallen to the pathogen's effects."

"Are you certain it's because of the passing meteor?" she inquires.

"Fairly certain," Elizabeth replies. "Why do you ask?"

"Well, I knew plenty of awful men before the meteor," Rigs says with a slight snigger and a hint of muffled laughter.

Elizabeth smirks and leans back in her seat. "Plenty of terrible women as well, Rigs."

"I suppose so……. get some rest, Doc; I'll wake you when we're close."

VIII

Memories

Clint sits alone in a quiet corner, his fingers idly tracing the rim of his cup as he savours the aroma of freshly brewed coffee and sweet pastries. The gentle hum of conversation and the distant clatter of porcelain have blended into a comforting white noise that acts as a backdrop to his wandering thoughts. Outside the rain-speckled window, life moves on without him. Figures pass by in hurried strides, and cars sound their horns in irritation and impatience. The door chime has rung several times as customers come and go, yet this time, the chime for some reason draws his attention. As the door swings open, the coffee shop is suddenly filled with loud laughter and chatter as two young women enter brazenly. His gaze lingers on the lively duo as he becomes almost entranced by the pair's actions. He covertly studies the pair over the top of his coffee cup as they exchange banter and giggles while perusing the menu. The pair effortlessly complement each other, sharing glances and synchronised laughter. Then, a hint of jealousy enters his mind.

Initially oblivious to his observant gaze, one of the women catches him in the act, and her exuberant voice cuts through the moment's ambience. "Want a picture?" The sharpness in her voice slices through the coffee shop, turning heads. Clint barely has time to react before she adds further embarrassment, louder this time, "Yeah, I'm talking to you." Her finger now points directly at him.

He feels a sudden heat creep up his neck as his grip tightens around the cup. His pulse quickens, and he shifts uncomfortably in his seat. *Smile and pretend nothing happened. No. Apologise. Oh, God, why?* He says nothing, managing a sheepish smile before diverting his attention back to the window.

"Creep."

"Yeah, what a loner." The other girl cruelly says.

Well, I wouldn't disagree with you.

The shop's atmosphere lingers, continuing to hold an awkward silence. Clint can feel that all eyes are still on him. *Just keep looking out the window.* He sips his coffee as he waits to regain his previous inconspicuousness, fixating on the world outside the window until he feels the ambience of the coffee shop finally begin to shift. As his embarrassment wanes, the pair leaves, throwing him a glare of shame as they exit, and he draws a breath of relief. Suddenly, the chair opposite him noisily slides across the floor, emitting a loud screech that reverberates through the building.

Oh, what now?

"Mind if I sit here?" Beside the vacant chair is a stranger, her eyes filled with curiosity and kindness.

He begins to shuffle awkwardly in his seat again. "No, not at all, please," he stammers, gesturing to the empty chair. In silence, he awkwardly sips his drink, peering at the new stranger over the brim of his cup as she settles herself into position and puts a couple of sugars in her drink.

"I'm Evie," she finally introduces with a warm smile.

"Clint," he responds, placing his coffee on the table.

"I hate people like that, making a drama out of nothing."

Clint chuckles, grateful for her understanding. "Yeah, that caught me off guard for sure.

"You were staring, though," she replies dryly.

"It was unintentional; I was more daydreaming than watching," he lies in response.

Evie nods in understanding. "Well, we've all been there. I just thought I'd rescue you from any coffee house judgement."

"Rescue accepted," he says with an appreciative grin.

As friendly conversation flows between the pair, the hands of the clock seem to skip forward heedlessly. They share laughter and stories as Evie's rescue turns into an encounter of genuine connection, the coffee shop becoming an intimate space where time seems to flow at its own pace. Clint's awkwardness has transformed into comfort as further time passes and the windows dim as the day begins to transition into evening.

Evie's watch alarm sounds abruptly, and she glances at her watch with a frown. "Damn."

"What is it?" Clint asks.

"Work", she responds disappointedly. "Wow, we've been here a while, huh?"

Clint checks his watch. "Blimey, yeah, we have, haven't we? Is it far to your workplace?"

"Only about a 10-minute walk."

"Well, how about I walk you," he offers, with a genuine willingness to extend their conversation.

"I would like that."

They leave their chairs in unison, exit the coffee house and step onto the bustling streets. The atmosphere shifts, and conversation momentarily eludes them. As they begin to navigate the lively crowds, Clint finds himself a few steps behind Evie, following her lead. His attention drifts, and he finds himself admiring her from afar. His cheeks flush with red as a sense of allure begins to overcome him. Her small stature, concealed by a long trench-style coat, seems to evoke a mysterious charm, and he feels an unexpected surge of attraction begin to stir within him.

She's not interested in you. Why would she be?

Spotting an opportunity in the bustling crowd, he navigates himself beside her silently. As they walk side by side, words continue to remain elusive.

Say something, you're making it weird.

Evie gives Clint a sly look and a slight grin. Before long, she stops suddenly outside a small, hip bar. Its vibrant neon sign spills through a large glass-fronted window onto the street, reflecting brightly on the damp pavement. Clint can hear the rhythmic beat of music through the windows.

"Well, this is me," Evie says, gesturing towards the entrance with a playful smile.

"Oh," Clint responds, attempting to play down his disappointment. "Seems like a lively place."

"Best cocktails in town."

"You don't say." *God I hate cocktails.*

"You don't strike me as a cocktail kind of guy."

"I could be." Clint lies.

"Oh really, what's your favourite?" Evie Challenges.

Oh Christ, why lie? "Erm." An awkward silence lingers between them again until Evie lets out a hushed giggle.

"I finish at midnight, in case you wondered, unless you know, that's past your bedtime."

"I suppose I could stay up past my bedtime, just this once."

"Well, I feel honoured." Evie has a menacing look in her eye. "Come a little earlier and have a drink first."

"Sure, why not?"

"How about sex on the beach?"

"Let's just have a drink first, he?" *Did I just say that?*

Evie gives Clint a coy smile before opening the door. "Looking forward to it."

Suddenly, like a violent surge, his senses jolt into a temporary and blurred awakening. Darkness surrounds him, and small light streams pierce through the obsidian void. Muffled voices reverber-

ate, distant and incomprehensible, like whispers from another dimension.

A surge of pain, sharp and intense, echoed through every fibre of his being as if the very essence of his existence had been shattered, and the fragments were now attempting to reassemble in the disorienting chaos. He tries to make sense of the shadows and whispers, his consciousness navigating through the haze with fragility.

Small streams of light flicker, casting fleeting glimpses of indistinct shapes and figures. Distorted and ethereal voices overlap in a cacophony that echoes the disarray within his mind, then darkness again.

The soft glow of lamplight casts a warm embrace over the room as he watches the door eagerly, listening to the metallic jingle of keys on the other side. Stepping through the door, Evie's presence instantly soothes his tired and weary soul. Slumped on the couch, his expression is prudent with frustration and disappointment. "Hey, babe," she greets him, her voice is soft, concerned almost, as she notices his downcast demeanour.

He forces a weak smile, but it falters shortly after. "I didn't get the job."

Evie places down her bags and crosses the room, sitting beside him. Her hand reaches out, takes his, and gently squeezes it. "I'm sorry, Honey."

"It's just... it's always the way. I thought I had it; I thought this was the one."

"There will be others," she responds, trying to remain positive. "It's a difficult time for everybody."

"I may as well work in a bar at this rate."

"Heeey," Evie squeals,

"Sorry, you know what I mean".

She listens further, her heart aching as he expresses his internal struggles. She knows all too well the toll instability in the job market has taken on him over the past few months, each position loss and redundancy massively knocking his confidence and sense of self-worth. Taking a deep breath, her eyes reflect a chaotic mix of emotions.

Do I tell him now? It's good news, isn't it?

She desperately wants to inject a glimmer of hope into the atmosphere. Yet, she hesitates for a moment before breaking the silence. She shifts close beside him, her fingers unconsciously tightening around his hand. There's hesitation in her words. "Honey," she starts softly, her voice carrying both excitement and uncertainty. "I have something to tell you, something good."

Clint lifts his head, drawn by the change in her tone. "What is it?"

For a moment, she admires him, memorising his face before she says it aloud. Then, finally - "I'm pregnant."

For Clint, time stills as the slow realisation dawns on him. His eyes widen in disbelief. "Pregnant?" he repeats in disbelief. "You're positive."

Evie nodded as she tried to suppress her smile, awaiting his true feelings. "Yes, after all this time, it's finally happened."

A surge of emotions washes over him.

Now, of all times.

Joy, disbelief, and a profound sense of gratitude.

"Are you going to say something?"

Evie's words pull him out of his trance. "Yes, sorry, just in shock," he says as he pulls her into a tight embrace.

As waves of joy and hope fill the room, he can feel his stomach turn as he begins to feel a cloud of doubt. Anxiety creeps into his mind as he ponders the thought of impending parenthood.

Of all the times, it happens now, why? I mean, it's great, look how happy she is, but money, clothes, food.

Evie immediately senses the shift in his demeanour and pulls away from the embrace. "Clint," she says gently as her hands cup his face, "I love you."

His eyes meet hers. "I love you too? I'm just a little worried about how I'm going to support us."

Evie's gaze held a reassuring warmth as her thumb brushed across his cheek. "Hey, listen to me. You will be an amazing parent, and we're in this together. Jobs come and go, but what matters is that we're a team. We can figure this out." A flicker of panic lingers in his eyes as Evie continues, "Parenting isn't defined by what you bring to the table; it's defined by being at the table. And, anyway, I can get some extra shifts for the first few months. It's not all about you, you know." She lets out a slight giggle.

Clint takes a deep breath as he absorbs her words. Her unwavering belief in him begins to chip away at any subconscious screams of self-doubt.

She smiles, "We've got this babe. You've got this".

IX

Cara

Clint slowly opens his eyes, wincing as the ember light burns his weary gaze. His body aches, and the murmur of distant voices reaches his ears. He tries to sit up, but a wave of dizziness washes over him, forcing his eyes shut once more.

Blinking away the remnants of sleep, he calls out for Ezra. He attempts to move, but his body is stiff. His arms feel heavy, but something is wrong; it's not his body's stiffness that's restricting his movements, but something else. He attempts to move again, more forcefully this time, but the truth hits him; restraints bind his wrists and feet. He lifts his head and searches his horizontal body. Panic begins to surge in as he wriggles violently, attempting to free himself, but the binds retain their firm grip.

As fear threatens to overwhelm him completely, Ezra's voice reaches his ears. "Dad, you're awake," he says softly, his voice trembling.

Clint's heartbeat pulses frantically as paranoia threatens to consume him. Ezra's face emerges from the shadows, and instantly, relief washes over him. Just as quickly as the boy had appeared, he was gone again. Clint attempts to follow his movements, but his eyes struggle to focus in the darkness, seeing nothing more than muffled blurs of erratic movements. Coming back into focus, the boy manoeuvres beside him and shuffles himself under his father's head, gently cradling it as he slides his leg partially under his neck. Ezra offers his father water from an old tin bottle, and Clint gratefully takes a few sips, his eyes remaining fixated on his son the entire time.

"Thank you. Why am I restrained? Where are we?" he questions, feeling the damp liquid on his lips.

Ezra gently places the small bottle by his side and strokes his father's head, as Clint had done so many times previously. "Dad, I need to give you your tests. I'm going to say a word, and I want you to tell me the thing word you think of, okay?"

"Okay." *He's remembered. Good boy.*

Clint stays silent and watches as the young boy ponders in his mind for the words he can use.

"Sunshine."

Clint furrows his brow as he considers the word "Warmth."

Ezra nods, "Good, now, Ocean."

Clint's eyes brighten as he visualises the sea. "Waves."

Ezra smiles, relieved by his father's ability to associate the words. He continues his test, offering a variety of words, some concrete and others abstract, as he assesses his father's ability to connect and perceive. With each response, Ezra observes his father, growing increasingly reassured by the signs of clarity, "Okay, Dad, last one, a riddle".

Do you know any riddles?

"The more I take, the more I leave behind. What am I?"

What? Who taught you that?

Clint searches his mind, his mouth moving as he releases silent words as he considers all possible answers. "Footsteps", he finally says, confident of his answer. "It's footsteps".

Without a word in response, Ezra gently removes himself from under his father's head, lies on the dusty floor beside him, and embraces him tightly, bursting into sobs that pull hard at Clint's resolve.

"Ezra? What happened?" he asks once the boy's sniffles have quietened.

The boy sits himself up, wiping his tears from his face in a clumsy fashion as he relays the events that had transpired while his father was unconscious. How he and the woman had come upon one another, and how she had offered to help in an act of compassion. However, and not to his surprise, she had insisted that he be restrained, wary of his sanity and their intentions. As Ezra unfolds all the details, Clint feels his admiration for his son growing, his heart swelling with pride as he listens.

"Ezra, you've shown incredible bravery. Thank you. Where is the Woman now?"

Ezra's eyes scan their dimly lit surroundings. " She left to go for a walk. She hates it here, but she promised to return soon."

"Is she the one who told you that riddle?"

Ezra nods, "Yeah"

"It's a good one."

Now more alert and awake, Clint examines his surroundings. The ceiling above is both an unusual and a fascinating sight. Thick branches are intertwined with one another and padded with layers of moss and leaves, forming a natural canopy: a living roof providing camouflage and protection from the elements. He notices small rays of sunlight that filter through the gaps in the foliage and admires the shadowed patterns they create on the soil walls.

"What is this place?"

"It's a den, like one that foxes use," says Ezra, gazing at the foliage above him.

"How long have you been here?"

"A few days, the woman helped; she patched up your wound but said you had to be tied up until she spoke to you. I didn't know what to do; I just wanted you to be okay."

Clint feels an overwhelming sense of guilt as he absorbs the information. "A few days, I'm so sorry," he says, looking longingly into Ezra's eyes. "I'm grateful for everything, even if it means being restrained for a while. You made all the right decisions, buddy, and I'm very proud of you."

Ezra moves again to the other side of the small den and busies himself with a task before quickly returning to his father and shuffling an arrangement of dry foliage beneath his head. Clint watches him as his young son tends to him, unaware of the added comfort that either Ezra or the Woman had arranged for him.

"Ezra, I'm ok. You don't need to fuss so much".

"I'm just making it a bit comfier," the boy responds bluntly, clearly annoyed at his father's statement. Then, he positions himself once more beside him and rests his head on Clint's chest.

Clint's eyes flutter open, adjusting once more to the dim light that filters through the makeshift roof of the hideout. His thoughts turn to Ezra, who still rests on his chest. For a moment, he contemplates waking him and asking to be freed, but finds himself torn between fear and worry; doing so may come across as irrational, and he doesn't want to undermine his son's unwavering support. He decides against the idea and returns to peacefully watching the slow movement of the shadows. Time passes slowly, the only sounds accompanying him being Ezra's breathing and the hushed movements of the unknown above the canopy.

This place is both beautiful and eerie; Ezra must have been frightened stiff. What am I doing? What am I trying to achieve?

His moment of peaceful self-reflection is abruptly disturbed when a small section of the foliage above begins to tear away. His heart begins thumping in his chest as he delicately tries pulling on his restraints once more. In a swift movement, a figure silently drops to the floor and then hastily repairs the entrance point. He watches in silence, awaiting a clear view of the new occupant. As she turns towards him, their eyes lock in an instant, and then, without hesitation, she makes a deliberate loud cough, instantly rousing Ezra from his slumber. Ezra sits up in a moment of panic, and his eyes dart between his father and the Woman.

With a firm voice, she addresses the boy, her words laced with caution. "Is your father's mind intact? Are you certain he has not been affected by the pathogen?"

Ezra's stare meets her demanding gaze, his young eyes fixated upon her like an animal stalking prey. "I'm sure."

Clint observes her intently. She is lean and agile and wears a tattered and dirtied denim jacket. The jacket clings to her body, accentuating her curves, and its sleeves are frayed at the edges. She wears ripped and stained jeans with faded patches that display a Greyish White.

Who the hell is she?

Her posture is sharp. Almost too steady and too controlled. Not like someone barely surviving, like someone used to being here.

"He's right. I'm as sane as I've ever been," he says, inspecting the Woman's features, her eyes are the colour of deep sapphire, drawing him in, and her cheekbones are defined. She studies them both, searching for any signs of deception or instability. Then, without warning, she flicks a small rock toward his face. Clint tilts his head, avoiding the small rock.

"Flinched," she mutters. "Good sign."

Clint exhales sharply. "What the hell was that?"

"Just a test," she replies bluntly. "I apologise for my caution, but I'm sure you understand".

"Strange test, but yes, I understand. I appreciate everything you have done for my son."

Her gaze softens as her initial scepticism gives way slightly. "Your son wasn't the one needing help," she responds bluntly.

"You're right. Thank you for helping me…. erm,"

"Cara."

"Thank you, Cara, I'm Clint."

Cara begins to busy herself arranging a small selection of rocks into a circle and then quickly starts a small fire. Surprised at her speed and resourcefulness, Clint wonders if she is incredibly well prepared or if his positioning has hidden elements of the den from his perception. Soon enough, the fire's smoke starts to vent through the overgrowth above. A carefully thought-out idea or an unintentional accident of genius, he's unsure.

"Cara, what is this place?"

"It's a hole, Clint." Her tone is sharp. "Obviously."

"Did you dig it yourself?"

She turns hastily towards him. "No, Clint, I didn't dig this hole by myself." Her tone hints at condescension. She turns back to her task and releases a long-drawn-out sigh. "While my father and I were travelling, I had a rather unfortunate accident and fell into this hole."

"Of course, that makes far more sense than you digging it."

"Why, because I'm a woman, can't women dig holes?" she says fearlessly.

"Oh, erm, that's not what I meant".

"I'm fucking with you, oh shit, sorry, Ezra, oh god." Embarrassment flushes in her cheeks. "Anyway, I injured my back. Dad tried to lift me out, but the pain was too much. So, instead, he reinforced the opening as best he could so we could use it as a makeshift recovery room until I regained my strength and mobility."

"Clever guy," says Clint, with a hint of jealousy. "He knew construction, perhaps."

Cara snorts as she lets out a loud laugh, "No, the hole was already here, how or why I don't know, and placing some branches across the top barely counts as construction."

"True," Clint responds. *I'm going to have to be more careful; stupid responses and questions are not going to fly here.*

"I never really understood my Dad's work," her voice still carries a trace of annoyance. "But he wasn't in construction, he was too soft for that."

"You seem well prepared. Have you travelled from somewhere, or perhaps, headed somewhere?".

"Dad was what people called an apocalypse hoarder. He always believed that we should be prepared for anything, always better to have it and not need it than to need it and not have it, he used to say."

Clint nods, his curiosity piqued. "I've heard about these, erm, preppers. Sounds like he took it seriously."

"Oh, he did. He had this whole system in place, cate-gorised bins, expiration date checklists, you name it. Our Garage was full of it. My friends and I used to tease him, but now, well, now, I appreciate his silly hobby more than ever."

He shuffles his position, attempting to sit himself slightly upright. Ezra's eyes are wide, and he stares at Cara with in-tensity.

Cara senses his stare, looks at him and holds his gaze. "Not yet."

"Where is your father now?"

Cara's voice tightens. "The madness took hold of him completely a few days ago."

Clint feels a heavy knot form in his stomach. *Ahh shit.* "I'm so sorry."

"Don't be," she replies, "I saw it coming. He'd been acting strange for days. At first, I thought it was just stress, but then one morning, he woke up... and couldn't say a sentence; he just mumbled. And when he looked at me... I knew."

"Again, I'm sorry," Clint repeats softly, gazing deeply at Cara.

"It's a good job I was pretty much fully healed, and we were about to head off. If I'd been unable to climb out of this hellhole, I'd be dead."

She must only be a teenager, early twenties at most. "

She turns to Ezra, and her expression softens. "Anyway, I'd like to show you something."

She stops tending to the fire and begins to search a back-pack that is perched against one of the walls. Searching within it, she retrieved a folded small piece of paper, its edges worn slightly. Gently, she unfolds it as she makes her way towards them, holding it outstretched against her chest so they can both view it. Clint's jaw opens as he gazes upon a hand-drawn yet detailed map of the surrounding area. It displays their current location with a simple circle and the word Den. It's rendered with skilful yet imperfect lines that seem to mark a previous journey that he assumes is that of Cara and her father. The landscape has been sketched with detail, showcasing the rugged terrain and untamed wilderness that surrounds it. It even seemed to show small elevation changes and winding rivers, giving a view of the vastness they had travelled.

"We lost our actual map crossing a river weeks ago. Dad drew what he could from memory, but paper is hard to come by, so he condensed as much as he could remember on this. This is our current location," she says, putting her finger on the location Clint spotted earlier. These dotted lines indicate potential paths or directions we were going to travel. The paths we have already taken have been drawn over and are now solid lines."

Clint's eyes remain fixated on the map as he finds himself captivated by its detail. Cara delicately traces the map's edge, unveiling a hand-drawn boat.

"This, Clint, was our destination. Dad wanted to explore this area for supplies first. Then he was adamant that a boat would be our saviour, that we could sail away, and navigate the sea for the remainder of our existence, I suppose."

Clint continues to examine the map, trying to memorise all that he saw. To his annoyance, Cara carefully folds the hand-drawn map again and stows it back in the backpack before returning her attention to the fire. His mind reels with unanswered questions: where had they travelled from? How old was she?

But before he can voice his questions, Ezra's curiosity piques. "What's that?" he inquires, as he watches Cara place a small silver bag into a metal tin and balance it on the fire.

"Those are ration boil bags," Clint answers quickly, his voice carrying a hint of pride. "You boil them, and inside, the food cooks."

"What food?"

"Well, they contain all sorts of things, but mainly proteins, vegetables, and carbohydrates, all the stuff your body needs"

Ezra's eyes widen as he approaches Cara and observes her pouring water into the small metal tin.

"Your dad's right. Once the water is boiling, the heat activates a chemical reaction that warms the food and makes it ready to eat within a few minutes."

"How did you get those?" Clint asks as Cara repeats the process, putting another silver bag in another small tin of water and setting it on the fire.

"As I said, Dad was always well prepared".

Silence consumes the den as Clint and Ezra watch Cara as she pokes at the contents of the small pots. She acts with precision, clearly having used the bags before, as she delicately opens the bags and pours the contents into each one, mixing them with the boiling water. She offers one to Ezra, warning him of the temperature beforehand, and then hands him an unusual spoon-shaped fork, the young boy scrutinising the utensil as he takes it from her. Cara settles onto the ground, crossing her legs on the earthen floor, and a hush falls over the small den as the pair partake in the nourishing meal. After several spoonfuls of his food, Ezra places his tin on the ground and moves into the same position he was in when giving Clint water, putting his leg under his father's neck. The young boy then takes it upon himself to feed his father. Carefully using the unusual utensil to scoop some of the meal and bring it towards his fathers waiting mouth.

"Thanks, buddy." Clint opens his mouth, allowing Ezra to feed him, feeling their connection deepening with each nourishing bite.

Cara finishes her meal first and puts her small metal tin on the floor beside her. "While your father seems sane to me, I ask that you keep him restrained until I leave in the morning," she says, looking at Ezra sternly.

With a mouth full of vegetables, the boy hesitates before voicing any response, torn between his loyalty to his father and his gratitude towards Cara.

Clint, however, understands the necessity of her caution and answers for his son. "It's all right, son. We'll abide by Cara's request."

Reluctantly, Ezra nods. "Where will you go?" he inquires between bites, his mouth still partially full. "You can stick with us, right, Dad?"

Clint gives Ezra a wistful look and then turns to Cara, silently urging her to address Ezra's question. However, she remains silent, choosing instead to inch towards one of the muddy walls. There, she unfurls a small blanket and settles comfortably, closing her eyes to rest.

As the night wore on, Ezra settled into an easy sleep with a full belly, his body nestled tightly against his father's side. Yet, the boy's comfort doesn't ease Clint's uneasy sleep, and he awakens intermittently.

In one of his moments of restlessness, a whispering voice breaks the silence. "I've been thinking... maybe you should leave now. Just disappear. Take the risk; leave Ezra with me."

Clint feels a terrible churning in his stomach.

"Madness will consume you eventually. He needs someone stable."

His brows furrow in the darkness as he struggles to answer such a suggestion. "I am fine; I can't just leave him. He's my son." Annoyance is prevalent in his hushed voice.

"Maybe at the moment, but eventually, you won't be, and then what?".

He sighs, conflicted by the weight of the unexpected conversation. "I can't abandon him. We're all each other has left."

"It's not abandonment if it's for his safety. You can watch over him from a distance. I'll make sure he's taken care of.

I'm sure you're a good father, no doubt one of the best, but just the two of you out there, isolated, what chance does he have if his only source of strength turns against him?"

Is she actually suggesting this?

The darkness amplifies the heaviness of the hushed words, and Clint finds himself torn between his paternal instincts and the harsh truth of Cara's words. He gazes at Ezra's peaceful figure sleeping next to him, and tears begin to well in his eyes. *What if she's right? What if Ezra wakes up one night to find me staring blankly at him, my mouth moving in senseless murmurs? Or worse.* He pictures Ezra backing away, calling his name, his voice trembling. But Clint - or whatever he has become - won't stop. He shudders. *No. No, I won't let that happen.*

The den falls into a heavy silence, punctuated only by the soft, sorrowful sniffles that manage to escape Clint's grief-stricken form. The weight of Cara's suggestion continues to linger, and a sombre atmosphere overtakes the cramped space. Eventually, he subdues his emotions, and a profound quietness settles upon the den as if the walls themselves mourn the problematic decision he faces. "Thank you, but no."

With the first rays of dawn, Cara gently rouses Clint from an eventual state of slumber. Yet not a word is spoken between the pair for a few moments. It is easy for Clint to conclude that the time has come for her departure, yet he voices no questions. His mind fills with gratitude for her assistance, but deep within, he also feels a nagging sadness. He respects her decision to go her own way, but the contemplation to ask her to reconsider Ezra's proposal to join them lingers. Her comments in the night circled his thoughts, and he knew, reluctantly, that she was right. Inevitably, he would succumb to the pathogen, and if she joined them, surely it would be the best decision for Ezra's future.

He studies her intently, convinced her eyes reflect a mixture of regret and sorrow. "Come with us," he finally manages to muster in a whispered voice. "I promise when it's time, I will go."

She freezes mid-step. For the first time, Clint's convinced he can see a crack in her expression. She glances at Ezra - just a second too long - before looking away. "There's a rucksack to your left," she says, her voice softer now. "It has everything I won't need," she responds, ignoring his request entirely. "Don't wake Ezra, I'd rather not deal with that goodbye".

She then equips a small backpack upon her shoulders, removes a small section of the woodland canopy and, with those parting words, slips into the early morning light, quickly scaling the wall using a frayed piece of rope that has deceived Clint thus far. As she begins to recover the small opening, her silhouette blocks the beam of morning sunlight. "Clint, when the time comes…when the decision needs to be made….I hope you make it in time". Then she covers the opening and disappears, leaving him and Ezra to face the next set of challenges that await them.

X

Arrival

The distorted voice of Rigs reverberates through the helicopter's headset. "10 minutes out, Doc," she announces.

The sudden intrusion jolts Elizabeth back to the reality of her airborne journey as the rhythmic thumping of the rotor blades had unwillingly become a lullaby during the flight. "Oh, Okay, thanks. How long have I been out?"

"A couple of hours."

"Really, Is that all? I thought it was further."

"Nothing's far when you can cheat gravity." Rigs responds sarcastically.

As the helicopter begins a gradual descent towards its destination, Elizabeth's mind starts to race with thoughts of the plans she had set in motion. Has everything gone as expected? Had the people she trusted come through at their respective ends?

This can't all be for nothing. But surely, we're not the only ones trying to do something?

The impending reveal of the makeshift facility holds a weight of uncertainty, and she can't shake the nagging doubt that gnaws at the edges of her thoughts.

"So, Doc, you haven't been here yet. How come?"

"I've been observing things, researching the pathogen's effects as much as possible from my apartment. Has everything gone well?"

"Yeah, I suppose so", responds Rigs bluntly, triggering a wave of scepticism through Elizabeth's mind.

"What does that mean?"

"Well, I didn't arrange all of this. I don't know what you're expecting."

Neither do I; I'm hoping for everything, and I'm expecting less.

She gazes out of the small window beside her. The landscape below has begun to reveal itself in glimpses of light from the helicopter's collision and navigation lights. The canopy of trees below creates the illusion of moss-covered concrete, just for a second, then darkness, then it's revealed for another second, again, and again. Suddenly, on the horizon, the ageing facility begins to come into sight, as the dim glow of a single light pierces through the darkness.

"Hell of a place you've picked here, Doc."

Looking out the window at the facility below, Elizabeth offers a small smile. "It's an ancient facility," she explains, "one of the first with a nuclear reactor underneath".

"No shit," responds Rigs, surprise evident in her tone. "I presume we aren't all going to melt from the inside out."

Elizabeth chuckles softly. "No, it's been safely decommissioned. But either way, anyone who knows of its existence, I doubt, would want to disturb it, and the nearest town is a few miles away and has pretty much been abandoned since the facility shut down."

"Living quarters for the workers?"

"Maybe. I'm unsure. It's a harbour town, a few shops, a launderette, a couple of bars, one school, that sort of thing."

"Not worth a potential supply run then."

"It's a possibility."

Once the helicopter touches down, Rigs begins to toggle switches and buttons, powering down the rotors, and the once-deafening noise gradually begins to subside. As Elizabeth prepares her belongings, the side door swings suddenly open, startling both Rigs and Elizabeth.

"Jesus, I've just shit a brick." Rigs angrily shouts.

The open door unveils the silhouette of a young woman standing eagerly. "Sorry"

As Elizabeth approaches the opening, she notices the casual attire of her welcomer: jeans paired with a plain, clean white shirt.

"Dr Stevens, I'm Alex. It's good to meet you," she says, extending her hand.

Elizabeth offers a genuine smile. "Alex, thank you," she replies, shaking her hand firmly.

"I'll meet you in there," says Rigs, with a gruff nod, as she continues to shut off various switches and toggles.

Elizabeth steps out of the helicopter, taking a small tumble. Instantly, she feels a flush of red creep across her face, grateful for the darkness that has concealed most of her embarrassment, until Alex shines a bright flashlight at her.

"Steady."

As the pair approach the facility, a single and large imposing light casts long shadows on the ground, creating an otherworldly atmosphere.

"Is that the best idea?" Elizabeth asks, gesturing to the light.

"Oh, it's only been on a few minutes; Rigs needs it to locate us; navigating the trees in the darkness, I can imagine, is quite hard; it will go off in a moment."

"I suppose that makes sense", Elizabeth responds, a little humbled.

Alex begins detailing efforts made to secure the area as they walk towards the facility.

"We've done our best to fortify against external threats," she explains as they walk across an open expanse of flattened grass. "The windows have been reinforced, and we have a couple of surveillance personnel set up to monitor the exterior surroundings. The off-grid setup is complete and fully operational using a mixture of wind and solar, and we also have a large generator at the rear of the property for emergency use," she continues, attempting to direct a flashlight towards that which she is talking about.

"Excellent work," Elizabeth responds, impressed with the facility's progress.

Approaching the door, Alex beckons her to enter the facility first, holding the door open. Upon entering the building, they begin to traverse a long and dimly lit corridor.

Alex begins describing the rooms and their uses as they pass. "The old communal room has been repurposed into sleeping quarters," she says matter-of-factly.

This sudden revelation takes Elizabeth aback, and she stops in her tracks. "What, why? What about the living quarters?" she questions, a mix of surprise and concern in her voice. Then, as she searches Alex's face, a realisation dawns on her. "Alex, how many people are here?"

"Well, you've met Rigs. We have two security personnel, Lana, our cook, and an engineer."

"Just a number will be fine," Elizabeth interrupts.

"Fourteen? " The number stuns her.

That's nowhere near what I had anticipated.

Her pulse quickens as she processes the implications. Had the others simply not made it? Had they refused? Or had something stopped them from getting here?

"But I told people they could bring children," she says, forcing steadiness into her voice. "I expected many more; that's why we picked this place.".

Alex, now looking visibly upset, responds with a heavy sigh. "Who knows, maybe it's better not to think about what could have happened."

"Has anyone come as a family, bought any children?"

"Would you leave your husband, uproot your family to come here?" Alex responds as she continues leading Elizabeth through the intricacies of the facility.

My mother wouldn't even do it. Was I stupid to presume others would? Is love that blinding?

As they proceed deeper into the facility, Alex reveals that a significant portion of the facility, particularly the lower levels, have been cordoned off completely.

"Given the size of the facility and the number of occupants, we've focused our operations within a more condensed space to conserve resources. We've limited access to the lower levels and put up barriers to separate the additional wings to make everything more manageable."

"Yep, that's sensible. Alex, please tell me we have a lab."

"Oh yes, definitely," she responds with a smile. "This way."

As they make their way further into the facility, Elizabeth uses the opportunity to learn more about her new colleague.

"How did you come to know about the plan? What's your skillset?"

Alex hesitates for a moment. "I don't have a skillset, to be honest. I am, or was, a math teacher and a friend of Sarah's from school. She shared the intel."

Knowing Sarah. You were, I suspect, a little more than friends.

"Well, I'm glad you're here Alex. We are going to need everyone we can get. Did you not have a family you could bring as well?"

Alex stops at a doorway just open enough for Elizabeth to see that they have reached the lab. "It was only me and my dad, so naturally….well, you know."

As they enter, Elizabeth immediately notices a small team of dedicated female scientists working hastily on a selection of tasks. Some familiar faces catch Elizabeth's eye, while others remain strangers. First, she notices an old colleague and friend, Dr Maya Simmons, a seasoned epidemiologist with extensive experience in studying diseases and their patterns. Standing beside her, Elizabeth recognises her close friend and fellow ex-government employee, Dr Sarah Chen, a microbiologist specialising in analysing microorganisms. Elizabeth approaches the pair.

Sarah offers her a welcoming smile as Maya extends her hand, excitement in her eyes. "Maya, it's so good to see you; it's been a while." Elizabeth greets warmly. "And Sarah, how are you?"

"Considering everything, I've been better. But what do you think of our makeshift lab?" Sarah continues cheerfully, not allowing Elizabeth to question the sentence's first statement.

"It's wonderful. it's just as I hoped it would be," she replies.

"Let me introduce you to the others," Maya says, beckoning for Elizabeth to join her.

Together, all three approach another pair of scientists. "This is Dr Elena Rodriguez. Elena is our geneticist."

Elena acknowledges her with a firm handshake. "Welcome, Dr Stevens. I trust my sister's flying wasn't too erratic."

"Rigs is your sister?"

"Unfortunately so," Elena responds with a wry smile.

Elizabeth examines Elena's features. Much softer than her sister's, with long, wavy dark hair and a youthful face bordering on childlike.

"And here we have Dr Michelle Baker, our biochemist," Maya introduces.

"Welcome," says Michelle, extending her hand to Elizabeth, who accepts it gratefully.

"Thanks, thank you for coming".

Although unfamiliar to Elizabeth, Elena and Michelle both exude an aura of authority.

"Would you like a quick tour?" Maya asks proudly.

"Absolutely".

"Great, follow me," she says, gesturing for Elizabeth to follow her once again. "So, despite its modest size, we have managed to equip ourselves with quite the array of tools and instruments.

I'm a little surprised.

"So, this is our central work hub," Maya begins, stopping and leaning on a single, large stainless-steel worktop. "We have a selection of high-powered microscopes, and then over here, we have our centrifuges." Elizabeth watches them quietly spin samples at high speeds. "Then we have a selection of Pipettes and micro-pipettors, with a refrigeration unit."

"This is wonderful," responds Elizabeth, a little overwhelmed with the team's organisation and resourcefulness thus far. "And all of this is working from the solar?" she questions, closely admiring a selection of Petri dishes containing agar plates on a nearby shelf, falling behind with distraction.

"Yep, backed up by a diesel generator. So shall we continue?"

Elizabeth suddenly feels Maya's lingering presence. "Yes, sorry."

"So, adjacent to our central work hub is an area we have designated for our molecular biology work, complete with a thermocycler for polymerase chain reaction analysis and a sequencer."

"Maya, this is superb," Elizabeth says, quickening her pace to catch up.

"It was hard work to organise, but over here, oh, this is the crème de la crème." Maya points to the far corner of the room. "We have even managed to get a biosafety cabinet with UV light sterilisation."

"Blimey, part of me anticipated us being lucky to have chalk and a chalkboard".

"Well, actually, not to disappoint, we do have this," Maya chuckles as she directs Elizabeth's attention to a large whiteboard mounted on the wall littered with diagrams, notes, detailed experiments, and research findings.

After Elizabeth has finished further exploration of the lab, the team gather at the work hub. "Thank you all for coming. It was a pleasure to meet you all. I'm knackered, so can I suggest we all get together in the morning to discuss every-thing? "

"Sounds like a plan to me," Sarah responds.

"Great, well, goodnight, everyone."

"Goodnight", the scientists respond in unison.

Alex, who has waited patiently at the door, guides Elizabeth out of the room and back through the corridors. "Dr Tomkins is due to meet you tomorrow," she informs.

Elizabeth lets out a dry chuckle. "I assume she couldn't be bothered to get up," but inside, a small knot of unease twists in her gut. If anyone could get under her skin, it was Jane.

"She's been overseeing some critical research on potential treatments." Alex continues. "It seems she's found some promising leads that she's eager to follow up on before her rendezvous with you."

Of course, she has. Typical Jane - always chasing breakthroughs but never quite catching them.

As they reach the sleeping quarters, Elizabeth thanks Alex for the information and help. "Rest well, Dr Stevens. Tomorrow is a new day," Alex says, smiling reassuringly as she returns to the corridor.

The following day, Elizabeth awakens feeling surprisingly fully rested. The darkness in the room the night before hadn't allowed her to pay much attention to its layout, but in the morning glow, she can see that the room's perimeter is lined with a wide array of bedding solutions. A single triple bunk bed is a focal point, towering in the corner. Nearby are a few single metal-framed beds alongside several wooden ones such as her own. Though practical, the room exudes a thrown-together feel, with a varied selection of patterned quilts and blankets. Being careful not to disturb those still sleeping, Elizabeth dresses and moves towards the door. As she steps into the corridor, preparing herself to face the new day's challenges, a whisper gently brushes her ear.

"Morning, Doc. Want a shower?" Alex offers.

"Oh my god, we have a shower, yes, of course"

"I thought you might," Alex chuckles. "Follow me."

Alex leads Elizabeth through the corridors once more, asking her how she slept.

"Very well actually, surprisingly. I assume everything was fine during the night?"

"Nothing to report," Alex replies, her tone steady. Shortly, they arrive at a large communal shower room just off the main corridor. Alex demonstrates how everything works. "Only one of the showers works, and it's stone cold," she remarks as she turns it on and tests the water with a slight shiver. "But it wakes you up."

Amused by the nonchalant attitude, Elizabeth nods. "I suppose it does."

"There's a selection of clothing in that cupboard if you need anything. We tend to share as much as possible around here, so if there's something you can add, it would be beneficial. Shall we meet in the canteen afterwards?".

"Sounds great, thanks, Alex".

Alex leaves Elizabeth to shower, who takes no time to begin enjoying the refreshing and brisk water. Once finished, she dresses quickly in an assortment of makeshift clothing, opting for a slightly baggy pair of jeans and a t-shirt branded with what she assumes to be a band. Then she makes her way down the corridor towards the canteen. The canteen oozes a dated charm. Its back wall contains makeshift shelving stocked with preserved foods, and a large wooden table and chairs, worn but functional, are proudly placed in the centre of the room where a few occupants sit together, sharing quiet conversations and sipping beverages. As Elizabeth enters, Alex's frantic waving catches her attention as she motions for her to join her in a corner.

As she approaches, another woman suddenly steps forward, blocking her path. "Morning, Dr Stevens," she says, extending her hand.

Elizabeth takes it cautiously.

"Lana, here is our resident cook," Alex interrupts with a raised voice across the canteen.

"Hardly a cook," Lana responds with a smile. "More of a food surveillance officer."

"Ah, yes, guardian of the beans," Alex jokes, laughing.

"I put a selection of things out for the day, rationing the best I can. If you want something cooked or warmed up, I handle that for you," Lana says with a smaile.

"Oh, okay, erm, thank you," Elizabeth replies, still bewildered by the sudden introduction.

"Can I do anything for you?"

"I think I'm okay this morning, thanks."

As Lana steps out of the way, Elizabeth closes the small distance between her and Alex, who is standing next to the arrangement of food items. Elizabeth notices steam coming from a large metallic jug. "Is that coffee?"

With a grin, Alex jokes, "Yep, but I hope you like it black. Milk's a bit scarce, and no one thought to bring a cow."

Elizabeth appreciates the humour, selecting one of the many mismatched cups from a nearby stack and pouring herself a cup, relishing the comforting aroma.

As she takes her first sip of the drink, enjoying its warmth, Alex leans in, "I was thinking, Doc, it might be good to show you around a bit, maybe meet our security personnel, you know, before you get to the science."

Elizabeth nods. "Yes, I suppose that sounds like a good idea."

Alex grins. "Should we start now, then?"

God, everyone's so keen, give me a minute. "Sure."

As Elizabeth follows Alex out of the canteen, she glances back at the others sipping their drinks, quietly chatting. The scene is almost peaceful. But the impending arrival of Dr Jane Tomkins leaves a lingering feeling of unease she can't quite shake.

XI

Tensions

As Elizabeth and Alex step into the early morning sunlight, the bright beams aim directly at them, temporarily blinding the pair as they exit the facility.

"So, what do you think? Now that you can see it in daylight?" asks Alex

"It's a little bigger than I expected. And older. That fence looks like it's barely standing."

"Yeah, the fences are mostly for show now. They're a good visual deterrent, but most of them would fall with the slightest push. The guard towers are just as old; we don't even bother with them. The cooling tower is our main lookout."

"Have any of the fences been secured?" Elizabeth asks, concerned.

"No, we thought time would be better spent fortifying the actual facility rather than the fences. We did fix some of the more obvious breaches, though."

"We?"

"Yeah, as a collective, most of us have been here a few weeks; only Elena, Rigs, and Beth, like yourself, have arrived more recently

"What about Jane?"

"Jane, she's been coming and going since the beginning."

"To follow up on this critical research?"

"Yeah, I would presume so."

"How is she travelling back and forth? I thought we had limited resources"?

"What do you mean by how?"

"Well, I assume she's coming and going somewhere to do this research?"

"Oh, you would need to ask Rigs. We only ever find out once she's already left."

Seems convenient and sly. Typical Jane.

Elizabeth basks in the feeling of the warm morning light on her face as she admires the facility's silent surroundings. "Those buildings? They look like they could collapse at any moment." She says, gesturing towards some small buildings on the fence's perimeter.

"Unfortunately, most of them are in rough shape. The old generator room is where we scavenged a few bits and pieces. The reactor is underground, attached to the main facility, but I'm sure you know all this.

"Some, but not all," admits Elizabeth. "I worked from diagrams mostly. I knew the facility was disused and, most importantly, safely decommissioned, but I've never actually been here before."

"Well, for what it's worth. I think it was a good choice".

"Thanks. I must admit, though, seeing it in the daylight, it almost feels ghostly."

"It is. But I suppose that's what makes it perfect," says Alex. The comment gives Elizabeth a hint of pride. "Since we're currently only occupying a small part of the facility, the perimeter is flawed, as I said, but we've made the immediate area, well, it's manageable."

As they walk along the outer edges, Elizabeth notices one of the attempts to barricade a wide opening. Improvised is a wall of sturdy wooden planks and metal sheets carefully arranged to form a barrier.

As they continue, they eventually reach the cooling tower base, and Alex suddenly calls out, "Hey, Kim!"

Looking upwards, Elizabeth spots a bright, cheerful face peeking over the tower's edge.

"Hey, Alex! What's going on?" Kim's voice calls back.

"Come down here for a second." Kim nods and begins to descend the metal staircase. Each step taken is met with the sound of creaking metal. As she reaches the bottom, Alex eagerly introduces Elizabeth to Kim, a female guard who is casually dressed but accompanied by an assault rifle,

"Kim here is one of our vigilant protectors. She and her security partner, Clair, rotate shifts to keep watch."

Kim nods and holds her hand out to Elizabeth in a gesture. Elizabeth accepts it, staring at Kim's calm demeanour, which reflects the discipline and seriousness required for her role.

"Thank you, Kim. Have you had to use that yet?" she asks, gesturing to the rifle slung across her shoulder.

"Not since I've been here."

Well, that's a relief.

"Anyway, it's been good to meet you," Kim continues, " but I'd better get back up there," she says, turning away from the pair.

"There's one last thing I would like to show you," Alex begins, leading Elizabeth back towards the main facility. Shortly afterwards, the pair stop at one of the old outbuildings. Alex fumbles around with a small metal keypad. She takes a couple of attempts to input the correct code, but, after a few tries, she finally enters the correct one, opens the door and gestures for Elizabeth to enter first.

"This is our armoury," Alex says, gesturing toward the shelves stocked with various weapons and ammunition. "It's not perfect, but it's better than nothing."

"Why aren't we keeping the weapons in the main facility?" Elizabeth asks directly.

"Some are," Alex replies, "but most are kept here for safety reasons."

Who's stupid idea was that? "Safety from who?" Elizabeth presses. "And who has the code?"

"Well, it's simple, 98789Y, so you do now," she says. "Kim and Clair know it, and so does Rigs."

"I'm not sure keeping our weapons hidden behind a locked door is the smartest move," Elizabeth comments angrily. She exits the small building. "And if that keypad stops working, then what?" Alex closes the door behind her, checking that it has self-locked and jogs a few steps to catch up with Elizabeth, who's already heading back to the main facility.

I can't believe that. I bet that was Jane's idea; she just has to have control of everything.

Falling into step beside her, Alex tries to lighten the mood. "So, diving straight into the science today?" she asks.

"Yes, that's the plan. What about you?" Elizabeth replies, anger still apparent in her voice.

"Oh, I'm sure they'll find something else to keep me busy," Alex says with a faint smile.

As they re-enter the facility, Jane Tomkins exits the canteen, surprising Elizabeth. Their eyes lock, and suddenly, she feels a wave of angst. Jane raises an eyebrow, her gaze steady and inscrutable.

Despite her doubts, Elizabeth squares her shoulders and approaches. "Jane."

"Elizabeth,"

Sensing the tension, Alex discreetly excuses herself, leaving the two alone.

Elizabeth outstretched her hand, "It's good to see you".

Jane's response is cold and direct. "Let's skip the pleasantries, Elizabeth. I did tell you they wouldn't listen."

"You did?"

Jane almost has a smug look on her face.

"You're a prophet." Elizabeth thinks, but the comment has already escaped her mouth.

"Still as petty as ever I see. So, shall we?" Jane says, gesturing for Elizabeth to accompany her.

The tension between the pair is palpable as they walk through the corridors side by side. Elizabeth attempts to correct her outspokenness by engaging in light conversation, "I have to be honest; I expected many more people."

Jane unexpectedly stops in her tracks, her gaze piercing. "How many people do you recognise?" she scolds.

Elizabeth blushes slightly. *Should have kept my mouth shut.* "Erm, Sarah."

"Precisely," Jane replies, her tone sharp. "This may have been a joint idea, but let's not forget who did ninety-nine percent of it. While you were swanning around, doing whatever it was you were doing. I was here, piecing all of this together, building fucking beds, moving wood and metal, risking myself to prepare this place."

The words hang in the air. Deep down, Elizabeth had hoped that the collapse of everything they had once known might have muted the past. However, it was clear that despite a collaborative effort in establishing the facility, the undertones of failure, rivalry and pride still simmered beneath the surface.

"I was doing all that I could; everyone was too consumed with the chaos that unfolded to listen."

"That's always been your problem, Elizabeth, too easily brushed aside. I should have been the one to present the findings; I would have made them listen. Now look where we are."

"Don't you dare try and blame me in the slightest", Elizabeth scolds back, tears welling in her eyes. "No one knew it would take effect so rapidly."

"I'm not blaming you for anything, I'm just saying, if things don't go your way, you make it so they do."

Jane continues through the corridor, ending the stand-off abruptly. Elizabeth shuffles her feet a few paces behind, trying to compose herself, before hurrying to Jane's side. Walking beside her, Elizabeth covertly studies the woman she once knew so well. A brilliant neurologist, one of the world's best, with a reputation that precedes her. Her posture and aura still exude a formidable presence, as they always have. Tall and composed, she carries a confidence that Elizabeth knows all too well borders on arrogance. Long Chestnut hair frames sharp features, and her once-soft blue eyes are now guarded and distant. Despite their history, Elizabeth won't deny the undeniable brilliance that radiates from Jane and the magnetism in how she carries herself. That damn magnetism. As they arrive at the lab door, Elizabeth anticipates a quick conversation about their approach to the pathogen. but, to her surprise, Jane walks straight in. She follows Jane into the lab, which is already filled with activity as the small team of scientists all work diligently at individual stations, analysing data, conducting experiments, and discussing findings. Jane navigates through the lab with familiarity, exchanging nods and brief words with each member.

Elizabeth follows suit, observing the team with curiosity and cautious optimism, when suddenly, Jane's authoritative tone cuts through the hum of activity in the lab, drawing the attention of the scientists with a loud clap of her hands.

"Right then, now that Dr Stevens has finally joined us, I would like to brainstorm some theories I have."

The scientists pause their tasks, set aside their equipment, and gather around Jane and Elizabeth.

"Until recently, I had been attempting to explore how this pathogen impacts men specifically, and I believe the target to be the Y chromosome."

The scientists start to share intrigued looks with one another.

"I understand how that might sound, but I have some theories." Jane paces a few steps, gauging her audience. "My first theory is Y Chromosome Specificity; simply put, the pathogen may have a unique and specific affinity for the Y chromosome, targeting either the genes or regulatory elements that play crucial roles in male development or brain function."

"That's a theory we discussed some time ago." Elizabeth retorts.

"Anyway, I believe this is achieved through specialised proteins or enzymes that have learnt to either recognise or interact with Y chromosome-specific sequences. My second theory," continues Jane, "is silent infection, simply put, to avoid detection and allow the pathogen to remain latent. Its effects don't manifest any noticeable symptoms until a specific trigger event occurs."

Sarah raises her hand frantically, and Jane acknowledges her with a gentle nod. "Would this be why the pathogen doesn't seem to influence male children?

"I believe so, but it's just a theory", Jane reminds her. "As you are probably all aware, the amygdala is the brain region involved in processing emotions and social behaviours; it's responsible for a person's 'fight or flight'. Suppose the pathogen specifically affects this brain region, which I believe it does. In that case, it will need to be activated or have its effects amplified once the amygdala has fully developed. This typically occurs around age twenty and could be achieved through various mechanisms, such as releasing specific toxins or viral proteins, which are only triggered at this certain developmental stage."

Elizabeth finds herself impressed with Jane's simplistic approach to the pathogen, almost forgetting that the theories mirror her own. "Jane", she interrupts, "This raises many questions about the pathogen's intent and why it would specifically target the Y chromosome."

Jane sighed, her voice now hinting at defeat. "Yep, you've prompted my final theory. If the pathogen is designed to target the Y chromosome specifically, then it could be trying to limit the reproduction and survival of males, thus affecting the overall population. However, it is extremely important that we remember the Y chromosome isn't purely responsible for the development of sex in humans; there are women with a Y chromosome and men without one. So, if that is its purpose, it does have a fundamental flaw".

"Can't we simply eradicate the Y chromosome?"

Elizabeth and Jane search the room for the colleague responsible for the question.

"I understand the scientific curiosity," Elizabeth begins to answer, still searching for a hint of the question's origin. "But removing the Y chromosome from humankind would be an immensely complex and ethically challenging task."

"But yes, it's a possibility," interrupts Jane. "There are already individuals with XX chromosomes who are biologically male" Jane sends a menacing sideways glance in Elizabeth's direction. "There's a condition is known as Swyer syndrome." She continues, "It's a mutation, or absence if you will, of the SRY gene on the Y chromosome, which is responsible for developing male sex characteristics. While these individuals have female chromosomes, they lack the Y chromosome and its key genetic components." Jane walks over to the whiteboard nearby, picking up a marker to illustrate her points. "During animal trials and research on individuals with Swyer syndrome, it has been observed that the absence of a Y chromosome can lead to several health complications, including dramatically increased risk of heart disease, Alzheimer's and cancer. The Y chromosome regulates many genes involved in various bodily functions." She drew a simplified chromosome structure on the whiteboard, highlighting the essential genes and their functions. "Genes on the Y chromosome contribute to the production of certain hormones, including testosterone, which plays a significant role in male sexual development, muscle mass, and bone density. The absence of these genes can lead to hormonal imbalances, but theoretically, yes, it is possible".

"However," interrupts Elizabeth, a battle of wills and opinion is now taking place. "Removing the Y chromosome from the entire human population would likely lead to severe health consequences for those who possess XX chromosomes without the Y chromosome's genetic components. It would disrupt the delicate balance of our hormonal and biological systems, resulting in various health issues and premature mortality. We would also need to develop highly advanced technology to selectively target humans only, then alter the DNA within every cell carrying the Y chromosome."

"Humans only? Why?" questioned Sarah.

"Well, if we eradicate the Y chromosome somehow without a selection design, we risk eradicating it in every living thing." Elizabeth holds out her hand, requesting the marker from Jane in a silent attempt to assert some dominance in the room. Jane complies, handing the marker over with a bewildered stare. Elizabeth sets the marker down, her expression grave. "The complexity and risks involved make such an endeavour far from practical and, most importantly, highly unethical. Our focus needs to be on finding a way to neutralise the pathogen's effects while preserving the essential genetic diversity that exists within our species. What we do or do not do here holds the potential to save countless lives, but it also demands responsible and thoughtful decision-making.

After a few seconds of silence, Sarah contributes her theory to the conversation. "May I also add another theory to the equation?"

"Please," responds Jane, welcoming the diverse perspectives.

"We observed a dramatic increase in behavioural episodes after the announcement of the pathogen. Reports of uncontrollable behaviour in men spiked. I have a theory that perhaps this specific trigger event that Dr Tomkins mentioned lies in trauma and stress."

"That would explain the sudden surge," Elizabeth interjects. "If stress can accelerate activation, it means we may have miscalculated the timeline. The pathogen could be programmed to wait for biological maturity - but under enough stress, the body might trigger it early as a survival mechanism."

"Surely we would have seen effects of the pathogen in children if this was the case?" Suggests Maya.

"A solid observation?" replies Jane. "But it could explain the different stages we have all witnessed; perhaps slow progressive infection is why verbal ability changes, creating these mumblers, and a traumatic response is responsible for the silent ones."

The thought of the silent ones sends a shiver down Elizabeth's spine. She had only ever seen one, and his eyes still haunt her dreams regularly. "The question is, how do we verify and test this hypothesis?" she interrupts.

Jane responds dryly, "Well, isn't it obvious? We need a male. Good work, Dr Chen." She then turns to leave the room.

Shocked by Jane's proposal of a live test, Elizabeth feels overcome with a surge of objection. After a few moments of processing, she can't contain her outrage and proceeds to chase Jane out of the room. "Absolutely not!" she shouts, her voice echoing through the corridor.

Jane, a few steps down the corridor already, stops instantly and calmly turns towards her. "Maybe if you were more willing to push boundaries, you wouldn't be stuck in your perpetual cycle of uncertainty. Haven't you learnt that a cautious approach could cost us more than you realise, Elizabeth?"

"I won't allow it".

"Allow it?" Jane scoffs. "Unlike you, I'm not constrained by hesitation and ethical handwringing." Her eyes are wide, her gaze unwavering. "I'll do whatever it takes to unravel this pathogen's secrets. And you're gravely mistaken if you think I need your, or anyone else's, permission to do anything." She steps closer to Elizabeth and lowers her voice. "Hesitation may well be the hindrance we can't afford." With that cutting statement, Jane turns on her heel and walks down the corridor without a second glance. Elizabeth watches her as she bravely attempts to hold her resolve, but tears well up in her eyes. Standing alone in the corridor, she grapples with the weight of their disagreement as the echoes of Jane's footsteps fade. Her heart pounds. She wants to believe that hesitation is strength, that caution is what separates them from madness. But as the weight of Jane's words lingers, she can't help but wonder: What if she's wrong?

XII

Burnt

Lying in his restraints, Clint can't shake the sense of interconnectedness that he felt had formed between himself, Ezra, and the woman named Cara. Guilt tugs at his stomach for not pushing her further to join them. He knew she had her own desires and that being around a man was dangerous for her, but for Ezra, and for him, a woman's presence would have been appreciated.

Was she afraid of them? Or afraid of what staying would mean?

He had not managed to return to sleep since her departure and had decided to allow Ezra to continue resting, the boy's grasp remaining tight against his side as if they had melted into one another through the night. Before long, boredom and the idea of freedom tore at Clint, and he let out a deliberate, loud yawn to awaken his son. The young boy arises, stretching his tired body. For a moment, he lies beside him, content and at peace, but as he sets his eyes upon his father's smiling face beside him, he immediately begins to tug, almost violently, at his father's restraints.

"Hey, hey, calmly," Clint says softly, "you don't want to make them any tighter."

Ezra stops momentarily and slows his erratic breathing. "Sorry."

He returns to the task, now cautious and measured, tackling his father's binds with small, clumsy hands. After a few moments of anticipation, the restraints on Clint's wrists finally give, allowing Ezra to feel the warming embrace of his father's love once more. The embrace can't last long enough.

Oh, Ezra, you've been so brave.

"Where's Cara?" the boy inquires, pulling away from the hug and searching the area.

"She left before you woke," Clint says, sitting up and tending to the restraints around his ankles.

"Oh, where did she go? Did she say when she's coming back?"

"I don't think she is buddy."

Ezra's expression changes, excitement and reunion replaced with sadness.

"Hey, pass me that backpack over there." Clint over-enthusiastically says, attempting to divert the boy's attention. "She said we could have it."

Ezra slowly retrieves the backpack, struggling on his first attempt to lift it; he doesn't try a second attempt and drags it across the floor. Clint shifts in his makeshift bed as he begins to sift through the backpack's contents, his fingers brushing over each item. It is clear that Cara and her father had prepared themselves for the challenges ahead, equipping themselves with a surprising amount of necessary survival tools. Still, he felt the expanse of the items she had left them was almost too generous.

Surely she couldn't afford to have left a full backpack, could she? I suppose there were two of them. But still.

He shifts through the variety of items. Water bottles, tinned foods, and a can opener. Boil-in-bags like the ones used the night before. A pocketknife, a couple of blankets, and mess tins - all essential items for any journey, along with the hand-drawn map. But it was the presence of the sidearm that caught him off guard. He knew that self-defence would be crucial, but he didn't anticipate finding a firearm among the provisions.

Ezra's eyes widen as he catches sight of the weapon. "Dad, are you going to take it?"

Clint hesitates, his fingers curling around the grip of the firearm. The last time he'd seen a gun; it had been aimed at him. He exhales and nods.

"We'll take it. But we only use it if we have no other choice."

Ezra nods in agreement.

As he rises to his feet, he feels a slight wave of dizziness and a deep aching in his side. The foliage ceiling brushes gently against the top of his head. He lifts his top and finds a neatly yet amateurishly made small row of stitches.

"I watched." Ezra says proudly, "And it didn't make me feel sick."

"Thank you, buddy, for looking after me." Clint gives Ezra's shoulder a light squeeze before placing the backpack securely on his back, stowing the firearm in the rear of his trousers, and placing the folded map in his pocket. " Let's say we get out of here."

He helps his young son navigate the exit rope, allowing him to work most of it out for himself. As he gradually emerges from the den, Ezra squints against the blinding daylight. Clint follows closely behind and experiences the temporary disorientation that days out of direct sunlight bring. His eyes feel as if they are burning in their sockets, and everything around him is a blur of colour. Clint inhales the fresh and crisp air, savouring the sharp scent of pine needles mixed with the faint sweetness of wildflowers. As his blurred vision finally begins to clear, the wilderness unfolds around him, showcasing a dense, untamed forest. Trees tower high into the sky, their branches filtering the bright sunlight into scattered beams. The underbrush is wild, filled with ferns, shrubs, and moss and grass that carpet the floor. Birds call out from the treetops, their songs echoing through the stillness as a gentle breeze rustles the leaves. He removes the map from his pocket and begins to assess it in the new light, his fingers tracing the solid lines that Cara said indicate her previous routes.

"So, where now?" asks Ezra, his curiosity evident.

"I suppose we follow Cara's plans and head for the coast," he responds, studying the map for the best route. *I have no other ideas.* "There might be signs of a safe place when we arrive."

"Oh, or a boat, like what Cara was going to do!" exclaims Ezra, excitement lighting up his eyes.

"Yeah, maybe," Clint chuckles, "but we could find anything. The coast has other advantages, resources, potential shelter, and maybe even a community of like-minded people" *Or everything we want to avoid.*

Ezra approaches his father and looks at him intimately. "Is it far?"

Clint considers the question, studying the map once again. "A few days' walk, I reckon. But we always, always need to be careful."

"Got it!" Ezra says, putting his hands on his hips, ready to embark on a new adventure.

"Excellent." *The coast it is then.* "But first, aren't you forgetting something?".

Ezra looks at him with a puzzled expression, "Oh yeah, Dad, I have a test for you".

With the new and comforting weight of the well-stocked backpack upon his shoulders, Clint begins to feel relief washing over him as the harrowing thought of having to turn back towards the city has completely waned. Yet, just a few steps into their journey, Ezra's discovery of the clearing and rooftops enters his mind, and he can't ignore an overwhelming desire to investigate.

"You know what, Ezra?" he says with curiosity. "Before we go too far, why don't we check out that clearing and the rooftops first?

Ezra looks at his father, puzzled. "Why?"

Because I'm not entirely set on the coast yet. "Because, according to the map, it's not too far from here, and who knows what we might find."

"Good idea, Dad. Can we take the road, though? I hate it in the woods".

Clint contemplates Ezra's request: "I don't see why not. Come on, this way."

The sun beats down harshly as they make their way through the undergrowth. Ezra has taken the lead, unknowingly, and it doesn't take long for them to come across the resting place of Cara's father. Ezra glides past with maturity, holding his head high, refusing to let curiosity get the better of him, but Clint feels a pang of guilt as he passes, opting to take a silent moment of reflection. Before long, they stumble across the road once more. Once upon it an increasing frequency of vehicles begin to litter its surface. They all display the same signs of ageing, with moss-ridden tyres, rusted paint jobs and broken windows; however, Ezra treats each one's arrival as a pivotal moment, peering within with excitement and wonder.

On the horizon, Clint finally spots the distant silhouettes of houses and increases their pace. "There is, come on."

Before them is a cul-de-sac-sized tiny village of 15, maybe 20 houses. He finds himself looking at the properties in awe, feeling a hint of jealousy enter his mind. "This is the sort of place I would love to have lived in," he tells Ezra.

The small village stands frozen in time, with more cars scattered along the overgrown streets. As they pass the first couple of houses, Clint notices they all bear the scars of looting, with shattered windows and doors either ajar or entirely missing. Turning to Ezra, he notices that his young son's pace has slowed as the boy eagerly observes something intently in the distance.

"What do you see?" Clint whispers, placing his hand on the sidearm secured in his trousers.

"That", replies Ezra, using his finger to try and direct his father's vision.

"I see it; what the hell?"

He hurries Ezra off the road and into the overgrowth, and together they begin to covertly approach Ezra's discovery. This particular property is different, with windows hidden by thick metal shutters. Although ivy has started to consume its exterior, to Clint's surprise, it looks almost entirely untouched. Large metal fence panels surround the rear of the property, almost wholly hiding the area from any outside viewing. Ezra draws his father's attention to a large opening in the metal panels, offering a peek into the hidden vicinity. As they draw nearer, Clint notices that a pair of large fencing panels lay on their side, instantly putting him on alert. He pulls out the small pistol and holds it clumsily out in front of him.

"What!" asks Ezra, alarmed.

Clint doesn't respond, his concentration remaining focused on their surroundings.

"Dad, what's the matter?"

Clint remains silent, but this time, he holds a finger to his lips, hushing any further questions Ezra may have. Clint, still carefully inspecting the area, points to some markings in the dirt nearby.

"Those look like tyre marks," he murmurs to himself.

"Look, there's rope tied around that post," Ezra responds.

Clint squats, running a finger over the disturbed dirt.

Days, maybe a week old. Recent enough to make me uneasy. "I don't think the people camping here were the ones who broke in."

Ezra stiffens. "So… someone else came?"

The boy's face sparks with fear, and he quickly moves to his father's side.

"Stay alert." Clint awkwardly tightens his grip on the small sidearm with both hands.

Stealthily, he moves through the opening with Ezra following closely. Stepping over the panels, they enter what was once a much-loved rear garden. A collapsed swing, partly hidden by bracken, is the focal point of one corner, and a large greenhouse stands in the opposite, with broken glass panels shattered and littering the floor nearby. The tell-tale signs of a makeshift campsite lay in the centre, with the remnants of a fire pit with large wooden logs placed around it, scattered food wrappers, and empty water bottles.

"Looks like someone was here not too long ago," he whispers to Ezra.

Ezra nodded, his eyes scanning the area for any signs of movement. "Why wouldn't they just stay in the house?"

An obvious observation but a valid one, Clint thought. As he turns towards the house, he feels Ezra grab the side of his shirt. He moves up the rear steps onto a large, decked area and examines the rear door.

"Look at the dents. Someone tried really, really hard to get in."

"That must be why they camped then, Dad."

"Agreed, that fence would have provided a nice hiding spot; I guess the fire attracted some unwanted attention."

"So, no one's here?" asks Ezra.

"No, buddy, not anymore, I don't think," he responds with relief.

Clint continues to explore the large decked area, checking the windows as he attempts to peer inside, oblivious that Ezra has quietly returned to the garden and has perched himself on a log in front of the fire pit. Clint manages to shift one of the windows, and through the small gap, he can see that the house's interior seems spotless, although dusty and abandoned. A large, comfortable sofa and an undamaged television are visible, along with a coffee table, neatly arranged bookshelves, and a vase containing the stems of long-dead flowers on a mantelpiece. As memories of the past come in waves, he feels defeated. He turns, expecting to find Ezra beside him. Panic sets in momentarily until he notices the boy sitting solemnly in the garden. He takes a moment to admire his son, feeling a wave of sadness overcome him as his thoughts become wild with scenarios of what could have been without the pathogen. He takes a deep breath, steps off the decking, and approaches the boy.

Ezra kicks at the dirt, frowning. "She didn't even say goodbye."

Clint ruffles his son's hair. "No, she didn't." He sighs. "But I think it was easier for her that way. Come on, let's keep moving."

The pair exit the garden and begin to search the remnants of the other open houses in the cul-de-sac. Each one is the same, with nothing to offer, except echoes of the past. Dust-covered furniture and empty rooms that tell tales of hurried departures. Before long, the repetitive process starts to become stale. Clint hoped that at least one dwelling would hold secret worth finding and continued to search despite Ezra's protests of boredom, in the hope of something. What exactly, he wasn't sure. After checking another couple of houses to no avail, Ezra's disappointment and lack of enthusiasm finally prompt Clint to quit the search. He places a comforting hand on Ezra's shoulder and offers a reassuring smile.

"I don't know about you, buddy, but I don't feel like sleeping in the woods again tonight. How about you pick a house, and we can stay in it for the night."

"That's so cool." The boy ponders his thoughts before picking. "That one."

"No, we've already been in that one. Pick one we haven't been in; that way, we can search it as well."

"Okay, then…that one."

As the duo approaches Ezra's chosen dwelling, the door, like most of the others, stands slightly ajar, inviting them inside. He glances at Ezra as a silent understanding passes between them. As he fully opens the creaky front door, his hand sits patiently on the sidearm holstered within his trousers. They slowly begin to make their way through the ground floor, Ezra following closely behind, searching, scanning, and mimicking the movements and observations of his father ahead of him. To Clint's relief, they finally find a few cans of preserves and an old kettle partially still filled with water, which he pours into one of the empty bottles from the backpack. After securing the lower floor, they begin to cautiously climb the stairs. He checks over each room, finding only the remnants of past occupants. Yet, as they open the final door, he notices signs that this room has had a more recent previous occupant. A makeshift bed lies against one wall, and empty cans and packets litter the floor.

"Is someone staying here, Dad? What if they come back?"

He doesn't respond as he checks the unusual situation. He lifts the thin duvet and sees in the light the dust particles that hover in the air.

"No, I think they are long gone, Ezra." He thinks for a moment, weighing the risks before walking to the room's window and peering through the makeshift blind at the sky above. "We'll stay here tonight."

Ezra takes no time settling into the bedroom, as his father barricades the door as best he can with the remaining furniture. Satisfied with his safety measures, he sits on the makeshift bed, removes the sidearm from his trousers and places it just within reach. As dusk begins to envelop the village, they huddle together, finding comfort and safety in each other's presence.

"So, are we going to take a car in the morning?" Ezra asks.

Clint sighs and shakes his head. "No, A car comes with its own set of risks. I don't know how to fix it if something goes wrong, and it would also mean sticking to the roads, which is dangerous."

"So, the woods are safer than the road?"

"I think so. There are more places to hide, and you never know; we might find hidden trails. Try to imagine yourself as an explorer."

As the night starts to cloak the village in darkness, he tenderly brushes his fingers through Ezra's hair and soothingly caresses his back.

"I know this has been hard for you buddy. Leaving the camp and the people we knew wasn't easy for me either. I miss them too, you know," he admits, his voice tinged with nostalgia.

"I'm more worried about you, Dad." Ezra's voice quivers as he replies. "I don't want you to change like... those people. I don't want to leave you and be alone."

Clint looks directly into Ezra's eyes, "I promise you; I'll do everything in my power to ensure that I stay in control; that won't happen to me. You know why?"

Ezra looks at him, uncertain, and shakes his head.

"Because you'll be there for me. You have a strength within you that I've always admired. If things ever get tough, you'll be the one to remind me who I am."

Ezra's eyes well up with tears. "You think so, Dad?"

"I know so," he affirms, pulling his son into a tight embrace. "You're my rock." *And I have just told a terrible, terrible lie.*

That night, sleep doesn't come for Clint. Ezra has drifted off quickly, curled tightly against his side with one arm flung across his chest. Yet, Clint lays there in silence, his eyes fixed on the ceiling above. The weight of his promise hung like a noose around his throat. You're my rock. He'd said it with conviction. Meant it, even. But he knew the truth behind the lie. Knew that fear lived just beneath his skin, growing each day. Hours pass in silence, save for the boy's soft breathing and the occasional creak of the settling house. He keeps staring toward the boarded window, unsure what he's waiting for. Hoping for nothing but dreading everything. Then, he hears them. Voices, distant and muffled. He tenses until curiosity overtakes him. Gently he shifts, lifting Ezra's arm from across his chest. The boy groans softly but doesn't wake. He inches away, his heart pounding, every nerve alight. He reaches, clasping the sidearm with a sweaty palm and tiptoes toward the window. He crouches low, just below the sill, and peers just enough to peer through the lowest part of the glass. His breath stills as he listens. Then, a flicker of firelight streaks across the glass, a torch beam, wild and wandering, gone as quickly as it had appeared. He ducks lower, pressing his back to the wall, listening. Footsteps thud against the tarmac—steady, deliberate. At least two people. Maybe three.

Then a voice, clearer this time: "...still fresh, that one. You see it too, right?"

A second voice, raspy and winded, replies, "Yeah. Wasn't here long ago. You think it's one of them?"

"No. I don't think so."

"Him?"

"Not sure."

Clint's throat tightens as he strains to catch more. *Are they tracking us? No... that doesn't make sense. Why would they?* He holds his breath. His pulse hammering in his ears as the voices continued, calm and steady, moving past the row of houses.

"When I find him, I'm going to gut him. Head to toe."

"Get in line, Si."

It's not us. He glances around the shadowed room, and the question returns like a whisper in his skull. *Who were you? Why were you here?*

Another voice cuts through the night, this one different. Female. Young. "It's been like two weeks. He's not gonna be around here anymore."

The sound of her voice hits Clint hard as guilt lances through his chest. Survivors. Maybe a family. He needs this. He leans forward, almost ready to speak.

"Oh, shut up, you little bitch. You helped him escape. You're lucky you're not next on the chopping block."

He freezes.

"I did noth-" A sharp crack was followed by a muffled cry.

"I swear, one more word. " The voice is low. Seething.

"She's just a kid, lay off."

"Yeah, dickhead," the girl spits, defiant.

"Oh, you vex me something fierce. I'm going to enjoy skinning you."

"Skin this," she snaps back.

Clint can't see it, but he doesn't need to. He can almost picture her middle finger raised, her jaw set, her eyes burning. The voices and footsteps begin to drift off, swallowed slowly by distance. Only when the silence returns does he crawl back across the room. The gun gripped in his hand. He settles beside Ezra once more, breath barely audible.

The morning after the voices, the world feels more disturbed than usual. A small spurt of rain has left a thin sheen across everything. The road appears slick, leaves glisten and puddles mirror a grey, indifferent sky. They eat a traveller's breakfast: stale cookies, tinned peaches. Sweet, soggy silence. Clint barely tastes it. His mind is still circling with the conversation from the night before, playing on a loop.

Who were they? Should I have done something? Could I have?

The voices seem to echo louder in daylight. The girl. Her defiance. Her fear. And the threat that followed.

"You're next on the chopping block."

He can still hear the venom in the man's voice. Can still feel the girl's fiery defiance.

"We'll check a few more houses before we head out," he says, disturbing the quiet.

Ezra nods, already energised from his father's passing of his three tests that morning. Clint had rattled off his answers without hesitation, and that had fuelled his son with confidence, blinding him of his father's confidence that had unravelled and frayed by dread and questions he didn't want to ask. Their footsteps echo down the empty streets, unnervingly loud. The village is too quiet. Too still. A place pretending to be dead. His mind races with possibilities. They reach another house. The final one, Clint told himself. Curiosity or fear? He doesn't know anymore. The air shifts as they enter, and a wave of rot hits them like a wall.

Ezra recoils, covering his nose. "What is that?"

"Stay close," Clint murmured as he stepped carefully, hand on his sidearm.

The smell thickens as they move through the hallway, pooling at the back of the house like something waiting. Then he sees it. A charred pile of bodies, burnt to ash and bone. The ceiling above them is blackened with soot, sagging and scorched by fire. He counts six... maybe seven. The details strike him with gut-punch clarity: strands of hair still clinging to scorched skulls, the curves of hips and chests distorted by flame but unmistakable. Mostly women. His knees threaten to buckle. He wants to scream, to turn back time, to do something. Anything. Instead, he swallows hard, holds the grief in his chest like a loaded gun, and steps in front of Ezra, shielding him with his body.

"There's nothing left for us here," he says, his voice strained but even. "Let's go."

Ezra doesn't question him. He simply nods trustingly. They walk away from the house and from the village.

As they put more distance behind them, Clint's thoughts begin to spiral again: *Were they alive when it happened?* He doesn't want an answer. He doesn't want to know. But the thought lingers, poisonous and persistent.

Why were they here? Why kill them like that? How close did we come to being next?

The road stretches on in silence. He tries to let the stillness settle over him, tries to let it calm his thoughts, but the quiet has started to feel less like peace and more like a pause before something inevitably worse. Hours pass until they come across a bus shelter, long abandoned and half-covered in moss. It's as good a place as any to rest. He shrugs off his pack and rummages inside.

Maybe now's the time for control, for grounding, for giving Ezra a piece of responsibility. "Ezra," he says, pulling out a folded cloth. "I want to show you something."

Ezra's eyes go wide as Clint unwraps the pocketknife. "Whoa! That's so cool! Can I use it for cutting wood and stuff?"

Clint nods, his tone firm. "Yes, but it's not a toy. It's a tool. For survival. You treat it with respect, always."

"I promise, Dad."

XIII

Oasis

Clint and Ezra have been heading towards the coast for a few days. Their progress thus far has been uneventful. When the road they initially followed took an unexpected turn the previous day, they abandoned its guidance and are now relying solely on the hand-drawn map given to them by Cara, and the pair are now meandering through a vast open expanse with no defined path. Since deviating from the road, Clint had silently begun to question either the map's accuracy or his ability to navigate it correctly. As his young son walks silently beside him, he notices that the boy's long strawberry-blonde hair has become more curled and unruly, no doubt due to the day's heat, as Ezra battles the constant casting of shadows that his fringe casts over his eyes. His features have started to bear the traces of their journey, with streaks of dirt on his face and blackness under his tiny fingernails. Yet it is the boy's gloomy expression that concerns Clint the most. His eyes give away his restlessness, darkened and heavy, and his clothes, which once held a shade of cleanliness and care, are now dirtied and smelling. The boy's steps, though still energetic, have slowed, and Clint feels a pang of parental concern as he observes his son's weariness. The open expanse before them seems to stretch endlessly, the horizon remaining an ever-elusive goal, and the hot sun creates wavering mirages in the distance, teasing with illusions of shade and rest.

"We'll find a good spot to rest soon," Clint says, in an attempt to reassure Ezra as he assesses the map once more. *Either I've miscalculated the distance, or I've read this thing wrong. Or am I putting too much faith in Cara's father? After all, how did he know where and what to draw?*

Amidst the solitude and the oppressive heat, He suddenly comes to an abrupt halt, fixating on a distant point, his gaze lingering in emptiness.

"Dad, what do you see?" DAD!

An unfamiliar flicker persists in his father's expression. Unheard and nonsensical, he mumbles to himself. Words seem to slip through his lips, but Ezra struggles to make sense of them. The boy's concern deepens as he observes his father, unsure of the look now dancing within his father's eyes.

"DAD!"

His shouts echo through the vast openness as he desperately attempts to grab his father's attention.

"DAD!"

Suddenly, Clint blinks rapidly, waking from his trance. His gaze refocuses on Ezra. "What? why are you shouting at me?" he asks, genuinely puzzled.

Ezra looks at his father with a mix of concern and frustration. "Why weren't you answering me?"

Clint furrows his brow. "What are you on about Ezra?"

"I was shouting at you."

"Yes, I know, but why?"

"Because you weren't listening."

What the fuck is he on about?

"I shouted Dad like three times."

Unaware of the unsettling mumbles that had escaped his lips, he shakes off the confusion and gives a reassuring smile. "Must've zoned out for a second, buddy, probably the heat." But his attempt at nonchalance couldn't entirely dissipate the uncertainty that lingers in Ezra's eyes. "Let's keep moving. We've got ground to cover."

What the hell just happened?

Ezra nods slowly "Okay," he says, Unconvinced by his father's lie.

The duo resumes their journey, and as more hours pass, the sun continues its relentless task of beating down on them. Clint eventually sees a glimmer of hope on the horizon. He squints his eyes as he tries to make out the distant transformation, as his mind fills with the idea of trees and the promise of shade and relief from the scorching heat. Convinced his desperation has played a cruel trick, he sighs heavily.

"Dad! Look!"

Clint squints against the sun again, towards the horizon, following Ezra's outstretched finger. "You see it too?" he asks, "I thought it was the sun playing tricks on me. We're getting there, buddy," he says with a smile, "Let's pick up the pace".

Eventually, a different yet familiar world unfolds as they reach the edge of the trees. The transition from the open expanse to the shelter of the woods brings a welcome change in the atmosphere. But at the woodland edge, Ezra halts, taking a moment to assess his new surroundings.

"What's up?" Clint asks.

As the boy glances at the line of trees before him, a thoughtful expression etches across his face. "I'm not sure which I hate more, the woods or the sun."

"Well, the woods will provide shade and be much more comfortable.

"Yeah, but it's scary, and the ground hurts my feet."

"I know, buddy. We can do another scavenger hunt".

"Oh yeah." An excited Ezra responds.

As they wander through the woods with a new scavenger hunt underway, they come across a single larger, majestic tree towering far above the others. Its sprawling branches cast vast shadows, blocking even the most stubborn sunlight dapples.

"Wow, that's the biggest tree I've ever seen," Ezra exclaims, his eyes wide in awe.

"It's impressive, alright, and that shade looks perfect for a break and a snack; what do you think?"

Ezra, already marching towards the tree, reaches its shade first. "It's perfect", he squeals.

The pair settle beneath its expansive canopy, and Clint begins to forage in the backpack, pulling out a packet of dried fruit and some dry biscuits. "Here, a little snack to refuel." *I need to ration better.*

Ezra eagerly accepts the offerings and takes a quick, unhesitant mouthful. However, his exuberance and excitement are short-lived, his facial expression changing as he swallows. "These are yucky," he complains, making a face.

Not stopping for long, they press on through this new wilderness as the heat persists and the air shimmers and wavers in the distance. Clint removes his shirt, revealing his thin yet muscular body. His frame is littered with scars from past battles and bears the marks of endurance earned through survival. His laceration from the fight with Cara's father is healing nicely. Thank God for Cara, he thinks, running his finger over the scar. His arms glisten with sweat, as do the hairs on his chest. His hair is damp and shimmers when sunlight breaks through the branches above. Despite his earlier unexplained episode, his eyes remain sharp and vigilant as he continuously scans their surroundings for signs of danger. Ezra, who follows closely, is now practising using the small pocket knife his father has entrusted him with. The boy's youthful face is flush from the heat, and he wipes sweat from his brow with the back of his hand. Clint stops for a moment, removes the backpack, and goes searching within his pocket.

As he does, he watches Ezra dart between the shade of two large trees and feels a content grin form on his lips before returning to his present task. Carefully, he unfolds the map and examines it again, his fingers tracing its lines. The coast, he guessed, still lay at least a day or two away. As he scrutinises the map, a minor marking catches his attention: a small circle and a tidily drawn fish symbol that he is positive resembles a pond or a small lake. A smile tugs at the corners of his lips as the idea of a refreshing oasis becomes too enticing to ignore.

He tucks the map back into his pocket and turns to Ezra. "Hey, buddy," he begins, "I've got a little surprise for you. We're going to take a small detour and check something out".

Ezra's eyes widen. "What is it, Dad?"

"You'll see".

As they walk, Clint eagerly scouts the horizon for his secret, still questioning himself about how Cara's father knew about the surrounding area so intently. However, after a short trek, his questions are answered as he spots an opening in the trees in the distance, and a smile tugs at his lips again as he decides to make the discovery a surprise for his son.

"Hey Ezra, come here," he says.

"What, why?"

"Because I asked."

His reply is slightly more parental than he expected. Softly, he places his hands over the boy's eyes and leads him towards the opening, walking carefully to avoid stumbling on any obstacles. When they finally arrive, he can't help but feel proud of the surprise he has in store for his son.

"Alright, you ready?" he says with a grin, stepping aside and revealing the sparkling expanse of the small lake before them.

A gasp of delight escaped Ezra's lips. "Wow! This is cool!"

The lake is surrounded by lush greenery and tall trees, providing the edges of the water with much-needed shade. At the opposite end of the lake is a small boathouse with a charming wooden dock that stretches over the water. Together, they stand in silence and admire the tranquil surface of the lake and its reflections of the beauty that surrounds it.

"I thought you might like it," Clint says with a smile.

"Like it? I love it!" the boy exclaims, his eyes sparkling with joy.

Holding out his hand, Clint awaits the feeling of his son's tiny hand before leading him towards the water's edge.

"Let's cool off and maybe explore that boathouse; what do you say?"

Approaching the water's edge, Ezra wriggles his hand from Clint's grasp and excitedly begins to remove his shoes and socks. Clint decides to follow his son's example, carefully picking up the boys' scattered footwear before removing his own. As they dip their feet into the refreshing water, he feels the worries and challenges of their journey momentarily fade away.

"What is this place?"

"It's called a lake, well, it's more of a pond really, like in the stories I used to read you at night."

"I didn't know they were real."

Sometimes, I forget that almost everything is new to you.

They walk along the water's edge towards the wooden boathouse, enjoying the oasis and playing together as father and son should. As Ezra darts eagerly ahead, he resists the urge to teach, observing quietly as Ezra exits the water and races excitedly along the newly approached wooden dock. At the dock's end, Ezra perches himself on the wooden planks, and starts swinging his legs back and forth above the water, desperately trying to skim the surface with his toes.

"Alright, buddy, I will take a quick look around. You stay there and enjoy the view, okay?"

Ezra nodded, his eyes still sparkling with amazement. "Sure."

He exits the water and walks towards the small boathouse, his footsteps leaving gentle ripples on the water's edge. As he approaches the door, he notices a sturdy padlock securing it. He studies its undamaged condition, with no apparent signs of tampering. After a brief pause, he carefully places the pairs of shoes at the entrance and reaches for the sidearm. Gripping it firmly, he carefully aims the butt at the padlock and, with a single swift strike, shatters the locking mechanism. The lock falls to the ground, its pieces lost, as they scatter to the floor below. Clint glances back towards Ezra, who is now lying flat on the dock with his feet still swinging above the water, before opening the door and stepping inside the boathouse. Its interior is dimly lit, with only small streaks of sunlight peeking through the gaps in the wooden walls and roof. His eyes adjust to the subdued light as he sees a rowboat resting on supports. Fishing rods and life jackets neatly adorn one wall, and the faint scent of damp wood and decay fills his nostrils as his gaze falls upon a stack of old newspapers in one corner, their yellowed pages telling stories from a bygone era. Determined to find anything of use, he rummages through the boathouse, discovering a rusted fishing net, a few empty gas canisters, and a tattered journal with illegible handwriting. After his quick search of the boathouse, he returns to Ezra. Who still swung his legs above the water.

He deserves this, just a moment of childhood, free from fear.

A memory stirs in Clint's mind, unbidden but welcome. He cleared his throat, a small smile forming.

"When I was about your age, my dad used to take me fishing. We would wake up early in the morning, pack our fishing gear, and head out to a small lake, a bit like this one. It was our special time together, just like this."

"What's fishing?"

"It's where you use bait to catch fish with a line and a hook."

"What's bait?"

"It's food for the fish. The whole point of fishing is that it's supposed to be peaceful. Just the sound of the water, the rustling of leaves, and the anticipation of catching a fish. My father and I would sit side by side, casting our lines and waiting patiently for a bite." He pauses for a moment, his expression softening. "Those fishing trips taught me patience and the importance of spending quality time with loved ones. It's something I'll always treasure."

Ezra leans closer, his eyes shining with curiosity. "Do you think we can go fishing here, Dad?"

Clint gently pats Ezra's back. "I'm glad you asked. I found some fishing rods in the boathouse, but I'll need to search again for the fishing line and something we can use as bait."

"You mean the food?"

"Yeah, you can use worms and insects, but if we can't find any, a small boy's toe would probably work. Now, where's that knife?" Clint says, chuckling loudly.

"Eughh, no, I don't want to fish anymore. Use your toe," he says in disgust, with a worried look in his eye.

"It's a joke, buddy. Now, how about we stay in that boathouse tonight? If I find everything we need, I'll show you how to fish in the morning."

Ezra's eyes light up with excitement at the prospect of staying in the boathouse and learning to fish. "Really, Dad? We get to spend the night here?" Ezra claps his hands in delight, unable to contain his joy.

Clint chuckles again, his heart swelling with love for his son. "I'm glad you're excited," he says. He stands up and extends his hand to Ezra. "Now, let's go swimming. Then I will take a look for that fishing gear."

"But I've never been swimming."

"Don't worry, there's time to learn."

As the night settles in, casting its gentle embrace over the boathouse, He watches over Ezra with a sense of contentment. His young son, who has chosen the perched row boat as his resting place, is nestled and wrapped snugly in a workman's blanket that they discovered while searching for fishing gear. Streaks of Moonlight have replaced the earlier sun that filters through the roof gaps, casting a soft glow on Ezra's peaceful face. The flickering of an old oil lamp on a nearby crate provides a warm and soothing light, adding to the moment's tranquil ambience, and the sound of crickets has begun to fill the air, blending harmoniously with the distant hush of the lake's gentle water. In this stillness, for the first time since they fled the city, Clint finds rest quickly. A noise. Soft at first, and barely audible hits Clint's ears. He stirs. Then another - a murmur, low voices carried by the breeze, and he's awake again. Water splashes, rhythmic and deliberate. His heartbeat picks up. He doesn't move, listening. He lay still for a moment, listening intently. The darkness envelopes the boathouse, the old oil lamp has diminished, and he's surrounded by darkness. He strains his ears, trying to discern the noise. Then, the tones of the voices, indistinct and low, reach his ears. Two distinct pitches, a conversation between men, but the words remain elusive. Carefully, he eases himself up, avoiding any sudden movements that might wake Ezra, and creeps towards the boathouse entrance. Opening the door ajar, he can make out vague silhouettes that move along the water's edge. Their hushed tones persist, snippets of conversation barely audible. He strains his ears again, hoping to catch any meaningful words, but the intermittent water splashing hides any clarity. He retreats quietly into the boathouse and retrieves a single piece of wood as he prepares for the possibility that these nighttime intruders may pose a threat. He waits a few tense moments until a strange feeling overcomes him; then, in silence, using the darkness as his ally, he leaves the boathouse.

XIV

Clandestine

A week has passed since Jane and Elizabeth's heated discussion about live tests, and the tensions between the pair have cast a subtle pall over the atmosphere.

Jane enters the laboratory with hurried footsteps approaching Dr Chen.

"Sarah, any luck with culturing?" she inquires, her tone is impatient.

Letting out a frustrated sigh, Sarah glances up from her microscope. "It's proving to be quite challenging. Culturing a foreign agent like this isn't giving typical results. The pathogen seems to be resisting our attempts to replicate it in controlled conditions."

Jane's face sterns as frustration simmers beneath the surface. "Without successful culturing, our progress is stunted."

"I'm aware of that, and I'm exploring alternative methods, but it's difficult and delicate to keep balance between gaining insights and mitigating potential risks."

"I don't need to remind you of the urgency. Time is of the essence. We can't afford to be held back by the limitations of culturing or your limitations."

Sarah, hurt by Jane's comment, lowers her voice. "I know, but we must proceed cautiously. There's still much we don't know about this pathogen, and rushing into uncharted territory could have severe consequences."

"The consequences are already upon us," Jane says abruptly, walking away, unimpressed with Sarah's lack of progress.

She seeks further insight from Dr Baker at the other end of the lab. "Michelle, please tell me you have made some progress in understanding how the presence of the pathogen is influencing the immune system."

Michelle looks up from her research and shakes her head solemnly. "It's an unusual situation. The human immune system seems to exhibit no response whatsoever to the presence of the pathogen"

"What, no response at all? You must be mistaken."

Michelle leans against the lab bench, clearly offended. "It's perplexing; the immediate assumption is that the pathogen's effects are concealed from the immune system. It's as if the system doesn't recognize the presence of a pathogen at all. This is why there was no immediate response, no sickness, no sign of men littering A&E departments."

Jane's mind races. "So, Hidden effects is what you're saying? Much like my theory on silent infection, but perhaps, even more sinister than initially thought". She ponders her thoughts momentarily, "It's a sophisticated evasion mechanism indeed".

"Agreed. I'm delving deeper into its molecular and cellular levels to try and understand this evasion tactic. If I can somehow decipher how it remains undetected, I might find a key to neutralizing its effects."

"Well, it appears you've at least made a little headway, unlike the esteemed Dr Chen over there," Jane quips, shooting a pointed sideways glance in Sarah's direction.

"Carry on." Jane begins to walk away.

"If I may," Michelle begins, halting Jane's escape. "There's another crucial aspect".

"Go on."

"We are all currently working solely from protein data. A complete DNA or RNA strand would benefit my research and advance our understanding."

"Finally, someone willing to do what it takes," Jane affirms, recognizing the subtle message in Michelle's words, "Thank you".

She doesn't bother to ask the others for their own insight, leaving the lab and walking down the corridor and towards the canteen. Along the way, she stops in a small side room where another colleague, Beth, is engrossed in inspecting an old generator machine. The generator, a relic in any circumstance, emits a faint hum as Beth diligently works on its internal parts.

"How's your progress?" Jane inquires, her eyes scanning the machinery.

"Yep, fine," Beth responds with a screwdriver in hand. Her short brown hair frames a focused, yet tired expression, and her clothing is oil-stained and carries the faint scent of machinery. "I should have it running in an hour."

"Excellent, and you know what to do once it's running."

Beth finally looks up from her work. "Yes, but I can't do it alone."

"Don't worry. I'll send Rigs your way," Jane reassures.

She continues down the corridor, passing by the familiar landmarks of the facility, the shower room, sleeping arrangements, and the canteen. Arriving at the main door, she swings it open, revealing a day engulfed in muted greys. Thick clouds, laden with moisture, obscure the sun's rays, allowing only small, diffused beams of light to highlight small areas across the landscape. The air holds a stillness which is only interrupted by the calls of birds overhead. She watches as they swoop past in unison, their feathers blending with the Greyed sky.

"Ah, Jane, perfect timing," says Rigs, interrupting Jane's adoration of the passing birds. "I have something I need to discuss with you."

"And I with you,"

"Could we attend to my thing first?" asks Rigs, a look of worry in her eyes.

"Certainly," replies Jane, detecting the unusual shift in Rigs' demeanour.

She closes the facility door behind her and falls into step with Rigs as they begin to approach the small outbuilding used as an armoury.

"We've got a problem", Rigs begins as she unlocks the door. "It's looking a little sparse, to say the least, and we're low on ammunition."

"Well, isn't that a revelation?" Jane responds dryly. "It's truly fascinating how many of our esteemed personnel arrived armed with spare pants and toothbrushes but not even a pocketknife."

"In all fairness, we did expect more equipment and personnel, you know, based on the original plan." Rigs retorts as she opens the door and gestures for Jane to enter.

"Yes, well, it seems like some of the invitations were wasted on the wrong people, too weak to get here."

Rigs is a little taken aback by Jane's biting remarks. Still, the comment did serve as a stark reminder that perhaps visions of a well-equipped, fortified facility were nothing more than wishful thinking.

"I wanted to make you aware of this," Rigs says as she directs Jane's attention to a humble piece of paper placed on one of the shelves.

Jane inspects the piece, finding a complete inventory and a handwritten account detailing each sidearm, assault rifle, and ammunition box. The writing is clear, but a certain lack of expertise is evident, suggesting that someone with limited knowledge of the products had written it.

Fury crosses her face. "I'll handle this," she declares with firm resolve.

Rigs arches an eyebrow, questioning. "Is that wise?" "Kim's taking Alex out tonight". Surely she'll notice if even a few items go missing."

Jane's frustration flares as she responds, "That's not the point. What's the use of an inventory? Will we meticulously check items off of this piece of paper during an attack? It's absurd."

Rigs absorbs Jane's irritation. "Alright, so what's the plan?" she asks.

"Nothing's changed; tell Kim to take what she needs. Then, I need you to go and give Beth a hand. I will deal with Elizabeth and her little list."

Elizabeth is enjoying light conversation with her friend Sarah in the canteen when they are abruptly startled by Jane's sudden entrance. Her footsteps are heavy and forceful as she approaches the pair. Upon arrival, she slams a piece of paper on the counter where they sit. Elizabeth's eyes widen as she notices the inventory.

"What the hell is this?" Jane's tone cuts through the air.

Caught off guard, Elizabeth stammers, "It's, it's an inventory of our weapons and ammunition. I thought it would be useful for everyone to know our available resources."

Jane glares directly at her, her frustration evident. "Useful? Is this a joke? We're facing a crisis, and you're playing librarian with our weapons? We need action, not paperwork."

Sarah attempts to mediate. "Jane, maybe Elizabeth was trying to ensure transparency and organization within the group."

Jane shoots a dismissive glance at Sarah. "Transparency? Organization? This isn't some bureaucratic office. We're dealing with a lethal pathogen, and this," she points at the paper, "is a waste of time and energy."

Elizabeth attempts to reconcile, "It's a harmless inventory; I don't see the fuss."

Jane responds angrily, almost shouting, "The fuss, Elizabeth, is that you called me, remember? And from what I can see, I've done almost all the work. Nearly everyone here is someone I recruited. You've bought her" pointing to Sarah, "who so far has been about as useful as this ridiculous piece of paper."

Elizabeth, taken aback by Jane's outburst, rises to her feet angrily. "Hey, we're all here for the same reason. If you want to talk about things being useful, explain the point in locking our weapons up anyway. Protection?

Jane's anger simmers beneath the surface as she retorts, the pair now in a standoff, "The weapons are there because that's where Kim and Clair patrol. Jesus, I'm not sure what's pissed me off more, your actions or the fact that I naively expected more from you."

With those damning words, Jane abruptly leaves before any response, her steps fast and furious.

Elizabeth looks at Sarah who's upset by Janes's remarks, "Ignore that bitch", she whispers as she comforts her friend.

Jane traverses the corridor angrily, her footsteps loud and deliberate. She glances into the small room where she briefly spoke with Beth and finds it empty, further frustrating her. Her walk through the corridor leads her to a quiet and secluded spot where the ambient hum of the lab's machinery and the conversations of the facility's occupants are distant, bordering on non-existent. She leans haphazardly against a wall made of wood, one of the facility's makeshift barriers and for a few moments, breathes deeply. Suddenly, with her frustration fuelling her strength, she pushes against the wall. It's heavy, but with determination, it eventually begins to swing open, and she disappears from the corridor, shutting the opening behind her. As she strides into the enveloping darkness, a distant glow of light draws her attention. Its subtle glow invited her further down the concealed corridor. As she navigates the mysterious darkened corridor, the shadows play tricks on the edges of her vision, adding an eerie atmosphere within the clandestine passage. As she continues towards the distant glow, it's not long before a string of lights strategically placed are intertwined above her. Her footsteps echo as she follows the illuminated path, the occasional flickering casting intermittent shadows on the passage floor until it guides her to a narrow stairwell. As she descends, she begins to hear the hum of distant voices. Pressing on, she follows the intermittent glow until it disappears through a thick and large door slightly ajar, where a warm radiance spills out from within, inviting her further. Without hesitation, she forcefully swings the heavy door open, its hinges creaking in protest. The sudden intrusion startles Beth and Rigs, their expressions caught in surprise.

"Christ," says Rigs. "I nearly died of fright."

"What?" says Jane, a hint of a smirk on her face.

She looks around the room, taking in the concrete walls that feel hard and cold. A thick glass panel fills the back wall, at least a few inches wide. Beyond it lies the old reactor room, shrouded in darkness and mystery. In the corner, Beth works diligently again on the now humming generator, its noise subdued by a few old dust-ridden blankets which have been thrown on top. Along one wall lies a tangled mess of thick, old electrical cables that snake across the surface.

"Excellent work," says Jane, acknowledging her partner's efforts as she approaches a workbench, her focus shifting and intensifying as she begins tinkering with some of the items on the workbench.

"What's that?" asks Rigs.

"This is an MEG; it's designed to detect and record the magnetic fields produced by neural activity," she says as she carefully checks each sensor, ensuring they are calibrated. And this," she says, moving to another piece of equipment, "is an EEG. It measures electrical activity in the brain by plac-ing electrodes on the scalp. Oh, that reminds me. I will need some other tools, knives, razors, etc."

"So, this is the night, huh?" Beth begins, a hint of concern in her voice. "I didn't think it would come to this so quickly."

"Well," responds Jane, "neither did I, but helping hands are far less than we predicted, and progress is painfully slow."

"And what about the Doc?" Rigs interjects

"You mean Elizabeth?" Jane remarks. "She's brilliant if she has time, but working to a deadline isn't exactly her strong suit; plus, I'm not sure she has what it takes to get any decent results."

"She won't be happy about this, or about you with holding equipment."

"I couldn't care less."

Jane says as she continues tending to the EEG machine, firing it up and ensuring it works seamlessly with a small laptop. Satisfied with the machine's performance, she turns to Beth. "Are our entrance and exit sorted?"

"Yes, it opens directly to the outside and is well out of view from where everyone is situated."

"I need a firearm down here in case things go south." Jane then says to Rigs, her expression serious.

Rigs nods confidently. "I can arrange that, but what about the Doc's list?"

Jane dismissively waves the comment off: "Forget the list. I only need a small handgun; take it from Kim's ones in the water tower if you're that concerned."

"Alright."

"I'm heading for some rest. It's going to be a busy night. I assume Kim's all set."

"All under control," Rigs responds. "How about meeting in the canteen at 2?"

"See you then," replies Jane.

Still sitting with Sarah in the canteen and joined by the other scientists, Alex approaches Elizabeth, looking coy and concerned.

"Dr Stevens, could I possibly have a word?" she asks, glancing around to check her surroundings.

"Sure, Alex. What's on your mind?" Elizabeth replies, gesturing towards an empty chair nearby.

"I would much rather speak in private," Alex asks, giving her a concerned look.

"Erm, Okay, Sure." Elizabeth rises from her chair and follows as Alex leads her outside the facility into the murky greyness. "What is it?"

"There's something you should know."

"Go on."

"I've been told by Jane that I'm to go out with Kim this evening to search the local area."

"Told?"

"Well, it certainly seems that way. I didn't get much of a say."

Confusion crosses Elizabeth's face. "Okay, but why have they asked you?"

"That's what I don't understand. Could you perhaps tell Jane I don't want to go?" she requests.

"Alex, I don't know. I'm already under scrutiny for playing librarian," she responds, using her fingers to quote inverted commas. "I understand your concern, but Kim is a professional. plus, there's nothing to worry about. We are miles away from what was once civilization."

"I suppose you're right."

"I want to know what you're up to, though. So come and see me tomorrow morning, okay?"

"Sure," says Alex, walking away with her head hanging.

In the shadows of the facility, Jane quietly navigates the dark corridors and slips into the canteen, unnoticed. She spots Rigs sitting at a table, bathed in the eerie glow of a two-way radios light. "Any news?"

"A potential sighting," Rigs responds mutedly, her eyes sharp with focus. "Just waiting on further updates."

The dimly lit canteen has now become the backdrop for their covert conversation and muted discussions. The impending night's operation weighs heavily on Jane's mind as she checks her watch, acutely aware of each passing moment. Time seems to drag as they await crucial news through the radio. Finally, the radio crackles with static, prompting Rigs to pick it up swiftly. She whispers urgently into the device, "Kim, Kim."

The static persists for a moment before Kim's voice breaks through, loud and panicked. Rigs quickly fiddles with the volume on the radio, reducing it to a barely audible level.

"Repeat, Kim," she instructs, her eyes fixed on the radio.

The pair exchange a tense glance as Kim's voice breaks through the static once more, "I discovered a group, maybe 7 or 8," she reports, her tone laced with uncertainty. "I'm not sure I can proceed any further. I'm not prepared."

In the background, a slight whimpering sound adds a layer of concern to the situation.

Jane, with a determined expression, snatches the radio from Rigs. "I only need one; kill the rest," she orders, her voice low and resolute.

Rigs glances at Jane, a hint of disbelief in her eyes. "Are you sure?" she begins to ask, but Jane silences her with a hush.

She spoke into the radio once more, emphasising her command. "I repeat, kill the rest." The air hangs heavy with tension as a brief silence ensues.

The radio crackles with static, breaking the silence once again. "Roger that.

XV

Captive

The night is coated in an inky darkness as Kim and Alex slip through a break in the perimeter fencing. Clouds dim the moonlight, helping to conceal their covert escape from the facility. Casually carrying an assault rifle over her shoulder, Kim moves with purpose and experience.

Alex, at her rear, however, is less at ease. Her eyes wide with fear as she struggles to comprehend the reason for their expedition.

"What exactly are we doing out here?" she asks, her voice barely above a whisper.

"I've been told your scientific expertise is rather, well, limited," Kim answers as her eyes scan the darkness for any signs of movement. "We have limited personnel, and Clair needs to remain at the facility. So, you're stepping into a new role."

Alex's eyes widened with a mixture of fear and realisation. "I'm not a soldier?"

Kim offers a menacing grin, her tone steady. "Oh, I know, but tonight marks the beginning of a new career path – one where you can contribute to the safety and success of the facility; now, point the damn flashlight in the right direction".

Alex contemplates a response but deems it wiser to withhold any disagreement.

As they venture into the wilderness, the safety of the facility at their back, dense foliage, and dry leaves begin to crack and break under each step.

"So, what's the plan?" Alex says, voicing her concerns again.

Kim spares a glance toward her, her eyes sharp in the moonlight. "When we find what we're looking for, I'll fill you in with the details. Until then, keep quiet, and keep that flashlight aimed in front of us," she replies with annoyance.

Minutes feel like hours until the wilderness gradually gives way to signs of civilisation. The trees become more sparse with each step, and paths seem to have magically emerged beneath their feet. The occasional glint of road signs reflect in the flashlight's beam, catching Alex's eyes as she wanders in silence, nervously surveying her surroundings. Old, redundant lampposts have begun to loom overhead, and stone walls now direct them towards old and abandoned dwellings. Still grappling with the revelation of her forced change in career, Alex walks in front. The occasional rustle of leaves and the distant disturbances of small nocturnal animals punctuate the quiet, causing her to continuously direct the flashlight away from their intended direction, frightened by each shadow and sound.

"Right, that's enough," Kim growls, catching up to Alex and snatching the flashlight from her. "You follow," she instructs as she clips the flashlight to the top of the assault rifle.

With purposeful strides, Kim begins to lead the way with Alex attempting to keep close behind as she tries not to focus on the sounds and shadows that trick her perception. Eventually, Kim comes to a sudden halt, directs the flashlight purposefully, and illuminates an old road sign indicating the distance to the town centre.

"What are we doing here?" Alex questions, in a calm plea for clarity, as she stares at the illuminated sign.

Kim, however, remains silent, her focus unwavering as she drops to one knee and retrieves a small radio from her gear: its dimly lit display only adding another eerie glow to the surroundings.

With familiarity, she adjusts the dials, finds a memorised channel, and then calmly speaks into the radio, "Destination reached."

The words hang in the night air, only increasing Alex's unease. Swiftly, Kim stows the radio back on her hip, not bothering to expect a response. Alex's confusion deepens. She clutches at her stomach as a knot of anxiety begins to take hold. After a short while, Kim turns to face her and patiently awaits as she closes the small gap between them.

Within proximity of each other, Alex notices in the dim moonlight that Kim has a small sidearm extended in her outstretched hand. "Take it," she says impatiently. "The safety is already off; just point and shoot."

Panic flickers across Alex's face. "Shoot at what?" she asks, her voice full of fear and confusion.

"Anything I tell you to," Kim replies bluntly, gesturing again for her to take the sidearm. Begrudgingly, Alex takes it, the cold metal of the weapon heavy in her sweaty and trembling hand.

"Kim, what the hell are we doing here?"

Kim meets Alex's gaze with a measured expression, her response deliberate and practised. "We need a live subject."

"The fuck are you on about? Alex almost shouts back.

"Keep it down", Kim loudly whispers back, shining the flashlight directly into Alex's eyes,

"What made you think I could do something like this?"

Kim's response is calm and dismissive: "Oh, calm yourself. I will do what's needed. You're just here as backup, you know, to watch my back."

"Couldn't this have been done in daylight?" Alex questions, her frustration evident.

"Darkness gives us more cover from prying eyes both out here and at the facility," Kim replies, her tone matter-of-fact.

"From the facility?"

"Are we supposed to announce that progress with the Pathogen is slow and that the only real way to get answers is to bring a madman within the walls?" Kim answers, maintaining her stern expression. "The people who need to know, know."

"So, is the whole lab team in on this?" Alex inquires, seeking clarity.

"It's on a need-to-know basis," Kim answers as she walks into the darkness.

Alex remains rooted to the spot, grappling with the information. With each passing moment, the situation tightens its grip on her mind. After a few paces, Kim halts abruptly, sensing Alex's hesitation. She turns to face her and points the flashlight and the assault rifle in her partner's direction.

"Are you coming, or would you rather stay here?" Kim challenges, her voice cutting through the darkness.

As Alex reluctantly follows her towards the town centre, their surroundings transform into a haunting portrayal of desolation. Rows of townhouses, their windows shattered and doors ajar, stand like silent witnesses to the recent chaos. What were once bustling main roads are now empty, as abandoned cars lie scattered haphazardly among the streets. Some are overturned, while others now lie as mere skeletons of rusted metal left from raging infernos. The air is thick with an unsettling stillness, save the occasional creak of a swinging store sign or the rustle of debris carried by the gentle breeze. The beam of Kim's flashlight cuts through the darkness, revealing only fragments of the abandonment that stretch beyond their immediate line of sight. In the darkness of the abandoned town, a momentary flicker of light catches their attention, and Kim acts swiftly, extinguishing the feeble beam emanating from her assault rifle's flashlight as she motions for Alex to huddle beside her behind the shelter of a vehicle's corpse. The sudden plunge into utter darkness intensifies the suspense; their surroundings now obscured entirely by the veil of night. Crouched beside Kim in the darkness, Alex presses her body closely against the frame of the vehicle. The air around her suddenly begins to feel thick, and she can feel each one of Kim's steady breaths - a soft, steady rhythm, unwavering. She dares not move, not even to glance at Kim; instead, she strains to listen beyond the shadows. Then, faint at first, came broken murmurs, garbled words and scraps of twisted laughter, barely human in their tones. The sounds drift closer, warped and unsettling. Curiosity grips her, and she edges forward, peering around her hiding spot. Two figures stagger into view in the faint glow of moonlight, their forms swaying and distorted as one erratically moves a flashlight beam. The pair sway as they move, their steps uneven and uncoordinated, like puppets whose strings had been cut and retied hastily. One of the men mutters something unintelligible, his voice cracking mid-sentence before slipping into a dark, hollow laugh that pierces her ears. The other, breathing heavily, responds in a tone too low to catch, the mumbled words melting into the night air. Her heart pounds, and as the beam of light suddenly sways in her direction for a moment, she glances at the man's eyes, vacant but still filled with a strange intensity, as if somewhere deep inside, something wild had come awake. A flicker of movement beside her pulls her back as Kim's fingers curl around her wrist and yank her from view. Gradually, the sounds begin to fade, and Kim tightens her grip on the assault rifle. With a subtle motion, she signals for Alex to follow her away from their cover. She falls in line immediately, matching Kim's movements without hesitation. But after a few paces, she notices that the echoes of the men's voices still linger, hanging in the night air, refusing to vanish entirely as she'd expected.

She tugs on Kim's jacket, whispering, "Where are we going?"

"We're following them. I'm waiting for an opening," Kim replies, her voice low and focused.

"Absolutely not, fuck this."

"Stay here alone then, I don't care."

As the pair stalk in quiet pursuit, their steps are cautious as they navigate the deserted streets. Alex clings to Kim's presence as the erratic beam of the madmen's torchlight dances ahead once again. Kim's gaze remains fixed, her senses attuned to the subtlest of sounds and movements as she follows the men with precision, each movement calculated and deliberate. Alex trails behind, her breath quick with a mixture of anticipation and dread.

Amid the hushed whispers of the night, Alex can't help but voice her unease. "This is mad", she whispers.

Kim, never breaking her stride, glances back at Alex. "We are making sure they're alone," she responds tersely, her focus returning to the task at hand.

With a swift motion, she moved ahead, finding refuge behind another structure in the eerie stillness of the town. Alex's breath catches in her throat as she continues to follow.

Kim crouches behind a low wall, using its cover as a shield as she strains to peer into the darkness. The faint sound of metal reverberates through the night, drawing her attention to a lone figure seated on a swing in an expanse of open terrain. With bated breath, she watches intently, her eyes fixated on the silhouette swaying gently in the darkness.

Alex huddles beside her, her breath shallow as she strains to catch any semblance of the dialogue escaping the man's mouth. The swing creaks softly in the night, the sound hauntingly accompanying the faint words of madness that reach their ears through the darkness.

"What now?"

"Shh," Kim responds, her focus intense as she scans the darkness, "where's the other one?" Frustration tinges Kim's movements as she adjusts her grip on the assault rifle. "Sod it," she mutters, deciding to proceed with final checks on her weapon.

As she stands ready to make a move, Alex releases a hushed gasp, urgently pulling on Kim's clothing. "There, look," she whispers, pointing just beyond the swing.

Kim follows Alex's gaze into the faint moonlight, where she spots the second figure emerging from the darkness. The silhouette wields a makeshift weapon, then emerges another, and another. Kim grits her teeth as she surveys the growing numbers in the darkness. She retakes cover, muttering a curse under her breath as the madmen's distant moans and erratic movements echo through the landscape.

"Shit." She peers over the cover once more, confirming her fears. "Shit."

"How many are there?" Alex asks, her voice barely audible in the tense night air.

"Seven, maybe eight," Kim responds with a heavy sigh.

Alex struggles to contain her fear, and a slight whimper escapes her lips.

Kim's fingers dance over her radio's controls; she lowers the volume before speaking into the device. "Come in," she murmurs, her words expressing urgency. Silence greets her plea, the only response a crackling of the radio waves. She tries again, but her tone is more insistent this time. "Come in," she repeats, her voice tinged with frustration.

After a moment, the radio crackles to life and a barely audible voice breaks through the static. "Repeat, Kim,"

"Discovered a group, maybe 7 or 8; not sure I can proceed any further. I'm not prepared." Alex's soft whimpers intensify. Kim silences her with a gentle hush as they both eagerly await a response.

Then it comes, and Kim's eyes flicker with a hint of concern as the radio relays a chilling directive. The voice on the other end is stoic, almost detached, delivering a stark command. "I only need one; kill the rest," the radio intones. The mechanical delivery left no room for negotiation. Alex shudders, her fears now mirrored in Kim's gaze. "I repeat, kill the rest."

"Roger that". Kim turns to Alex, her expression serious. "We stick to the plan."

"What fucking plan?"

"One target, and we get out. Stay close and stay quiet," Kim instructs, her voice a low murmur for Alex's ears only. With determination in her eyes, Kim readies her assault rifle, preparing to navigate the treacherous path ahead. The pair approach the group of men, moving silently in the darkness. The moonlight intermittently casts a glow upon the figures through shifting clouds, emphasising their dishevelled appearances. Kim signals them to stop behind another dilapidated car, its frame offering concealment. The men, absorbed in their disjointed ramblings, seem oblivious to the approaching duo.

Kim looks back at Alex, her eyes conveying caution as she raises her index finger to her lips, urging silence. "I want you to follow me, watch my back. See the one on the swing who's separated from the others; he's our target," she says, her voice barely above a whisper.

With tears streaming down her face, Alex responds, "I can't do this."

"You're going to have to. Let's go."

Stealthily, Kim gets closer to the group, her assault rifle in the ready position. Alex reluctantly trails behind, doing her best to muffle her sobs and control the trembling in her hands as she holds the small sidearm. As they draw closer, the swing-set creaks rhythmically with their tactical movements and her trained eyes scan the surroundings, searching for hidden signs of further danger. The men's disorganised ramblings continue until Kim suddenly releases a single shot, startling the group and Alex. A lone figure collapses, sending shockwaves through the remaining men. Chaos ensues as they react with frantic movements, their mad screams and incoherent threats filling the night. Amidst the confusion, another shot echoes from the darkness, claiming another victim. The distorted silhouettes of the men tense up but do not scatter. Instead, they huddle together, their deranged gazes scanning the surroundings for the unseen assailant. Alex tries to follow Kim's movements, frantically scanning her surroundings, her hands trembling. Kim skilfully picks off another victim, her shot precise in the darkness, but just as another target falls, a sudden shift in the clouds exposes them to bright moonlight, betraying their careful approach. At that moment, Alex glances at the swing, noticing it is now devoid of its previous occupant. She freezes as the moonlight bathes the scene, her gaze fixated on the haunting image of the swing swaying alone. Fuelled by a frenzied fury, the remaining men catch sight of the two intruders and, without hesitation, charge towards them, their erratic movements and guttural cries echoing through the night. Kim fires off a couple of quick shots, but still, the charging men approach. Alex, gripped by fear, raises her sidearm, her hands trembling as she aims at the approaching madness. Yet, in this critical moment, she realises that her fixation on the vacant swing has unwittingly created a small but dangerous gap between her and Kim. As the men, consumed by madness, relentlessly charge, they reach Kim first, forcing her into a desperate dance as she attempts to evade their frenzied onslaught. With every swing of her fists and the butt of her assault rifle, she manages to repel the attackers momentarily as she releases sporadic shots that echo through the moonlit night. Her lethal tool fails to be as effective as before, her shots merely slowing the relentless advance of the remaining attackers rather than becoming instantaneously effective. Alex stands frozen, her sidearm aiming at the chaotic scene. Kim's erratic movements and the madmen's frantic advance make her hesitant to pull the trigger. The melee intensifies as the strained breaths and guttural cries of both Kim and the madmen create an atmosphere of impending doom. Yet, as Alex holds her breath, frozen in place, she suddenly feels an intense pain in her chest. She clutches at her breast, the source of agony, her hand finding an unfamiliar feeling, cold and metallic. Panic and confusion set in as she looked down, her eyes widening in horror at the surreal sight before her. A sinister chuckle echoed from behind, sending shivers down her spine, and a cold breath on her neck made her skin crawl. She turns slowly, her gaze meeting the crazed eyes of one of the madmen, a wicked grin etched on his face. The moonlight reveals his deranged features as he presses the tip of his nose against hers, adding an unsettling intimacy to her scenario. Time slows down, elongating her torment as his features begin to turn into a grotesque and blurred visualisation of madness. Staggering under the weight of her pain, she fights to stay on her feet, the agony intensifying with each passing moment. Suddenly, the madman grips the protruding piece of metal embedded in her chest and unrelentingly twists it, forcing Alex to release a guttural cry of pain that echoes through the night. As the twisted metal is torqued further, agony courses through her body. Her vision begins to darken, and the world begins to spin around her. She focuses on the moving lips of the madman as they relay unheard twisted mumblings as he continues his torment. Suddenly, the surging pain began to dissipate, leaving her with a strange numbness. The strength in her legs abandons her, and she collapses backwards. The madman, still gripping the protruding metal with relentless determination, maintains his hold as her body slides off the gruesome impalement. Kim's veins pulse with adrenaline as she watches Alex crumple, her silhouette replaced with the ominous figure of a madman brandishing a bloodied metal object with menacing intent. Fuelled by anger, Kim takes a final shot, eliminating her final attacker and then raises her assault rifle. The remaining madman stands over Alex, undeterred by his counterpart's aim. Kim's instincts urge her to pull the trigger, but the mission demands a different outcome. As the pair stand in a silent standoff, Kim begrudgingly lowers her weapon, her fingers tightening the grip. She cannot risk losing this live subject, especially after the mission's cost. Cautiously, she approaches the scene, her footsteps echoing in the chilling silence. He remains eerily still as she cautiously approaches. His wild, bloodshot eyes dart around with an unhinged zeal, and his pupils are dilated in the grip of lunacy. Strands of dishevelled hair cling to his sweaty forehead, and every muscle in his body appears tense. His lips part in a sinister grin, revealing missing teeth; those remaining are stained with the remnants of his brutality. Now, standing in the unsettling proximity of this embodiment of madness, she could sense the volatile energy that was emanating from him. She glances down at Alex's lifeless form, her body ruined and bloodied, yet there's a sense of peace that has settled upon her. As she lifts her gaze, her attention refocuses on the madman standing before her. Undeterred by the gruesome scene, she takes another step forward, only to be met by a faint, sinister laughter that reverberates in her ears, but her expression remains stern, her resolve unshaken. Suddenly, with a swift movement, she brings the butt of her rifle down on the madman's shoulder. Yet, the strike only leads to his laughter intensifying. The madness in his eyes was undiminished. With a determined grit, she delivers another strike, causing him to stumble. Now, his laughter morphs into a twisted melody. Blow after blow, the dance between aggressor and madman unfolds. Kim's breath catches as she observes his surprising lack of self-defence, his actions almost goading her on, as if inviting her to unleash her full force, taunting her to do her best. The twisted dance between them takes on an eerie rhythm; each strike from Kim is met with an unsettling blend of laughter and resistance until she narrows her focus, determined to end the performance. She steadies herself, rifle in hand, and delivers a series of calculated blows. This time, the man makes a feeble attempt to shield himself, instantly falling short, and his once-formidable laughter begins to wane. A flicker of doubt crosses Kim's mind.

Is this a trap? Is he luring her into a false sense of security? The madman's laughter once again morphs into a haunting chant, his words a nonsensical mix of disjointed phrases and fragmented memories. Undeterred, she presses on, her strikes growing more forceful until she senses a change in the madman's demeanour - a shift from taunting amusement to a darker, more primal desperation. As the intensity of the struggle reaches its peak, Kim summons her strength for a final blow. Battered and broken, the madman lies sprawled on the ground; his laughter ceased, replaced with an unsettling silence. She stands over the fallen figure as her chest heaves with exertion. The weight of the mission, the loss of Alex, and the unusual and brutal encounter with madness all settle upon her shoulders as the world around her seems to hold its breath, waiting for her next move.

As Jane and Rigs navigate the dark corridors, the weight of apprehension hangs heavy in the air. Rigs forces the sturdy metal door open, allowing the early dawn light to spill into the passage. Standing a few feet away, Kim eventually comes into focus, her weariness evident.

"Where is he?" Jane inquires, her voice urgent and authoritative. Responding silently, Kim points to her left, and Jane follows her direction until her gaze spots the figure, bound, bloodied, and forced to their knees. Cautiously, she advances towards the captive, kneeling and examining him closely. His visage is marred - bruised and swollen - with one eye entirely sealed shut and blood staining his matted hair.

"Christ," she murmurs, glancing at Kim for confirmation.

A subtle nod from Kim affirms the unspoken truth.

"Alright," she says, rising to her feet. "Take him downstairs."

Efficiently, Kim raises the man to his feet and guides him through the doorway.

Rigs quietly observes the procession down the corridor before briefly scanning the surroundings outside. "Where's Alex?"

XVI

Awakening

The sky is painted with soft hues of orange and pink, casting a gentle glow over the landscape. The air is crisp, and the scent of dew-kissed grass penetrates his nostrils. Grogginess clouds his mind as he struggles to sit up, the stiffness in his limbs giving him flashbacks of his restriction in Cara's den. Suddenly, A realization hits him like a sudden jolt - he's outside, though the reason eludes him. He examines his surroundings: the peaceful water before him and the small boathouse nearby. Marks on his clothing draw his attention, and he traces his fingers over the unusual stains on his trousers, the texture foreign beneath his touch. As he touches the new markings, his eyes widen in disbelief as he sees the telltale signs of dried blood and blackness on his knuckles. Confusion and unease grip him as he tries to piece together what's happened.

What the hell?

Slowly, he rises to his feet. His body ached as if he'd aged ten years in a single night. He gazes out over the landscape as the soft hue of dawn continues to paint the sky in a palette of pastel colours. The water before him reflects the morning light like a mirror, and its surface shimmers with gentle ripples. The wooden boardwalk beside him stretches out into the calm waters, and he traces its path as it seems to vanish into the shimmering sunlight. The Surrounding foliage is alive with the sounds of nature - the birds chirp once again, and leaves rustle in the breeze.

He takes in the scene until a concerning issue enters his mind. "Ezra," he says to himself.

With a sense of urgency he rises and bolts towards the nearby boathouse, reaching the door in a few significant and hurried strides. Yet, at the threshold, he hesitates momentarily, his mind racing with the thoughts of what may lie beyond.

Please be ok, please.

As he cautiously opens the door and steps into the boathouse, he notices the light filtering through the gaps in the wooden planks. The floorboards creak beneath his feet as he silently searches the boathouse's interior. He approaches the small boat perched on stilts, his apprehension growing with every step, his heart beating faster with each second as the weight of uncertainty presses down on him.

Please.

Reaching the side of the boat, he takes a deep breath, steeling himself for what he might find. As he peers over the edge of the boat, a wave of relief washes over him as he notices Ezra sleeping soundly, wrapped in the warmth of the workman's blanket.

Thank god.

The tension in his shoulders eased instantly, and he took a moment to watch Ezra sleep, a wave of gratitude washing over him. He brushes a lock of the boy's hair from his face, but in doing so, further questions enter his mind as he again notices his bruised and darkened knuckles.

What the hell has happened? why can't I remember?

Turning away from the boat, his mind races with unanswered questions. Leaving Ezra to rest, he exits the boathouse, stepping outside. He takes a moment to breathe in the crisp morning air and feel the warmth of the sunlight on his skin. With each passing minute, the memories of the previous evening begin to stir within his mind like fragments of a shattered mirror. He tries to piece them together, but clarity remains elusive, slipping through his grasp like a wisp of smoke. He wanders through the tranquil surroundings, lost in thought as the rhythmic lapping of the water against the wooden boardwalk provides a soothing backdrop to his contemplation. He desperately searches his mind for clues, hoping something may shed some light on his missing memories, but to his annoyance, they remain stubbornly out of reach. Despite his growing frustration, he finds solace in the tranquillity of the morning. The beauty of his surroundings gives him a sense of peace amidst the chaos of his thoughts. He approaches the water's edge, takes a moment to remove his shoes, and rolls up his trouser legs as he prepares to wade into the cool embrace of the pond. He enters the water, feeling the soft, silty texture beneath his feet. He wades further into the pond, the water rising to his calves as the silt is replaced with the feel of gentle weeds and plants tugging at his toes. He searches his memories once more, hoping for a clue of the events from the night before, but they continue to remain shrouded in darkness, elusive and intangible. Was this the onset of the pathogen's effects, he wonders? Was his mind beginning to succumb to its insidious influence? The thought sent a shiver down his spine, and a sense of unease crept into his heart. He pushes the troubling thoughts aside, focusing instead on the sensation of the water against his skin. As he stands in the water, feeling the sensation on his skin, a sudden movement catches his attention. Something brushed against his toes, sending a ripple of unease through him. He looks down, staring at a faint reflection of himself shimmering on the water's surface, but the image is unsettling. His features seem contorted in a grotesque mask of agony, and his face has aged far beyond how he remembered. His eyes bulge with terror, and dark bruises mar his neck. Touching his neck, he notices the reflection doesn't mimic his movement. His heart pounds in his chest as he stares at the reflection, a sense of dread settling over him like a heavy cloak. With trembling hands, he reaches in to touch the water, but the image remains unchanged, a face staring back at him with hollow eyes. A chill runs down his spine as the realization sinks in: this is not a mere reflection but a glimpse into something far more sinister lurking beneath the pond's surface. *Oh fuck.* A chill runs down his spine as he realizes the truth - the face staring back at him isn't his own, but that of someone else concealed beneath the water's surface. Panic grips him as he recoils from the disturbing sight, his mind racing with a flurry of unanswered questions. In shock from his unsettling discovery, he hurries back to the safety of the boathouse, his mind reeling with a tumult of questions and fears. Each step feels heavier than the last. As he reaches the door, his fingers tremble as he swings it open, its hinges creaking in protest, as he steps inside. Noticing that Ezra is unmoved by his sudden intrusion, he closes the door quietly behind him and leans heavily against its wooden frame. His chest rises and falls rapidly with each laboured breath, and his heartbeat pounds in his ears.

Did I do this?

He assesses his hands once more, his thoughts whirling like a fierce storm. As he struggles to make sense of the fragmented memories that flicker at the edge of his con- sciousness, images flash before his eyes - the shimmering re- flection in the pond and the face distorted and unfamiliar. After catching his breath, his gaze shifts toward the small wooden boat where Ezra lies peacefully, and his mind churns with a whirlwind of emotions. He pushes his feelings aside as he approaches the cluttered shelves of the boathouse, scan- ning the disarray for something useful. He spots a coil of weathered rope tucked away in a corner among the various tools and supplies and snatches it, feeling its rough texture against his calloused hands. With a determined nod, he takes the rope, heads back to the door and steps back outside into the morning light, closing the door quietly behind him. His moves are swift, his mindset focused on the task as he weaves the rope through the remnants of the broken padlock latch and secures it tightly, barring entry or exit of the boathouse. Satisfied with his makeshift solution, he steadies his breath, his heart heavy with the weight of his actions. He knows keeping Ezra locked inside the boathouse isn't the safest action. Still, he needed to know. As he approaches the water again, his hands tremble with violent uncertainty. He wades into the water again, scouring the water's surface until he notices the face below the surface staring back at him once more, distorted by the ripples of the water. Without hesitation and with a deep breath, he plunges his hand into the cold depths and wraps his fingers around the submerged figure. With a firm grip, he brings the unknown out of the water, his muscles straining with the effort. As the figure emerges, water cascades off their form. He kneels beside the figure, his hands shaking as he reaches to touch the person's face. His features are unfamiliar, a stranger's, yet hauntingly serene in its unconsciousness. He estimates the man's age to be in his late sixties. His skin is now pallid with wrinkles accentuated by its waterlogged condition. Strangulation marks encircle the man's neck, and his eyes are clouded and lifeless. The effects of being submerged in water have already begun to take their toll on the man's features.

Why is his skin not swollen and discoloured?

Despite the grim scene before him, Clint remains desperate to uncover the truth behind this man's demise. With a heavy heart, he searches the man's pockets for clues, discovering only a few meagre possessions: a pocketknife, a small packet of beef jerky, and a worn-out wallet. Opening the wallet, he finds it devoid of anything, no identification or remnants from a once functioning society, save for a single piece of paper tucked inside. His fingers tremble as he retrieves the item, its edges frayed and stained from its time in the water. Tears begin to well up in his eyes as he gazes upon its contents. Despite the water damage, the image remains discernible - a young child. A pang of sorrow and empathy courses through him, and tears blur his vision as he gazes at the photograph, mingling with the water droplets on its surface. With a heavy heart, he carefully returns the picture to the wallet, handling it with the utmost care, and closes the wallet, tucking it delicately back into the pocket of the deceased man's clothing, in a silent gesture of respect. He rises to his feet, his mind ablaze with thoughts that crash against his consciousness's walls like relentless waves against the shore. In his mind, the photograph paints a picture of someone who still clung to control and cherished memories despite the encroaching darkness of the pathogen. And now, here lies that person, robbed of life and broken by forces beyond their control.

I know why you're not bloated. That takes time. Did I do this?

The question lingered in his mind longer than he wanted, suffocating him with its implications. Though the events of the previous evening remain shrouded in darkness, he senses the truth lurking within the recesses of his fractured memories. Tears continue to blur his vision as he gazes upon the lifeless body before him, his heart heavy with guilt. Each breath he takes is a struggle, each heartbeat a painful reminder of the consequences of his actions.

How could I?

His mind churns with decisions as he continues to gaze upon the lifeless form before him. Ezra would awaken soon, and this was not a sight he should bear witness to. Giving the stranger a proper burial tugs at Clint's conscience, but he knows the effort, time, and tools required would only complicate matters further. After moments of agonizing deliberation, he decides to return the body to its watery grave. With a heavy heart, he begins to drag the lifeless form back into the water, each step a painful reminder of the pathogen's potential that lurks within him. Removing the makeshift boundary, he enters the boathouse and closes the door softly behind him. He sits quietly on the floor, his back against the door and reaches for the nearby backpack, rummaging through it. Finding the map, he unfolds it, and his eyes traces the familiar lines that mark their location and the path toward the coast. As he studies it, a sense of urgency grips him. If he was indeed succumbing to the pathogen, time was now of the essence, and every moment he wasted was a step closer to losing himself completely. Hastily, he repacks the backpack, raises to his feet and places it upon his shoulders.

Standing beside the small row boat, his hand gently shakes Ezra's shoulder. "Ezra, wake up," he says softly.

Ezra stirs, blinking sleepily as he sits up and rubs his eyes. "What's going on, Dad?" he asks.

Clint forces a small smile. "Morning, buddy; we need to get moving," he replies, his tone serious.

Ezra furrows his brow, puzzled. "Why?" he questions, confusion evident.

Clint hesitates for a moment, struggling to find the right words. "No reason," he lies, his voice trailing. "We should just get moving."

As Ezra climbs out of the boat, he notices a subtle change in his father's demeanour, an unfamiliar shift in his expression that sets his nerves on edge. Despite his father's reassurances, there's an underlying tension in the air that the boy can't ignore. He gathers the blanket that has comforted him through the night and clutches it tightly to his chest as if seeking comfort in its familiar warmth.

"Can I bring this with me?"

Clint nods as he removes the backpack and begins rearranging the items to accommodate Ezra's blanket. "Sure," he says absentmindedly, his mind preoccupied with their next steps.

"What about breakfast? And you promised we could go fishing today." Ezra says innocently.

"We'll eat on the road, and there's no time for fishing," Clint responds curtly, his tone harsher than intended. "We need to get moving."

"That's not fair; you promised."

"I made no such promise. Now, let's go." Clint's voice is stern, fatherly.

Ezra's shoulders slump, and disappointment etches across his face, but he reluctantly and silently accepts his father's decision.

Clint remains silent, his actions speaking louder than words as he secures the backpack and hoists it onto his back. He extends his hand, waiting for Ezra to grasp it, offering a silent gesture of reassurance amidst the tension. Ezra hesitates, staring at his father before reluctantly taking his hand, his head remaining bowed with disappointment, and together, they step out of the boathouse and into the morning sunshine.

The boy's gaze lingers on the water with longing as they walk. "I really wanted to try fishing," he murmured, his voice a disappointed whisper.

"I know," Clint responds gently, his tone filled with regret as he guides them back toward the wilderness. "I'm sorry."

They tread through the wilderness in silence for what feels like an eternity, the weight of their unspoken thoughts heavy upon them. After a few hours, Clint decides to halt their journey and take a brief respite. He unloads the backpack's contents onto the woodland floor, organizing the food into small piles. As he surveys their dwindling supplies, a frustrated sigh escapes him.

Clint then unfolded the map once more and studied it intently. "Two more days, and I think we will be there," he says as his finger traces the map's route.

"At the coast?" asks Ezra.

"Yes," Clint confirms. "The coast and this town," he adds, pointing at a spot on the map. He then repacks the contents into the backpack, leaving out a single packet of food and the map.

"What's that?" asks Ezra.

Clint tears the bag open and pulls out a dry wheat biscuit. "Cookies," he responds, hoping to excite Ezra. He offers one to the boy, who, without any hesitation, takes a large bite.

"Ergh, worst cookie ever," he says with a grimace.

After their short break and snack, Clint is eager to resume their journey, readying himself. As he slings the backpack upon his shoulders again, he turns to Ezra, who has found companionship in a large stick, "I think it's time for you to give me my tests."

"In a minute, Dad", Ezra responds nonchalantly.

"Ezra", Clint growls, "Now".

XVII

Storm

A whole day has passed since Clint and Ezra left the boathouse, and his mind continues to replay the events by the water's edge in a relentless loop. Each time he drifts into his thoughts, the image of the man's lifeless body would haunt him. Worse, he was convinced that Ezra, usually brimming with questions and boundless energy, had begun to observe him with quiet intensity, and he found it unnerving. Was it merely his guilt and paranoia magnifying Ezra's scrutiny, or does his son truly sense the turmoil within him? Whichever it was, he couldn't shake the feeling that something had shifted between them, and a subtle undercurrent of tension seemed to hang. He wonders if his son's recent silence and reluctance to engage in conversation or woodland games are masking the boy's doubts and fears; the thought alone that his young son may be feeling this way towards him tears deep within his soul.

Perhaps he's just really upset about the fishing.

As they sit together on the woodland floor, the usual chatter that fills the air is conspicuously absent. He glances at Ezra, searching for any sign of the carefree innocence that usually defined him, but only finds a solemn expression that mirrors his troubled thoughts. A whisper of doubt echoed in his mind as he watched Ezra. Is he projecting his fears onto his son? Or has there truly begun a shift in Ezra's perception of him? Only time will tell. The scent of impending rain hits Clint's nostrils. the sunshine of yesterday is nowhere to be found, replaced by a thick blanket of heavy, grey clouds that stretch across the sky like a sombre shroud. The woodland around them even seemed to sigh under the weight of the impending storm, usually alive with insects and colour. The ground now lies muted beneath the gloomy sky, its colours drained. As they ate their simple meal, food seemed to have lost any semblance of flavour amidst the atmosphere. He glances at Ezra, noting the solemn expression on his son's face. Even the chirping of the birds, usually a cheerful backdrop, seemed subdued, as if the natural world itself was mourning the atmosphere surrounding them.

"We'll be at the coast today," he murmured to Ezra, hoping to ignite some of the excitement that once filled the air.

Still, Ezra's response is a simple nod and a noncommittal hum, his gaze fixated on a distant point in the woodland.

"What's up, buddy?" he prods gently, his voice laced with concern.

"Nothing," Ezra snaps back, his tone is sharper than Clint had anticipated and with a huff, he rises to his feet and wanders a few paces away, his movements restless and agitated.

Clint felt a pang of frustration rising within him, a reflexive urge to scold Ezra for his attitude. But as he watches his son retreat into the solitude of the woodland, a wave of empathy washes over him. At that moment, he understood that Ezra was grappling with an internal struggle, just as he was, and with a heavy sigh, he decides to let Ezra be, allowing him the space to navigate his emotions in his own time. Finding a sanctuary for Ezra has become an increasingly pressing task that was weighing heavily on his mind. He can't shake the feeling that he is failing his son, that the looming shadow of the pathogen is closing in on him with each step he takes, and an overwhelming sense of guilt twists painfully in his gut. Throughout the day, he has convinced himself that he can feel the effects of the pathogen, feel its subtle tendrils of influence creeping into his mind. Still, even as he grapples with the fear of it overtaking him completely, a question lingers in the back of his mind: Has Ezra witnessed things that his mind is hiding from him? The thought sends a shiver down his spine. Could he have said things in moments of delirium that he can't remember? Has he unknowingly placed Ezra in danger without even knowing it? A surge of panic overwhelms him as he considers the possibility. Should he have taken Cara's offer, letting Ezra seek refuge in her care? As the notion flickers in his mind, he swiftly extinguishes it. The mere idea of being separated from his son is unbearable, both now and forever.

Fed up with the torment of his internal struggles, Clint rises to his feet, a determined expression on his weary face. "Time to get moving," he calls out to Ezra, who hesitates for a moment, reluctance evident in his posture, but eventually replies with a nod.

Clint takes the lead, forging ahead. He glances back regularly, keeping a watchful eye on his son's progress a few feet behind. As they draw closer to the coast, the signs of humanity's footprint begin to emerge amidst the untamed wilderness as it gives way to a narrow single-track road that they now follow. Cracked tarmac peeks through the overgrown grass and foliage that has reclaims its territory in the absence of vehicles. Remnants of fencing line the roadside, weathered and worn from neglect, while rusted gates stand sentinel to large open fields that have long since been abandoned to nature's whims, and road signs, once vibrant with colour, now faded by the relentless sun, offering cryptic clues to new travellers. As they continue navigating the narrow road, its gradual incline stretches endlessly towards the heavens - each step forward feeling like a struggle against gravity. Ezra, who has been mostly silent throughout the day, is now audibly expressing his fatigue through ragged huffs and puffs as he trudges behind. Hearing Ezra's fatigue, Clint comes to an abrupt halt, allowing his son to catch up.

With a soft sigh, he slides the backpack around, wearing it on his front instead, and kneels to Ezra's level. "Come on, on you get," he encourages gently, extending a hand to help Ezra hoist himself onto his father's back.

The backpack's weight presses against his chest, but he ignores the discomfort. Without a word and without hesitation Ezra clambers upon his father's back, his silent acceptance speaking volumes. Clint straightened up, feeling the added weight of his son settle against him.

This was a bad idea; I can barely hold myself up.

He doesn't falter, and with a deep breath, he slowly but surely resumes the uphill trek along the narrow road. As they walk another couple of miles, the summit finally comes into view. He pushes himself harder, feeling his muscles strain with the effort as he suppresses the urge to breathe heavily, silently hoping to communicate his fitness and strength as a father figure to his son. As they reach the summit of the narrow road, he pauses, drops Ezra to the ground and takes in the captivating scene that unfolds before them. From their vantage point, the horizon stretches, revealing an open expanse of ocean and a small seaside town nestled along its coastline. The town appears both haunting and mesmerising. Its streets appear deserted, devoid of the hustle and bustle of life that would have once defined them, and a tower rises above most of the rooftops. The harbour itself, no doubt once a hive of activity and trade, lies eerily quiet. The soft light of the overcast setting sun casts long shadows across the landscape and paints the buildings, deserted streets, and everything beyond it in hues of muted gold and amber. His gaze drifts from the view of the abandoned seaside town to Ezra standing beside him, quietly absorbing the scene.

A small hint of a smile tugged at the corners of the boy's lips, bringing a wave of relief to Clint. "It's pretty." He says as he takes in the view.

Clint's eyes roam the landscape, searching for any signs of life or shelter in the distance. Then, he notices a small farm dwelling not too far from where they stand - a single farmhouse with a cluster of outbuildings surrounding it.

"Hey, look," he says, drawing his son's attention to the distant farmhouse. "Perhaps we should check out that farmhouse. Maybe stay there tonight and recharge. We can make our way to the town tomorrow."

Ezra looks at him, then back at the town in the distance, his expression thoughtful.

As Clint awaits Ezra's response, he feels a drop of moisture on his face. He wipes it away, his gaze drifting upwards to the sky. Suddenly, rain begins to pour down in torrents, soaking them both within moments. They exchange a glance, their decision made for them by the weather, and with a nod, they wordlessly agree to seek shelter in the farmhouse. Together, they quickened their pace, determined to reach the sanctuary of the abandoned dwelling before the storm grew fiercer. They trudged along the narrow road, searching for an opening in the hedgerow to the farmhouse. Finally, they spot an old farm track veering off from the road, and without hesitation, they dart towards it. The track, overgrown and littered with debris, presents a challenge. Still, they navigate it with determined agility, their feet splashing through puddles and mud. As they draw closer to the farmhouse, the remnants of farm life materialize around them. Rustic wooden fences, weathered and worn, crisscross the landscape, enclosing neglected fields. Tangled vines creep up the sides of the dilapidated outbuildings, their tendrils reaching out like ghostly fingers. The farmhouse looms ahead, standing as a solitary figure against a sudden stormy sky. As they approach the porchway, Clint slows them to a gentle walk. He holds his hand out as a silent signal for Ezra to follow his lead and, with a practised motion, removes his sidearm from his trousers. He holds it at the ready, his senses attuned to any potential threats. Slowly, he ascends the small wooden steps leading up to the door, his movements deliberate and careful. He peers through a small side window, scanning the interior for any signs of movement. Satisfied with the stillness within, he cautiously reaches out and attempts the door handle. To his surprise, the door creaks open with ease, revealing the dimly lit interior of the farmhouse beyond. He holds his breath for a moment, his senses on high alert as he peers into the darkness, searching for any signs of danger. As his eyes adjust to the dim light, his gaze sweeps across the room, taking in the abandoned remnants of a life once lived. Furniture sits silently in the shadows, and a few cobwebs hang from the rafters. Despite an air of neglect that hangs heavy, there is a sense of quiet serenity within the building's walls. He exhales slowly as his grip on the sidearm relaxes as he steps cautiously over the threshold. Ezra follows closely behind, his movements mimicking his protectors as they explore the small living space and kitchen area. Clint methodically checks each drawer, his hands searching clumsily within as he tries to feel for anything of value. To his surprise and relief, he uncovers a few treasures amidst the dust and debris: a half-empty box of matches and a couple of tins of canned peaches, their labels faded but still intact. With their newfound provisions stowed away, he turns to the small utility room at the base of the stairs and enters. He approaches the rear door, his brow furrowing as he tests the handle, finding it stubbornly locked. He then motions for Ezra to follow as he ascends the creaking staircase, each step protesting in the silence of the abandoned dwelling. As they reach the top, he pauses, his senses on alert as he listens for any signs of movement or danger. Sensing nothing amiss, he motions for Ezra to continue. Upstairs, they discover a bedroom, a bathroom, and another smaller bedroom, its decor hinting at the presence of a child similar in age to Ezra.

As Clint enters the smaller bedroom ahead of Ezra, he takes note of the familiar trinkets scattered about - a small toy car garage, a collection of well-loved stuffed animals, and framed artwork adorning the walls. Ezra follows Clint into the room, his eyes alighting with curiosity as he takes in the surroundings. Without a word, he settles himself on the floor in front of the toy car garage, his small fingers tracing the worn edges with intrigue. Rummaging through his pockets, Ezra retrieves his treasured photograph and, with great care, sets it down beside him on the floor.

"Stay here," Clint says softly, shutting the door behind him as he leaves Ezra to his own devices.

With his sidearm still ready, he returns downstairs. As he reaches the ground floor, he pauses momentarily and listens again for any sounds that might indicate a threat. Satisfied with the farmhouse's vacancy, he sets down his sidearm on the kitchen counter, leans the backpack against a cabinet, and then returns to the front door. He peers outside again, observing the relentless torrent of rain and the ominous clouds looming on the horizon.

Looks like we're here for a while.

Closing the door behind him, he begins to barricade it, shifting pieces of furniture from the living room, dragging them across the floor and arranging them with methodical precision. Once satisfied with the barricade, he takes a step back to survey his handiwork and settles himself into an armchair in the living room, its worn upholstery emitting a cloud of dust as his weight sinks into it. Leaning back against the faded fabric, he lets out a weary sigh as the tension in his muscles slowly eases; the only sound accompanying him is the storm raging outside.

XVIII

Frank

Clint awakens, startled by a large bang. He sits apprehensively in the darkness, his mind racing as he tries to familiarise himself with his surroundings. Frantically, he searches the dimly lit room, his eyes falling upon the makeshift barricade he had meticulously arranged earlier. But in the darkness, his eyes struggle to adjust, and the details of the living room remain shrouded in shadow. His heart races as he notices a faint light emanating from the small utility room at the base of the stairs. His senses sharpen as he listens intently to the huffs, puffs, and groans that echo from within. He rises and considers calling out to avoid any shocks, but the room seems to close around him as any words clog in his throat. As the seconds tick by, anxiety mounts, and adrenaline begins to course through his veins. With bated breath, he stares into the darkness, his muscles coiled like springs, ready to react immediately. He watches as the beam of light suddenly freezes, casting an eerie glow through the doorway and into the kitchen, illuminating his backpack and sidearm in a surreal display. His breath catches in his throat as he watches the light illuminate his belongings, and his heart begins pounding erratically in his chest. A thought grips him: Why didn't he wake up sooner? He was a light sleeper, always on edge. Had he truly been that exhausted, or... had something changed?

Shit.

A jumble of thoughts and emotions hit him all at once.

Suddenly, a voice pierces the silence, sending a shiver down his spine. "Get out."

The words hang in the air. Sane words.

He remains silent in response to the callout as he contemplates his next actions. His hands form into fists, and then he hears it - the undeniable sound of a firearm being loaded, and he holds his breath.

The light again fixates on his belongings, illuminating them in the darkness.

"I said, get out?" the voice demands.

The blockage in his throat subsides, and his voice cuts through the darkness, his words carefully chosen.

"My name is Clint," he declares, his tone steady. "My son is upstairs. We are seeking refuge from the weather."

For a moment, there is silence, and now it is his words that hang heavy in the air.

"And it's just the two of you?"

Clint nods to himself. "Yes," he confirms, his voice carrying across the room. "The door was unlocked."

As he continues to speak, he notices the beam of light shifting, its glow illuminating the kitchen even more. His pulse quickens as he prepares for whoever emerges from the darkness. Then, a figure appears in the doorway, bathing him in a blinding light. Clint's eyes narrow as he attempts to adjust and assess the figure in the doorway, taking in the silhouette. The person appears a little larger and more rotund than he expected, their stature short and stocky.

As he considers his next move, the person demands, "Call your boy."

Clint's jaw tightens at the command. "What?" he asks, surprised.

"Call the boy, show me," the person insists, their tone leaving no room for negotiation.

He weighs his options carefully, knowing that his response will determine the outcome of this tense standoff.

With a deep breath, he raises his voice. "Ezra, come downstairs now." His heart pounds as he listens for movement upstairs; he calls again, louder and more frantically this time, "Ezra".

"If a man appears at the top of those stairs, I will shoot you both."

Suddenly, he hears panicked footsteps, which cease at the top of the stairs.

"Come down, don't worry," he says calmly.

He imagines his son's frozen stature and the look of surprise and fear that must be on his face. "It's okay, come down". he reassures again, desperation in his voice.

Slowly, Ezra begins to descend the stairs, his movements cautious and deliberate, as the torchlight swings and illuminates him.

Clint watches anxiously as his son comes into view, relief flooding him as Ezra draws nearer. "What's happening?"

The boy's voice trembles with uncertainty, his eyes searching his father's face for answers.

Clint takes a deep breath, steeling himself for what comes next. "Come to me, son," he urges, his voice surprisingly steady despite the fear gnawing at his insides. He gestures towards the darkness surrounding him, hoping to draw Ezra's attention to the safety of his embrace.

As he cautiously approaches in the darkness, the figure's torchlight follows him, casting long shadows across the floor. Clint can feel the weight of the intruder's gaze upon them. Finally, Ezra reached his side, his presence a comforting anchor in the darkness. Clint subtly moves his body to shield Ezra, his instincts sharp. He can't read this man yet. The figure's torchlight shifts again, illuminating the pair in its harsh glare. Clint squares his shoulders, his jaw set as he meets the figure's gaze head-on. They stand together, father and son, bathed in the unforgiving light, as they wait for the figure to make his next move.

"Boy, is this man your father?" he questions, his gaze fixed on Ezra with a penetrating intensity.

Ezra's brows furrow in confusion as he looks to his father for guidance, seeking reassurance in Clint's steady gaze.

"Don't look at him; look at me."

Ezra startles at the demand, but he finds the courage to respond. "Yes," he answers firmly, his voice quivering slightly.

The figure pauses, thoughtfully contemplating Ezra's response. "Why are you here?" he asks, his tone demanding an explanation.

"We are headed to the coast," Ezra explains, his voice faltering again slightly as he recalls their journey. "But then it rained."

Clint watches his son closely, pride swelling in his chest at Ezra's courage in uncertainty. The stranger lowered the flashlight beam, and a wave of relief washed over Clint at the unexpected event.

"Okay," the figure remarks, a hint of relief in his voice.

Clint exhales heavily, his shoulders sagging with the weight of tension released. The person approaches Clint slowly and then extends his hand. He hesitates momentarily, his gaze flickering between the offered hand and the figure's face. There's a moment where he wonders if it's a trick. If he should strike first. But then, with a sense of cautious trust, he firmly clasps the offered hand.

"Clint," he introduces, his voice steady despite the lingering adrenaline coursing through his veins. "And this is Ezra."

The figure nods in acknowledgement, as their hands meet in a firm handshake. "Frank," he introduces himself, his voice gruff yet warm. "Hard to trust people these days," he mutters as they shake hands. "The last ones who found their way here weren't as civil."

"What happened to them?"

Frank looks at him for a long moment. "They left."

By their means or by yours.

"I will be right back," he declares, his voice cutting through the lingering tension.

With that, he turns and heads back towards the utility room, leaving Clint and Ezra in bewilderment in the darkness. He exchanges a glance with Ezra, both uncertain of what to make of their encounter with Frank.

He seems almost a little too trusting. What's the play?

They remain rooted to the spot, wary of spooking their newfound companion. In the following silence, Frank disappears out of view. Clint strains to hear the faint sound of him fiddling with the lock on the rear door, then moments later, he reappears, a small backpack slung over his shoulder and a lantern in his hand. He returns to them again, placing the lantern on a nearby unit before plopping himself down on the seat where Clint had been resting earlier.

"Please," Frank says, gesturing towards the adjacent small settee.

Clint and Ezra exchange glances before complying, moving towards the settee and taking a seat. "Relax," Frank urges, his voice calm and reassuring. The pair take a deep breath, allowing themselves to unwind slightly in the presence of their unexpected host.

"Are you living here?" Clint asks, his voice cautious but genuine.

"Always have, always will," Frank replies, his gaze drifting towards the barricade constructed at the front door. "That explains that then," he remarks, a note of understanding in his voice.

"It was unlocked," Clint added, feeling the need to clarify their presence in the farmhouse.

"Yes, deliberately. Saves it from being kicked in."

Either a calculated risk or a stupid one.

"Were you in my grandson's room?" Frank asks, catching Ezra off guard.

The boy stares back at the older man blankly, uncertainty flickering in his eyes.

Before Ezra can respond, Frank reassures him, "It's fine. It's been a long time since anyone has enjoyed that room. You can go back up if you like. Everything's fine."

Ezra looks to Clint, seeking reassurance from his father.

"It's fine, son," he assures him gently. "Frank and I have to talk."

With a cautious nod, Ezra rises from the settee and returns up the stairs. Halfway up, he pauses, looking at his father again for further reassurance. Clint offers him a nod and a smile, giving him the encouragement he needs to continue.

As Ezra disappears back upstairs into the darkness, Clint turns his attention back to Frank.

"So, what's your story, and where are you going?" the man asks, his voice low and steady.

Clint shifts uncomfortably. "Honestly, I'm not entirely sure," he admits. "We were in a safe camp for a while, but it was overrun. We had to flee, and since then, we've been wandering without much of a plan."

Frank nods in understanding, and sympathy is evident in his expression. "I'm sorry to hear that," he says, his voice soft. It's a crazy world out there."

Clint nods in agreement, his thoughts drifting back to the safety and security they had lost. "Yeah," he agrees quietly. "But I'm not giving up. We stumbled upon a woman, Cara, she gave us a few supplies and a map, and I decided to head for the coast."

Frank considers Clint's words for a moment before speaking again. "And what do you hope to find there?" he asks, his voice gentle yet probing.

"Safety, I suppose", Clint responds, his voice filled with conviction. "Something similar to what we've lost. A place where Ezra can be safe."

Frank nods in understanding, his expression mirroring Clint's determination. "I can respect that," he says quietly. "In this world, safety is a precious commodity, but you won't find it here."

"Is that how you have managed to stay here all this time? I assume the place is derelict; it looked it."

"Yes, I suppose so. That's probably only part of it; the rest is hard work and not taking any prisoners," Frank replies. "You are lucky you answered me when you did. I was a few seconds from blowing your head off."

"Well, that's reasonable.

Is it?

"And you're by yourself?" Clint asks.

"I am now."

As their conversation continues, Clint and Frank find themselves opening up to each other, sharing stories of loss and resilience in a world forever changed by the pathogen. As the night wears on, they find comfort in each other's company, united by the shared desire for safety and security in a world fraught with danger and uncertainty.

But suddenly, the atmosphere turns unexpectedly when Frank poses a question at the heart of Clint's fears. "Clint," he says, his voice taking on a solemn tone, "can I ask a personal question?"

"Erm, Sure", he responds, surprised.

"How are you coping with this virus or madness thing? Do you ever think that in trying to protect your son, you might become his greatest threat?"

Clint's breath catches in his throat, his mind racing to grapple with the weight of Frank's inquiry. "That's a question I wrestle with in the darkest corners of my mind every day," he answers, "and it's a fear that I'm reluctant to confront head-on."

Frank nods, understanding Clint's answer.

"I saw a motto, or a saying if you like," Clint continues, "painted on a wall long back when this all began; it said, your true test lies not in the ability to fight the external threats but in your ability to conquer the demons within." With a heavy heart, he turns to face Frank, his expression grave. "I didn't really understand it when I first read it, I assumed it was a religious thing, but it's something that lives in my head daily now," he admits in a whisper. "I take every moment as it comes, but yes, to answer your question. I do wonder if I'm putting Ezra in harm's way."

Frank nods in understanding, his gaze filled with empathy. "It's a burden no parent should bear," he says softly. "Stay vigilant, young man, trust your instincts, and never underestimate the strength of a father's love. Mine got me through hell and back."

Clint takes Frank's words to heart, and a thousand new questions enter his mind. Was he a father? What's happened to his child or children? Why does he stay here? How does he stay here?

Frank gets up from the chair and opens a small ottoman, taking a small blanket. "You take the bed upstairs," he says, "I will stay down here."

Clint rises to meet Frank and extends his hand in gratitude. "Thank you," he says.

Frank responds with a nod, his expression unreadable.

Slowly, Clint proceeds towards the kitchen, collecting the backpack and the firearm from the kitchen side.

"Not the gun," Frank says from across the room. "We don't know each other that well."

Clint gives Frank a sly smile and proceeds up the stairs. *Well, he's definitely sane.*

Before heading to sleep, he decides to check on Ezra and finds the boy sleeping soundly in a single bed. He watches him sleep momentarily as a mixture of love and concern swells in his chest. For the first time since the boathouse, he felt a strange feeling, peace. He lowers the backpack to the ground and quietly sneaks in beside Ezra, wrapping his arm around him tightly. Ezra startles, waking abruptly.

"It's just me." He whispers as he settles in beside his son.

As he lies beside him, Frank's words stick stubbornly in his mind.

Do you ever think that in trying to protect your son, you might become his greatest threat?

He swallows hard, staring at the ceiling: his body aches, and his mind races. Yet again, he thinks back to the man in the water – the marks on his throat, the struggle he can't remember. He sees flashes of his own bruised knuckles, the blackened stains. He clenches his fists, checking them. Was that blood from defending himself or something else? Ezra shifts beside him, murmuring in his sleep, blissfully unaware. Clint exhales, his breath shaky. The storm rages outside. But the real storm - the one he's truly afraid of - is the one growing inside him.

XIX

Exposed

Days have passed since Alex's disappearance, leaving Elizabeth restless and consumed by a gnawing sense of unease. With each passing hour, her suspicions grew. She's convinced herself that the facility was filled with whispers and furtive glances and that all eyes seemed to follow her every move. This morning, she has made the decision to try and uncover the truth, to face Jane's wrath with equal strength. As she enters the facility's canteen, the hushed murmurs of the research team catch her attention; their voices are low and secretive as they cluster together in a small group. As they notice her, the team's whispers cease, their attention now fixated on her, observing her. Something is amiss; she can feel it in her bones. The team's gazes shift awkwardly as she draws near, their eyes flickering with apprehension.

"Good morning," she greets them, her voice steady.

The team remains entirely silent, all but Maya, who finally responds, "Good morning".

"What's going on?"

The group exchange uneasy glances, their expressions guarded as they shift uncomfortably, and a tense silence settles over the room again, broken only by the soft hum of the canteen's fluorescent lights. Sarah catches Elizabeth's attention with a troubled expression as her gaze shifts towards a small tape player resting in the centre of the table.

"Come on, what's the secret?"

Sarah speaks in a low, urgent tone. "We were just about to convene a meeting," she begins.

"Bullshit, you're already in a meeting," Elizabeth responds curtly. She expected more of her friend.

"Please, just sit down." Sarah requests. "Jane's whereabouts this morning are currently unknown, but still, I think it's time to share this."

Elizabeth nods as she sits, a silent signal for Sarah to continue.

"I keep this small radio on MW, recording everything," she elaborates. "In case of any communication attempts. I think you need to hear what's on it," she says, pressing a button.

The tape recorder whirs to life, and a static sound fills Elizabeth's ears with an eerie ambience; she waits with bated breath as Sarah handles the device, rewinding the tape with practised efficiency and then pressing the play button.

Static crackles again, interrupted by occasional bursts of interference, before a voice, tinged with worry and urgency, pierces through the canteen. "Is anyone out there? Can anyone hear me?" The voice is female, her tone frantic and trembling with fear.

Elizabeth's heart skips a beat as she leans closer, straining to catch every word.

"We thought... no, we knew those affected by the pathogen had some form of camaraderie," the voice continues, breathless and panicked. "But we were wrong. It's... It's much worse. They seem to recognize each other somehow. They're forming packs; we're calling them legions. Large groups, roaming the streets like... like animals."

The gravity of the revelation hits Elizabeth like a physical blow. The implications were staggering, the reality of the situation more dire than she could have imagined. She glances at the team, the weight of the recorded words hanging heavily among them. As Elizabeth and the team listen intently to the recording, Jane's sudden entrance brings a momentary pause to their collective focus.

Elizabeth's gaze shifts to Jane, her expression taut with urgency, just as Sarah pauses the tape recorder.

"You need to hear this."

Jane studies her, noting the barely concealed panic in her eyes. Without a word, she pulls a chair from a nearby table and settles beside the rest of the team. Elizabeth gives a curt nod.

Sarah rewinds the tape swiftly, her fingers steady despite the weight of the moment. "That wasn't everything. There's more."

More? God, what I've already heard is enough.

The room seems to hold its breath as the recording begins anew. Jane listens, her expression tightening with each passing second as the familiar voice delivers its grim message once again. Then, something new. Something neither Jane nor Elizabeth had yet to hear.

"The virus is airborne! It has to be! There's no other explanation! Reports are coming in - out-of-control males in isolated zones, sealed facilities - places far, far from the meteor debris! Governments worldwide are reporting a systematic collapse. Infrastructure is failing - female military forces are stretched too thin. Borders mean nothing anymore. It's in the air, it's everywhere!"

Wide eyes dart across the room, silent questions hanging in the air.

"God help us - war is on the horizon. Nations are on edge, accusations are flying, and retaliation is imminent! If you can hear this - stay inside, seal your homes, abandon all men, DO NOT let - "

The tape abruptly clicks off.

Elizabeth scans the room, her colleagues' expressions mirroring her own - fear, disbelief, and something deeper. Something darker. No one speaks. After a tense moment of silence, she speaks up, breaking the stalemate that had settled over the room. "Jane?" she asks, her voice heavy with apprehension.

Jane pauses, her brow furrowing in thought as she considers the implications of the recorded message. "I've seen this, pack, behaviour," she begins slowly. "But never in numbers as large as this person is speaking of. I always thought it was just a subtle influence, much like the behaviour of teenagers testing boundaries."

Elizabeth struggles with the notion that the pathogens infected were organising into large groups, akin to packs or legions, as the message called them.

"How and when have you seen this?" Questions Michelle, normally the silent one of the group. "Wouldn't it have been an idea to share this information?"

"As I've just said, I thought it was similar to teenage mentality," Jane responds sharply.

Ahh, there's the Jane we all know and love.

Michelle continues her out-of-character outburst. "Well, I think we should remain focused on our primary objective: finding a cure," she continues, addressing the table. "We don't have the resources to embark on an entirely new field of study," she continues. "Our priority must be to continue our efforts to understand the pathogen's mechanisms of action and develop effective treatments or vaccines to combat its spread. Every moment we spend diverted from our research is a moment wasted."

Elizabeth's voice rings out with conviction, challenging her colleague's assertion. "With all due respect, I must disagree. While our progress has been limited thus far".

Jane scoffs. Elizabeth ignores her.

"Simply continuing down the same path without considering new avenues of research may not yield the breakthrough we need." Her gaze sweeps over each member in turn. "The key to defeating this pathogen lies in understanding its mechanisms of action and identifying its vulnerabilities," she continues. "If we can uncover the signalling mechanisms used to facilitate this group mentality, we may be able to disrupt or neutralize them." Elizabeth's words seem to resonate with the team as they begin to stir with a sense of possibility. "Imagine the impact if we could prevent the formation of these infected 'legions' by targeting the signalling pathways." Her voice gains momentum. "It could mean the difference between isolated skirmishes with individual infected and full-blown outbreaks involving dozens or even hundreds of them." She pauses, allowing her words to sink in before concluding her point. "Our goal remains the same: to save as many lives as possible. But to do that, we must be open to exploring new approaches and pushing the boundaries of our research". Elizabeth's words prompt a thoughtful pause among the team. She turns to Jane, seeking her perspective on the matter. "Any input from you?" she inquires.

Jane ponders for a moment longer. "Well, considering the entire world seems to be going to shit anyway, I believe you're both correct," she says, her voice measured. "Our primary focus should remain on finding a way to eradicate or at least diminish the pathogen's influence. However, It's crucial that we consider all aspects, even with our limited resources." she continues, her expression serious. "Given this information and its urgency, I recommend that Dr Baker shift her focus to investigating the pathogen's signalling mechanisms. Understanding how it communicates could provide valuable insights into its behaviour and help us develop more targeted strategies for combating it."

Elizabeth considers Jane's suggestion carefully before nodding again in agreement. "That sounds like a prudent course of action," she concedes. "

Michelle, I trust you are happy to lead this effort," Jane asks.

Michelle nods in affirmation. "Of course," she sighs defeatedly. "I'll begin immediately."

Jane rose to her feet. "Excellent, well, I have pressing matters to attend to." She then proceeds to the canteen's makeshift coffee station.

The rest of the team apprehensively begin to follow suit, as conversations buzz with discussions about their upcoming tasks for the day and the tape recordings of new information.

As they disperse, Elizabeth stands alone at the table, her thoughts still swirling. She watches as Jane makes herself a drink on the other side of the canteen, observing her seemingly unwavering confidence intently. As Jane begins walking towards the canteen exit, Elizabeth feels a surge of bravery wash over her, and without hesitation, she calls out.

"Jane!"

Startled by the sudden interruption, Jane stops in her tracks and turns to face Elizabeth with a curious expression in her eyes.

With brisk steps, Elizabeth closes the distance, her gaze fixed upon her counterpart. "Jane," she says out loud again, her voice clear and assertive. Her next manoeuvre catches Jane off guard as Elizabeth strides past her towards the canteen exit. Curiosity mingles with apprehension as she tries to understand the strange behaviour; then, sighing heavily, she follows, uncertain of what will come next.

As Elizabeth exits the canteen, she pauses momentarily and glances up and down the hallway, ensuring they are alone. Satisfied with her assessment, she returns to the canteen door and firmly closes it, effectively sealing them off from the rest of the research team. Their proximity is now uncomfortably close as Jane searches her face for any indication of what has prompted this sudden action. Her expression is a mixture of confusion and curiosity.

"I want to know what's going on. Alex didn't return from her trip with Kim, and I'm not buying the excuses anymore."

Jane's eyes widen in surprise at her directness, but before she can respond, she presses on. "I've also noticed your frequent disappearances," she continues, her voice unwavering. "I want to know where you've been going. We're supposed to be a team, and it feels like secrets are being kept."

Jane remains silent for a few moments before letting out a defeated sigh. "I think it would be better to show you," she says.

Following Jane through the corridor, Elizabeth allows her to keep a few feet in front, until eventually, Jane leads her to a secluded spot where she leans against a makeshift wooden barrier that separates them from the rest of the facility.

"What is this?" Elizabeth's voice is tinged with unease.

Jane remains silent, her gaze fixed beyond Elizabeth, searching for unwanted followers. Then, with a forceful push, she opened the doorway hidden within the barrier. Elizabeth's breath catches in her throat as she gazes into the darkness.

"Jane," she says, her voice barely above a whisper, "what have you done?"

Jane turns to face her, her features bathed in shadows. "What's necessary."

Elizabeth hesitates, questions and doubts flowing through her. Summoning her courage, she steps through the doorway. As she enters, she's enveloped by darkness, the only light filtering in from a small, narrow opening in the distance. Jane abruptly closes the doorway behind her and proceeds a few paces ahead of her again. With cautious steps, Elizabeth navigates the dimly lit space. She can hear the faint hum of machinery and the distant echo of voices, but she can't discern their origin. As she is led through the new and unfamiliar corridors of the facility, she can't shake an overwhelming feeling of dread, her eyes darting nervously around the dimly lit passageways. As the pair begin to descend the stairwell, the air grows colder, and her skin prickles with apprehension.

I should have known Jane would do something like this; I should have known better.

Jane's continued calm demeanour only adds to Elizabeth's sense of unease. "When you called me at the beginning of all this, I already had ideas of what would need to be done," she begins to say, her voice low and steady.

"What do you mean?" her voice barely above a whisper.

"I knew it was airborne; it had to be; it was too fast, too deadly."

Shit, did I miss this? Am I that naïve? No, I was focused.

"I knew war would be on the cards, madmen in charge, hovering their already fat, clammy hands over the nuclear buttons. It was bound to happen."

I know Jane always had an issue with the way society's roles were handed out, but not to this extent.

"I thought, when you called, that we would be on the same page after all these years."

So did I.

"But we're not, so I took matters into my own hands, as I knew I would have to, and I've discovered something even worse."

This day just gets better.

"The pathogen's effects are far less amplified when not in a live host," Jane explains, her tone matter of fact. "We, well,

I, stupidly assumed that what we saw in our tests was its full capability, but I was wrong. Very wrong."

Elizabeth's mind races as she tries to process Jane's words. The implications were staggering - could it be possible that they had underestimated the pathogen's true potential all along? And if so, what did that mean for their research? Eventually, they reach a heavily sealed door. Jane stops, resting her hand on the cool metal surface, using her arm as a barrier and sighs heavily. Then, purposefully, she knocks on the heavy door with a closed fist. Elizabeth's heart hammers in her chest with anticipation. The seconds stretch on, each one feeling like an eternity as they wait for a response. Finally, the heavy door opens. Elizabeth's eyes strain to adjust to the sudden flood of light. In the doorway stands the silhouette of a figure, initially indiscernible in the brightness. However, the voice that greets them is unmistakable.

"Jane," says Rigs, the familiarity of her voice washing over Elizabeth like a wave. She glances in Elizabeth's direction, acknowledging her presence with a nod. "And Elizabeth," she adds, her tone neutral but with a hint of curiosity.

"Everything's fine," Jane affirms, her gaze shifting momentarily to Elizabeth before returning to Rigs.

With that assurance, Rigs steps out of the way, and Jane steps into the room with Elizabeth closely behind. Rigs closes the door with a heavy thud. Elizabeth's gaze sweeps across the room, taking in the tools and equipment occupying the small workspace. She notices several devices designed for pathogen detection and prevention, each meticulously arranged with care. One apparatus catches her attention - an advanced pathogen scanner with an array of sensors and monitors. Beside the pathogen scanner, she spots a series of containment units equipped with airtight seals and deconta-mination protocols for safely handling and storing pathogen samples. As her gaze drifts towards the large window at the far end of the room, her thoughts turn to the imposing struc-ture beyond - a relic of the facility's past. She's just about to scold Jane for hoarding vital equipment and using valuable resources when her eyes fall upon another scene within the room, instantly giving her an understanding of the reason-ing for the secrecy. A single chair is bolted firmly to the floor. Its occupant sits peacefully, their head slightly bowed. Her gaze inspects him and the intricate network of wires and sen-sors that adorn his body. Thin cables snake across his skin, attached to various points on his arms, chest, and temples. She follows them to a small laptop that's perched on a small desk beside the chair, where the sensors record vital signs, such as brain activity and other physiological indicators. Be-side the chair, a small makeshift workbench holds an array of scientific instruments. The laptop hums softly, its screen illu-minated with a cascade of data charts and graphs. She recog-nises the EEG and fMRI monitors among the equipment, along with other measuring devices that clutter the tabletop, their blinking lights and digital displays attesting to the con-stant monitoring and recording of the subject's physiological responses.

Elizabeth's gaze shifts from the subject to Jane and back again, the silence in the room palpable. "Infected?" she asks, her voice barely above a whisper.

Jane nods solemnly, her movements deliberate as she approaches the makeshift laptop beside the subject. "Yes," she confirms.

"And Alex?" Elizabeth inquires.

"I think you know", Jane replies.

I knew, but why didn't I mention it sooner?

There's silence again as every second stretches with tension. "Do you realize the danger of this? Do you understand the panic this will cause?" Elizabeth demands, her voice rising with each question. "Why on earth would you think it's a good idea to keep an irrational and unpredictable individual within these walls?" Her frustration boiled over completely, transforming her words into a shout. "What the hell were you thinking?" she demands of Jane, her tone a mix of incredulity and anger.

"I was thinking that a live subject would provide more answers," Jane states firmly, her volume matching Elizabeth's intensity. "And it has. Because of my actions, I now know that the pathogen's effects are amplified within a live host. The presence of the pathogen within a living organism enhances its virulence, leading to increased severity of symptoms."

Elizabeth opens her mouth to interject, but she gets cut off.

"And there's more. I discovered that the pathogen's impact is further intensified by trauma - both psychological and physical." Her expression reflects a mix of determination and something Elizabeth can't quite grasp. "Exposure to trauma triggers an escalation of the pathogen's activity within the brain, leading to heightened aggression and irrational behaviour; this means that the pathogen's presence elicits a cascade of neurochemical changes within the brain, resulting in aberrant neuronal activity".

Elizabeth attempts to interject again, but Jane continues relaying her new information.

"Furthermore, I know now that trauma induces a stress response, activating the hypothalamic-pituitary-adrenal axis and triggering the release of stress hormones such as cortisol, which exacerbate the pathogen's effects on neural circuits associated with emotion and cognition."

Finally, Jane takes a deep breath, no doubt steeling herself for a barrage of inevitable questions.

"How do you know trauma amplifies the pathogen's potency?"

The question is asked calmly. Too calmly, Jane's eyes flicker towards Rigs, seeking support or validation.

"Jane?"

Elizabeth is demanding her attention.

Jane tries to evade it, remaining silent, but her expression betrays a hint of inner turmoil.

A sickening realization creeps over Elizabeth as she stares at the bound man. She knew the answer before she even asked the question, but she wanted to hear Jane say it. The bruises, the thin, wiry tension in his muscles - it wasn't just the pathogen that had done this to him.

"Torture?" her voice rises slightly, her accusation hanging heavily in the air.

Jane meets her gaze but offers no response, her silence speaking volumes.

"I've done what's necessary to obtain results," she eventually declares, her voice unwavering. "And what I've discovered is crucial; I can now confirm that trauma significantly amplifies the pathogen's effects, meaning any previous efforts with the samples upstairs would have been futile, as they only contained approximately 5% of the pathogen's full strength."

Elizabeth's head sinks into her hands, fingers pressing against her temples as if to contain the whirlwind of emotions swirling within her.

"When this subject first arrived, he mumbled, laughed erratically, spoke curses and incoherent sentences." she continues, "but now. I've broken him even further." There's pride in her expression. "He's silent, consumed entirely by the pathogen, and I have the change recorded, from start to finish."

Elizabeth's mind races with questions, anger, and sheer disbelief, each thought fighting for dominance. She began to pace the room, her footsteps echoing in the tense silence. Mumbling to herself, Elizabeth utters words neither Jane nor Rigs can discern. Then, abruptly, she halts in her tracks, her eyes fixating on the desk where the laptop sits. She strides towards the workstation, and her fingers begin to navigate the keys and mouse as she scours through Jane's research.

Jane watches in bewilderment, unsure of her intentions. "What are you looking for?"

"If we accept the premise that the pathogenic agent is indeed heightened in potency through exposure to trauma and integrate this finding with the observed behaviour of group dynamics alongside our conjecture regarding a putative signalling mechanism, what are the implications?" Elizabeth asks, her voice commanding urgency, her words precise and analytical.

"I'm not following," Jane admits.

Elizabeth persists, her tone unwavering. "Considering the potential for the pathogen to discern its kind through signalling mechanisms, could it be hypothesised that one entirely consumed by the pathogen may elicit a distress signal?"

"Considering we only found out about the potential for signalling today, how would I have known to look for it?" Jane asked, her tone tinged with surprise and frustration.

"Exactly," Elizabeth retorts sharply. "How would any of us have known? This is precisely why you don't operate in secrecy or without consultation. Your subject not only sits in the most dangerous state, but he could now be a distress beacon for all we know."

"That's highly unlikely," Jane begins, but Elizabeth cuts her off.

"Is it?" she counters, almost shouting. "We've made minimal progress, and you're telling me that our efforts have been futile against a subdued version of a colossal threat, yet you want to dismiss a possibility. I want this subject released or deceased, I don't care which, but I want it done now."

For the first time, Jane hesitates. A flicker of something - shock? Defiance? - passes over her features, but it's gone in an instant. She crosses her arms, standing her ground.

"NOW!" Elizabeth demands, her voice reverberating through the room.

XX

Uncharted

Clint sits at the weathered dining table, savouring each bite of the hearty breakfast Frank has created for him. Cooked mushrooms, fresh tomatoes and fried potatoes all grown proudly by Frank, who had spent much longer explaining the processes of how he grew each one than he did cooking them. The weight of the previous night's events had almost entirely lifted as companionship seemed to form between the pair through the simple pleasure of sharing a meal. Clint pushed any reservations and doubts to the back of his mind as he carefully examined the man sitting opposite him. While Clint appreciated his hospitality, something seemed off; calmness and generosity were not something that were easy to come by in this day and age. again, Clint pushes his doubts back. As Frank continues to relay the growth processes of Tomatoes and potatoes, Clint can't help but steal glances towards the staircase as he eagerly awaits the appearance of his young son.

"It's all about keeping the soil healthy," Franks says proudly.

"How have you managed to stay here uninterrupted all this time?" Clint interrupts, desperate for a change of topic.

Frank pauses, his full mouth, and a wry smile plays at the corners of his lips. "Uninterrupted?" he manages to say, before swallowing his food. "I've lost everything and everyone; this place is all I have left."

Clint's fork stills, Frank's response was unexpected, sharp, and now there's a hint of pain in his eyes for the first time. His usual smile fades, replaced by a solemn expression.

"This place is my home," he begins, his voice now heavy with emotion. "I've lost my loved ones, my friends, everything I held dear. It's not just bricks and mortar; it's memories, and I will cherish this place as long as I'm able".

Clint listens silently, his heart heavy with empathy for the man across from him.

"In some ways, you and I are alike. Waiting for this thing to consume us. The difference is that I've accepted it, almost welcomed it, but for some reason I am prolonged to spend my days with my memories, and my grief, intact."

Clint feels an overwhelming sense of guilt. He senses there's more to Frank's story, a tale of struggle and sacrifice hidden beneath the surface. further.

"Don't look at me like that; I've made my peace with it", Frank continues, "I may have lost much, but this farm, this small piece of land, is, I suppose". He pauses. "Well, I suppose it's my last stand, you know, in some stupid way."

Clint nods, mulling Frank's words.

"Besides, what are my options?"

"You could leave, start new memories." The words come from Clint's lips before he can stop them.

"Where is there to go?" Frank answers; his tone is contemplative. "You're driven, Clint, but even you admit you're wandering without direction."

Frank's observation settles heavily on Clint's shoulders, stirring a disquieting uncertainty. "I just want safety for Ezra," he confesses.

A quiet hum of agreement underscores Frank's understanding. "Seems to me, young man, that safety may not take the form you expect." He muses, leaving Clint questioning everything and every decision he's made thus far. "If what they say holds true, and all men are doomed, maybe it's not a place you're seeking, but a presence."

Cara's voice instantly enters his mind.

I've been thinking... maybe you should leave now. Just disappear. Take the risk; leave Ezra with me.

"Perhaps you're right, but I fear I've missed that opportunity", he concedes softly.

Frank removes himself from the table, "Sometimes, Clint, the weight of the choices given to us can be so heavy that it clouds our judgment. Your boy may not see it, but the strength of his father's character, of your character, lies not in the ease of your decisions but in the courage you have to stay true to your commitment." Frank's words pierce Clint's heart as he takes in the man's wisdom.

"But what if my commitment is to the wrong thing. Like you've said, if it's a presence I seek rather than a place, I may have already blown it."

"Another opportunity will present itself, just make sure you recognise it for what it is when it does. Now, come, there is something I would like to share with you."

Curiosity takes hold of Clint, and he quickly finishes up, placing his plate on the kitchen side. Frank enters the small utility room, opens the side door and beckons for Clint to follow. He obliges, suspicious and unsure of what to expect. The morning after the storm had left the ground damp and soggy and the sky above a dreary expanse of Grey. Frank leads Clint around the entirety of the building back to the front of the house, where he awaits, gazing thoughtfully towards the horizon.

"You can only really see it on a good day," Frank begins, pointing to the town's silhouette, barely visible against the gloomy backdrop. "But beyond the sea, on the horizon, there's more land. About 20 or 30 miles away, as the crow flies."

Clint listens intently, curious about the purpose of sharing this information. "Okay, and?"

"On that land, to the East, there's a lighthouse," he explains, "If you look to its left closely, you'll notice a groove in the terrain, like a shallow V in the landscape."

"Okay, what are you trying to tell me? "

"There's an old nuclear facility, buried in the hills. It had been decommissioned before I was a Kid".

"Seems like the sort of place to avoid. " Clint responds dryly.

"Well, it is, but shortly after the virus or illness, whatever it is, became common knowledge, I saw a helicopter go backwards and forwards a few times, not our usual coastal safety one either, but something else".

Clint listens intently, processing the revelation. "How recently?"

"Oh, not recently, nothing for years in fact."

"So why are you telling me this?"

"Well, I'm sorry to say your idea of the coast and its expectations have fallen short. There's not much in town, a small supermarket and a handful of shops on the harbourside, which have been empty for years. So, maybe you'll want somewhere to head afterwards, I don't know really."

Clint nods, taking in the information. "How long a walk to the V you mention? Once on the other side," he asks.

"Only a few miles, I reckon." Simultaneously, the pair turn around as a gentle knock interrupts the conversation.

As they glance up at the window, Ezra's bright and cheery face greets them, the boy waving. They both return the favour, smiling and waving back until the young boy's face disappears.

"Anyway, that's enough for now. Let's feed that boy of yours". Frank says.

As they enter the house again, a well-rested and happy Ezra eagerly awaits them at the kitchen table. "Sleep well, young man?" Frank asks.

"Yes, thanks, do you have anything to eat?"

"Ezra!" Clint scolds.

"Oh, it's fine, young hunger waits for no man," Frank responds as he begins collecting ingredients from somewhere in the utility room.

Clint's mind races again.

Where's he getting this food from? Did I miss it last night, or did I just not look properly?

"What's that in your hand?" Frank asks Ezra inquisitively, noticing something in the boy's grasp as he re-enters.

Ezra looks at his cherished photograph and then slowly holds it out to Frank. Suspiciously, he accepts the boy's offering, looks at it longingly and then passes it back, saying nothing but offering him a subtle smile. "Mum?" he simply asks.

"Yeah." The boy solemnly answers, putting the photograph in his pocket.

As Ezra eagerly tucks into his breakfast, humming softly between bites, Frank stands from the far corner of the room and gestures to Clint with a quiet wave of his fingers. No words. Just a look. The kind that says now. Clint hesitates, his eyes flicking to Ezra, then rises, following Frank to the same couch they'd sat on the night before. The morning light filters weakly through thick curtains, casting the old man's face in a weathered half-shadow.

Frank doesn't waste time. "I've appreciated your camaraderie, young man," he begins softly, his hands clasped before him. "But I must insist… that you move on."

Clint nods slowly as his eyes narrow. "Oh."

He had expected it. Eventually. But so soon? After just one night?

Frank lets the silence stretch before continuing. "You're good people. I can tell. Your boy's got more light in him than I've seen in years. But this isn't about kindness."

Clint shifts in his seat. "It's about safety."

Frank's jaw works for a moment, then he sighs and leans forward, placing his elbows on his knees. "Exactly. You understand then. We don't know each other. And I've survived this long because I keep it that way." He glances toward the kitchen table, where Ezra swings his legs idly beneath the chair, licking something from his fingers. His voice drops to a whisper. "We don't know what'll happen tomorrow or the day after. I can't risk it."

Clint nods again, slower this time. "I get it. You've made it this far by being smart. Cautious."

Frank looks him square in the eye. "Yes. But it's also this infection. It's not just you, it's me, having your boy around two men, it's tempting fate, it's.."

"Increasing the danger," Clint finishes.

Frank says nothing. He doesn't have to.

Clint rubs at his wrists, where faint scars from his restraints still linger. "I feel fine." Clint lies.

"I don't doubt you," Frank replies. "But it's not now, that's the problem. Maybe not today. But I've seen men snap. Seen them smile at their daughters one night, and then they slit their throats the next. Not because they wanted to. But because it made them." His face drops, and his lip shudders.

Clint swallows hard. There is something Frank's not telling him, a history he's keeping hidden. "When do you want us gone?"

Frank looks back toward Ezra. "Let him finish breakfast. I'll pack you some food for the road."

Clint's voice drops, and something hard slips into his tone. "Have you ever had to tell a boy that shelter is temporary? That kindness has an expiration date?"

His tone is argumentative.

Frank doesn't answer right away. Then he says quietly, "Would you rather I tell him that keeping him safe from you is kindness too?"

The two men lock eyes. Clint breaks first, glancing back toward his son. "I understand," he says finally. "I don't like it. But I understand."

Frank stands and slowly wanders towards Clint. His hand reaches out. Clint instinctively flinches as a hand is placed on his shoulder. "I wish things were different."

Clint offers a hollow smile. "So do I."

Then Frank makes his way towards the kitchen. "I'll fetch you some rations."

Clint doesn't look at him. He just watches his son eat.

As he rustles through the backpack and prepares himself, Frank once again reappears from the utility room "These are a few things I can spare," he explains.

Excited, Ezra eagerly reaches into the box, retrieving a small wind-up torch, and begins to fiddle with the device, testing its functions. Curious, Clint peers into the box, finding several bottles of water and a couple of tinned goods.

Is there a secret portal in that damn room?

"Thank you, Frank, this is more than generous."

Frank kneels beside Ezra. "Why don't you go upstairs and grab any clothes that will fit you, perhaps a toy?" he suggests kindly.

"Really?" Ezra responds, his eyes lighting up with excitement.

He glances at his father for confirmation and then promptly dashes up the stairs.

As Clint watches Ezra hastily fumble up the stairs, Frank disappears into the utility room. A second later, he returns, but this time, he's holding something new. Clint's muscles tense instinctively. His hand instinctively searching the back of his trousers.

"Eight rounds," Frank says, holding up a shotgun. "That's all I can spare. It'll be a better deterrent than that little thing you carry."

Clint exhales, his heart racing as he reaches for the weapon.

"More effective, too."

Clint accepts the shotgun from Frank, his hands feeling the weight of the responsibility it carries. "I've got to ask, where the hell do you keep getting this stuff from?"

"Ah, well, perhaps that's a secret best kept. Anyway, just pump, point, and shoot. Oh, and watch the kickback, that thing will dislocate a shoulder," he instructs.

Clint nods silently, grateful for the guidance, and with a smile to Frank, begins loading the new supplies into the backpack. He slings the bag over his shoulder and positions the shotgun securely over one arm with the strap. Then, he extends his hand to Frank, which is met with the older man's firm grasp. "Thank you again for everything."

"Of course."

"Ezra, time to go." He calls, and soon enough, the boy begins descending the stairs, still adjusting his new outfit. A pair of black jeans and a taupe overcoat paired with his trusty grey hooded top.

As Ezra reaches the bottom of the stairs, Frank extends his hand, "It's been a pleasure, young man," he says warmly. Ezra looks at him, puzzled, not knowing how to return the gesture.

"Are you coming with us?"

"Time to go," Clint announces, saving Frank from having to fashion a child-friendly excuse.

"You can help me move this barricade first," Frank informs Clint.

With the barricade removed, the pair bid Frank farewell and stepped out onto the farmhouse steps. The pair trudge their way back to the narrow single-track and begin towards the harbour town. It doesn't take long into their descent down the hill for the road to widen, and a solitary metal barrier now separates two lanes. The sky has remained a dull Grey, casting a sombre tone over their surroundings as scattered scraps of paper and other debris flutter by in the breeze like ghostly whispers of the past. Buildings eventually start to appear, standing in various states of disrepair, some with shattered windows and crumbling facades, while others have almost collapsed entirely, leaving only piles of rubble in their wake. As they enter the desolate streets, Clint peers through a few of the broken and boarded windows of shops and buildings, scavenging for further supplies, while hoping to avoid any surprises. Approaching a crossroads, they spot a single large building standing stark against the dreary backdrop. The supermarket car park is a shadow of its former self, with abandoned cars still occupying some of its spaces. Cautiously, they approach the central doorway, where a large panel of glass once welcomed shoppers in search of groceries. He readies his new shotgun and signals Ezra to stay close as they approach the entrance. Stepping over the broken glass and into the building, they are hit with a stale scent that hangs heavy in the air. The once bustling supermarket lies in ruin; its aisles strewn with debris and the remnants of looting. Dust particles shimmer in the air, caught in the dim light filtering through gaps in the high ceiling. Once stocked with various goods, the shelves now stand empty or overturned, their contents long since pillaged.

After a thorough search, Clint finally puts the shotgun back over his shoulder and concedes defeat.

"Just like Frank said, nothing's here, buddy".

Ezra ignores his father, preoccupied as he attempts to upright an overturned shopping cart.

Clint helps, unaware of Ezra's intentions, until the boy clambers into the cart and sits clumsily. "How about you push me the rest of the way?" he suggests playfully.

Clint chuckles. "I don't think so. I don't have a license."

"What's a license?"

"It's nothing." Clint sighs, then he begins giving the cart a gentle push, then, with a mischievous grin, he suddenly starts to run, increasing his speed as he rushes the cart down one of the aisles.

Ezra bursts into laughter, the sound filling the space of the abandoned supermarket.

Skilfully, Clint navigates the shopping cart around one end of the aisle, while Ezra's laughter erupts, beckoning his father to go faster. Clint picks up more speed down the next aisle, using the cart like a battering ram to clear debris from their path. As they reach the end, he tries to manoeuvre the corner as smoothly as he had done before, but this time the cart tips over unexpectedly, sending them both flying.

There's a moment of uncertainty before Clint groans, and more laughter erupts from Ezra. "Yeeeaah let's do that again!" he giggles with a spark in his eye.

Clint pushes his aches aside and joins in the laughter. After dusting himself off, he extends a hand to help Ezra up. "Come on, that's enough. Let's keep going," he suggests.

"Ahh, but I don't want to," the boy argues.

Once more, they begin to traverse the labyrinth of forsaken structures, the echoes of their footsteps reverberating against the worn pavement. Eventually, Clint begins to hear the distinctive sound of boats knocking together, each collision echoing like a solemn drumbeat. As they emerge into a spacious clearing, they face a decrepit combination of a marina and harbour, where a selection of once vibrant boardwalks now sag under neglect, the salt-weathered wood creaking mournfully with each gentle gust of wind. The boats moored alongside are a sorry sight; their hulls battered and splintered, with masts askew and their rigging tangled. Several larger ones lay partially submerged in the murky waters, their decks barely visible below the water's surface. Other vessels list precariously to one side, their hulls breached and waterlogged, while others lie entirely sunken, the only evidence of their existence being masts that protrude awkwardly from the water like skeletal fingers reaching desperately for the sky. Amidst the desolation stands a large clock tower; its imposing structure starkly contrasts the shabby surroundings. Though now weather-worn and partially obscured by time's relentless advance, its grandeur is undeniable. Clint recalls seeing its silhouette from the hilltop, a looming presence on the horizon. As they stroll along the harbour edge, gazing into the murky depths below, the horizon stretches before them, cloaked in shades of Grey. Clint begins to wonder if Frank's mention of additional land beyond the sea was truthful as he struggles to see anything other than muted darkness and mist on the horizon. Suddenly, his eyes catch sight of a smaller, more carefully prepared boat in the distance, its appearance unlike all the others. Unable to contain his excitement, he points it out to

Ezra, grabbing the boy's hand and quickening his pace toward the vessel. As they draw closer, he notices the stark differences between this boat and the others. Ropes lay neatly coiled on the deck, and the windows and doors remained intact. Clint scans the area with a sense of urgency, his mind racing with questions. Were there still occupants on board? Had they docked for supplies, and where are they, if not aboard? He checks the back of his trousers for the small sidearm, confirms its presence and readies the shotgun again, silently beckoning Ezra to his side.

"Anyone home?" His words echo across the quiet harbour, but there's no response. He takes a deep breath and tries again, speaking louder, "We're just looking for safety, perfectly sane here." Still, there's only silence in return, leaving him wondering about the fate of whoever owned this seemingly well-kept boat.

With no sign of anyone around, He decides to cautiously board the vessel, motioning for Ezra to stay put on the dock. Carefully, he approaches the single-entry door leading into the bow and opens it slowly. Peering inside, he sees a cramped interior. Its walls are lined with aged wooden panels, and the floor is covered in worn linoleum, scuffed and faded from use. It is arranged in a functional yet compact manner. A modest seating area occupies one side of the bow, featuring a single corner bench with faded cushions. Across from the bench is a tiny galley with a small sink and a compact stove. He tests the boat's utilities, flipping switches and turning knobs, to no avail. Frustrated, he exits the bow and returns to the deck, where he sees Ezra waiting anxiously on the harbourside. Clint looks up at him and shrugs, then he spots the outboard motor.

As he inspects the motor, he is surprised to find it still contains fuel. "Well, I'll be damned," he mutters to himself, a glimmer of hope flickering within him. "Ezra, come on."

Ezra hesitates, looking uncertain. "What if they come back?" he asks, worries etched on his face.

"That's why we're going now," Clint replies eagerly.

He sets down his backpack and shotgun and motions for Ezra to climb aboard, holding his arms open to assist the boy. "Go and sit inside," he instructs, eager to get underway before their luck runs out.

Ezra enters the boat's bow and sits patiently on the bench as Clint reassesses the small outboard motor. He attempts to start the engine, yanking haphazardly on the motor's starter cord, but the first attempt yields nothing. With a deeper pull, the motor still fails to start, much to his frustration.

Come on, you bastard.

He wipes his hands on his trousers and takes a deep breath, trying to keep his composure despite his mounting frustration. With a third, much stronger pull, there's a sputter, then a cough, and finally, the motor roars to life. He exhales in relief, and a smile spreads across his face as he looks at Ezra, who eagerly watches his father progress from the bow's small doorway.

"We're in business, buddy," he says, his voice filled with confidence.

Ezra grins back, his eyes wide with excitement. Quickly, he throws any mooring ropes onto the harbourside and then carefully guides the boat alongside the boardwalk and away from the dock and begins navigating through the still waters of the harbour. As they move farther away from the shore, the sounds of the abandoned town begin to fade into the distance, replaced by the gentle lapping of the waves against the hull and the hum of the small motor. Sitting beside the motor, Clint watches Ezra lean over the boat's edge, entranced by the waves, his small fingers trailing in the water and A rare, genuine happiness flickers in Clint's chest. Then, he sees it. A figure. Standing still, waving. His breath catches, and his pulse pounds in his ears. He doesn't move. For a second, his fingers gripped the boat's controls. Turn back? Just for a second? Ezra laughs, unaware. Clint swallows hard. *No.* He keeps going. As the dock disappears, so does the figure, shrinking into the distance, swallowed by the bleak Grey.

XXI

Darkness

His eyes flutter open. A disorienting darkness greets him. The sound of raindrops penetrates his ears. A calm wind whispers through the air. He blinks rapidly, as confusion grips him. His memory offers only fragments, disjointed images of their departure from the harbour town and the sun attempting to cast long shadows through the grey skies. Yet now, darkness reigns supreme, shrouding his whereabouts in obscurity. He pushes himself up, his body aching as he shuffles himself across the deck to the edge of the boat, dampness seeping through his clothes. Now, in a partially upright position, he can not only feel the rain, but see its reflective glimmers as it falls. Squinting into the darkness, he rattles his thoughts for the missing fragments. Wearily, he rises to his feet, his heart hammering in his chest. Then, a surge of panic courses through him.

Ezra.

Hastily, he makes his way to the door leading into the small boat's bow, struggling to keep his footing in the swaying echoes of the night. As he steps into the cabin, he is met by even further blackness. His breath hitches as he swiftly scans the cramped space, frustration and fear gnawing at him with each passing second. In a frenzy, he rushes back to the boat's deck, moving frantically along the edge, using the structure as his guide in the dark until he stumbles. Desperately groping in the darkness for what tripped him, he finally feels the backpack and urgently begins to rummage through it, feeling its contents. Finding the small wind-up torch, he cranks it frantically. With its brief flicker of light, he hurries back to the narrow doorway, sweeping the dim beam across the darkened bow in a desperate search. Fear tightens its grip around his chest and squeezes the air from his lungs as the room appears empty. Pain pierces his heart, sharp and relentless, as the internal grapples of uncertainty begin. But, almost immediately, sadness starts to wash over him in waves, heavy and suffocating, swirling and twisting his thoughts as he struggles to make sense of the surreal nightmare unfolding before him. With a sudden thought, he rushes back onto the deck, his heart pounding so hard he was sure it was going to erupt from his chest. His hands shake as he rummages through the backpack contents again, tossing aside food and supplies in a desperate search for a trace of his son. As panic rises within him like a tidal wave, the gravity of the situation sets in, and he slumps against the boat's edge with a heavy sigh, his back pressing firmly against the cold wood.

He buries his face as he struggles to contain the flood of emotions threatening to overwhelm him. Tears slip through his fingers, mingling with the raindrops that trace down his cheeks. His mind becomes a whirlwind of doubt and self-blame, each thought a dagger piercing his shattered heart. As he sits alone, swaying in the ocean, surrounded by darkness and silence, the feeling of failure and overwhelming guilt consumes him. He knew, deep down, it had happened again, but this time he had truly become what he feared most - a danger to his son. Tears begin to blur his vision as his harsh sobs start to pierce the silence. The thought of harming Ezra, of losing control and becoming a threat to the one person he loves above all else, fills him with horror and despair.

What did I do?

The rain lashes against his skin, each droplet stinging. He casts a wary glance out into the abyss of the night, where the inky blackness seems to stretch on endlessly.

What the fuck have I done?

The rain becomes heavier and louder; its relentless drumming on the deck floor and bow roof echoes in his ears as he winds the torch once more and begins crawling along the deck. He searches the scattered debris of the backpack, unsure of what he's searching for, then he remembers and reaches for his waist. Manoeuvring himself back to the boat edge, he leans against the damp wood again, resting his arms heavily on his knees, the small sidearm feeling unusually heavy in his trembling hand. Each breath feels harder, more of a struggle, as if the air itself had become thick with sorrow and regret. Memories of Ezra begin to flood his mind like the torrential downpour surrounding him, each one more painful than the last. He sees Ezra's bright smile, can hear his infectious laughter, and feels the warmth of his embrace. His hands tremble uncontrollably as he checks over the sidearm, his fingers fumbling with each movement, the weapon feeling heavier with each passing second. With each click of its mechanisms, his heart pounds heavily.

"I'm sorry," he whispers, his voice barely audible over the sound of the rain and the waves lapping against the boat's hull.

A solemn admission of defeat. He can't bear the pain any longer, not wanting to face another moment of this unbearable agony. Slowly, almost mechanically, he raises the sidearm to his face. His breath caught in his throat as he felt the cold steel against his skin, the barrel pressing against his temple. He closes his eyes as the world around him narrows to a single point of focus. At that moment, time seemed to stand still, the rain, the wind, and the ocean all silenced by the steady rhythm of his heartbeat. His mind, just a moment ago, was a whirlwind of conflicting emotions, a tumultuous storm raging within him; now, even his mind had been silenced. He tightens his grip on the sidearm with a trembling hand, his finger hovering delicately over the trigger. He takes a deep breath and then, with a sense of determination. squeezes the trigger. He waits, expecting the deafening roar of a gunshot, but there is only silence. The sidearm remains motionless in his hand, its chamber empty, its purpose unfulfilled. His eyes snap open in shock, his heart pounding in his chest, the sound of the rain and the lapping of water almost deafening. For a moment, he remains frozen in disbelief, unable to comprehend what's happened. Carefully, he lowers the sidearm to the deck, his hands shaking with the weight of what should have been. His shoulders heave with grief as the sound of a father's sobs are lost to the patter of the continuous rain. After a few moments, he once again readies the sidearm, checking its barrel, clocking it, and holding it firmly against his temple. Ezra's voice calls out to him with a softness that fills him with longing and dread. He curses his mind for tormenting him with the cruel illusions, but still, he can't help but hope. He opens his eyes, his hand shaking violently as it holds the weight of the firearm against his skin. He blinks, trying to make sense of the silhouette kneeling before him. Through the watery blur, he sees faint features begin to take shape, a face framed by waves of strawberry blonde hair and eyes that hold a familiar warmth.

"Daddy," Ezra's voice comes again, so real and so close that he swears he can feel the breath on his face.

His heart aches with longing as he slowly lowers the sidearm and reaches out, desperate to hold onto the illusion.

Only it's not a trick of his mind. His fingers feel the damp fabric, and as he reaches for Ezra's face, it's tangible and real.

"Ezra," he utters, his voice trembling with disbelief, as he cradles the boy's face.

"What can you never eat for breakfast?"

Clint blinks, confusion etching across his face. "What?" he stammers, caught off guard by the unexpected question.

"It's a test," Ezra patiently explains. "What can you never eat for breakfast?" he repeats.

Clint's mind races, struggling to comprehend the surreal encounter. "Is that you?" he asks, his voice barely above a whisper. "Where, how?"

But Ezra ignores his questions, his gaze fixed intently on his father's face. He repeats his question again, this time with a sense of urgency.

Clint realises he must answer. "I don't know," he admits, frustration creeping into his voice.

Ezra's expression tightens with worry, his eyes pleading for his father to understand. "Think," the boy urges, his voice barely above a whisper.

Clint closes his eyes, searching his mind for an answer. After a few moments, he opens his eyes again, savouring the darkened sight of his son before him, eagerly awaiting his response. "Lunch or dinner," he finally says, "You can't eat lunch or dinner for breakfast."

Ezra's lips begin to broaden, forming a faint smile. "Good." The boy collects the small wind-up torch from the deck floor, stands up, and outstretches his hand towards his father.

Clint takes Ezra's tiny hand in his own and pushes himself up from the sopping deck. The sidearm he still holds makes a noise against the wooden surface, drawing his attention, and he stares at it momentarily, then pushes it away with a determined gesture, sliding it along the wet wooden floor.

As Ezra guides his father into the cabin, he shines the small flashlight's beam within the cabin. Clint's eyes begin to scan the compact space, taking in as much detail as possible. As Ezra manoeuvres himself about the cabin, a momentary passing of the flashlight's beam draws Clint's attention to the small bench seat. But it's not as he remembers; it now lies askew, revealing a small compartment beneath it.

"You were in there?" he asks.

Ezra responds with a soft hum, confirming his father's observation.

"Why?"

Ezra moves to the small bench seat, adjusts the ajar wooden top, and indicates for his father to sit. Moving slowly in the darkness, Clint approaches the small bench seat and obliges.

"We were happy, on our way, somewhere", Ezra begins, his voice soft. "But when I spoke to you, you ignored me". As Ezra settles onto the bench seat beside his father, his voice trembles with emotion as he continues to recount the experience. "Then you started talking, but I couldn't hear what you were saying," he confesses, his eyes flickering towards the small wooden compartment beneath him. "I got scared, so, I came here looking for a hiding place."

Clint's heart aches at the admission, and tears start to stream down his face again. "I'm so sorry," his words are choked with emotion.

Ezra shakes his head, his tears glistening in his eyes as he winds the torch for light once more. "I didn't know what to do or how to help," he continues.

Clint reaches out, his hand trembling as he attempts to brush away a tear from Ezra's cheek, but Ezra retreats almost violently. Petrification in his eyes.

"You did the right thing, buddy," Clint assures him. "You're so brave, and I'm so sorry."

Ezra's shoulders shake with silent sobs as he struggles to contain his emotions. "No, I'm not," he insists, his voice barely above a whisper. "I hid like a baby."

Clint's heart breaks. He reaches out to the boy again, slowly. "You are brave, Ezra," he whispers as he tries to envelop the boy in damp reassurance.

For a moment, Ezra hesitates again, his body tense with uncertainty. But then, overcome with emotion, his body collapses into his father's arms, clinging to him tightly.

Clint's mind swirls with thoughts and feelings as they sit locked in their emotional clasp. The severity of his situation dawns on him. The weight of the pathogen's effects loomed over him like a dark cloud. But now an even darker thought enters his mind. What if he had succeeded with his intention on deck? Fear grips him like a vice as he leans back against the wooden cabin's wall, still holding Ezra tightly. With trembling fingers, he brushes through Ezra's hair, attempting to comfort the boy amidst the rhythmic sound of rain drumming against the cabin's roof. As Clint cradles Ezra in his arms, he closes his eyes, allowing his mind to drift between thoughts of the future and the haunting spectre of what might have been, and determination courses through him as he makes a silent plea for redemption.

A loud bang reverberates through the boat, jolting Clint and Ezra from their reverie. Ezra's startled cry pierces the air, and Clint's instincts kick in as he almost violently disentangles himself from Ezra's embrace. He rises to his feet and hastily makes his way to the cabin door in search of the source. Stepping onto the boat's deck, his eyes are drawn to the hint of sunrise that paints the horizon, signalling the end of the night. As his gaze sweeps across the water, he spots a landmass, sparking the recollection of their purpose for embarking on the boat; his heart quickens with anticipation as he leans over the boat's edge and confirms their arrival at the distant shore. Yet, his excitement is quickly tempered by the rocky and barren coastline before them, offering no clear path to land. He calls out to Ezra, reassuring him that everything is alright.

Ezra joins him on the deck, "What was that?" he asks, his voice uncertain.

"Land," Clint replies, a note of triumph in his voice. "We've made it to the other side."

Quickly, he shifts his focus to the practical matters at hand and moves towards the small outboard motor. With determined resolve, he attempts to start the engine, pulling the cord with all his strength. Yet, despite his efforts, the engine remains stubbornly silent, refusing to come to life. Undeterred, Clint tries again, each tug of the cord echoing with a sense of urgency and determination. His heart sinks as he checks the fuel tank, finding it disappointingly dry.

"Shit." His hands on his hips, he paces back and forth, his mind racing with possibilities.

"I'm sorry," Ezra says, breaking the silence with a sense of guilt that Clint immediately recognises.

"No, no," he interrupts, his voice gentle as he approaches Ezra, kneeling to his level. "This isn't your fault," he re-assures the boy, his hand resting softly on Ezra's shoulder. "We'll figure something out."

Ezra looks at him, his eyes filled with concern. "So, what now?"

Clint sighs, his gaze drifting back to the rugged coastline before them. "I'm thinking," he responds, his tone thought-ful.

Kneeling beside the outboard motor again, he begins ma-nipulating its various components. He checks the fuel line for any signs of blockage or leakage, his mind recalling any ba-sic mechanical knowledge he can think of. While his hands work, his gaze drifts across the rugged landscape before them. The rocky coastal terrain offers few clues for their next move, but he knows they can't afford to stay stranded. As he scans the horizon, searching for any sign of civilisation or a potential route to safety, his eyes catch the subtle decline of the terrain in one direction, the gradual slope hinting at the possibility of finding a more accessible path or a beach if they follow it. He quickly relays his observations to Ezra, urging him to check the boat for any signs of damage. Ezra nods, understanding the urgency in his father's voice. With nimble movements, the young boy scours the vessel, inspecting each side meticulously. Clint's frustration mounts as he tugs on the outboard motor's cord, hoping against hope for any sign of life; then, just as desperation threatens to overtake him, the motor sputters to life. His heart leaps with relief as the engine roars to life, its familiar hum a reassuring sound. His tinkering with the fuel line seems to have paid off, providing enough fuel to ignite the engine. He instructs Ezra to hold on tight as he rushes to the front of the boat. He dangles his legs over the edge and uses every ounce of his strength to push the vessel away from the perilous rocks. As the boat gradually glides into clearer waters, he swiftly returns to the outboard motor, his movements frantic and urgent. He carefully and precisely adjusts the motor, aligning the boat toward the terrain's decline. He knows maintaining momentum is crucial, especially if the engine fails again. Taking a deep breath, he opens the throttle, the engine roaring as the boat surges. As the boat skims across the water, his gaze shifts between Ezra and the landscape ahead. He scans the rocky shoreline beside them, yearning for a glimpse of opportunity. Then, as they navigate a protruding rock formation, he spots a narrow opening leading to a small beach. Ezra's excited gesture confirms his observation. He nods silently in agreement as he studies the beach intently, searching for signs that there may be a path leading further inland. He's wary, hoping desperately that the secluded spot isn't a dead end.

He guides the boat towards the beach. "Hold on!"

Ezra clings desperately to the cabin door as the boat grumbles and scrapes against the grainy, grey shingles, the outboard motor taking a beating in the process until the boat comes to a sudden and abrupt halt.

"Let's go," Clint declares to Ezra, his voice charged with adrenaline.

Ezra watches him intently as his father strides purposefully into the cabin, brushing past the boy heavily. Moments later, he emerges with the backpack on and the shotgun slung over his shoulder.

"Ready?" With a confident nod from Ezra, Clint leaps over the side of the boat, plunging into the water with a resounding splash.

Ezra gasps at his father's bold move, rushing to the boat's edge to find Clint waiting for him, arms outstretched. As Ezra hesitates, Clint scoops him up under his arms, holding him securely as he wades through the shallow water towards the water's edge. Gently, he sets Ezra down on the shore and collapses beside him, and they both catch their breath. Clint surveys their surroundings, squinting at the early morning sun as it rises on the horizon. He leans forward, places his hands on his knees, and takes in a few deep, laboured breaths as the adrenaline begins to ebb away.

Ezra scans the beach, kicking at the shingled floor beneath his feet. "That's a lot of stairs," he remarks, pointing towards a narrow staircase carved into the landscape.

Following his gesture, Clint traces the stairs with his eyes, his gaze climbing towards the top. "You, my boy, are a genius."

Ezra smiles proudly, momentarily forgetting all that transpired during the night.

"Let's just take a minute before we climb them."

"Okay," Ezra agrees, settling on the beach's gritty floor beside his father.

After a few moments, Ezra breaks the quiet, "I know what's going to happen to you," he says.

The comment is unexpected, raw even, and Clint feels a pang of sadness overwhelm him, but keeps his composure.

"I know you do," he replies softly, wrapping his arm around his son's shoulders.

"Does it hurt?" Ezra asks, "When it happens?".

Clint feels its weight settle on his chest like an anvil. He takes a moment to gather his thoughts, meeting Ezra's gaze.

"No," he answers softly, "It's like drifting into a deep, peaceful sleep."

Ezra nods, his expression thoughtful. "Okay," he responds quietly, his voice tinged with unwilling acceptance.

Eventually, Clint rises to his feet, brushing the sand from his clothes. He offers Ezra a reassuring smile, hoping to convey a sense of calm despite the tumultuous thoughts swirling in his mind.

"Come on, buddy," he says, his voice gentle. Ezra doesn't protest, but there are shadows of worry that linger in his eyes.

It's at this moment that Clint notices a fierce shift has taken place, replacing the carefree innocence of childhood. As they make their way from the shore towards the looming cliff edge. He offers to hold Ezra's hand in a silent gesture of solidarity.

"I'm fine," Ezra insists, his words cutting. Clint nods, respecting Ezra's decision but remaining close by in case he's needed.

The staircase carved into the rock face looms ahead, its narrow steps winding toward the unknown. As they begin their ascent, they come upon a small opening adorned with a lone wooden bench. Clint gestures for Ezra to take a seat, and they both settle onto the weathered wood, weary but grateful for the chance to rest. The early morning sun casts a warm glow across the landscape, painting the sky in hues of gold and amber. Far in the distance, the town they left behind begins to stir, its buildings bathed in the soft light of dawn. The silhouette of the clock tower stands tall against the backdrop. Ezra runs his fingers over a weathered plaque affixed to the bench, tracing the engraved letters.

Clint joins him, reading the inscription aloud. "For Dan, Forever Fishing. It's a memorial plaque," he explains softly. "Someone called Dan must have cherished this spot, found solace in its quiet beauty. Their loved ones placed this bench here to honour their memory."

"Mum doesn't have a bench," Ezra murmurs, his voice heavy with longing.

Clint's heart clenches at Ezra's words, the ache of loss seeping into every corner of his being. He reaches out, his hand finding Ezra's shoulder in a gesture of solace.

"No, she doesn't," he replies, his voice is gentle and tinged with sorrow.

Ezra's eyes remain fixed on the plaque. "I don't want us to be alone," he admits, his voice barely above a whisper, but each word echoing with profound vulnerability.

Clint's grip tightens. "You won't be," he lies, "We'll find somewhere safe together."

Ezra's gaze meets Clint's, and he seeks reassurance in the depths of his father's eyes. "No, I mean don't want you to be alone, or me, like mum," he confesses.

"Neither do I," says Clint, rising to his feet, hoping to continue the journey and stop the heartbreak. "Come on, we're nearly at the top."

As they ascend to the summit of the staircase, a vast expanse of open fields unfolds before them. Clint's eyes scan the landscape, tracing the gentle slope of the valley that leads to the outskirts of a much larger town than the one across the water. He follows the contours of the land, searching for the distinctive silhouette of the lighthouse mentioned by Frank. Laying eyes on it, his gaze scans the horizon, searching for the telltale V-shaped indentation, but it remains elusive. Frowning in concentration, he studies the distant town, formulating their next move.

"Come on," he says to Ezra.

"Where are we going?" Ezra asks, his curiosity piqued.

"This way."

XXII

Sewer*

Reaching the outskirts of the town, the streets around them lay desolate. Charred remnants of buildings dot the landscape, their frames reaching from the ground like twisted fingers, while others lie entirely crumbled. A children's park lay in ruins, its playground equipment twisted and mangled. A set of swings sway eerily in the breeze, their chains squeaking and creaking. Amidst the wreckage, he notices skeletal remains lying nearby, then others, their remains twisted and broken. Throughout the town, the scene is similar; more skeletal remains are ravaged by time, yet others seem more recent. His grip tightens on his shotgun as they continue, his senses on high alert for any sign of danger.

Ezra walks cautiously beside him, with eyes wide. "What happened here?" he whispers.

"Something terrible," Clint responds, his tone grave. "Stay close and keep your eyes open."

They navigate the streets with caution, venturing further as the devastation intensifies. Now, entire rows of buildings lay in ruin, walls charred and crumbling, and debris litters the streets while broken windows gape like empty eye sockets. Clint continues his scanning of their surroundings, warily, taking in the scenes.

Eventually, he spots a signpost that catches his attention. 'Ferry.' "This way."

As they continue to walk, the young boy suddenly tugs at his father's arm, causing Clint to turn back in surprise.

"Jesus, what's up?" he asks, his heart pounding.

"Listen," instructs Ezra, his expression tense.

Clint strains his ears to hear, tilting his head slightly. At first, he hears the distant sound of barking dogs. "It's just dogs."

Thank God.

"They're probably arguing over food or something," he says to Ezra, reassuringly.

"No, listen." The young boy's face is etched in fear.

Clint listens once again. This time, he notices the barking growing louder. Each one echoes through the empty streets. But then, beneath the canine voices, he hears something else, a faint chorus of manic screams rising and falling in a terrifying crescendo, and his blood runs cold.

"Shit," he mutters under his breath.

Frantically, he searches the area before spotting a nearby building, still standing, still with walls, and he wastes no time taking action.

"Quickly," his voice is urgent as he grabs the boy roughly by the arm and runs for the building.

Using the butt of his shotgun, he carefully clears away any sharp remnants from a single window frame before lifting Ezra through the threshold. He hoists himself through the window and into the building swiftly, glass crunching beneath his feet. Once inside, he ushers Ezra to the rear, his eyes darting furiously from side to side.

"Stay close," he whispers to the boy, his grip tightening on the shotgun as they move deeper into the building.

As they reach the back wall, his heart sinks as he realises that he has unwittingly cornered them.

Fuck.

They're trapped, with no other way out of the building except for the boarded-up door and the single window they have entered through. He gestures for Ezra to get down to the ground, as he quickly surveys their surroundings again. Despite the outside desolation, the shop's interior appears relatively well. Empty shelves adorn the walls, although no longer stocked.

With a determined expression, he turns to Ezra, "Stay here."

"No, don't leave me." Ezra's fear is palpable, both in his expression and his tone.

Clint pauses, weighing his options. After contemplation, he sits on the floor beside his son, leans the backpack against the wall, and sets the shotgun on his knee at the ready.

Okay, we'll wait here.

Together, they listen as the barking grows louder, a cacophony echoing through the lonely streets. Clint estimates there are maybe five or six, their dew claws rapidly clicking against the pavement as they close in on the shop. But it is the sound of the madmen in pursuit that sends a chill down his spine. As the dogs thunder past the shop, their frenzied barks reverberate off the walls, causing Ezra to cower and bury his head in his knees. Following closely behind are the madmen, their shouts filling the air with incoherent obscenities and guttural screams. Clint holds his breath, hoping they continue to pass by without noticing their hiding place, hoping they stay set on the dogs for whatever grievance they feel they have. He glances at Ezra. The boy's eyes are wide, wider than he's ever seen them before. He tries to place a reassuring hand on his son's shoulder, but Ezra retorts almost violently. Scared and on edge as the procession of madmen continues, their numbers multiplying with each passing moment. Clint peers towards the window and watches intently as some stumble and lurch past, their movements erratic and disjointed. Others move with predatory grace. He tries to keep track of their numbers, but quickly loses count as they blur together in a nightmarish haze.

Too many.

Far more than he could have imagined encountering. He tightens his grip on the shotgun, his knuckles white with tension. The pair remain still, listening intently as the chaos finally begins to fade into the distance. The barking and screaming grow increasingly faint until they are little more than echoes. After the sounds recede further, to a barely audible whisper, Clint motions for Ezra to rise. Cautiously, he leads the boy through the shop and towards the window, the shattered glass crunching beneath their feet again. Clint leans out, scanning the direction of the Madness. When his gaze shifts to the other direction, a sudden and violent surge of pain causes him to stagger, the unexpected blow sending him reeling backwards. Disoriented and off balance, he collides with Ezra and the pair crash to the floor in a tangle of limbs. Stars dance before his eyes as he struggles to regain his senses. Through the haze, he sees a dark silhouette framed against the broken window looming over them. Adrenaline suddenly surges through him as he fights to push himself upright. As he staggers to his feet. The figure climbs through the window and then stands menacingly still, his only movements being uncontrolled twitches as he observes him with bloodshot eyes and a feral intensity. The man's face is gaunt, his cheeks hollow, his skin pallid. His clothes hang loosely on a bony frame, tattered and stained with dirt and grime and an array of god knows what, and his unkempt hair falls in matted tangles around his face. Clint stands entirely still, observing his assaulter. The madman's lips curl into a twisted grin, revealing yellowed teeth that seem too large for his mouth. Then he emits a low, guttural growl. His appearance is dishevelled, but there is a primal strength to the man's stance, a predatory readiness. Clint's heart pounds quicker with every flinch of the madman's erratic movements, every nerve in his body ready to react in anticipation of the madman's uncontrolled twists and jerks.

"I don't want any trouble," Clint says, his voice wavering slightly despite his efforts to sound confident.

The man remains silent, his gaze locked upon him with disturbing intensity. Clint backs away slowly, urging Ezra to shuffle along the floor and retreat further, but the boy is frozen with terror. His mind races as he desperately tries to determine his next move.

"Just let us pass," he pleads again, his voice deep and guttural.

He scans the area frantically, searching for any sign of the shotgun or another means of escape. But the man remains rooted in place, a silent sentinel blocking their only escape path. A stand-off takes place. Silent. Testing. Clint momentarily glances at Ezra, unwillingly giving the madman a window of opportunity. With a sudden, violent lunge, he charges, catching Clint off guard, and the pair crash to the ground in a bundle of flailing arms and legs. Clint grapples desperately with the madman, the struggle intensifying with each passing moment. The madman remains entirely silent, the only sounds are Ezra's terrified cries, and his father's grunts of exasperation. Despite Clint's efforts, the madman's strength is unyielding; his attacks vicious. He waves his arms uncontrollably, scratching and punching at Clint's cowering form. Ezra's screams pierce through the chaos, the sound driving his father to fight harder. With a surge of adrenaline, he pushes the madman off momentarily and scrambles to his feet, searching for anything he can use as a weapon, desperately needing an upper hand. Suddenly, without hesitation, Clint lunges for a nearby pile of rubble, pulling hard on some sort of cable. It rips it from its security clips like buttons popping from strain. Gripping the cable tightly, he turns to face the madman again with fierce determination and braces himself for the next onslaught. But the madman doesn't move, almost goading Clint to strike first, but he knows better. After a few seconds in another stand-off, the madman lunges at him once more. Yet, this time, he anticipates the attack, sidestepping it swiftly and, with a precise and calculated movement, wraps the cable around the man's neck. He pulls him off balance and sends them both crashing to the ground. The impact jars Clint's body, but he maintains his firm grip on the cable. The man's frantic movements batter his body, his nails leaving angry red welts on his face. Clint grunts with effort as his muscles strain against the weight of the madman. But he refuses to slacken his grip on the cable. He can feel the man's desperate gasps for breath beneath him, and after a few seconds of frantic, unpredictable thrashing, the madman's struggles begin to weaken. Sensing his opportunity, with a final surge of strength, Clint pulls the cable as tight as he possibly can. The madman's desperate movements slow further, until eventually, they cease altogether, his body going limp in Clint's grasp. For a moment, the room is filled only with the sound of Clint's ragged breathing as he refuses to loosen his grip. After a few moments, his grip in his hands gives, trembling with exhaustion and relief. With a heavy sigh, he rolls the lifeless body off him and staggers to his feet, his gaze immediately seeking out Ezra. The boy watches wide-eyed from the far corner of the room. Clint's heart pounds in his chest as he moves slowly and painfully through the shop, scanning the area, his eyes darting frantically. On the floor a few feet away, partially obscured by the overturned shelves, Clint spots the shotgun. He reaches for it with a sense of urgency and scoops it up, his fingers fumbling as he pumps it for action. His breath is short, coming in uneven and ragged gasps as he tries to steady himself. Taking a deep breath and calming the racing thoughts in his mind, he makes his way back to the lifeless body of the madman. He stands over the body, his grip on the shotgun tight. Blood leaks from the man's mangled eyes, staining the floor in dark, small, viscous puddles. Clint feels his stomach churn at the sight, but he pushes aside his revulsion, focusing on the task. With steady hands, he raises the shotgun, aiming it directly at the madman's head. His finger hovers over the trigger, his gaze fixed on his target, then he squeezes the trigger. The blast echoes through the room, its force sending the madman's body jerking backwards. Clint winces in pain as the recoil reverberates through his shoulder. He and the surrounding area are covered in a wave of blood and bone as the force of the shot obliterates any trace of humanity that the madman had left. Clint stands there momentarily, the ringing in his ears drowning out all other sounds. Slowly, he lowers the shotgun, his hands still trembling with the aftermath of the adrenaline-fueled encounter.

He takes a deep, shuddering breath, trying to steady himself as he looks around the room, spotting Ezra, who continues to watch from the corner.

"It's okay," he finally says, his voice gentle but firm. "We're safe now."

Ezra's silence hangs heavy in the air, his eyes locked on his father, searching for something. Clint approaches the boy, extending a single arm, offering the comfort of an embrace. Still, Ezra hesitates, his gaze fixed on the bruises and blood that mar his father's features.

"It's okay," Clint repeats, the words sounding hollow even to his ears.

"Trees."

Clint's heart skips a beat, but quickly he responds, "Leaves."

Good boy.

"Beach"

"Sand"

Ezra's mouth hints at a smile as he accepts his father's hand.

"Are you okay?" Clint asks.

"Yeah, are you?"

After locating the backpack and retrieving the shotgun with laboured movements, Clint climbs out of the window. Ezra follows closely behind, his small frame managing the climb with determined effort. Once back on the street, they continue their journey. Clint's pace has slowed, each step sending jolts of pain through his battered body. Ezra notices his father's discomfort and offers a small boy's attempt at help. Clint accepts, putting his arm on Ezra's shoulder with one hand while maintaining a vigilant watch and holding the shotgun at the ready with the other. He checks each building and doorway they pass, his senses heightened by the recent encounter. Ezra walks beside him, his eyes scanning their surroundings with wary curiosity. After a while, they begin to hear familiar sounds, the gentle lapping of water and the occasional cry of a seagull. Clint's heart quickens at the sounds, a glimmer of hope igniting within him. Up ahead, a break in the buildings reveals an expanse of blue sky and a clearing in the distance. Relief floods through him as they draw closer to their destination. He tightens his grip on the shotgun and uprights himself.

"Are you sure you can do it?"

"Ezra, I'm fine buddy, thanks for helping me."

As they reach the end of the road, the marina stretches before them, eerily silent, its waters contrasting with the harbour across the sea, almost empty. It's vast in size, with multiple boardwalks extending out over the calm, glassy surface of the water. Rusted mooring posts stand sentinel along the edges, with chains trailing into the depths below. A single boat seems to have suffered the same fate as the buildings, its hull charred and blackened from fire, while the rest lay partially submerged in the murky depths. In the distance, Clint's gaze finally descends upon the lighthouse. With it, in the vast distance, beyond the valley and the sprawling ruins of the town, he spots the unmistakable V-shaped indentation that

Frank had mentioned. Yet, his moment of triumph is short-lived, shattered by the sudden interruption of shouts and violent screams that begin to echo through the air once again. His breath catches in his throat as he catches sight of the fear reflected in Ezra's eyes.

Run.

Clint grasps his son's hand tightly and begins to run, his heart thumping with each step as they make a desperate dash for safety. As they navigate through the marina's maze of lobster pots and other debris, a sudden metallic clang reverberates beneath his feet, halting him in his tracks. Ignoring Ezra's protests and cries, he swiftly sets down the shotgun and begins to wrestle with the stubborn sewer cover. With sweat trickling down his forehead, he struggles to get a decent grip on the cover. Its shape and close fit make it awkward to remove. Thinking quickly, he threads the shotgun strap through the small metal grab handle and, with a determined grunt, uses the strap as leverage, pulling with all his might until the cover shifts.

"Go, Ezra! Get down there!" he commands, his voice urgent but controlled.

Ezra peers into the darkness, hesitant.

"NOW!"

Ezra hesitates no longer and quickly begins descending the rusted ladder into the darkness below as Clint hoists the shotgun over his shoulders. With a final effort, Clint lowers himself into the shaft, battling with the protruding backpack as the ladder creaks beneath his weight. He strains and huffs as he replaces the sewer cover, its weighty clang sealing them from the impending chaos above and devouring them in darkness.

XXIII

Secrets

Jane stands in the small, once-secret makeshift laboratory, the shock of Elizabeth's callousness regarding the live testing lingering heavily in her mind. It's not just disappointment she feels; it's a profound sense of annoyance.

"I was naive to believe that Elizabeth was ready to push boundaries." She says under her breath.

She was convinced that sharing her discoveries about the pathogen would serve as a wake-up call. But Elizabeth's reaction had shattered those hopes. Instead of embracing the potential breakthroughs, she had seemed to dismiss them almost entirely, opting only to highlight the potential flaw in signalling. As Jane pores over her notes, frustration begins to intertwine with anger, presenting her with a challenging dilemma. On one side, she could persist in her work despite Elizabeth's directives. On the other hand, she could take a bold stance, confronting the attempt at authority and sharing her findings with her colleagues.

Or there's option number 3.

She doesn't waste time dwelling on her achievements. The real question isn't whether she'll continue her work, but where, and who will stand beside her.

"Well, that didn't go as expected," Rigs mutters, breaking the silence.

Jane exhales sharply. "I don't know what I thought would happen. Elizabeth has always been rigid about rules and ethics. This is on me."

"So, what now?" Concern lines Rig's face.

"I gather the team. Share my findings before Elizabeth twists the narrative."

Rigs nods. "Yeah, I think that's best."

"And those who agree with me can come with us."

Rigs blinks. "Come with us?"

Jane scoffs. "You didn't think this was my only contingency, did you?"

Rigs frowns, unease creeping in. "What the hell are you talking about?"

"This pathogen is global. You really believed everything hinged on just this team?" Jane shakes her head. "There are other teams, doing their own work, all over the world."

"Wait.. wait a damn minute."

"Rigs, it's not complicated. We're women, not just mothers, sisters, daughters. You, of all people, should understand that."

"Of course I do," Rigs snaps. "But why didn't you tell me?"

Jane levels her with a hard stare. "You know how it works. There's still a hierarchy."

Rigs let out a bitter scoff. "Right. And the rest of us are better off in the dark."

"Oh, Grow up."

Jane doesn't wait for a response, strides out of the small lab and ascends the stairs back to the main facility. She slips through the camouflaged doorway and re-enters the facility's main corridors, where, to her surprise, there's no sense of urgency. No chaos. Maybe Elizabeth hadn't spread the news as fast as she feared she thought. Near the laboratory entrance, the small group of researchers huddle, speaking in hushed voices. Jane narrows her eyes as she notices Sarah discreetly signalling for them to move inside, trying to her gaze. Annoyed, Jane quickens her pace, slipping in just behind them. The entire team is there. So is Elizabeth, her expression calm. Too calm.

"What's going on?" Jane asks, voice sharp.

Elizabeth gestures toward the door. "Close it."

Jane hesitates, then complies. Turning back, she meets Elizabeth's unreadable gaze. "Is this an ambush?"

Elizabeth chuckles, a sound that only fuels Jane's suspicion. "Actually, I thought you might want to share your discoveries. Perhaps we can smooth things over and get back on track."

What is she playing at?

Jane keeps her expression neutral. "Erm, Okay, so." She begins taking small steps, almost pacing on the spot. "I know it wasn't discussed; in fact, when it was mentioned, Elizabeth shot me down entirely, but through live testing, I've uncovered some crucial information."

She scans the room. No outrage. No immediate push back. Surprising. Encouraging.

"This pathogen does something to the amygdala. I'm not sure what, but it causes massive inflammation. That, combined with the body's natural response mechanisms, then leads to severe neuroinflammation. The result? Dysregulated neurotransmitters."

"That would explain the aggression, fear, and hallucinations, " Elena says, nodding. "None of it is controlled."

"That's my understanding, yes. I believe it suppresses aggression toward the infected while heightening hostility toward the uninfected. A self-preservation mechanism."

"Fucking hell," Michelle murmurs. "So it is using signalling."

"Great, so we have a fucking homing beacon downstairs," Elizabeth interjects.

"Wait, we have a downstairs?" Sarah questions

"No, there's no evidence of that", Jane continues, ignoring Sarah's remark. "These gatherings could just be herd behaviour. They recognise each other and decide to stick around. Simple, really."

Elizabeth raises her hands, palms up. "Does anyone have an issue with Jane secretly conducting live tests?" Silence.

Maya speaks instead, ignoring Elizabeth entirely. "So, a cure would need to be antiviral, antibacterial, and anti-inflammatory. On top of restoring neurotransmitter balance. How the fuck do we even do that?"

Jane's voice is steady, cold. "We don't, we, this team, can't" She meets their gazes, unwavering. "But I have a team that might."

Silence follows Jane's declaration. Then, "What do you mean, you have a team?" Michelle's voice is sharp and demanding.

Jane exhales, steeling herself. "There are other teams, obviously, there are other teams. Are you all seriously that self-centred?"

"How do you know?"

"I helped set them up," Jane responds, a hint of pride in her voice.

A murmur ripples through the room. Sarah's eyes narrow. "Set them up? You knew about them this whole time?"

"Of course," Jane says firmly. "The more teams looking at this from different angles, the better. "

"You're telling us now?" Elena snaps, incredulous. "After everything we went through to set this place up, everything we've been through. The People we've lost?"

"I did what I had to." Jane's tone is controlled, but the tension in the room thickens.

"You had to?" Sarah's voice cuts through, laced with disbelief. "We've been here, desperate for breakthroughs, thinking we were alone in this fight, and you knew otherwise? How long, Jane?"

Jane clenches her jaw. "Since the beginning."

Outrage erupts.

"Since the beginning?" Sarah nearly shouts. "Jesus Christ, Jane! You let us believe we were humanity's only shot!"

"No, I didn't. You all assumed you were!" Jane fires back. "But being honest. If you knew, thought someone else would figure it out, would you all have pushed as hard? Would you have risked as much?"

"That wasn't your decision to make," Michelle seethes.

Elizabeth remains silent, watching, assessing, as if she's waiting for this storm to play out.

Elena folds her arms. "Who are they? Where are they?"

Jane exhales. "There are teams in Europe, South America, and Asia. Different specialisations, different approaches. Some focused on genetics, others on immunology. We had no way of knowing who would get there first, but..."

"And who controls them?" Sarah cuts in. "Who decides what gets shared? What if they've already found something?"

Jane doesn't answer immediately.

"Oh my God," Sarah breathes. "You don't even know, do you?"

A new kind of unease settles over the group.

Michelle shakes her head. "I trusted you, Jane. Fought beside you. And the whole time, you were keeping this from us?"

"I did what was necessary," Jane repeats, but even she can hear the defensive edge creeping into her voice.

Elizabeth finally speaks, her voice deceptively calm. "Necessary for whom?"

The room is in chaos.

Voices rise in overlapping shouts, as a tidal wave of anger and betrayal crashes in Jane's direction.

"You kept this from us?"

"All this time, and you never said a word?"

"Who do you work for, Jane? Who are they?"

The fury is raw, Relentless. The noise spills into the hall, and more people begin gathering, drawn by the commotion, and murmurs begin to ripple through the crowd, the weight of their stares pressing down on Jane like a physical force. Just down the corridor, Lana and Beth exchange hushed words, watching intently. They don't intervene. They don't have to. Everything is unravelling on its own.

Suddenly, Elena pushes forward, her expression stormy as she makes a beeline for her sister. Rigs, who had slipped in almost unnoticed moments ago, stiffens.

"You knew, didn't you?" Elena accuses, her voice low but razor-sharp.

Rigs doesn't respond. Instead, she looks away, her silence speaking volumes.

Then, Elizabeth moves, crossing the room with quiet purpose, stepping into Jane's space, close enough that she can feel her breath against her skin. "This," Elizabeth murmurs, voice laced with something sharper than anger, "is exactly why I left you. "

Jane exhales slowly but doesn't move away. Elizabeth tilts her head, eyes searching Jane's face. "You always kept things from me. From everyone. You thought love, marriage, meant trusting someone with everything except what mattered."

A muscle tightens in Jane's jaw, but she says nothing.

Elizabeth's voice lowers, almost a whisper. "You say you did this for the greater good. But deep down, it's the same thing it's always been with you. Control."

Jane's hands curl into fists at her sides. "And you never understood that some secrets keep people alive."

Elizabeth lets out a quiet, bitter laugh. "No, Jane. Some secrets destroy everything." She pulls back just enough to meet Jane's gaze. "And that's exactly what you've done here."

XXIV

Alone

The lab is silent except for the hum of overhead lights and the rhythmic beeping of the monitors. Jane sits perfectly still, her elbows resting on her knees, her face inches from her captives. She watches him, unblinking, searching for any flicker of recognition, any sign that he's still in there.

"Why do you cease to even mumble?" Her voice is low, almost coaxing. "What happens?"

Nothing. His wrists twitch in their restraints, digging into his skin, but Jane doesn't flinch. He could lunge at her if he wanted to, not that it would do him any good. He's secure. Contained.

She tilts her head, studying him. "Nothing to say, nothing to complain about."

She lets out a small, humourless laugh. "Shame you have a dick. You'd be quite attractive otherwise.

The strong, literal silent type." Since the truth about her research and the knowledge of other teams had come out, everything had shifted. Jane wasn't barred from the facility; no words to that effect had been said, but they might as well have been. Elizabeth had seized her opportunity to seize a little more control, and the tide had turned. People spoke to Jane less now, moving around her most of the time, as if she weren't there. Those she thought were some of her closest companions, like Rigs and Michelle, met her gaze with silent accusations. Fuck them. Others, like Sarah, simply avoided her altogether. Elizabeth, on the other hand, had thrived without Jane's constant belittling, almost becoming something of a leader. People seemed to have gravitated toward her, drawn in by her newfound steadiness. Elizabeth had always had a way of winning people over, of making them feel safe. That had once been one of the things Jane loved about her. Now, it just pissed her off. But in truth, the unspoken resentment had started to bother her more than she'd expected. So, she'd withdrawn. Choosing to work alone, secluded in what had once been her secret lab, but was now just another room everyone knew about. Though few dared enter. When she did visit the upstairs of the facility, she moved through its halls like a ghost, slipping through the corridors in the quiet hours when most were asleep. Even the canteen had become a place of avoidance. She waited until late at night. It was easier that way. Less noise, less judgment, and less pretending she gave a damn about what they all thought of her. At least, that's what she told herself. Jane shifts in her chair, her focus returning to the captive in front of her. His breathing was steady, his eyes fixed forward. Still silent. Still waiting.

"Must be nice," she muttered. "Not giving a damn about anyone."

And for the first time, Jane found herself wondering if she envied him. Then, A sound breaks the silence. A distant echo. A deep and resonant bang. She lifts her head and frowns, annoyed at the intrusion, but then, there's another. She rises from her chair and moves instinctively toward the heavy metal door that seals her off from the rest of the facility. She pulls it open just a jar. Then she hears it again, sharp, rapid cracks that slice through the stillness.

Gunfire.

Again, there's another crack, and again, in a controlled, relentless rhythm. She turns sharply, scanning her lab. She crosses to the far wall, where a small metal box sits on one side. Twisting its dial, she unlocks it quickly and yanks it open. She rustles within it until she finds it. Her contingency plan, originally meant for her captive. She searches within it again, and snatches up a loaded magazine, slams it into place and chambers a round in one fluid motion. Then she bolts. Up the stairs, two at a time, the pounding of her feet drowned out by the rising chaos above. The gunfire is increasing, faster now, louder. No longer in controlled bursts, now it sounds frantic, desperate, and that's when the screaming joins it, high-pitched and raw, deafening. Emerging from the lower levels and into the facility, the corridors stretch before her, but something is wrong. She expected panicked scientists to be scrambling and injured bodies to be dragging themselves to safety. But there is nothing. No Kim or Clair wild-eyed shouting orders, and no Elizabeth. Just a sterile emptiness. But then she hears it again. The relentless gunfire and the screams, and that is when the realisation crashes into her. The gunfire isn't coming from inside the facility. She pivots, sprinting down the corridor toward the main exit, the sound growing louder with every rushed step. As she reached the door, she threw her hand out to grab the handle, when suddenly, the door swung open violently, slamming into her and sending her staggering back. Jane barely catches herself before hitting the floor.

"Jane, fuck!" Beth says dishevelled, breathing hard, her eyes wide with adrenaline.

Jane steadies herself, clutching at her wrist. "What the fuck is going on?"

Beth's gaze flicks behind her as if she doesn't have time for this conversation. "What do you think, Jane?" she snaps. "Fuck's sake, get out there and help!"

Jane clutches at her wrist as pain flares through the bone. She's certain the impact from the door had fractured something, but now wasn't the time to focus on that. She forces herself forward, stepping into the open air. The facility's outer perimeter is alive with movement, as she watches people duck behind crates, overturned tables, and whatever else they can find. Some fire blindly into the darkness, while others grip their guns so tightly their knuckles shine white in the moonlight, unsure whether to shoot or wait for orders that will never come. The gunfire is erratic and uneven, a mixture of frantic bursts and hesitant single shots.

This isn't a tactical defence. It's fear.

She scans the area, searching for someone who knows what the hell they're doing, noticing Rigs, who is crouched low behind a bundle pile of metal and wood, one of the makeshift barricades. Her rifle is firm in her grasp, and her face is set with hard focus. Jane moves fast, diving beside her just as another shot cracks through the night.

Rigs doesn't even flinch, barely sparing Jane a glance before muttering, "Nice to see you finally crawled out of your hole."

Jane ignores the jab, her breath still heavy from the sprint. "What's happening?"

Rigs keeps her eyes locked ahead. "Kim made a shot, we thought it was a one-off, a single madman on a charge. But then more appeared."

Jane risks a glance over the barriers of rusted metal. The facility's single large floodlight was on, casting an eerie beam across the grass, just falling short of illuminating the treeline. But she can see them, the figures moving in the darkness. Some are cautious, exposing themselves only briefly before retreating back into the foliage. Others charge without hesitation, sprinting full speed toward the facility, only to be cut down mid-run. Jane watches as another figure bolts from the trees, arms pumping, mouth open in a silent scream before a bullet takes him down, his body skidding across the dirt. For a moment, nothing happens.

Then another shape shifts in the trees. Watching. Waiting.

They're fucking testing us.

"How many? Jane asks.

Rigs shakes her head. "No idea. Could be fifty, could be five hundred."

Jane's grip tightens around her pistol. "And the others? Where's Elizabeth?"

Rigs jerks her head toward the far side of the perimeter. "Trying to hold things over there with Michelle."

Jane exhales sharply. "They're going to rush eventually."

Rigs nods. "And when they do, we won't hold them for long."

The decision is made, and suddenly Rigs stiffens, feeling the unyielding metal pressed against her back. Jane's stomach drops at her own actions. "Get me the fuck out of here." She whispers.

"How the fuck am I meant to do that?"

"The chopper, now. Move!"

XXV

Shot

The sewer air is thick with the stench of damp and decay and a slight hint of faeces. The darkness feels oppressive, suffocating almost. Clint fumbles around in the backpack, finding the wind-up torch and winding it until a gentle dim beam of light begins to break through the Black. Immediately, he notices Ezra, who is sitting hunched with his knees drawn to his chest, staring blankly ahead. Clint exhales, winding the torch a few more times, before searching up and down the narrow tunnel.

Crouching beside the boy, he raises his hand in front of the beam, curling his fingers into shapes. A rabbit. A dog. A bird and making their silhouettes dance across the sewer wall.

"Remember these?" he asks softly, shifting his hand to make another animal. "I used to do these for you when you were a baby."

Ezra doesn't answer. His face is blank, his body rigid. Clint sighs, lowering his hands, conceding to failure.

Water drips somewhere in the distance, the sound eerily rhythmic against the silence.

"Dad." Ezra finally whispers.

"Yeah, buddy."

"Is it going to happen to me?"

"Is what going to happen to you?"

"You know the bad stuff."

Clint considers lying. The boy is already wary of him, and he knew, even if Ezra didn't admit it, that he was scared.

"I don't know."

Not entirely a lie, not entirely the truth either.

"It doesn't affect children, only adults, so there's a lot of time."

"Lots of time alone, you mean."

Ezra's comment rips at Clint. Such a mature observation, for such a young boy, and brutally honest. He's aware of what's happening, aware of the time frame. Aware of it all.

What do you say when nothing can be said?

"Come on, let's get moving."

For what seems like an eternity, they navigate the narrow tunnels. Clint's body aches, the aftermath of his most recent skirmish, combined with this new, not upright, but not entirely crouched walking position, caused aches and cramps in his back. Eventually, to his relief, they come across a service ladder leading up and with it a space to stretch fully. He pulls on the rungs, testing them. "I'm going to go first, okay. I will make sure it's safe, and then I will call. Here, take the torch."

"Okay, are you sure about this?"

"Well, we can't stay down here forever," Clint responds, fumbling with the backpack, the shotgun and the small sidearm in his trousers, securing everything.

Slowly, he begins to climb the service ladder in darkness, ensuring his footing and grip on each rung until his head clobbers unexpectedly against hard steel.

"Ah, shit."

"Dad, what is it?"

"Nothing buddy, just hit my head," he responds, rubbing at yet another source of pain.

With a single strong arm, he pushes hard against the steel. A faint glimmer of light protrudes from its edges as it rises, but then his strength gives, sealing them in darkness again. He takes a few moments, breathing deeply and mustering his strength before attempting again. This time, he lets out a loud verbal cry as he lifts the steel clear, blinding them in daylight. As he emerges from the underground, the air is fresh but tinged with smoke. They're at the town's edge, near the ruins of an old market, but the coast seems clear.

"Come on up, Ezra." He says, pulling himself out of the opening.

Ezra fumbles with the torch as he struggles to fit the hard plastic into his tiny pocket. His breathing becomes increasingly rapid as he plunges himself into darkness. It takes the boy a few seconds to familiarise himself with the ladder, but quickly he gets the grasp. As he reaches the top, Clint offers a hand, but he refuses it, either preferring to do it alone or untrusting of the help. Buildings lean against one another, broken and hollow, while rusted-out cars remain frozen in place, littered with overgrown weeds. They move cautiously, keeping low as they slip through the old market. Clint moves slightly ahead, trying his hardest to step lightly on the cracked pavement. His eyes constantly dart between the ruined stalls, the abandoned storefronts and the alleys that stretch into shadows. Ezra trails behind, mimicking his movements. Clint pauses at the edge of a collapsed stand, scanning the road ahead.

"Stay close," he mutters.

Ezra nods, gripping the strap of the backpack for security, his fingers fidgeting along the frayed webbing. A faded tarp flutters weakly, startling the pair in unison as it barely holds on to the rusted nails that pin it to a splintered stall. Another low sound echoes in the distance, and both of them freeze. Then, listen intently until they hear another noise, but closer this time. A scraping, like something being dragged across the ground.

Ezra inches closer, his breath shallow. "What is that?" he whispers.

Clint doesn't answer. Instead, he motions for them to move, quickly and low, as he holds the shotgun at the ready.

They cut across what used to be a butcher's shop, its sign hanging by a single chain. The windows are smashed, with jagged glass clinging to the edges of the frames, and A dark stain mars the threshold, old but unmistakable. Clint moves faster now, pulling Ezra along.

"Just keep moving." Then, from the alley up ahead, a shadow shifts.

Clint brings them to an instant halt, causing Ezra to go crashing into his rear. The shadow shifts again, and Clint fires! A scream tears through the quiet. A woman's scream, high-pitched and filled with pain. His stomach plummets as he lowers the shotgun just in time to see a figure crumple to the ground, hands clutching her side where the shot has torn through flesh. Blood darkens her shirt, pooling beneath her as she gasps in agony.

"Fuck, what have I done?" The words tumble from his mouth before he even realises he's spoken them.

Ezra stares, trembling. Then, his face crumples. "Why did you do that?" His voice cracks, thick with tears. "She...she wasn't even..."

Clint is already moving, dropping to his knees beside the woman. "Shit. I didn't know. I thought..."

His hands hover uselessly over her wound as her body begins shaking violently. She's young. Mid-twenties, maybe. She's riddled with pain, her breathing sharp, coming in shallow gulps.

"Please, " she chokes out.

"I didn't mean to."

Clint swallows hard as panic claws at his throat. He presses his hands against the wound in an attempt to stop the bleeding.

"I thought… I thought you were…."

But then something even worse. A sound that shatters his frantic haze like a hammer through glass. A manic cry, then laughter, faint but unmistakable, and his stomach knots.

The shot. They heard it.

The woman on the ground sobs.

Clint grips the shotgun tightly. "Ezra. Run. "Move!" He grabs Ezra's hand.

But Ezra resists, digging his heels into the pavement. "We can't leave her!" he wails, as he claws at his father's grip, trying to pry himself free.

"We don't have a choice!" Clint growls, but Ezra is fighting with everything he has, twisting and pulling with rage and grief.

"You shot her!" Ezra screams.

Shrills echo behind them. Then another. With a grunt, he yanks Ezra forward, overpowering him easily. The boy is no match for his strength, but he still fights, trying to rip away.

"Let me go!" Ezra thrashes against him, tears streaming down his dirt-streaked face. "We can't leave her!"

Clint grits his teeth. The noises behind them are multiplying. "Enough," he snarls. In one swift motion, he scoops the boy up, slinging him under his arm like a sack of grain.

Ezra shrieks, swinging his fists against Clint's grip. "Put me down! Put me - mmph!" Clint clamps a hand over his mouth.

"Shut up!"

The weight of the boy, the backpack, the gun, it's almost too much. He's already exhausted, and his muscles burn. Sheer determination and fear are what're driving him now. The ruined stalls blur past as he barrels forward, weaving clumsily through debris as he tries to put as much distance as he can between them and the nightmare behind. The road opens ahead, exposed and dangerous, but there's no other way. Just before he reaches it, he risks a glance over his shoulder. But there's nothing. No madmen spilling from the bunched stalls. No movement on the horizon. Just the eerie, unnatural stillness of the ruined market. His pulse hammers in his ears, and he slows, just for a second, his breath heavy, his body aching.

Maybe.

Then the woman screams a raw, bloodcurdling wail of pure agony. His body instantly stiffens again. They've found her. Or maybe she's just dying in insufferable pain because of him. He doesn't know. And he's not willing to wait to find out. He forces his legs to keep moving, but the burn in his muscles is unbearable. He staggers a few times, nearly tripping over his own feet, and his grip on Ezra falters for half a second before he regains control. His young son trembles against him, his muffled sobs vibrating against his palm. Eventually, the sounds behind them seem to have disappeared, lost to distance and wind, and now all that surrounds them is eerily quiet. Clint slows his pace, giving in to his lungs that are screaming and the ache in his arms that are barely able to hold the weight any longer. His hand is still pressed firmly against Ezra's mouth, but the boy's struggle has dwindled into exhausted hiccups. It's not long before they reach a crumbling row of buildings, and an old laundromat with open window frames catches his attention. He mounts the window in a deliberate and powerful movement, carrying himself and Ezra inside. He works his way past the derelict machines to the rear wall, where he presses his back against the concrete, his chest heaving. Finally, cautiously, he lowers Ezra to the ground and removes his hand.

Ezra gasps sharply, sucking in air, then glares up at him with tear-streaked fury. "You left her," he hisses.

Clint drags a hand down his face. "Ezra, I thought she was one of them," he says, almost pleading. "I saw the movement, and I reacted. I didn't know."

Ezra glares at him, tears still streaking his dirt-smudged cheeks. "You killed her"

He swallows hard, as guilt presses against his ribs like a weight he can't shake. "I know," he says, barely more than a whisper. He leans his head back against the concrete and shuts his eyes tight for a second. "I fucked up. I fucked up bad. I wanted to help her. I swear to you, I wanted to. But the shot... they heard it. We wouldn't have stood a chance if we stayed."

Ezra drops himself to the floor and hugs his knees to his chest, his small frame shaking. "I hate you."

Clint presses his lips together, looking away. He doesn't argue. Doesn't try to justify it further. He just stands there, the words settling over him like lead.

"Rest for a second," he says, forcing the emotion from his voice. "Then we keep moving."

XXVI

Elizabeth

The lab felt like it shook with every impact, every echo of gunfire, every scream seemingly reverberated through its walls. Elizabeth stood frozen, leaning heavily on a workstation as her heart hammered against her ribs, her hands trembling. Once the madness had attacked in unison, they had run, retreated like frightened children, enclosing themselves in the lab that now felt more like a tomb. Beth was hunched against the door, panting, her eyes darting wildly, reacting to every noise. Sarah and Lana lingered towards the back of the lab, whispering frantically, their voices nothing to Elizabeth but distant murmurs. She clenches her fists. She could still hear them fighting. The ones who had stayed. Kim was the first she had seen fall, firing with lethal precision until the last bullet in her assault rifle was replaced with a sudden click. She swung the weapon like a club, bashing heads, but more had already reached her. They ripped, slashed, screamed and laughed in harmony as they dealt out their pain. Kim's screams mingled with the sounds of flesh tearing and bones snapping. Sending outright terror through the facility's occupants and causing widespread panic. Clair and Elena fought back-to-back, cracking shot after shot into the horde, each bullet sinking into skulls and throats. Elena ran out first, reaching for her knife as the slide of her gun locked empty. She slashed wildly as they closed in until her blade was turned against her, but she didn't stop.

She fought until she had nothing left.

Elizabeth didn't have the stomach to see what happened to Clair. But the sounds told her all she needed to know as she fled back to the facility.

The door rattled from the force outside. "Quickly", Beth screams, "Get the tables, chairs, anything."

Without hesitation, Elizabeth and the others start sliding tables across the floor, pushing and throwing the meticulously arranged apparatus to one side, sealing them inside. The madmen were relentless as their fists pounded against the frame, their guttural screams and laughter reverberating through Elizabeth's mind.

Lana's loud, panicked voice broke through the cacophony of sounds.

"What the fucking hell do we do now?"

No one answered. The room was filled with nothing but heavy breathing and fear.

Beth pressed her forehead against the wall. "There's no way out," she muttered. "The only window is barred shut."

"What about the vents?" Sarah asked quickly. "Maybe we can squeeze through one."

Beth turned, shaking her head. "There's nothing. I checked when we first got here. The lab's air filtration system is too small. None of the shafts are big enough for any of us."

Lana exhales sharply, running a hand through her hair. "Then we're screwed."

Elizabeth grits her teeth. "No. There's got to be something," she says, scanning the lab, her mind racing. "Weapons? Chemicals? Anything?"

Sarah starts pacing. "There's a storage closet in the back. I don't know if there's anything useful, but.."

"Check it," Elizabeth orders. Sarah nods, rushing toward the back of the room.

Beth clenches her jaw. "Even if we arm ourselves, we can't stay here forever. We need a real exit."

A few moments later, Sarah returns, her arms full of metal canisters and various vials of liquid.

"I found some of the pathogen research samples and some old chemical agents."

Elizabeth's gaze locks onto the canisters. "What kind of chemical agents?"

Sarah places them down on the floor. "Ethanol, hydrogen peroxide, ammonium nitrate... some kind of dispersal agent Jane was working on."

My god, Jane.

"If we mix them the right way, we could make a blast."

Beth frowns. "Wait, you're not saying..."

"We're on an external wall," Elizabeth cut in. "If we can create an explosion, we might be able to blow a hole through it."

Lana shakes her head. "That's insane. We don't even know if it'll work."

"What about Jane?" Elizabeth turns to Sarah. "Has anyone seen Jane?"

"Screw her," adds Beth angrily. "Leave her with her pet."

"You can't be serious; we need everyone we can."

Beth squares to Elizabeth. "So, blow a hole in the wall, go around the facility, downstairs, find Jane and then what?" Elizabeth can't answer; something is withholding her from agreeing.

Jane wouldn't leave us, would she? Yes probably.

"Can you mix something that will do the job?" Beth asks Sarah.

Sarah hesitates before nodding. "If we use the dispersal agents properly, we might be able to generate enough force. But we'll only get one shot."

Beth exhales sharply, rubbing a hand over her face. "Fuck, then let's make it count."

"Won't we just be creating a way in?" Lana questions.

Shit, that's a point.

"We will have to make sure we're quick, don't stop running for anything," Elizabeth responds, her sternness surprising even her.

Sarah begins work quickly, pouring and mixing as carefully as her shaking hands allow. She measures out the hydrogen peroxide and ethanol, whispering calculations under her breath as she does. Then packs the ammonium nitrate tightly within a repurposed oxygen canister to maximise its pressure.

Elizabeth crouches near the back wall, noticing a small air brick. "Here," she says. "It has to go here."

"Okay, it's done," Sarah confesses as she carefully lifts the makeshift bomb off the floor and gingerly walks it to Elizabeth.

Amateurishly, she secures it against the wall using a mess of medical tape. "We need a trigger," she mutters.

Beth holds up her pistol. "Already sorted."

Everyone steps back, towards the lab's main door. The Madness of the other side intensifies, as if they know what's about to happen. Elizabeth's breath feels shallow as she locks eyes with Beth. Frozen seconds seem to pass between the pair, then she nods. Beth raises the pistol, aims, and wastes no time squeezing the trigger. A gunshot rings out. Then the explosion. Far bigger than they expected. The force sent them flying backwards into the door and the wall behind them. Elizabeth felt the heat blast across her skin as debris rained down from the ceiling. Smoke and dust filled the air, causing her to cough as she began to push herself up, her body aching from the impact. Dimly, she registered the others groaning around her, struggling to recover. Then the cold night air hit her skin. The entire section of the lab wall was gone. Open to the outside.

Beth, coughing beside her, let out a breathless laugh. "Fuck me… that worked."

Lana groans, staggering to her feet. "Next time, let's go smaller."

Elizabeth searches the lab for Sarah, finding her lying still on the ground, slumped unnaturally.

For a brief, foolish second, Elizabeth thought she was catching her breath. But then she saw the jagged metal shards that had pierced through her chest and abdomen, and her breath caught in her throat. "No…"

Beth's gaze falls upon the scene, and she tumbles toward Sarah. Her eyes are open, but vacant, her body limp. She had been just a fraction closer to the blast. Just unlucky.

Lana presses a hand to her mouth upon realising the scene. "Shit…"

Elizabeth swallows the grief of her fallen friend. "We can't stay here."

Beth hesitates, kneeling beside Sarah's body for just a second before clenching her jaw and standing. "Yep. Let's go."

They turn toward the open night, their hearts pounding. But then another explosion. This time, it comes from beyond the facility, in the distance. A deep, rumbling blast that sends a fresh wave of smoke and fire curling into the night sky.

XXVII

Rigs

"Drop your weapon on the floor. Now!"

"You can't be serious," Rigs mutters under her breath. Then she feels another sharp jab in her back, and her fingers instinctively drop her rifle.

"Deadly serious," Jane says, her voice laced with her usual terrifying conviction. "Now move."

The air is thick with smoke and gunfire. The facility is under siege, and yet her only concern is saving herself.

Rigs cast a glance over her shoulder, her heart pulsating as she glances at the sight of Elizabeth, then Kim, her sister Elena, and the facility's other occupants as they release frantic shots into the tree line.

"This is insane, Jane. Do you think I'll just fly you out of here?

Jane doesn't answer immediately, and Rigs wonders if reflection is crossing her mind, then she feels the gun harder against her spine.

"That's exactly what's going to happen."

"I don't have the keys."

"How stupid do you think I am?"

"What about the others?" Rigs asks, "We just gonna leave them all to die?"

"They made their choice. I'm making mine."

"You're a real piece of work, you know that!"

"Spare me any sort of morality speech Rigs. Just get me to the chopper." Jane's voice is calm and measured, but now there is something else behind the words and a wild unpredictability in her eyes.

Gunfire roars behind them as they begin to move. Thoughts rush through Rigs' mind. She can hear Elizabeth's voice as she barks orders frantically over the chaos, the words blending with the screeches of the madmen surging forward. Suddenly, a bloodcurdling scream breaks through the cacophony, and she knows it's someone, one of her comrades, a friend, but she doesn't look back. Then it's cut short with a sickening gurgle. Rigs pushes forward, Jane following behind, holding the weapon at her back. Ahead, the fence looms, its rusted frame reinforced with its makeshift barricades, piled crates, sheets of old iron, anything they could scavenge to keep the madness out. Now, it was in their way.

"Shit," Rigs mutters, hands instinctively grabbing at the barrier's chain links.

Jane presses the gun harder against her back. "We need to move faster."

"I'm trying!" Rigs snaps as she yanks at the rusted wiring.

Then she spots them. Distant shapes that dart between the trees, near the helicopter, shifting like hungry predators waiting for a chance to strike. "I'm not sure this is a good idea."

Jane's voice is sharp. "Just shut up and get on with it."

She gives up on the chain linking and begins to tear at a piece of corrugated metal, and the barrier groans as it shifts. Each sudden crack of gunfire pulls at her resolve, each sound making her flinch. Finally, with a grunt, she shoves a large piece aside, and then an avalanche of materials falls.

"It's open."

"Let's go." Jane's voice has no hesitation as she shoves Rigs forward through the gap.

The pair move as quickly and as silently as they can, staying low to the ground as they run. The helicopter, the treeline, and the shifting shadows were getting closer with each step. Rigs' boots crunched against the earth, and her breath came in shallow gasps. She can still hear the battle raging behind them, gunfire, screams, the guttural howls of the mad, but out here, between the facility and the tree line, it feels like they had entered another world, one filled only with deafening dread. Her mind races, tangled in cowardice and doubt. Is she really going to let Jane dictate to her like this? Let her steal the only way out? It made her sick, the way she was being pushed along like a prisoner. But with the barrel pressed against her spine, she doesn't have much choice.

"Keep moving," Jane mutters, scanning the darkness ahead. "We're almost there."

Rigs clenched her fists. If she was going to do something, it had to be soon. The helicopter was just ahead now, perched near the trees like a sleeping beast, its rotors still and waiting. Then. A shrill and maniacal laugh erupts from the darkness. She freezes as the madman barrels toward them from the treeline, his eyes wide and gleaming in the fractured moonlight. His arms flailed wildly, and his tattered clothes were smeared with dirt and blood. Rigs panics. No weapon. No way to defend herself. Her breath catches in her throat as the madman lunges, his hands outstretched. Then, A gunshot shatters the night. The sound exploding in Rigs' skull, deafening. A sharp, piercing ring fills her ears, drowning out everything. Her vision blurs, and her balance wavers as her hands instinctively shoot up to clutch at her head. Everything around her becomes a distorted mess of muffled noise and dizziness. She can feel Jane behind her as each forceful shove against her back prompts her to keep moving forward. Rigs blinked, disoriented, and through the haze, she noticed the madman now lay still on the floor, a fresh bullet hole clean through his forehead. A precise and accurate shot. Jane's pistol still smoked. Rigs couldn't hear the words Jane was saying, her voice nothing but a distant murmur, lost in the chaos inside her own head. But she could feel the pressure and the heat of Jane's pistol at her back yet again; Jane wasn't giving her a choice. As they reach the helicopter, her hearing begins to return in fragmented bursts. She can hear the distant gunfire, the static hum of the night and the sound of Jane barking orders.

"I said get in," Jane snaps. "Now."

Rigs hesitates only a second before climbing into the cockpit, her hands shaking as they find familiar grips. Jane follows, immediately slamming the door behind her.

"Start it up," Jane orders, pistol still in hand and her eyes scanning the darkness outside.

Rigs feels her autopilot kick in, and she begins to flick toggles and flip switches. Familiar sounds begin to fill the air. The priming of the fuel, and the engine engaging, and then a deep mechanical whir begins to fill the cockpit as the rotor blades groan in protest before beginning their slow rotation. Her hands worked fast, but her mind was still spinning. Every part of her wanted to refuse, to stop this. But Jane's presence looming beside her was a silent and armed reminder of her lack of choice. In the distance, the facility's main floodlight flickers to life, and the grounds are bathed in harsh white light. Gunfire flashes like sporadic lightning on the horizon. Moving figures darted through the shadows, some running, others shambling, drawn by the chaos. Jane's voice cut through her thoughts.

"Get us in the air. Now."

As the helicopter's rotor blades gained speed, the mechanical whir growing louder with each second, Rigs' pulse hammers in her ears. The floodlight has illuminated the facility grounds, shining a stark white against the chaos unfolding in the distance. Figures moved erratically, some with purpose, others with the jerky, unnatural gait of something that no longer seemed human. Jane's grip tightened around her pistol as she scanned the perimeter.

"Come on, come on..." she muttered under her breath.

Rigs' fingers worked through the final pre-flight checks, her muscle memory overriding the static haze in her mind. The engine roars louder as the chopper begins vibrating beneath them. Just a few more seconds and they'd be airborne. Then, the first one hits.

A figure sprinted out of the darkness, launching itself at the cockpit. The impact rattled the windshield as a man, wild-eyed, with blood smeared across his face, clawed desperately at the glass. His mouth opened in a silent scream, his teeth bared as his hands slammed hard enough to crack the surface.

"Jesus!" Rigs yelped, jerking back.

Jane swung her pistol up, but before she could fire, a second and third body slammed into the side of the chopper. The force rocked them sideways, the skids scraping and sliding across the grass. Then a fourth hits, his hands tearing at the cockpit door, before grabbing Rigs' arm through the open side. Nails and fingers dig into her skin as she's yanked violently toward the exit. She let out a strangled yell, instinctively jerking the cyclic stick in her struggle. The tail swings sharply, the rotor blades shrieking as they clip low branches nearby.

"Get control!" Jane shouts, releasing another single shot beside her temple.

But Rigs can't. The damage had been done, and the chopper lurches sideways, its balance thrown. The half-mad men cling to it, refusing to let go, their weight adding to the already unstable aircraft, throwing it further off its axis. The rotors scraped across the grass, digging into the earth, bending and snapping as they headed towards a fence before shearing through the metal in a violent burst of sparks. Then came more trees. The tail boom clips the first one, and the force spins them violently into a second one that takes them full force, splintering wood so violently that it sounds like fireworks. The world turns sideways, then upside down, as metal screeches and branches snap beneath them until a sudden impact hits like a sledgehammer. The windshield shatters, and glass slices at exposed skin. For a moment, everything is a blur of noise, screaming metal, the deep, echoing thunk of bodies being thrown, and then stillness. Rigs blinked, dazed, and a deep ringing filled her ears. Smoke curls through the shattered cockpit, and theirs the scent of burning fuel thick in the air. The world is tilted at an unnatural angle, and branches and wreckage are scattered around them. Jane groans beside her, shifting in the twisted metal.

"Rigs… you still with me?" Her voice has lost its authority, almost seemingly friendly.

Rigs doesn't answer, her gaze fixated on the blurs of movement outside, fear crossing her face as she watches dark shapes stagger between the trees, drawn to the wreck. Smoke curls through the shattered cockpit, the acrid scent of burning fuel getting stronger. The helicopter lay on its side, metal groaning as it settled into the wreckage. Jane coughs, pushing herself up with trembling arms. A sharp pain stabbed through her ribs, but she ignored it.

"Rigs!, Rigs! Talk to me!"

There's a ragged breath, followed by a weak, pained voice. "Jane..."

Jane twists, blinking through her haze before noticing that Rigs is slumped against the fractured windshield, her arm wedged between the twisted frame and the unforgiving ground outside. Blood smears her forehead, and her chest rose and fell in uneven gasps. Jane curses under her breath.

"Shit, okay. Hold on. I'll get you out."

Then a sound in the distance made her freeze. Figures move between the trees. Slowly at first, then faster, drawn by the crash and Jane's heart slammed against her ribs.

"They're coming," she whispers.

Rigs let out a bitter laugh, coughing. "Yeah... figured."

Jane pushes against the crushed door frame, trying to force it open. It didn't budge.

"We don't have time for this, Rigs. I need you to help me. Move your arm."

"Can't. It's pinned good."

"Then I'll..." Jane stops mid-sentence as Rigs shifts slightly, her free hand slipping into the pocket of her cargo pants, where her fingers wrap around something and she pulls it into view.

Jane's breath caught in her throat. "Rigs!"

"Just Go."

"No. No fucking way. We can get you out. I just need..."

Rig's eyes lock onto Jane, calm. Resigned. "Fine, then stay."

For a second, neither of them moves. Then. Click. Jane knows the sound, the unmistakable sound of a pin being pulled, and panic surges in her chest.

"Fuck!" She turns, scrambling for the exit.

She squeezed through the twisted wreckage, its jagged edges tearing at her jacket. Her leg catches on a piece of bent metal, holding her in place. She hears it. The soft clatter of the pin hitting the floor.

"No. No, no, no.." Jane wrenches her leg free, pain shooting up her calf as she stumbles forward.

She runs her breathing erratic. *BOOM.* The force of the explosion sends her sprawling as the heat licks at her back, as fire erupts behind her.

XXVIII

Hate

The world seems quieter now. It has been a day, maybe two, since the market, the shot, and since he had carried Ezra, kicking and screaming, into the unknown. Now, they walk in silence, the crunch of dirt and gravel beneath their feet the only sound between them. The road stretches ahead in a winding, broken path, cracked and overtaken by nature as weeds crawl through the pavement. Cars sit rusted along the roadside in their usual manner, windows shattered, seats torn and decayed, their insides picked clean. Ezra walks a few steps behind, his small frame hunched, his arms angrily crossed. He has barely spoken, and when he has, it was in short, clipped answers. Never a question. Never a complaint. Mostly, he ignored Clint entirely. Clint adjusts the shotgun slung over his shoulder and clears his throat.

"Ezra, you need to drink something. Do you want to make a stop?" But theirs no response. He exhales through his nose, stopping in his tracks. "Come on, buddy. You need your fluids."

Ezra stops but doesn't look at him. His arms remained folded in a protective barrier.

Clint sighs, reaching into the backpack and pulling out a water bottle. He holds it out. "Just a few sips."

Ezra hesitates, then snatches the bottle from his hand without a word. He unscrews the cap and takes a single sip, barely enough to wet his lips, before shoving it back at his father and trudging forward.

Clint takes it, watching him for a long moment before following. "I'm sorry." Ezra still didn't answer. "I get it," Clint continues. "What happened back there, but I'm still your dad. I just made a mistake."

"She was begging," Ezra mutters, his voice so quiet that Clint almost missed it.

"I know."

"And you left her."

"I know."

Ezra kicks a loose rock down the road. "I hate you."

The words sting, but Clint doesn't react. He just keeps walking, trying to engage in conversation, "You have every right to be angry."

"Good."

A gentle breeze drifts through the trees, sending leaves dancing across the pavement. "I was trying to protect you."

Ezra scoffs. "By killing someone?"

"By making sure you didn't die, Ezra. By making sure we didn't die."

Ezra shook his head, his steps slowing. "I don't want to end up like you."

Clint stops walking and swallows hard, his throat suddenly dry. "What's that supposed to mean?"

Ezra turns to face him, his expression unreadable beneath the dirt and exhaustion. "Sick."

Clint feels something deep in his gut twist. "Ezra, you're a kid. You don't understand"

"I do" The boy's voice trembles, but there is a fire beneath it. "You're turning bad, like all the others, because of the sickness. I don't want you to be bad. You're a good daddy, not a bad one."

"I'm trying my hardest."

The boy's lips shudder, and Clint knows he is holding back tears. "I miss mummy."

The words cut Clint sharply. Ezra doesn't wait for a response, and he turns and starts walking again, leaving his father standing there, alone with the weight of his son's words. For a long moment, he doesn't move, finding comfort in the grooves of the tarmac as he stares at the ground, at the cracks running through it like the fractures in his mind.

So do I.

"I know".

With a quiet sigh, he starts walking again. Because what else was there to do but keep moving? The road stretches ahead, cracked and uneven as nature continues its relentless attempt to swallow it from the outside in. The wind carries the scent of damp earth, but Clint can taste something else on his tongue, something worse, something rancid, festering. He moves himself ahead of the boy, his shotgun tight in his grip. Ezra follows behind, back to not talking to him, not forgiving him. Clint wishes that he would, and then Frank's words echo in his head.

A groove in the terrain, like a shallow V in the landscape.

Ezra finally speaks, his voice small. "How much longer?"

"I don't know."

They continue to walk in silence until the road curves and an industrial estate looms ahead. Clint notices faded signage that clings to rusted fences, their letters barely legible through years of wear and decay. In the distance, warehouses stand like empty mausoleums, doors hanging ajar. Then he sees them. The bodies, hanging from the entrance arch, swayed slightly in the breeze. Some looked fresh, others not. Ezra's breath hitches as he catches sight of them.

Clint grabs the boy's arm and pulls him forward. "Don't look."

But his son recoils almost violently at his father's actions.

His small hands curling into fists, his nails biting into his palms. "Get off?"

Clint doesn't retaliate, just keeps moving, passing beneath the entrance arch as the smell of decay and rot thickens, almost choking. Inside the estate, the silence feels different, watchful. He tightens his grip on the shotgun as the pair weave their way through a sea of rusted machinery and debris, eventually spotting a faint trail of blood that leads into the shadows, disappearing beneath a bent loading bay door.

Absolutely not!

Then, a low sound rumbles from deep behind the door, something harrowing, something moving. Clint motions to Ezra for silence, and they move faster, slipping through the maze of broken buildings and machinery until they reach the other side. Finally, beyond the metal and concrete, the horizon opens again. Trees stretch across the land ahead, tall and dark, broken only by a distinct, unmissable gap, an opening in the treeline on the horizon.

Ezra sees it first. "There."

Clint nods, exhaling a heavy breath. "Yeah. Keep going."

The road gives way to dirt as the ground becomes more and more uneven as they near the treeline, and Clint tries with the boy again. "You doing okay?"

"Fine." Ezra's response is blunt and clipped. Just like all the others.

Clint runs his hand down his face as he glances ahead at the opening in the trees. The sight should be reassuring. But it isn't. "Not far now," he mutters, more to himself than to Ezra. "Frank said this was the way."

Ezra doesn't respond again, walking with his head down and his arms tight to his sides. Clint swallows, forcing the thought down before it can take root. But it comes anyway.

What if Frank was lying?

He'd never questioned it before. Never thought to. Frank had given him a direction when he had none. But now, after everything, after trusting his gut, he felt as though he had led them to nothing, and in the process, to terrible consequences.

What if Frank has sent us to our deaths?

He shakes the thought off as they reach the trees. Clint enters, the shade surrounding him, while Ezra stops dead. Clint slows, turning back. "What's wrong?"

Ezra's gaze flicks up to the towering trees. "I don't like the woods."

"I know. But it's the way we have to go." Ezra still doesn't move. "How about another scavenger hunt? We can..."

"No."

Clint blinks. "Ezra"

"I don't want to." There is no anger in his voice. No tantrum. Just exhaustion.

Clint rubs at the back of his neck. He is tired, too. Too tired to argue. "Alright. No scavenger hunt. Just walking."

Ezra takes a small step forward, eyes locked on the ground.

Clint nods. "That's it. Just one foot in front of the other."

"I know how to walk!"

The wilderness swallows them quickly, their surroundings suddenly becoming darker beneath the canopy of leaves and branches. The air is cooler here, damp, and thick with the smell of earth. Every step, once again, is carefully measured. Clint watches the ground for roots, loose stones, and anything that might trip them. Ezra stays quiet, his breathing shallow, his eyes fixated on the horizon. He keeps close, but never too close, just close enough for Clint to feel his presence. A shadow trailing him, silent and small. The hours drag and the trees blur together until Clint can't tell how far they'd gone. Time seems meaningless now. They were just moving. Always moving. Night falls quickly, and Clint eventually finds a patch of ground near a fallen tree, clearing it as best he can.

"We'll stop here for the night." Ezra doesn't argue but doesn't agree either.

He simply curls himself up on the ground without a word. Clint sits nearby, resting the shotgun across his lap. He stares out into the dark, listening to the forest groan and creak around them. Sleep comes in brief, haunted stretches. He would drift, then startle awake at every snap of a branch or rustle of leaves. But nothing comes. Just the trees and the dark.

Morning arrives grey and cold, and he nudges Ezra gently. "Hey. Time to move."

Ezra, blinking slowly and bleary-eyed, rises to his feet without protest, and they begin to walk again, pushing deeper into the wilderness. Before long, the trees begin to thin as the sun rises, but with it, Clint feels his chest ache with each step; the weight of the past few days was finally catching up. After what felt like hours, he tried with the boy once more.

His voice cracks from disuse. "Ezra?"

But the boy doesn't answer. He forces another breath.

"I'm... I'm sorry, Ezra. For everything."

Still, silence, his young son not even glancing his way. Clint swallows the knot in his throat, staring down at the dirt beneath his boots.

What's the point?

The words loop in his head.

What's left for me if he's already gone?

He didn't know if he was talking about death anymore. Ezra hadn't just stopped speaking. He'd stopped looking at him, stopped trusting him. he could feel it, like the bond between them had frayed to the thinnest of threads. And any second now, anything could snap it.

What would she think?

The thought clawed its way through his mind, unwelcome and sharp.

If she could see me now... would she even recognise me? Or would she see what Ezra sees? Just another madman with a gun and a trail of bodies behind him.

He blinks hard against the sting behind his eyes as he keeps walking, until the sun shifts overhead, the trees grow sparse, and finally, through the last of the branches, he sees it, concrete. A building, Large, silent, still.

"Ezra," he rasps. "Look." Ezra's head lifts, his expression still unreadable. They stand there, at the edge of the woods, staring at the structure. "Come on."

XXIX

Vacant

The building loomed from the treeline, silent and forgotten. Clint slows his footsteps, allowing Ezra, who trails behind, to catch up, his eyes wide as they take in the ruin of whatever this place had once been. There are no signs. no markings. No hints of government or officiality. Just crumbling concrete and bent steel. Clint notices a large entanglement of metal, a water tower, or what is left of one. Its rusted frame collapsed in a heap, surrounded by foliage growing through its wreckage. In the back of his mind, he wonders who built it and why it had fallen. The pair move cautiously over the open grass towards it. The perimeter fencing is shredded, sagging in places, and entirely gone in others. Gaps yawned wide where something, or someone, had forced their way through long ago. Metal posts lean at awkward angles, barely held together by the remaining brittle, rusted wire that clung to them. The grass grew wild and thick, tall enough to hide whatever stories the earth still held. But it was there, half-lost in the green, that he saw them. Skeletons. Not many and not obvious, but they were there, scattered and half-buried by time. Bones bleached white by the sun, ribs protruding through the foliage like warning markers. Clint stares, his throat dry.

What... happened here?

Ezra says nothing, but Clint knew he had seen them because now the boy stayed close, holding the strap of his father's backpack tightly. Clint forces his legs forward, past the broken fence, past the skeletons and towards the building's edge. Whatever it had once been, it wasn't built to be found. No markings, no welcome. Ahead was more metal, twisted, and burned out long ago. Large shards of metal are half-buried in the dirt. He keeps his shotgun close, listening for any sounds other than the wind that was sending cold shivers down his spine. As they round one corner, he sees it, a gaping hole in the wall. A way in. He leads the pair toward the jagged edges of the blast-scarred concrete jutting out like teeth, and he runs his hand lightly across the rough surface, blackened and brittle. With light steps, he enters through the breach, instantly feeling a change in the air, heavier inside, still and unmoving, thick with the smell of rust, decay, and something chemical. The room's remnants are sprawled out before him. Rows of rusted stainless-steel counters line the walls, streaked brown with age and neglect, and strange machines sit dormant, their wires frayed, and panels cracked open like gutted corpses. Dust coats everything in a thick, undisturbed layer.

Ezra hovers just inside the hole, staring wide-eyed at the alien landscape. "What is this place?"

Clint shakes his head slowly. "I don't know, but we're too late."

Glass crunches beneath his feet as he approaches a large whiteboard on one wall where strange symbols and scrawled notes still partially cling to its surface. Others, though, look pristine and fresh. In the centre of the room, a large metal table dominates the space, and rusted restraints lie open at its sides. Clint inspects it, drawing his fingertips across the floor, tracing the table's drag lines.

Someone's been here!

Ezra's voice trembles. "Is this… a hospital?"

"No," Clint rasps. "Not any kind I've ever seen, come on, stay close".

He moves toward the far side of the lab, spotting a single door set into the wall. Its surface is streaked with grime, but the handle is still intact, and he tests it. Locked. He presses his shoulder against the hardwood surface and shoves hard. A metallic clank answers him from the other side. The dull rattle of a chain restraint.

"Shit," Clint mutters.

He rams the door again, his shoulder instantly aching from the impact. Again, the chain groans under the pressure, but to his annoyance, it holds. He steps back, breathing hard with sweat beading on his brow.

"Ezra," he says, glancing back. "Cover your ears."

Ezra nods quickly, his hands flying up to his ears as his father raises the shotgun, aiming square at the door's handle. He exhales slowly, then fires. The blast is deafening in the confined space, bouncing off the walls like a thunderclap. Ezra flinches but remains rooted in place, but Clint doesn't wait; he pumps the shotgun and fires again, splintering the door and decimating the handle. Smoke and dust fill the air as he lowers the gun, coughing. He takes a deep breath and shoulders the door one more time. He grits his teeth, and with a final burst of strength, it gives, and he stumbles forward, crashing awkwardly into the dark beyond, landing hard on one knee. Instinctively, he raises the shotgun again and blinks into the shadows. A hallway stretches ahead to his left and to his right, narrow, suffocating, the walls streaked with grime and dirt.

Ezra peers cautiously through the smoke and doorway. "Dad?"

Clint grunts, forcing himself up. "Stay there."

But Ezra doesn't. He inches forward, refusing to be left behind as his father steadies his breathing and stares into the dark ahead.

What the fuck is this place?

Standing in the dim, stagnant air, he listens as silence presses in on him from all sides, until a sound, almost too soft to hear, reaches his ears. He draws the shotgun to his shoulder and listens. The noise comes again. A scraping, distant, but distinct. Ezra hears it too, and his eyes shoot to his father, wide and fearful. Clint motions silently for him to stay put, then turns toward the left corridor. He moves carefully, taking a few steps before another sound, much closer this time and from behind, startles him. He turns, shotgun at the ready, and sees Ezra at the doorway.

"Don't leave me."

The scraping came again, much closer this time. Metal on concrete, and the boy bounds frightfully to his father's side. Clint pauses, listening. Then the sound stops. Slowly, he creeps forward again. The narrow hallway feels endless as the walls seem to press in. Another sound echoes faintly ahead, and he feels Ezra tug hard at the backpack, but he pushes forward, his heart hammering. Something shifts in the darkness, too quickly for him to catch, and his heart skips a beat. He freezes, his hands tight on the shotgun. His breath catches in his throat, but he forces it out.

Come on, Clint. It's just your mind playing tricks... just a shadow.

But even as he says it, the feeling of being watched tightens around him, gnawing at his spine.

You're imagining shit. Pull it together.

He passes other doors, some hanging ajar while others are sealed tight with chains. Dried blood stains the floor beneath one, streaked in a smear toward the darkness. He tries not to look. The corridor feels like it narrows, feeling as if it is barely wide enough for him to pass. Then, at the far end, an opening in the wall awaits, with nothing but darkness beyond. The sound comes again. Louder. Just beyond the opening. He hesitates, his breathing coming fast now.

What the fuck am I doing? Turn around. Leave.

He lifts the shotgun, his finger twitching near the trigger.

"Alright…" he whispers to himself. "Let's see what the hell you are."

With a grunt, he leans in, peering through the opening in the wall. Something explodes from the darkness in a flash of movement. Then, instant pain, White-hot and blinding. A violent strike connects with his face, something snaps, metal, bone, he can't tell. His head snaps back as the shotgun clatters to the floor. Darkness swallows him whole. His last sight, a panicked flash of Ezra's face. Then nothing.

XXX

Degloving

Clint's head throbs in dull, rhythmic pulses where each beat sends a fresh wave of pain through his skull. His eyes flicker open, then slam shut again, as a sharp light sears his vision. He tries to move, but his limbs resist, and he can feel the tension as something cuts into his wrists. Restraints. Again. He forces himself to breathe, slow and steady, pushing back against the rising tide of panic. The air smells stale and tinged with something chemical. He opens his eyes again, and beyond the brightness, everything is murky. Thick concrete walls loom around him, their cold, unyielding presence pressing inward, and a large single window frames an abyss of darkness beyond. He blinks as his vision adjusts, the overhead glare no longer as blinding. He notices movement as a blurred figure shifts at the edges of his perception, and his pulse instantly quickens, elevating his headache. A memory claws its way to the surface, rough rope biting into his skin, and the den where he had been held before and his stomach twists at the thought of Ezra. As the figure approaches, stepping closer, a face begins to materialise in the dim light. A female with sharp features, worn, and tired. Her eyes are cold, appraising almost, and a scar traces the line of her jaw, disappearing beneath the collar of a dark, utilitarian jacket.

"You're awake," she says. No surprise in her voice, no sympathy either. Just an observation.

Clint swallows against the dryness in his throat. "Where's my son?"

The woman tilts her head slightly, considering him, "Interesting."

He can feel a fresh wave of anger surge through his veins, and he tugs at the restraints, testing them. Finding them tight with no give.

"Answer me," he growls, his voice raw. "If you've hurt him, you're as good as dead."

The woman's expression doesn't waver. "You're not in a position to demand anything."

He sets his jaw, forcing his breathing even. He knows panic is useless. He needs information and to figure out where the hell he is, who this woman is, and most importantly, where Ezra is.

The woman takes another slow step forward, her presence now looming over him. "You're far more alert than I anticipated. That makes you interesting. Let's see if you're useful too." She says, reaching for a nearby table.

Metal instruments clink softly against one another, catching the light as she shifts through a collection of unknown items.

Clint's fists clench instinctively, his arms tugging hard at the restraints that hold him firm.

"You want answers?" she muses, lifting a small device with wires trailing like veins. "Fine. Let's start with the basics. My name is Jane. This facility, well, it was supposed to be salvation. A haven of research, knowledge, and control. As the world went to hell, we studied the pathogen here, tried to understand it as it took everything. And I was on the verge of something. A breakthrough. A way to stop it."

She presses something cold and adhesive to his temple, another to his chest, sliding a cold hand down his shirt. Her fingers are deft as she attaches the monitoring equipment.

"I'm all that's left, with nowhere to go, and no way to get there if I did."

She taps on a keyboard and screens flicker to life behind her, jagged green lines pulsing with his heartbeat.

"So, I've continued my research. And you?" she continues, adjusting a dial. "You're exactly what I need. A man still in control. A man I can break. Do you understand what that means?"

Clint doesn't answer.

"It means I can watch the pathogen work from the beginning. Study its progress. Observe how sanity crumbles in real time. And if I can control that? If I can isolate the process, the triggers? Then maybe, just maybe, I can cure it."

She steps back, examining the readings, then turns, selecting a thin, curved blade from the table.

"But first, I need data. I need to push. I need to see how long you last."

Without hesitation, she moves to his left hand, gripping his fingers tightly, and he instantly attempts to recoil.

"I wonder how much pressure it takes," she murmurs, slipping the knife beneath his fingernail.

A small twist. A deliberate, slow push. Fire erupts in his nerves as his jaw locks. He stares at her, fear, anger and pain crossing his features until eventually he releases a guttural sound. The noise barely escapes his throat as she slides the blade deeper, lifting his nail away from the tender flesh beneath in a slow, methodical motion. Blood wells instantly, thick and dark, spilling down his fingers. Jane watches the monitors.

"Heart rate's spiking, but no screaming. You're holding back. Let's see how long that lasts".

She rips the blade free, and his chest heaves sharply, his chest heaving, muscles rigid against the restraints.

"Good. You're strong. That's what I need."

"Where is my son?"

Then, she moves blurringly fast, throwing a punch with full force that connects with his temple. His head snaps to the side, and stars burst into his vision. Then, another hit, her knuckles cracking against his cheekbone, the sharp sting of split skin following and blood trickling from his mouth.

"Your pain tolerance is impressive," she notes, flexing her fingers. "Tell me, have you experienced the pathogen yet. What's it like? That moment when you feel something inside you give. When do you know it's over?"

Another punch rocks him, somehow harder and more forceful, and a dull roar fills his ears. Blood pools in his mouth, and he spits to the side, the red splattering against the cold concrete floor. His breathing is heavy, ragged, but his eyes remain locked on hers, defiant.

Jane smirks. "Not bad. But we're just getting started."

"Numb," he suddenly says. "It feels numb."

Her eyes narrow slightly, her smirk faltering. "You've felt it?" Her voice suddenly softens.

Clint lets his head rest back against the chair and stares at the ceiling. "I've felt it. I know it's coming."

She studies him for a moment, her expression unreadable. "Then this shouldn't take long."

She turns back to the table, selecting something new. Clint watches his breathing slow until he sees her pick up some pliers.

"Is this necessary?" For the first time, he heard it, the fear in his voice.

Jane approaches him again, gripping his hand and wrapping the cold steel around his smallest finger.

"Yes, it's necessary and unfortunately for you, bones snap before minds do." Her words sound almost absent. "So, let's see how many it takes."

Then, with a sharp and precise movement, she twists. The first break is clean and controlled. The second is slower, deliberate. A sickening pop echoes through the sterile room.

Clint grits his teeth, allowing only a strangled sound to escape his throat. But his vision blurs and his body trembles.

"Where is my son?" he rasps again.

She ignores him, releases his hand, stands back and watches the way his mangled fingers twitch involuntarily. The monitors spike, warning of his body's distress, and she tilts her head, intrigued.

"Interesting," she murmurs.

Then, without a word, she grabs another finger. Another snap and Clint's world tilts.

Darkness begins to creep at the edges of his vision, swallowing the fluorescent light above and drowning Jane's face in shadow. He drifts between consciousness and oblivion, the pain anchoring him, pulling him under only to rip him back again. He could barely register the cold, the silence, or the overwhelming ache as his mind floated in the void, detached, resisting the pull of reality. When he finally surfaces, the room is empty. Darkness. No movement and no sound except for the weak rasp of his breath. His muscles are stiff and unresponsive, and he struggles to even turn his head. The restraints he could feel were still there, unrelenting against now bruised flesh. His body yearned for rest, but the pain wouldn't let him. He lets his eyes slip shut again, and the blackness swallows him whole. The next time he wakes, Jane is there, standing in front of the monitors as she scrolls through the readings, studying the jagged lines of his heart-beat and his brain activity.

"Men are normally so easy to break," she muses, almost to herself. "Weak. Designed for war. You lash out, you rage, you destroy, but you can't endure. Not like us."

Clint doesn't move. He barely breathed.

She turns, her lips curled into something too dangerous to be called a smile. "I suppose I should thank you for being an exception," she continues. "For not making this easy. I expected less from you, but I shouldn't have."

She approached the table, running her fingers along the cold steel instruments. Choosing. Deciding.

"I never thought to ask your name."

"It's Clint", he wearily responds.

She approaches him, leaning forward, hands on her knees. "Well, Clint." Her eyes are rageful. "I'm going to break you now".

His breathing instantly comes in shallow, ragged gasps. His body internally screams with every nerve flaring with pain, and now he prays for unconsciousness again, knowing what's coming. He can see it in her eyes, a hunger and a need to dismantle him piece by piece, to unravel him down to his most base, primal self, so she could see the pathogen at work. Jane straightens and steps back toward the table. Her fingers glide over her selection of tools with meticulous deliberation.

"Tell me, Clint, have you ever heard of degloving?"

She lifts a slender pair of small forceps, turning them in the bright light.

"It's one of the more overlooked methods of pain inducement, but I've always found it to be... intriguing." Her gaze flicks to his hand, battered and broken. "I haven't done this before. So, you will have to forgive me if I do this wrong."

Clint tenses as she reaches for his hand and pries open his fingers, ignoring the way they twitch involuntarily.

"You're enjoying this, aren't you?" his voice is hoarse, and his breath ragged.

She doesn't look up. "Enjoying it? No." Her tone is devoid of emotion. "I'm doing what's necessary. Do you have any idea what a vaccine would be worth?"

Clint huffs out something between a cough and a laugh. "So that's it? You're putting me through this... for money? In this world? And men are supposed to be the crazy ones."

Jane's eyes flicker, something in her carefully crafted resolve cracking, and her fist snaps out before he can react, connecting with a vicious strike that sends his head jerking to the side, sending a fresh burst of pain splitting through his skull.

"Don't you dare insinuate that I'm the crazy one." Her voice has sharpened. "You're just another man who thinks the world ceases to exist without him. But when I find the cure, the world will recover. And when it does, I will be at the top. The saviour of men."

He lets out a slow, wheezing chuckle, feeling at his swollen lip with his tongue. "The saviour of men," he repeats, his voice thick with mockery. "And still just a bitch." He spits bloodied saliva that hits the floor between them.

She doesn't flinch, not reacting at all, only wiping her knuckles against the fabric of her sleeve and exhaling slowly as she reaches for the forceps again.

"Let's get back to work, shall we?" she murmurs, her voice returning to that same measured calm. "I think we've wasted enough time".

"Where is my son?" Clint's voice is desperate, cracking.

"You know, it's an amazing thing, skin," she muses, ignoring him completely and positioning the forceps at the base of his index finger. "It's like the pathogen in ways, it stretches. tears. peels away. If done well enough, it won't even bleed much at first. Just a slow, agonising separation. Like shedding a layer of yourself you never wanted to lose."

Clint barely has time to brace himself before she pinches the tool down, trapping a sliver of flesh near the edge of his nail.

With an excruciating pull, she begins to peel and A raw, strangled sound tears from Clint's throat as the first layer of skin comes free, his nerve endings shrieking in white-hot agony. His body lurches involuntarily against the restraints as his muscles lock in sheer, brutal resistance. The pain is suffocating and dizzying. Jane lets out a quiet hum as her eyes flicker toward the monitors.

She twists the forceps slightly, lifting another section. "You pretend to be strong, but strength isn't just about what you endure. It's about what you give up."

Clint's jaw clenches so tightly that his teeth threatened to crack. Sweat drips down his temples, mingling with the blood and bruises that smear across his face. But still, he refuses to scream.

Jane sighs, shaking her head. "Men. Always so stubborn".

Clint lets out a mumble, the words unclear, and she leans in closer, her brow furrowing. "What was that?"

Again, he mumbles words, but no words, his lips forming shapes without sound. A flicker of something unfamiliar creeps into Jane's expression, dangerously close to hesitation, and she turns sharply, rushing to her monitors, her fingers flying across the keyboard.

Data scrolls across the screens in rapid succession, jagged lines of brain activity fluctuating wildly. She taps, clicks, recalibrates, scanning for anomalies, for something, anything, that explains what was happening. Another mumble. This time, the words were clear. "Where is my son?"

She stills, the rhythmic clicking of keys coming to an abrupt halt. Slowly, deliberately, she turns back to him, "You should be worrying about yourself, Clint," she murmurs, her voice dipping into something almost gentle. Almost pitying. "Not about a boy who's already dead."

Clint's fingers twitch against the restraints. His breathing shifts. Deeper, uneven. Even beneath the swelling, the bruises, and the raw agony searing through his body, his eyes lock on Jane, burning with something unbroken. Something defiant.

Jane studies him for a moment, then exhales, shaking her head. "You still don't get it, do you? None of this is about him. It's about you. Your body. Your mind. Your limits."

Then something shifts. A realisation, and a slow, creeping grin tugs at the corner of her lips as she steps closer, lowering herself until he can feel the warmth of her breath against his ear. "Oh, Clint, I've been going about this all wrong," she whispers, her voice coiling around him like a noose. "Physical pain won't break you. But emotional pain? That just might." She pulls back, her eyes gleaming with something dark, something cruel.

Without another word, she turns and strides towards the door. The heavy metal slammed shut behind her, the final sound echoing through the cold, empty room.

XXXI

Lost

Time ceases to exist as Clint sits alone in the room. Barely tethered to consciousness, he winces at every slow pulse of agony. His body feels like a collapsed ruin, his limbs no longer his own, just aching reminders of what has been done to him. His hand throbs as he looks down at the mangled, useless thing attached to the end of his wrist. He lets his eyes drift to the ceiling, tracking cracks in the concrete, trying to piece together something from them, a shape, a meaning, anything to focus on that wasn't the wreckage of his body. His mind pulls him elsewhere, out of this place, this room, this existence. Ezra's voice, distant, is there. The weight of a small hand in his own, the warmth of it and the smell of the damp earth after a storm, and campfire smoke that curls into the air. He holds onto it for as long as he can, knowing that the moment he lets go, a cold reality would return, the walls would press in, and with them the pain. Suddenly, a sound reaches his ears, forcing him to focus, his breath shallow. Footsteps. Slow and purposeful. Then the door creaks open, and Jane enters without a word, her expression stern. No scalpel, no thinly veiled monologue about her research. Just her presence, heavy and controlled. Clint braces himself for what will come next. The words, the questions, the sharp edge of her voice carving into him as effectively as any of her instruments. But she says nothing. She simply steps closer and, without hesitation, takes his broken hand in hers. Her touch is almost gentle, but the moment she begins wrapping the bandage around his shattered fingers, white-hot agony flares again. He sucks in a breath through clenched teeth, as his body locks up as the pain tears through him. Then it happens, before he can stop it, before he can bury it. A whimper, soft and barely there. Jane's hands don't pause. She continues wrapping methodically and precisely. He keeps his gaze fixed on the ceiling, refusing to meet her eyes, ashamed of the sound that has escaped him. She reaches for an old rag, stained with things he didn't want to think about, and wipes the blood from his face. No malice. No mockery. Just the mechanical efficiency of cleaning up a mess. Then, as quickly as she had come, she was gone, and the door slammed shut. In silence and breathing hard, he blinks against the haze of confusion clouding his mind. Further time stretches. He thinks he slept, but there was no rest in it. His body continued to refuse to settle, and his mind continuously circled the same thoughts over and over, like a wounded animal pacing a cage. Was this another game? Was Jane softening him up just to tear him down again? That was what made the most sense. The moment she wiped the blood from his face, he felt it. The smallest shred of something human. But Jane wasn't human, not to him. Not in the ways that mattered. She was a scalpel, a machine hellbent on breaking bodies and minds in the name of progress. But then why bandage his hand at all? Why bother? Maybe she wanted him alive. Maybe she needed him to last longer. Then footsteps. Quick, frantic, and the door bursts open.

Arms wrap around him, small, desperate, shaking. Sobs wracked the fragile frame pressing against him, gasping, choking, barely able to speak between ragged breaths.

"Daddy."

Clint feels his whole body lock. The pain didn't matter. The restraints didn't matter. Nothing mattered except the warmth against his chest, the familiar scent, the way tiny fingers gripped at him like they'd never let go.

It's possible. She has done it. She has won.

But the sobs kept coming, shaking against him, and a heartbeat, rapid and frantic, pounds against his chest, real and alive. His head tilts forward, his forehead pressing against the crown of Ezra's hair. He squeezed his eyes shut as if that might stop the tears from coming, but it was useless. Then Clint breaks, and A sob rips from his throat, raw and jagged. His body shakes as the weight of everything, the pain, the fear, the hope, the impossible reality of this moment, crashes down on him. He turns his head just enough to press his lips to the top of Ezra's head. He doesn't know how or why. But Ezra was with him, and for the first time in a long time, he allowed himself to cry.

But then there's another voice. "See, I told you he was fine."

Clint's breath shudders, his eyes snapping open as she enters the room, and he braces for her usual cruelty, for the cold precision of her words. But this time, there is none of it. Instead, she crouches beside Ezra, her voice warm and soothing. A doctor's voice.

"You're very brave, Ezra," she says gently, offering a small smile. "Your father has been helping me with something very important. Something that could save people."

Ezra sniffles, his small hands still clinging to Clint's arms. "Save people?"

Jane nods. "I'm very close to a cure. But your dad..." She sighs and tilts her head as if in admiration. "He's strong. He's been helping me. But we can't do it alone."

Clint's breath catches. His vision tunnelling on Ezra's face as his son wipes his tears and lifts his head, listening.

"I need someone as brave as you," Jane continues, her voice honeyed, patient. "Someone who can help me make the world better. Your dad is already doing his part."

Ezra pulls back just slightly, his brows furrowed. "I can help?"

Clint's blood runs cold, and his wrists twitch against the restraints. He wants to scream, to shake Ezra, to tell him to run, to not listen. But his voice, his body, betrays him. He can only watch. Ezra nods, eyes wide, hopeful.

"Tell me how."

"No", Clint suddenly burst. "Don't listen to her Ezra."

"Now, Clint, Ezra knows you are already under the pathogen's influence, he knows not to listen to you, and that you will say strange things. I'm here to help."

"She's going to help you Daddy."

"No Ezra, listen to me."

"Right, Clint that's enough," Jane shouts, pulling a gun out and aiming it at Ezra.

"What's happening?" Ezra shouts.

Jane's voice is sharp. "What's happening, Ezra, is that your father is confused. The sickness inside him is fighting back, pushing him to say whatever he thinks will stop us. But it's not really him talking anymore, is it?" Her gaze never leaves Clint, even as she speaks softly to the boy.

Clint growls low, teeth clenched against the pain. "Bullshit... you're twisting everything. Ezra, look at me. Look at me!"

But Ezra can't. The barrel of the pistol lingers too close, and his body is frozen in place.

Clint shifts, struggling against his bindings, biting into his flesh. "What is this, huh? You gonna kill him now? Is this really necessary?"

Jane's lips curl, somewhere between a smirk and a snarl. "Is this really necessary?" she mocks. "That's rich, Clint. Necessary? All of this is necessary. I'm the only one left who can fix it."

Clint spits blood. "Fix it? You're stuck here. If you could've left, you would've. So, tell me, who exactly will you sell this cure to, huh? You got customers waiting out there?" He laughs bitterly. "There's no one left."

For the first time, Jane falters, and he can see a flicker of something behind her eyes, doubt, maybe. Or just anger at being called out.

"You don't know anything," she snaps. "There are people. Survivors. Networks. They're out there, waiting. And when they come looking, when the world tries to piece itself back together, they're going to need this. They're going to pay for it. And I'm going to be the one holding the key."

Clint stares at her, breathing raggedly. "You're delusional. Do you think anyone's coming back for this place? For you? How long have you been here, huh? You're rotting down here, and no one is coming for you."

"Enough," she hisses, turning the gun toward him. "You don't get to ask the questions."

Ezra starts crying, loud, messy sobs that echo through the cold concrete. "Stop it! Stop shouting!"

Jane grits her teeth, annoyed. "See what you're doing? You're scaring him, Clint. You can't even hold yourself together."

His eyes are locked on her, and his voice is low and broken. "If you hurt him… If you even think about it, I swear to God."

"You'll what?" she snaps. "Die? Because that's the only card you've got left."

The room fills with Ezra's crying, and the sound claws at Clint's soul as Jane stares down at him.

Slowly, she finally lowers the gun, just enough, before leaning in closer to Clint, her voice a venomous whisper.

"We can do this my way, or we can do it my way with your son dead. Either way, the boy helps me. You understand that, right?"

"Oh, I understand just fine. But, you know what I also understand. I understand that even if you get a cure or your vaccine or whatever, you won't sell it, and the world will never know about it, because you're alone here, you're too scared to go out there, and you're too weak to quit."

Her face twitches. Just for a second, but it's enough to let him know that his words have hit home. Then, without warning, she whirls on Ezra, the gun snapping back up straight at the boy's head.

"Shut that noise," she snarls.

Ezra flinches, his sobs cutting off into strangled hiccups.

"Please," Clint starts, but she cuts him off with a glance so sharp it could flay skin.

"Enough. You want me to prove I'm not bluffing, Clint?" she spits. "You think I won't do what's necessary?" She takes a step toward Ezra, gun still raised. Then another. Until she's towering over the boy.

Clint begins to thrash hard against the restraints, his wrists tearing open. "Don't you fucking touch him?"

"Oh, I'm going to," she sneers, and in one smooth motion, she grabs Ezra by the collar and yanks him across the room.

Ezra cries out, stumbling, as she drags him to the far corner of the room. "Stay there," she commands.

Ezra's chest heaves as he presses his back against the concrete wall, his small hands balled into fists at his sides.

Jane watches him for a long, calculated second, then turns sharply and stalks toward the monitors. Her fingers dance lazily over the controls, the screens flickering, and she mutters something under her breath, clearly unimpressed, her eyes cold and distant.

Clint barely moves as blood drips from his wrists where the restraints have torn at his skin. His gaze locked on Ezra.

Jane clicks her tongue in frustration, the sound sharp as a whip crack. Then, as if bored, she turns her head, her gaze falling lazily back on the boy. Without hesitation, she crosses the room and backhands Ezra across the face. The sound echoes, sharp and brutal and Ezra gasps, a wet, choked sound as his head snaps sideways. His knees gave, but the boy caught himself with trembling hands.

Clint loses it. "I will fucking kill you," he bellows, almost a roar. More beast than man. He thrashes, and the chair groans as his body strains against its limits. "You fucking touch him again."

Jane doesn't flinch. She smiles. "Good," she murmurs, almost to herself again. She turns her back on them both and strolls casually toward the monitors again. She taps at the screens, brows furrowed, unimpressed by whatever data she is checking.

Clint's breathing is ragged, his chest heaving. "You're dead. You hear me? You're dead the second I get out of this chair."

Jane doesn't respond. Not right away. She simply glances at him, almost bored at his threats. She strides forward. Ezra whimpers, his small frame shrinking against the wall, but it doesn't stop her. With a brutal, effortless swing, she backhands the boy again, this time with enough force to send him sprawling sideways, crumpling to the floor like a discarded doll.

The room goes silent. No screaming from Clint. No cursing. No thrashing. Nothing. Clint just stares.

Jane looks down at Ezra, then glances at Clint, expecting the rage, the explosion. But he doesn't move. Doesn't speak. He just watches, his face blank, his eyes empty. Jane approaches the monitors, her posture relaxed, one arm resting against the console as she glances between him and the monitors. No struggling. No screaming. Just... stillness. And it thrills her. This was what she'd been waiting for. The moment the line blurred and the last threads of self-preservation, of fatherhood, of sanity had snapped. The quiet acceptance of madness. She taps idly at the controls and then glances back, expecting the usual: a mumbled descent, the cracked whispers. But Clint doesn't speak. He just stares, his eyes hollow.

"Strange..." she murmurs, amused. "You skipped it, didn't you? Straight past the muttering... straight to the silence."

She steps back, biting her lip as if savouring the moment. Finally, softly, like a breath dragged from the deepest pit of his chest, Clint releases a mumble. The sound is more than a word. Jane stiffens and her head snaps toward him.

"What was that?" she whispers, stalking forward now, like a predator closing in.

Clint remains motionless, but the mumble comes again. A fractured syllable. Meaningless.

Jane inhales sharply, the thrill of discovery lighting up her eyes. "There it is... right there." Her voice trembles with excitement as if she's teaching a room of students. "The moment it takes hold." She kneels, inches from his face, studying him like a prize specimen. "Do you feel it? That little voice... not yours anymore, is it?"

Ezra sobs in the corner, but she doesn't even glance his way.

Her whole world was narrowing to Clint and the pathogen. "You performed... perfectly," Jane breathes. "Denial. Anger. Bargaining. Thank you." She straightens slowly, beaming like she's just won the Nobel prize. "You're gone now, Clint. You understand that, don't you?" Her voice softens as if explaining to a child. "There's no coming back from this. You're lost. And he," she flicks her eyes toward Ezra, "he needs to know that." Her attention turns fully to the boy. "Ezra," she calls sweetly, with that poisonous, syrupy tone. "You need to listen now. Your father's gone. What's sitting here?" she gestures lazily to Clint's slumped frame. "That's not him anymore. That's what the sickness does. You've seen it before, I'm sure."

Ezra trembles, wiping his sleeve across his bloody cheek, staring at his father like he's trying to see him through the ruin left behind.

"He's not your father anymore. He's a husk. The sooner you understand that, the better."

She gives Clint one final glance, expecting, almost hoping for a reaction. But there's nothing. Just that blank stare. Satisfied, she turns her back on both of them and busies herself with the monitors again, hands moving quickly. Ezra doesn't move, doesn't speak, just stays frozen in place, his wide, tear-filled eyes locked onto his father. He flinches at every flicker of his father's erractic wrist movements, but his gaze refuses to leave him.

The room is thick with silence, broken only by Jane's soft tapping and Ezra's shuddering breaths. Then.

"Hello? Anyone there?"

XXXII

Bullet

"**D**own here!" Ezra's scream comes quickly, shattering the silence, his call echoing off the cold concrete walls.

Jane spins on him instantly, her face twisting with fury. "What the hell do you think you're doing?" she snaps, striding forward. She storms across the room, her hand shooting out and grabbing his arm in an iron grip. "You are a stupid, stupid boy!"

Ezra flinches but doesn't shrink away. His chest rises and falls in rapid bursts, but his tear-streaked face is locked in stubborn defiance.

Jane's nostrils flare. "Do you have any idea what you've just done?" she hisses, shaking him slightly. "Do you even understand what's at stake?"

Then there's the sound of movement. Whoever had heard Ezra was coming.

Jane's eyes flick toward the doorway, then back to the boy. Her grip tightens on his arm, and before he can react, she yanks him in front of her and presses the cold muzzle of her pistol against the side of his head.

"You're going to keep your mouth shut," she murmurs into his ear, voice sickly sweet with venom. "Or you'll be the first to go."

The small boy's body trembles against her hold. After a few tense moments, a shadow breaks through the dim light of the doorway, and a figure steps inside.

Cara. Her rifle is raised, her eyes sharp as they sweep the room in an instant. They land on Clint first, strapped to the chair, slumped, releasing the occasional incoherent mumble as his head twitched ever so slightly. Then her gaze locks onto Jane and onto the pistol pressed to Ezra's skull, and her entire body goes rigid.

"What the fuck is going on?"

Jane barely reacts, her expression remains eerily calm despite the gun pointed at her, and her grip on Ezra doesn't loosen.

"Who the hell are you?"

"Lower the gun, now," Cara orders, stepping further inside.

"You have no idea what you're walking into. This isn't what it looks like. I am standing on the cusp of our salvation. You don't understand what's at stake here."

"What I understand," Cara shoots back, "is that you've got a child at gunpoint, and that makes you the only fucking threat in this room. Let him go."

Jane's fingers twitch against the trigger. "I'm close, so close, to something bigger than all of us. A cure. A way out of this hell".

"Bullshit." Cara's jaw tightens. "If you had a cure, we wouldn't be having this conversation. You'd be out there, saving the world. Instead, you're in here, holding a kid hostage like a goddamn coward."

Before Jane can respond, Ezra's voice cuts through the standoff.

"She's lying!" he blurts, "She just hurts people!"

Cara's eyes fall back to Clint, and her stomach twists at the sight of him. "Ezra, did she hurt you?"

Ezra nods frantically, tears welling in his eyes. "She hit me. She, she." He sucks in a shuddering breath. "She's mean."

Jane's grip on the gun falters briefly. "Ezra, I know you're scared, but you have to understand."

"Don't talk to him!" Cara snaps, stepping forward, her finger tightening on the trigger. "I swear to God, drop the gun, or I drop you."

Jane inhales deeply, her composure returning like a mask slipping back into place. "You don't get it. He was already exposed, like all men are. The pathogen was in his system. But he was doing well at resisting it. He held on longer than anyone I'd seen before. He was my first opportunity to see the full stages of its progress. I needed to see what exactly it would take to break him, to trigger the pathogen."

Cara's lips curl in disgust as she assesses Clint's quiet form. "So, you tortured him."

"I pushed him," Jane corrects, her voice eerily calm. "For results. And I got them. It may look like sadism. Some twisted game, but it is research. And I think I finally understand how to stop it."

"You're saying you learned something from this? From him?"

Jane nods. "His resistance. His mind. The way he fought off its effects for a while. It all showed me something I hadn't managed to fully see before. The trigger. The process. Something I can isolate." She exhales sharply, shaking her head. "I was close before, but now, now I think I know how it works. I just need more time."

Cara's expression twists, uncertainty flowing through her. Could it be true? Could this hellscape have an end in sight? Could Clint's suffering have meant something?

Jane saw it, the hesitation. The tiniest sliver of doubt, and she latched onto it. "You don't have to understand. You don't even have to believe me. But think for a second. If I'm right, if I really am as close as I think I am, then what happens if you kill me? It all dies with me."

Cara swallows hard.

"There's just one problem," Jane continues, her voice turning sharp again. "I still need the boy."

Cara's grip on the rifle tightened. "The fuck did you just say?"

Jane still doesn't waver. "Children are immune, you know that. The pathogen doesn't take hold in kids, but it mutates in adults. If I can study that, track it as he grows, I can find any missing pieces." Ezra lets out a small, terrified gasp, his body trembling at Jane's words.

Cara takes a step forward, her entire body now radiating fury. "And use him like a goddamn guinea pig? I think not."

Jane's grip on the boy didn't loosen. "He's necessary."

"No," Cara growls. "He comes with me, or he dies in a cage with you. And that? That's never gonna fucking happen. Let him go." Cara's grip on the rifle firms, her knuckles white as she stares down her opponent.

Jane's breathing remains steady and measured, as if she is speaking to another petulant child rather than a woman ready and holding the barrel of a rifle her way. "You don't get it, this isn't cruelty. This isn't about power or control. This is science. This is the only way forward."

"You keep saying that like it justifies all this bullshit, like it makes up for what you did to him." She flicks her eyes toward Clint, still slumped in the chair, his muttered words lost between the argument. "Like it gives you the right to keep hurting people."

Jane shakes her head. "You think I wanted this? You think I wanted to be here all alone, that I enjoyed pushing him that far? I needed to understand it."

"You tortured him," Cara snaps. "You played God. And now you think you get to do it again, with him." She nods toward Ezra.

"Children are immune. His body holds answers that no adults ever could. With time, with observation, I can understand it even further, find what I've been missing."

Cara lets out a short, bitter laugh. "Observation? You mean keeping him locked in here like a fucking lab rat? Watching him grow up, while you pick apart his blood and poke at his brain?"

Jane's lips pressed into a thin line. "That's not quite how it works. But, if it means saving humanity, then yes."

"That's not saving humanity," Cara growls. "That's sacrificing it. And for what? A shortcut? Do you think you're the only one trying to figure this out? If you're this close, then so is someone else, someone out there who didn't have to torture a man to get there. Someone who isn't holding a kid at gunpoint."

Jane's grip on Ezra tightens. "We don't have years to wait. The world has crumbled, and we need results now. You're willing to gamble that someone, somewhere, is just as close as I am?"

Cara's jaw clenches. "I'd rather it takes years and be done right than let this be the cost."

Her eyes narrow. "Ezra's coming with me now. And you're going to let him. If you try to stop him… well."

Ezra trembles on the spot for a moment, eventually taking a hesitant step toward Cara, his eyes locked on hers like she's the only solid thing left in the world. Shockingly, Jane seems to let him. For a breath, but then, without warning, her arm snaps up and a deafening sound reverberates through the room. For a heartbeat, no one moves. Then, Jane stumbles, her mouth opening in shock. Her gun slips from her fingers, clattering to the floor. She gasps, looking down as dark crimson begins to bloom beneath her collarbone.

"Jesus Christ," Jane breathes, falling hard to her knees, clutching her shoulder, and blood pours between her fingers. Ezra freezes, staring wide-eyed at Jane, then back at Cara, still standing firm, rifle steady, smoke curling from the barrel.

"I warned you."

Jane wheezes, trying to catch her breath, swaying where she kneels. "You... you shot me."

Ezra's lip quivers as he forces himself forward, stumbling the last few steps and barreling his body into her legs. "You're okay," she mutters into his hair, her rifle still trained on Jane. "You're okay, kid."

Jane glares up at her, rage and agony twisting her face. "You... you just destroyed everything... everything I built...for what, for a kid."

Cara takes a shaky breath, steadying the gun. "I should finish you off. Right now." She takes an angry step forward, pulling Ezra with her.

Jane coughs, spitting blood. "Do it, then... but you'll never know what I found. You kill me, it dies with me."

Cara takes another step forward, hesitating, her finger tightening on the trigger.

Ezra buries his face against her side, whimpering. "Please," he whispers. "Don't... don't kill her."

Cara's jaw works, but slowly, slowly... she lowers the rifle. "You're not worth the bullet."

Jane slumps, gasping, blood soaking through her shirt. "You're a coward"

Cara ignores the comment and picks up the strewn Pistol from the concrete floor. It's heavier than it looks, and she slides her thumb over the cold steel as she checks the chamber. One round.

She swallows hard, turns, and walks back to Clint, Ezra trailing beside her, his breath shaky, eyes locked on his father. Cara crouches in front of Clint's slumped form. There's no resistance. No fight. Only an unnatural stillness. "You stole my boat," Cara says, her voice cracking as she forces a weak smile. "Remember that asshole?" He doesn't move. Doesn't blink. Just stares forward, vacant, breathing slowly but heavily.

Ezra steps closer, his small frame trembling. "Daddy..." His voice is a whisper, barely there.

Cara notices the man's eyes flicker at the sound. Only slightly, but enough. Ezra reaches out and presses his tiny hand against his father's rough knuckles. "Please... please come back," he chokes out. "I'm right here."

Cara's heart pounds in her chest as she shifts, slowly untying Clint's good hand. Half expecting him to lash out, to strike, to kill. But he doesn't. His free hand just drops heavily to his side, his fingers twitching as if the impulse to strike is there, but something else is holding him back.

She stares at them both for a moment, her throat tightening. Slowly, with shaking hands, she places the pistol into Clint's free palm. Placing the cold metal against his cold skin. "It's loaded," she whispers. "One bullet... It's yours". Clint's fingers twitch, curling lightly around the grip. Cara forces the words out, barely audible. "It's your choice, Clint. No one else."

Ezra stares up at her, his lips trembling, before turning back to his father. He takes a shaky breath and leans in, resting his forehead against his father's, Cara watching carefully for any signs of erratic and sudden movement.

"I love you, Daddy," the boy whispers. "I... I love you so much."

For a second, just a second, Clint's eyes flicker again, and that dull, distant gaze softens. And then... a single tear slips down his cheek, cutting through the grime and blood. Ezra sobs, but there's no more pleading. He knows. Deep down.

Cara's voice cracks. "We... we have to go now, Ezra."

Ezra hesitates, then slowly reaches into his pocket. The sound of rustling fabric filling the heavy silence. With trembling fingers, he pulls out the worn, creased photograph, his mother's face staring back at him, smiling from another life. He looks at it one last time... then gently places it on Clint's lap. "So you're not alone." Then turns away before his courage shatters.

Cara scoops him up, holding him tight, and backs toward the stairs. She doesn't look back.

XXXIII

Epilogue

The road stretches endlessly before them, shimmering in the midday heat, its cracked tarmac littered with debris. Cara runs, her breath ragged, her feet pounding the ground in sync with Ezra's lighter footsteps beside her. He is taller now, still thin, still fragile, but stronger than before. The road ahead is blocked with a mess of rusted metal sheets, barbed wire, and stacked fences that rise like a wall against the horizon. Ezra sprints beside her, his breaths sharp and controlled, but Cara can begin to hear the strain in them. Then. A single gunshot cracks through the air. Cara spins, instinctively pulling her rifle up. But the shot hadn't been for them. She watches as one of their pursuers staggers, his arms flailing before he crumples to the pavement in a heap.

Ezra skids to a halt beside her, chest heaving. "Who?"

Cara doesn't answer, scanning the surroundings, the wrecked cars, then back to the wall. before she begins sprinting toward it again. The sound of heavy boots thundering behind them, their pursuers relentless, gaining. "Faster, Ezra!" she urges, her lungs burning, every muscle in her legs screaming. Another shot. Then another. Each one followed by a grunt, a moan, and a dull thud as bodies hit the pavement. Whoever was out there, they were thinning the herd. The barricade looms closer now. Tall, rusted, and stitched together from scraps of a world long gone. *If we could just reach it. If we could just.*

"Stop." A voice rings out, sharp and commanding, cutting through the chaos like a blade.

Ezra falters, his feet skidding against the tarmac. Cara catches his arm, forcing him to keep moving.

"Stop now, or the next bullets will be for you." This time, she has to listen. Now it is Cara who skids to a halt, dragging Ezra behind her. She turns and raises the rifle, her breath coming fast. In the distance are further pursuers, closing fast. Shots ring out, Cara's rifle along with their strange defender. The dust hasn't even settled from the fallen men when the voice from behind the barricade makes another command. "Drop your weapons," the stranger orders. Cara turns back to the barricade. The shots have stopped, now replaced with an apprehensive silence that thickens the air. Behind her, the bodies of their pursuers lay still, blood seeping into the cracks of the road. Cara's fingers tighten before she forces them to loosen. With a slow and deliberate motion, she unhooks her rifle from her shoulder and lets it fall to the ground. "And you," the voice orders. Ezra hesitates. Reluctantly. Cara nods once. The boy exhales sharply and kneels, setting his weapon down. It wasn't much, barely more than a relic, but it had made him feel safe. Now, stripped of it, he felt smaller and thinner, as his ribs pressed against his too-tight shirt. Silence continues to thicken the air as the pair stands, unarmed and unprepared for what will happen next. Another sound, then a loud bang fills the air, and the barricade rattles, metal scraping against metal. Another deep bang echoes, then another, followed by the sharp ping of something loosening, and a door within the towering wall begins to open, as the metal shifts and a thick, rusted sheet peels away. Beyond it, A passage. A way in. "Inside. Now, leave the weapons." Cara glances at Ezra, who is already looking at her for reassurance. Waiting. She takes his hand, her breath catching in her throat. She steps cautiously forward, Ezra's small hand gripping hers tightly as they enter through the opening. A road stretches out before them, pristine and untouched by the decay of the world they'd left behind. No rusted-out vehicles, no overgrown moss devouring the pavement, just a smooth, clean stretch of tarmac lined with houses. People move between them, chatting, carrying baskets of supplies. On one porch, a woman sits shelling peas into a bowl, rocking gently in an old chair, and a group of children dart across the street, laughing, chasing a faded leather football. Their voices rang clear in the air, untainted by fear. Ezra's fingers clench around hers, and she glances down, seeing his face, wide-eyed and slack with disbelief. Behind them, the metal door clangs shut. The stranger who had led them inside approaches, rifle still slung across her back, stepping forward, watching them closely. "Wait here, don't move a muscle."

Cara tenses, her instincts curling her fingers into fists. "We're not here to start trouble."

The stranger studies her, then flicks their gaze to Ezra. Something softens in her expression. "No," they murmur. "You're here to survive."

For the first time in years, Cara wasn't sure what to do next. She shifts uneasily, her fingers flexing at her sides as the stranger disappears back towards the steel wall. The massive structure looming over them. Time seems to stand still as they wait until a figure begins to approach them from the distance, her steps measured, deliberate. A long coat drapes over her lean frame, and her eyes are sharp as she scans Cara and Ezra with an unreadable expression. For a moment, neither of them spoke, awaiting her arrival. The woman comes to a slow stop just a few feet away, dust lifting gently at her heels. Her hair is long, pale gold, swaying slightly in the breeze, and it gleams under the sun. She kneels, lowering herself gracefully to Ezra's height, her coat pooling around her like a shadow. Ezra stiffens, uncertain, but doesn't step back. Her hand rises and moves gently through his tangled, strawberry-blonde hair, dirt and all, brushing it back from his brow with careful fingers. He flinches at first, but says nothing.

"Welcome," she says simply, her voice soft but firm, like someone who rarely repeats herself. Then she straightens and turns her full attention to Cara. Her eyes lingered for a moment, reading everything without asking a question. Then she extends her hand.

Cara hesitates, her instincts screaming to stay guarded, to expect betrayal. But there is something in the woman's gaze that's clear and unflinching. Slowly and cautiously, she accepts the hand. "I'm Cara," she says, her voice a little hoarse. "This is Ezra."

The woman's grip is strong but not aggressive, and she nods once. "Elizabeth." Behind her, the settlement hums with quiet life. A wind chime made from silverware tinkles in the breeze. Somewhere, a dog barks, and someone laughs. The road ahead curves between rows of small, well-kept houses, disappearing into the horizon, wide open and full of something that almost resembles hope. Elizabeth lets go of Cara's hand and steps aside, gesturing to the road. "No doubt, you've come far," she says. "You're safe now. But this place..." she pauses, her tone tightening just slightly, "it has rules. You'll be given food, water, and shelter. But you'll have to earn your place here." She turns her gaze to Ezra, "Especially you, young man."

"He knows," Cara replies immediately. "We don't expect anything for free."

Elizabeth's mouth curves in the faintest smile, the kind that doesn't quite reach her eyes. She studies them for another moment, then nods once more. "I believe you."

Acknowledgements

First and foremost, my deepest thanks go to Sarah. Thank you for putting up with the late-night typing, the constant clacking of keys, and my grumpiness while I stared blankly at the screen. Your patience, belief, and faith in me kept this story from ending up like so many of my other endeavours, in the "someday" folder.

To my parents—thank you. Without you having me, I never would have had the chance to procrastinate for years before finally writing this book.

To Dionne—thank you for your early feedback and scientific expertise. Your insight gave this book a brain to go along with its beating heart.

To Sue—I was honestly scared to share this with you, but you had nothing but kind words, despite me constantly bombarding you with questions while you tried to serve customers at The Sawmills. Thank you for your time, your patience, and encouragement - it meant more than you'll ever know.

And to you, the reader—thank you for giving this book your time. Out of all the questionable ways to spend a few hours, you chose this one, and I'm deeply flattered.

Finally, from me, this book has been a long time coming, a mix of stubbornness, caffeine, and a bucket-list dream. Whether it stands alone or becomes the first of many, I'm glad it found its way into your hands.

Matt

Fractured Horizons is the debut novel by **SP Mercer**, a writer whose journey into storytelling is as unconventional as the world he creates. With no formal qualifications in literature and no prior experience in creative writing, SP spent nearly three years bringing his vision for this novel to life. A story born from passion rather than expertise, *Fractured Horizons* is the result of a relentless drive to explore the depths of human survival, resilience, and the fragility of society.

In his day job, SP Mercer is an online retail product manager, where he oversees the complexities of e-commerce, but his professional life is as diverse as his creative one. He is also a qualified electrician and runs his own business, applying the same problem-solving skills to both circuits and narratives. This combination of practical knowledge and boundless curiosity fuels his writing, allowing him to craft worlds with gritty realism and emotional depth.

When he's not immersed in the world of online retail or tinkering with electrical systems, SP can be found with his head buried in a notebook, building complex characters, and imagining the collapse of worlds—both physical and emotional.

SP Mercer lives with his family and continues to write, always seeking to explore new horizons in his stories, and proving that anyone, no matter their background, can become a storyteller.